"Couldn't sleep, I take it?"

Meg shook her head, unable to respond in voice for the unexpected lump in her throat.

"Nor could I, as I am sure is apparent in my presence here with you," Richard answered in his delicious timbre.

Sensing that anything she might say aloud could never come out as she intended, Meg simply glanced up at the canopy of sky above them; it was filled with stars.

"It is beautiful," Richard murmured huskily, "but you are chilled." He lifted his arms slowly and held them wide, inviting her to share the warmth beneath his cloak. But she hesitated.

Richard seemed to read her thoughts. "I am warm and you are not. Joining me under the shelter of this cloak will be a very simple solution—and innocent too, if that is what you fear." But then something shifted in his gaze, flaring to dangerous life as he added in a murmur, "I promise to make an effort to behave myself."

"What if I did not want you to?" The bold question escaped her before she had time to hold it back, and she saw the heat in his gaze flicker higher.

"Did not want me to what?"

"Behave."

MARY
REED MCCALL

Beyond Temptation

THE
TEMPLAR KNIGHTS

AVON BOOKS
An Imprint of HarperCollinsPublishers

AVON BOOKS
An Imprint of HarperCollins*Publishers*
10 East 53rd Street
New York, New York 10022-5299

Copyright © 2005 by Mary Reed McCall
ISBN: 0-06-059368-7
www.avonromance.com

First Avon Books paperback printing: June 2005

Avon Trademark Reg. U.S. Pat. Off. and in Other Countries, Marca Registrada, Hecho en U.S.A.
HarperCollins® is a registered trademark of HarperCollins Publishers Inc.

Printed in the U.S.A.

10 9 8 7 6 5 4 3 2 1

For Cynthia Bunal Dyer . . . we became best friends on the first day of kindergarten, when you got on the bus and sat next to me—and the fun hasn't stopped since. Thanks for being you, Cin . . . no matter how much time or distance intervenes, you'll always be my "best-est friend."

And for Dawn O'Reilly Smouse . . . British by birth, American in marriage, and a true friend of the heart. Thanks for the company, the conversations, and as many cups of perfectly made tea as I can drink! Meeting you on the very first day that our eldest daughters entered kindergarten was a stroke of happy fortune for me . . . and I am so grateful for your friendship.

Acknowledgments

My sincere gratitude:

To Stephanie Koch, a wonderful young woman and former student . . . my children adore you and John and I do too! Thank you for everything this past summer . . .

To all those who offered me their time, ideas, or a thorough critique of this manuscript, including May Chen, Lyssa Keusch, Meg Ruley, Annelise Robey, and, of course, my dear parents, David and Marion Reed . . .

And finally—in acknowledgment of all the good and principled men who fought with honor, lived with conviction, and died with courage under the crimson cross of the Templars . . . I salute you.

Non nobis, Domine, non nobis,
sed Nomini, Tuo da gloriam . . .
*(Not for us, Lord, not for us
but to Thy Name give glory . . .)*

MOTTO OF THE KNIGHTS TEMPLAR

When I look back now, I cannot believe that any of us survived that day, no less the weeks and months that followed. It came to be known as Black Friday—and inky black it was when we finally claimed a moment's rest from the evil that had been unleashing itself all around us since dawn.

Aye, it was as dark as a soul scorched in the raging fires of hell . . .

The letters of Sir Richard de Cantor
The year of our Lord, 1315

Beyond Temptation

Prologue

The woodland just outside Montivilliers, France
Friday, October 13, 1307

Rain slashed down, the wind sounding an eerie moan as it swept over the leafy grove where Richard de Cantor crouched, gasping, next to the shuddering flanks of his horse. He waited for the others to reach him and seek shelter here as well. His head ached and his heart pounded, but nothing could ease the sick disbelief that flooded him anew with each breath. It came whenever he paused long enough to think about what had begun at the break of day— what was still happening now.

They were being hunted like animals.

It was the same, it seemed, everywhere in France. The Templars were being hunted. He and his three closest comrades in arms—John de Clifton and Damien and Alex de Ashby—had been the only knights to escape St. Simeon's

1

Preceptory when the attacks by King Philip's soldiers had begun this morn.

In truth, he had no idea why they were being set upon. As Templars they were the most renowned warriors, the most respected and feared military order in all Christendom. It made no sense. None of it did. He'd wanted to face their pursuers and force an explanation. He'd wanted to do battle with them as his finely honed instincts demanded, but there had been too many. There wasn't a whisper of a chance at surviving those numbers, and Templar law forbade him to try. For the terrible truth was that their enemies here were Christians, soldiers under the French king—and fighting other Christians for the sake of pride was a grievous sin.

As for surrendering . . .

A Templar Knight never surrendered, not while there was still breath left in his body to fight.

The swish of wet branches and cracking of underbrush drew Richard's gaze, and he tensed, gripping his weapon's hilt in readiness. John rode into the clearing, followed shortly after by Damien, who led a bound Alex behind on his mount. Cursing under his breath, an action that earned him a sharp look from Damien, John dismounted and approached Richard. Every now and again a slice of moon shone feebly through the rain, providing them with shadowy light.

"What now, Richard?" John rasped, turning as he did to look toward Damien, who was pulling his manacled brother from atop his steed. Once they'd steadied, Damien led Alex nearer to the other two, his expression tight in contrast to the anger sparking behind Alex's eyes.

"That depends. How close are the gendarmes?"

"A mile—two at most," Damien said lowly. "They will not cease their pursuit of us. The rain will help our cause, perhaps, as will the darkness, but it is likely that we have less than a quarter hour's rest before they will be upon us again."

"It would help our cause immensely if you unshackled me, don't you think?" Alex grated. "Dragging me behind as the prisoner you've made of me since we left Cyprus does nothing but slow us down."

Damien stood rigid; a muscle in his jaw twitched and his gauntleted hand clasped tight the chain leading from his older brother's bound wrists. But he said nothing, keeping his attention on Richard in an obvious show of ignoring Alex.

"Of course your insistence on continuing to wear that damned surcoat does not help either," Alex continued, clearly bent on being acknowledged by his brother. "They're after us because we're *Templars*, Damien, don't you understand that? Blessed Christ, listen to me for once in your life! You might as well offer yourself up as a sacrifice to their arrows, with that scarlet cross emblazoned on your—"

"Enough!" Damien growled, swinging his dark blond head to glare at his brother. "You sin in using God's name so, but do not suggest that I forsake Him as well by removing the visible signs of our calling. I will not do it."

"Then you will likely die this night," Alex muttered, "but I do not intend to go quietly along with you. Release me so that I can have a fighting chance." He skewered Richard, then John with his gaze. "You know I am right. We have gone all day like this, and we are losing ground."

Richard met Alex's gaze unflinchingly. His friend had a point, he knew, and yet they'd been placed under strict orders to deliver Alex to the grand master Jacques de Molay himself, to be judged for carnal transgressions committed during their time in Cyprus. But that had been before the madness of this day . . . before the entire Templar Brotherhood had come under attack.

As if he sensed his wavering, Alex added, "By the blood we've spilled for God and each other, Richard, release my bonds. Whatever my sins against the Brotherhood, I am not the enemy this night. The French are. Let me do my part in keeping us from their grasp."

"He may be right," John said in a low voice, glancing to Damien's stony face for but an instant before fixing his gaze on Richard again. "We could use Alex's skill if it comes to outright battle. The horses are tiring. We've pushed them as hard as we can, and who knows how much farther we will need to go?"

"The coast lies but a few miles beyond here," Richard answered, jabbing his hand through his rain-damp hair. "And yet a few miles might as well be the length of France if we are caught before reaching it." He paused, the thoughts flooding through him, swift and sharp. "If we are to survive this, we must do the unexpected."

"What—surrender?" Damien rasped, heat palpable in his eyes. "Do not consider the thought, Richard; I will not do it."

"Nay, Damien, not that, but something almost as surprising for Templar Knights. We must separate. Divide our force and make our way to the coast on our own, to board ships for England."

"That is all well and good, except that I have no coin for a crossing fee, as well you know," Alex said sharply. "Along with my surcoat, I was stripped of my status as Templar Knight. I haven't a farthing to my name."

"That will be remedied before we leave this grove. You will have enough to buy passage, never fear, Alex." Richard met his fallen friend's gaze. "You still need to answer for your crimes against the Brotherhood, make no mistake on it. But our survival must come first. I think we are all in agreement on that point, are we not?" He glanced first at John, who nodded, then at Damien, who looked angrier than before, but who nonetheless jerked his head in reluctant concurrence after a moment.

"It is settled, then," Richard continued. "Once we set foot on English soil, we must needs make our way to safer ground to see what will transpire. Hawksley Manor lies not many days' travel inland; I had not intended to return to my former home in this lifetime, and yet it is our best choice for a safe haven right now."

All the men fell silent for a moment after he was finished speaking; the weight of the day's events combining with the dire circumstances they faced now created an increasing sense of doom that would not be shaken. Trying to suppress the feeling, Richard approached his mount and pulled a pouch of coins from his saddle. He tossed it to Alex, who caught it with both bound hands. Nodding, Richard murmured, "Undo his shackles now, Damien. We haven't much time."

Tight-jawed, Damien set to the task. In a moment, Alex was free. But as his brother rubbed his newly freed wrists, Damien suddenly stalked back to his own mount, swinging astride and then reining it around to face the others for an instant.

"There is no need to dally longer here, then," he called, looking at each of them in turn, though his gaze glanced more quickly off Alex. "May heaven grant us all safe journey to England." With a jerk of his chin, he added, "Until we meet at Hawksley." Before Richard could say anything in response, Damien wheeled his mount toward the entrance into the clearing, dug his spurs into its flanks, and bent over its neck as he galloped back out into the storm.

John was the first to break the stillness Damien left behind. "We should all go, before the soldiers are upon us," he said, clasping Richard by his forearm. "Godspeed to you, friend."

"Aye, to you as well," Richard echoed, turning in the next moment with the intent of offering Alex the same sign of encouragement and alliance.

But Alex was already remounted, his expression enigmatic and his dark blue gaze seeming alight in the shadows. Thunder boomed, and Alex murmured to his skittish mount, barely keeping him under control. When he'd restored his balance, he called over the noise of the storm, "I cannot let that foolish brother of mine ride out without protection of some kind, Richard. I will stay far enough back to maintain separation, but near enough to watch his back. You understand, I'm sure."

Without waiting for a reply, Alex raised his arm in salute and cocked his familiar half grin, riding out of the clearing as he called, "To England, lads!"

John shook his head, looking serious as he mounted and headed in the same direction. Just before leaving the clearing, he met Richard's gaze one last time; they nodded to each other, and then John galloped from the glen. Soon after, Richard left as well. The force of the rain slashed down on him as he rode hunched over his steed's neck; he managed to keep John's shadowy form in his sights for a few moments until the black of the stormy night swept everything up in its embrace, blocking out all light and forcing him to give his destrier its head in leading them toward the coast.

And then he rode—rode hard and fast, blocking the shriek of the wind, the sting of the rain, and the relentless blackness from his mind by pure force of will—hoping that the plans he'd just made with his comrades in arms would bear fruit . . . and that he hadn't just sent them all to face violent deaths alone, at the hands of the army that was even now breathing hellish flames at their backs and swinging sparking, gory blades at their heels.

Homecoming

Chapter 1

Hawksley Manor, East Sussex
A week later

By all the saints, it was too soon to be happening again. Another cry rang out, thin and desperate, echoing off the walls of the main chamber as Meg rushed from where Willa, the cook, had come to find her in the buttery. The sobbing that rose up after that cry bit into Meg's soul, and she hurried the remaining steps into the large hall. Aye, it was too soon for another spell. Eleanor's last one had been but a sennight ago.

In the dim light it was difficult to locate her cousin Eleanor's wasted form, but the sobs drew Meg to the spot soon enough; she crossed to where Eleanor was huddled, weeping and rocking in the shadows behind the massive carved chest that held some of the family's silver.

"Hush now, Ella," Meg said gently, crouching and wrap-

11

ping her arms around the woman's thin shoulders. "All will be well."

But Eleanor continued to moan and fidget, and Meg saw with a start that her cousin's arms were empty of their usual burden. *Of course.* Meg did a quick glance of the area to see if she could spot the bundled bit of rags and thread; there was nothing. She gathered Eleanor closer against her, wishing that the comfort would be enough this time. That Ella would calm and allow herself to be led back to her chamber. And for what seemed like the thousandth time since she'd come to this godforsaken manor two years earlier, Meg cursed the one who had been the start of all this suffering—a man she'd never seen but about whom she'd heard countless tales.

She didn't need to have seen Sir Richard de Cantor to know the truth of what he'd done: He was a man like every other, who did as he pleased without thought or care to the results.

White-hot emotion shot through her, startling her with its virulence, and she went rigid against the dull aching she knew would bloom afterward. When it passed, she silently berated herself for allowing her own long-buried pain to creep out into the light again . . . for allowing the shadows of her past to muddy the waters of what was happening to Ella here and now. Her own history had nothing to do with this and no real connection to Eleanor or the husband who had abandoned her nearly half a decade ago.

Reclaiming her sense of composure by force of sheer will, Meg directed her attention back to Eleanor and whispered words of comfort, stroking her cousin's brow and brushing the tangled strands of her hair from her face. Eleanor's eyes remained wild and unfocused, grief having etched premature lines of worry between her delicate brows.

Tight-lipped, Meg coaxed her to stand. Hugh would need to be called in to take the watch again. Eleanor's last spell like this had come to near disaster; she'd broken free of her chamber to climb toward the danger of the crenellations, driven there by the ghosts in her mind. She'd almost flung herself over into oblivion then.

Perhaps it would have been a blessing to end her torment so.

Meg sucked in her breath, stifling the sinful whisper. Nay, her cousin deserved far better, both in this life and the next. No matter how difficult the struggle of each day, they couldn't risk such a possibility again.

"Peace now, Ella, there is naught to fear," Meg murmured, supporting the woman's fragile weight and pulling her close. At times like this it was difficult to remember that her cousin was the younger by two years; neither of them had yet reached thirty, but Ella's bones felt as sharp and pronounced as an old woman's to Meg's touch.

Meg guided her to the corner of the stairs, tugging her along, at the same time sharing a look of pained understanding with Willa, nodding her head to the woman with a wordless command to continue looking for the poppet and bring it above stairs as soon as it was found.

Within a half an hour, she'd managed to help Ella swallow a draught of wine laced with valerian. Then she'd eased her out of her soiled bliaud and made sure she donned fresh robes before tucking her under a blanket in her favorite chair by the fire. With the bundle of rags returned at last to the crook of her arm, Ella had fallen asleep, though even in the peacefulness of that release, a perpetual frown marred what remained of her once legendary beauty.

Sighing, Meg went out into the hall, latching the door shut behind her. She nodded to Hugh. He'd arrived a few moments ago to take up his old post at the door, his somber eyes kind. A simple man and a smithy by trade, Hugh had been one of the few loyal villagers to remain on the land after Hawksley's master had abandoned them. Ella would be safe from harm while he kept the watch.

Perhaps now she might finish the chores she'd only just begun when all this had started, Meg thought as she made her way back down to the main level of the house. The cheese wheels needed to be turned and the bags of apples picked through for rot before Brother Thomas came and—

"Meg—oh, Meg! Hurry, by the Holy Savior, Mary, and Joseph—you have to come quick!"

Meg had just taken the final step into the main hall when the cry rang out, bellowed by young James, one of the tanner's sons. He'd come bursting into the hall from the back door near the kitchens, and now he gasped for breath, leaning over to brace his palms on his knees as he struggled to convey the remainder of his message.

"I tried to get here fast as I could fly," he panted. "I wanted you to have some warning. A knight's come to Hawksley . . . he rode up to the village gates a few moments past and came right through. A powerful big knight he is, bearing on his shield the cross of—"

James's words were cut off by a rattling bang as the thick, oaken door opposite him swung in and creaked to a stop against the stone wall. Silhouetted in the sun-drenched opening stood a warrior of impressive height and bearing. Yet rather than a drawn blade, he held some kind of large leather sack in his left hand, knotted tightly closed at the top. Meg's heart gave an erratic beat, her startled gaze taking in the chain mail, gauntlets, and cape that covered the imposing stranger. Even with his face cast in shadow from the streaming light behind him, she could see that his head was bare; dark hair brushed his shoulders and slid across the stubborn line of his jaw, sooty with a beard of several days' growth.

Trying to appear far more confident than she was feeling, Meg mustered her own regal bearing and straightened, readying to snap out a command for an answer to this intrusion. But the knight suddenly altered his stance, jerking back a bit as if he would return whence he came, before he finally strode across the threshold and into the great hall.

Meg stiffened even more than before, something about the full sight of this travel-worn warrior niggling at the back of her mind. He was familiar, and yet she knew she had never seen him before. Nay, she couldn't have. She'd have remembered otherwise. His eyes were mesmerizing, making her think of misty green forests and sweet, dark honey, blended to a flawless hue.

Shame followed hard upon the thought; she knew better than most the penalty to be paid for indulging in such silly, romanticized notions. She buried the whim with ruthless zeal, preparing to remedy her unusual reticence with action. But before she could do anything, the knight came to a halt mid-chamber. He ceased his perusal of the hall's other occupants to stare straight at her, stilling her breath under the force of his gaze. And when he finally spoke, his words threatened to stop her heart from beating altogether . . .

"It seems that you wear the mantle of authority here at present, lady, so it is you I must needs address. Answer me this, then: Who in God's name are you . . . and what have you done with my wife?"

The servants' whispers rose in the moments following the dead silence that had greeted Richard's question; he saw a latent shock of recognition sweep over the striking face of the woman standing before him, and it set off a strange, twisting sensation inside. She knew him, then. Or at least *of* him, which was nearly the same—and from her expression, what she'd heard had been less than complimentary.

"You are Sir Richard de Cantor?" she clipped out, her voice entirely too accusatory for his liking.

"Aye, that is one name by which I am known, though I have also been called a Knight of the Temple of Solomon . . . and most importantly where you are concerned, lord of Hawksley Manor."

He watched her lips purse at that, feeling a sense of dismay when he failed to avoid focusing on their lush hue and fullness as she did. Pulling his gaze back up to her eyes, he raised one brow. "I have satisfied your inquiry, and yet you have still not answered mine. I will have it now. Tell me your name and the whereabouts of my wife."

"You refer to Eleanor? A lady whom you have neither seen nor sought word concerning for nearly half a decade?"

Wrong though she was in that assumption, Richard nevertheless felt the sting of her barb, but he didn't reply, instead letting the ice he'd become so adept at summoning these past years sift into his gaze. The woman responded accordingly, her look of condemnation altering to one tinged with wariness. Aye, that was better. It seemed she'd suddenly remembered the extent of his power as lord of this demesne—and the dearth of her own.

She glanced to the blade dangling at his side and then back up to his face before licking those full lips to respond, "I am Margaret Newcomb, youngest daughter to the Earl of Welton, and Eleanor's distant cousin. I serve as her companion here. At the moment she is above stairs, resting."

Richard concealed a start of disbelief upon hearing the woman's societal rank. Distant relative or nay, what in God's name was an earl's daughter, one who looked as if she should have been long ago overseeing the care of her own home, doing at his humble, fortified manor house? But the answer to that would needs come later, he reasoned, after he'd had a chance to gain his bearings. He steeled himself for his next question.

"Is Eleanor ill, then, to be resting midday, *Lady* Margaret?" he asked, using the title she deserved by birth but seemed to have deliberately left off when making her introduction.

She winced almost imperceptibly, he noticed. Then she glanced away.

"Eleanor has been . . . unwell for quite some time. It has been necessary for me to take over management of the household in her stead."

The news sank like a stone in Richard's gut. It was what he'd feared. But oh, God, he'd hoped—by all that was holy, he'd prayed every day in the best way he knew how, with his blood and body as the sacrificial offering— for Eleanor's return to health in the time he'd served with the Templars. He had been encouraged by the dearth of painful detail within his brother's letters during the past two years, but it seemed it had all been for naught; his sin had been too great to allow such a boon.

Suppressing that wrenching thought, he jerked into motion, giving Margaret a curt nod. "I will see her by the by, then, when she awakens. In the meantime, I would like to bathe away the dirt of my travels. Have warmed water sent up to the second best chamber, as I do not wish to disturb her rest."

"Nay—that cannot be done."

Richard stiffened.

"I did not mean the bath, sir," Margaret added hastily, her hands fluttering for a moment like bird's wings before she squeezed them tightly to her bodice, "but rather that it cannot be brought to the second chamber. That is where Eleanor is sleeping."

"Why there, instead of in her own room?"

"The first chamber is—it is difficult for her to rest there," Margaret answered, her words halting and her face flushed, making Richard wonder just how much she knew of the dark and horrible truth behind his leaving and Eleanor's madness. "Though it is smaller, she sleeps far more peacefully in the second chamber," Margaret added, "so I had her things moved to accommodate her need."

Richard nodded, his jaw tight. "I see. Send the bathing water up to the first chamber, then, within the half hour. I will settle my belongings there until further notice, so as not to disturb Eleanor's comfort. And send word to Brother Thomas at the preceptory. He was appointed steward of this estate when I left England; he continues in that role, does he not?"

"Aye."

He noted the tight edge to her voice in delivering that single word, but he was feeling too raw—too on edge right now to pursue why.

"Then bid him to come and sup; I have much to discuss with him."

Lady Margaret flushed again and looked as though she was about to say something further, but she abruptly stopped herself and nodded in return.

Brushing past her, Richard made his way across the great hall, not looking right or left, though acutely aware of the weight of stares pressing upon him as he went. He gripped his leather bag more tightly, reaching the stairs leading to the upper floor in another six strides.

Once at the top of them, he at last approached the portal to the first chamber. Dark memories of the past had been pummeling him ever since he'd set foot onto Hawksley's grounds. Now they surged up again with a vengeance. He gritted his teeth against their onslaught and pushed open the door, slipping into the dimly lighted room and dropping his bundle to the floor before shutting out the rest of the world behind him. Only after he'd secluded himself did he allow a moment to acknowledge the pain.

Then he leaned back against the unyielding wood, holding himself rigid as he fought to bring his emotions under control. Blindly, he looked around the chamber, finding no respite there; it too was filled with old ghosts—images that flashed into his mind's eye, taunting him, tormenting . . . memories in snatches of time . . . of the sweet scent of violets and the gentle caress of the sun's warmth on long and silky dark tresses . . . of tinkling, little girl's laughter that played over his soul and left in its wake a sweet agony of loss and self-loathing . . . of much, much more that he could not bear to relive, but could not stop from coming anyway . . .

Closing his eyes, Richard tipped his head up, his breathing shallow and his heart aching. Resuming his old life as master of Hawksley Manor, even for a short time, was going to be a grand and horrible penance, he knew. One that promised relentless struggle and agony far worse than anything he'd endured on the battlefield, in dungeon holes, or under the baking desert sun during the past five years. But it was his duty to see it through. He had no other choice in the matter, he thought, clenching his jaw as he finally pushed away from the door.

God help him, he had no choice.

A half hour later, Meg stood outside Sir Richard's door—
her door, she reminded herself—her mind swirling with dark
thoughts. She'd presumed he'd have immediately stormed
out, uttering commands upon seeing her possessions scattered about the room he'd chosen to occupy. But he hadn't.

In truth, he'd remained unnaturally quiet and secluded inside, even when two of the kitchen boys came back and forth
carrying numerous pails of steaming water to fill the washtub.
According to their talk, Hawksley's lord had found the
wooden vessel himself, turned on its top as was usual in the
corner where Meg made use of it as a table between baths.
He'd brought it out, flipped it over, and bid them to fill it. She
hadn't allowed herself to think beyond that point. It had been a
deliberate decision; she couldn't bear imagining in too much
detail how his strong, masculine, very naked body would be
filling her tub. It was far too intimate an image to entertain.

Now here she stood outside the chamber, wondering what
she should do. It had been some time since the lads had carried the last jug of water in to him, and yet still no sounds issued from the chamber. No splashing or knocking about.
Was he waiting, then, for her to come and assist him?

As acting lady of the manor, she had that duty, she supposed, and yet she didn't want to. She was furious at Richard
de Cantor for barging into their lives like this without warning.
He was an errant husband. A man who had caused great misery to his wife if the tales she'd heard were truthful, and she
had no reason to believe otherwise. Not with Eleanor as tragic,
living proof. But honor demanded that she fulfill her obligations to Eleanor by aiding him, whether she liked it or not.

Resigned to what she would have to do, Meg tightened her jaw and scratched softly on the door, gripping close to her chest the folded bundle of fresh linen towels and pot of softened soap she carried. A muffled answer came through the thick wood, and she held her breath as she lifted the latch string and slipped inside.

The chamber was quite large, but she knew it well. A pang swept through her to see it; it had been her refuge and place of peace for nearly all her time at Hawksley. It took only a moment to locate the tub in the far corner, opposite the curtained bed. Richard himself, however, was nowhere to be seen. The spicy scent of borage petals swirled up from water that still steamed with curls of heat, the fragrance of the herb spreading through the chamber from beneath the canopy that hung over the tub to ward off chills.

"Do you require something of me, lady?"

The quiet, masculine voice came from the shadows behind the bed, and Meg started, her gaze snapping to the spot. How foolish of her to forget about the door leading to the connected wardrobe chamber. Richard had apparently been inside the little storeroom.

Looking for contents of value, no doubt.

The thought came unbidden, and she knew she should chastise herself for the less than Christian thought. But she wasn't sorry. He was a Templar, after all, and as such he was surely well-versed in the costliness of many goods, though forbidden by the vows of the Brotherhood from keeping anything of real worth. Still, she'd known many of the order—knights, sergeants, and clerics alike—who made a habit of bending such rules. Brother Thomas, the Templar who had been placed in charge of Hawksley in Sir Richard's absence, was such a one. In fact—

"Did you hear me, lady? Is aught amiss?"

Though she still couldn't see him, Richard sounded less patient than before, and she realized she had yet to answer his initial inquiry. Still hugging the folded linens to herself, she pursed her lips and veered away from his voice toward the bathing vessel, trying to keep her attention on the task at hand. She set down the towels.

"Nay, there is nothing amiss," she answered, adding the pot of soap to her little pile near the tub. "I've only come to assist you with your bath. It is my duty, since Eleanor cannot."

"It is unnecessary."

"Of course it is necessary, and proper as well. You are the lord of Hawksley, and you have been abroad for a goodly time. This service is your right as well as—"

"But I have already bathed."

His voice was a warm rumble close behind her. Too close. With a gasp, she whirled to face him, her startled gaze meeting his. How had he reached her so quickly, and with nary a sound? But he'd spoken true; he was clean-shaven, wearing fresh garments, and his dark hair was still damp, its wetness waving down to his shoulders. When he stood so close, she was struck anew at how tall and powerfully built a man he was. Taking a step back in instinctive response, she bumped the backs of her legs into the tub. The canopy wavered dangerously, and water sloshed over the sides.

His expression enigmatic, Richard reached past her head to steady the draped covering and prevent it from collapsing on its poles into the drink. The movement brought him even closer to her . . . near enough that she could smell the delicious, spicy scent that lingered on him and feel his warmth against her in contrast to the chill of the room. *Perhaps it is simply the moist heat from the tub,* she reasoned. But she took a gulp of air nonetheless, dismayed to realize that she'd stopped breathing from the moment he'd lunged forward to aid her.

"Forgive my clumsiness," she murmured, afraid to move again. "It is just that I—I did not expect you to be finished in so short a time."

"I became accustomed to bathing quickly while in Cyprus. There was little time to indulge in pleasurable pursuits." He lowered his arm from the now-steady canopy to look down at her, and she couldn't help noticing that his eyes were even more beautiful than she'd realized in the great hall.

At a loss for what to say, and feeling more than a bit disconcerted under the force of his attention, Meg cleared her throat. He took a step back then, seeming somewhat ill at ease himself, and the tension in the air shifted. His head moved subtly to the side, his gaze indicating the sweep of the room. "It appears that I have demanded use of the chamber you had made your own."

"It is of little matter. As lord here, it is only proper now that you've returned home. I will move my things before nightfall."

"You seem to be quite concerned about doing what is proper, Lady Margaret."

She tried not to wince again at the sound of her true name. Standing straighter, she answered, "There is no shame in doing right, Sir Richard. And as the issue has presented itself, I must tell you that I do not relish being addressed by my formal title. I have long asked that the servants of Hawksley Manor and those from the village refer to me simply as Meg."

"Meg?"

He sounded incredulous, but she avoided his stare.

"Aye, it is my request."

"But you are the daughter of an earl, are you not? You have just schooled me on the virtues to be found in following the limits of propriety. As a simple knight, I am of a far lesser standing than you. Such informality can hardly be construed as proper—"

"And yet it is the way I would have it," she broke in, lacing her fingers tightly in front of her.

"Why?"

The question startled her, and she found herself unable to answer right away. The truth behind it all wouldn't do, that much was certain. She would have to gamble that he would be gracious enough to accept the meager reasons she *could* voice. Evenly, she answered, "With the exception of Brother Thomas and the others residing at the Templar Priory to the west of Hawksley, the people of this demesne feel more at ease around me and I them when there is no chasm of title between us. This aids me in my role as Eleanor's caretaker, for I often need to ask them for assistance. If you would be so kind as to honor my request, I would be most . . . grateful."

Richard continued to study her, and she glanced up at him again then, only to feel hard-pressed in deciding whether his hazel eyes held amusement or pique.

"Very well," he answered at last. "I concede to your wishes, though it will be uncomfortable until I become accustomed to it." His expression remained bemused as he added, "Naturally, I must require you to share in my discomfort. It would be ludicrous to maintain my title of address in our conversations, when you have forfeited your own. Agreed?"

She paused for just an instant, a tiny shiver slipping down her back; she'd never known any man to willingly forgo a title owed him. Most were far too overweening to see the possibility as anything but insult. But without comment, she dipped her chin. "Of course." Then, straightening her shoulders, she prepared to move past him. "Now, as it seems that the task for which I came is no longer required, may I leave? You must be weary from your journey, and I can return for my belongings after you have rested."

"Nay. We must discuss something further before you go."

Meg stiffened, willing herself to maintain her calm demeanor. Here it was, then. What she'd feared since he first appeared in the doorway below stairs; he was going to tell her that she was no longer needed to care for Eleanor. Now that he'd returned home, she would be free to go, not only from this room but also from Hawksley altogether. He would release her.

And then . . . and then . . .

Her palms felt damp, and so she twisted them in her skirts.

"You haven't yet said *where* you intend to take your possessions," he continued. "Unless you are willing to share the smaller chamber with Eleanor, the only other choice would be to bed with the servants below stairs, and that would not be prop—" He broke off mid-word, flashing a glance of exasperation. "Such a circumstance would not be *seemly* for one of your birth. You are an earl's daughter, whether or not you wish to use the title that accompanies that ranking."

Meg flushed. If this was his way of trying to get her to offer to leave on her own, he was sadly mistaken. She'd bed down with the chickens first.

"Sharing the second chamber with Eleanor will suit quite well, my lord," she answered sweetly, doing her best to hide her fear and animosity.

A scratch suddenly sounded at the door, making Meg jump. Frowning at the interruption, Richard called out for entry, and Willa shuffled in, looking both discomfited and fierce all at once. Meg felt a swell of gratitude toward this woman who, after an initial period of adjustment, had been more like a mother than a household servant to her during her time at Hawksley; it was clear that Willa had noticed the length of time she and Richard had been closeted in the bedchamber alone. Like a mama cat with her kitten, she had come in to make certain that all was well.

Richard looked at Willa in question as she took up a position near Meg.

"Pardon, sir," Willa murmured, nodding in deference. "I came to tell you that your message to Brother Thomas has been received. He sent word back that he will be arriving as soon as is possible."

"I am glad to hear it, mistress . . . ?"

"Willa, sir. Just Willa."

"Aye, that seems a common theme in this house," he said under his breath, adding more loudly, "I do not recall having seen you before, Willa. What position do you hold at Hawksley?"

"I am cook and general housekeeper, milord, and have been for near three years."

"I see. Then perhaps you can assist Lady Marg—I mean, *Meg,* in moving her belongings into the second chamber after the evening meal."

"Into the second chamber?" Willa looked aghast. "With Lady de Cantor? But she cannot—"

"It is quite satisfactory, Willa." Meg kept her tone even, though she threw the cook a sharp glance. "You shall help me set up everything to ensure that my cousin is not disturbed by my arrival."

"Why—is there some further difficulty of which I am not aware?" Richard asked, frowning again.

"Nay, all is well. The arrangement will suit just fine." Meg knew her voice sounded tight, and she struggled to paste a bland smile to her face. But though Willa remained silent now, she glowered like a thundercloud before shaking her head enough to set her jowls jiggling. Then with a mumbled by-your-leave, she departed the chamber.

"If that is all, then?" Meg allowed her words to trail off and backed away from Richard to the door as she did.

He nodded his permission this time, still looking serious, his gaze piercing her with heat—with the warm, tantalizing brush of awareness . . .

Quickly, Meg slipped out into the hall, closing the heavy wooden slab behind her. Then she breathed a sigh of relief, sagging against the wall for a moment.

Hawksley's lord had agreed to let her stay, and that was what mattered most. The rest would need to be worked out in time, for though residing in the same room with Ella was sure to prove difficult, it would at least allow her to stay. She would try to serve as a buffer between her cousin and this man; he seemed dangerous somehow, and not only because of the stories she had heard about him. Nay, it was more than that. Something akin to the way he made her heart race, the way her skin seemed to tingle and take on a heated flush when he was near. It was unsettling and unwelcome.

Glancing back over her shoulder at the door that concealed him from her sight, Meg tightened her jaw and set off with purpose down the hall. One thing was certain, she thought;

she'd feel much better as soon as she got back to work . . . and put as goodly a distance between herself and the disturbing lord of Hawksley Manor as was possible.

Richard held himself very still as he watched Lady Margaret Newcomb—*Meg*, as he had agreed to call her, by all the saints—steal out of his chamber. He could do little else but remain so as he tried to regain his bearings. She had startled him, had shaken him from his usual sense of balance, not only with her forthright manner but also with the sharp pangs of desire her very presence had sent spilling through him; the feelings had been wholly unexpected and certainly unwelcome, but they were there.

When he had stood so close to her near the bath . . . when he had been forced to reach out to prevent the canopy from collapsing into the water, it had been all he could do not to allow his hand to brush against the softness of her hair instead. Even so, he had not been able to keep himself from breathing in the heady sweet and spice fragrance of her. Nay, he had been too weak. And for the first time in years he had been gripped with the stark and raw need for a woman's touch. For *this* woman's touch. He had been possessed with a yearning to touch and embrace her as well—a sharp, biting ache that made his breath catch and his stomach drop in a way that was far too pleasant to be allowable.

He clenched his jaw hard, savoring the tightness . . . aware that it echoed the hollow throbbing of guilt that was even now churning in his soul. He was a married man, by God, only newly returned home. A man married to a wife stricken with madness, it was true, but wed nonetheless. And even were that not so, he knew without a doubt that he was a man to whom no woman should find herself bound in any way, ever again. No female deserved that miserable fate. He had proven not once but twice that he was unworthy to know the bliss of a woman's love and the comfort of a tender embrace. By this point he had thought himself well accustomed to that knowledge.

But that had been before the Lady Margaret Newcomb had stepped into his life.

With a grimace, he walked over to the table in his solar and sat down; then with much deliberation, he reached for the sack of Templar treasure he had managed to protect during his flight from France. As he sorted through its contents, Richard tried to forcibly direct his thoughts away from the maddening path they had been taking; achieving that goal was proving far more challenging than he cared to admit, but he would make it so. He had to—for he knew better than anyone the kinds of difficulties the coming weeks were going to bring.

Because when all was said and done, it was quite clear that he had more than enough to contend with here at Hawksley Manor without adding a dangerous and forbidden attraction to the mix . . . a temptation that could come to naught but heartache, to a heart that had already been trampled enough under the heavy boots of guilt and regret.

Chapter 2

Richard paced his solar, waiting for Brother Thomas to arrive. The Templar priest had been delayed, missing the meal altogether—a result that was probably for the best anyway. Supper had been a strained affair, to put it mildly. Though his years with the Brotherhood had accustomed him to silence while eating, the dagger-edged stares coming at him from all directions were another thing altogether.

Eleanor would not be descending from her bedchamber to partake of the meal, Meg had informed him, a circumstance that, he learned upon asking, was not at all unusual. The chilly exchange had only served to highlight more clearly to him, and everyone else in hearing distance, he wagered, how precious little he knew about the stranger who had shared his name for the past eight years.

Not that he'd ever truly known Eleanor, he reminded himself. He walked over to the hearth and squatted down, warming his hands and staring into the twisting flames. The memories churned, and though they sent a renewed aching through him, he found that he couldn't block them from his mind as he'd been able to when he was in Cyprus.

His thoughts reached back to the very beginning with Eleanor and the first time he'd seen her at court, all golden hair and wide, thick-lashed blue eyes. Even then she had been delicate and somehow ethereal, seeming beyond the realm of his understanding. He had no more been able to predict her moods or read the workings of her heart than he could say when the wind would blow. But she had needed him. It had been what had first drawn him into their marriage vows those many years ago.

There had been little else, he'd been forced to admit later. Aye, she was undeniably beautiful, but he had entered their union because she was a woman yearning for comfort, protection, nurturing—for many things. He'd fallen into the required role so easily . . . done his best to fill that emptiness for her. And in truth, she'd seemed content in him as her choice.

But in the end the woman he'd married had become a stranger to him, alternately cold and silent or weeping and inconsolable. It was what had driven him to join the Templars, desperately seeking redemption and a sense of peace he'd never found.

Now, after almost five years away, he didn't know her at all.

Richard stood, his breath exhaling in a heavy sigh. He needed to go and see Eleanor face to face, much as he dreaded the moment; until she awakened, he was granted reprieve, but he dreaded it nonetheless. Even more, he knew, than he did the discussion that was about to take place between him and Brother Thomas, the master of the local Templar Preceptory, who had been placed in charge of Hawksley during his absence.

Running his fingers through his hair, Richard walked over to the prie-dieu near the sole window of the chamber. Perhaps he should try to pray. He'd have felt far more comfortable driving himself to physical exhaustion with training, but at the moment such an outlet did not seem feasible. Besides, there was always hope, as unlikely as it was, that this time the praying would work. A voice brought him up short in the act of kneeling.

"Sir Richard, forgive my tardiness."

So be it.

"It has been too long since last we met," Brother Thomas continued, "though I confess that I had expected your return to Hawksley Manor nearly a year ago, after your official term as a Templar Knight was completed."

Richard turned slowly from the prie-dieu to face the cleric, vaguely annoyed at the tone of the man's censure. Brother Thomas stood in the shadows of the open doorway, and so, tipping his head, Richard indicated that he should come in the rest of the way. Though he didn't voice the idea, he couldn't help thinking that Brother Thomas looked rather more prosperous in his dress and bearing than he had the last time they had met.

"I saw no reason to give up my service so abruptly, Brother," he answered aloud, "when it was clear I could continue to be useful to the order."

"And what of your wife?" the priest asked as he approached. "Did you not consider her?"

Richard paused for a strained beat before answering. "Letters from my brother led me to believe that Eleanor has been well cared for in my absence. I understand, however, that as of this moment she is . . . unimproved in her affliction and may very well not know me."

"Aye, that is so," Brother Thomas murmured, shaking his head. "Quite surprising, in view of your considerable sacrifice to God."

The Templar cleric looked away then, and Richard couldn't tell whether he'd offered the statement as additional censure. It didn't matter. The implication of the truth that had greeted him upon his return to Hawksley was clear as water: His sin was so great that not even five years spent offering body and soul to God as a weapon of vengeance could expiate it. He hadn't been punished enough. If he'd been forgiven, Eleanor would have been healed. She would be whole.

"But be that as it may," Brother Thomas added, bringing him back to the task, "you should not tarry too long in your reunion. It would not be seemly."

"And yet I do not wish to upset my wife by waking her from sleep to greet me after so long an absence. Her cousin made it clear she was resting and shouldn't be disturbed."

"Aye, well, Lady Margaret is very resourceful in her protection of her cousin—perhaps too much so," Brother Thomas said. "You would do well to curtail that woman's influence here now that you've returned."

Richard paused again, absorbing the hostility Brother Thomas seemed to feel for Meg—a woman who appeared nothing but devoted to Eleanor from what Richard had observed. He was careful to keep his voice neutral. "Do you know her story? It seems unusual for the daughter of an earl to waste her youth far from society to live as nursemaid on a distant relative's country estate."

"Just the contrary; she is fortunate to have a place here, sinful creature that she is."

"*Sinful?* How so?"

"Not in a manner that would bring harm to your wife, rest

assured," Brother Thomas offered. "Lady Margaret is simply a true daughter of Eve." He lifted his gaze to Richard. "I received few details when she arrived here two years past, but I know prior to that she had engaged in an illicit union with a man of lower birth. The temptress willingly abandoned her virtue to him."

Richard kept hidden the surprise that shot through him at the information. "What brought her to Hawksley, then?"

Brother Thomas made a noise deep in his throat. "As expected, the earl her father was none too pleased with her transgression. He secluded her in a nunnery as penance. It was only upon the death of Lady de Cantor's former nurse that Lady Margaret was pressed into service here. The earl hoped that this humble position would go farther to teach her obedience and remorse for her licentious behavior." He shook his head. "It has done little good, I fear."

"Aye, well, she does not strike me as particularly remorseful, I'll grant you that," Richard murmured, remembering Meg's passionate words and fiery glares.

"Precisely. She is far too proud, considering her circumstances. But under your authority, I trust her demeanor will improve, and that you will make progress where I could not. My journeying to Hawksley each week to administer her correction has been less than ideal, I will admit."

Richard felt another lance of surprise. "I am not sure that I understand what you mean."

"Lady Margaret's physical penance, of course," Brother Thomas said, sounding confused in the face of Richard's query. "Weekly mortification of the flesh in an effort to expunge her soul of the dire sin she brought upon herself. It is common in cases such as hers—a blessed and wholly sanctioned way of bringing oneself back to God after grave transgression." He fixed Richard with his gaze, his brows knit with consternation. "As a fellow Templar, you cannot be unfamiliar with the practice."

Richard didn't answer at first, instead walking over to the hearth again to stir the coals and add more wood to the blaze. His chest felt tight with memories of exactly what Brother Thomas had just described . . . regular beatings delivered at a preordained time by the master of the preceptory to cleanse the soul of sin. Sometimes the penance was delivered in sharp blows to the back or palms with a wooden rod, other times, it involved strokes with a biting lash. He wondered which Meg had been made to bear, and he was unable to keep his fists from clenching at the thought that she'd been forced to suffer either.

Glancing over to the cleric, he struggled to bring his reaction under control. "The practice is familiar to me, of course, Brother. I just did not realize that Lady Margaret had been consigned to it. She has been here already for two years; it seems a long term for such atonement."

"Her failing was severe, placing not only her immortal soul in reach of the flames, but also depriving her father of the fortuitous marriage he had arranged for her. It was he who recommended the penance to the abbess with whom she was originally placed, and I was instructed to uphold the practice upon her arrival here."

"I see." Tossing a final log on the fire, Richard straightened and stood with his back to the hearth, knowing he would do nothing of the sort, even as he added, "It appears, then, that I must oversee this . . . *duty*. And yet you should be aware that I do not know how long I will be remaining at Hawksley. I have not received instructions from the grand master concerning my future activities, nor have I been officially released from my service with the Templars."

Brother Thomas frowned anew. "The grand master . . . aye . . . he is another matter which I had hoped to discuss with you further today."

"Have you heard anything, then? Was he able to escape France?"

"There has been some news. Just yestermorn, in fact."

"What is it?"

"To my great sorrow, I was told that Jacques de Molay was brought into custody on the morn of October thirteenth, along with several thousand other Templar sergeants, preceptors, knights, and brethren, all taken before nightfall." Brother Thomas's expression flickered almost imperceptibly as he added, "Though your reputation for unmatched skill with blade and shield is widely known, Sir Richard, it nevertheless seems that you were very fortunate . . . one of only a handful of brethren, whether warriors or otherwise, to escape France on that day of infamy."

Richard looked away, his jaw clenched as the dark memories rose up again, painful flashes of his storm-swept flight through Normandy. They pricked at him, renewing his feelings of anger and impotence.

"The grand master's arrest on the thirteenth was a double injustice," Brother Thomas continued, "perpetrated only one day after he had been granted a position of honor at the funeral of King Philip's sister-by-marriage, Catherine de Valois."

Richard bit back the curse that rose to his lips at that, forestalling it to grate out the question that had been burning inside him since the black day of the arrests. "But why the Templars? On what charges?"

"Heresy and the immorality of the order as a whole."

"*What?*"

Brother Thomas shook his head again, moving toward the solar's window to look out. "I know . . . it is beyond belief, and yet it is so."

"Has not the pope stepped forward to demand an end to this?" Richard asked hoarsely. "No earthly king has authority over the Templars. Why has His Holiness not condemned King Philip's actions against the order?"

"He has, but the charges are vast . . . shocking in content." He turned his face from the window to meet Richard's gaze. "Clouding the matter, some of those in custody have already admitted guilt in the crimes charged against them, no doubt thanks to the ingenious means employed by those appointed to extract their confessions."

"Torture."

Richard uttered the word more as a statement than a question, but Brother Thomas responded with a vehemence that revealed his anger over the truth of it—and perhaps his dread.

"Aye. The French king has placed no limits. It is profane, and yet, if more Templars capitulate, the tide will continue to rise against us . . . and perhaps spread to our shores."

Richard fisted his hand where it rested on the mantel. All this news was not unexpected, and yet to hear it said aloud made it that much more difficult to stomach.

"What in heaven's name will we do, if our own King Edward takes up the call of France's monarch? He is young and new to the throne . . . mayhap he will be too easily swayed to join in the outcry against us," Brother Thomas continued after a moment, his gaze haunted. "The vast number of brethren in England, myself included, are not of the warrior class. We have never wielded a weapon in our lives. It was the same in France, and they fell as lambs before the wolf. What will become of us?"

Richard remained silent, coming to the realization of the answer only an instant before he spoke. "I can only say what my own course will be, Brother. I fled once in order to protect some of that which belongs to the Templars—and to preserve myself, I confess it freely. I will not flee again, even should the Inquisition march to the very gates of Hawksley."

That seemed to shock the cleric from his stupor; he flashed a pointed stare at Richard's clean-shaven jaw. "And yet you have chosen to rid yourself of the beard required of those in the order. Perhaps your mind will change about leaving England as well, as the evil tide laps closer?"

Richard fought a surge of shame. Shaving his beard had been an unwelcome but necessary action, taken in an attempt to buy a little more time to reach the coast after separating from Damien, John, and Alex on the night of the arrests.

"As you have already pointed out," he said, suppressing the emotion, "my mandated term with the Templars ended a year ago. Nevertheless, my commitment to the Brotherhood remains strong. My Templar comrades and I did what was necessary to keep our freedom, and in truth we had more than our own lives to protect. We were charged with the safekeeping of goods given us by the preceptor of Normandy himself, Geoffrey de Charnay. He was traveling toward Paris to greet the grand master and was with us when the arrests began. I and my three friends only just managed to escape with what he handed over before King Philip's soldiers were at the door."

"I see." A gleam lit Brother Thomas's gaze for an instant before he looked away. "There has been much talk of the Templar treasure in France being spirited away before the arrests. Might that comprise some of the goods of which you speak?"

"I do not know."

"Did you not look at the items you were handed?"

"Aye, though that was of little matter at the time." Richard leveled a hard stare on him. "We were simply fulfilling our duty by attempting to carry the sacks to safety."

Brother Thomas nodded, seemingly unaware that he had sounded so avaricious. "I ask for no other reason but that I intend to offer use of the preceptory for storing the treasure—" He broke off, looking apologetically at Richard and tilting his head in deference. "If indeed you would qualify the contents of the sacks as such. It would be far safer on Templar property."

"Hawksley Manor *is* Templar property—it became so upon my acceptance into the order."

"Only half of it. You entered for but a fixed term, and as a married man; the rights to the remaining half of the estate must be retained for the sustenance of your wife," Brother Thomas reminded him.

He was correct in that, Richard knew, but it didn't change the fact that in his own mind he'd consigned Hawksley Manor to the Templars long ago. He rubbed his hand along the cool, smooth wood of the finely carved mantel, savoring the feel of it. Giving over Hawksley had been another sacrifice, an attempt to aid in expiating his sins. The estate had been a gift from the king himself . . . a reward that he'd later learned had been earned at too great a cost.

Brother Thomas shook his head again. "Nay, Hawksley Manor is not the best place to store Templar valuables should the arrests begin in England. If it goes the way of France, the soldiers will surely claim right to goods found on any properties associated with the Brotherhood."

"Then how will the preceptory provide a safe haven?"

Richard asked, moving away at last from the warmth of the hearth. "An official Templar holding seems far more suspect and likely to be ransacked. We saw many such preceptories in France suffering that indignity on our flight from the countryside to England, but few secular houses."

"Ah, but I haven't told you all. Long ago I discovered an alcove near our burial grounds. None know of it but myself and another of the retired brothers—the man who was with me when I stumbled upon it. There was little in it but some scraps of cloth and a few broken chalices, but it is a sturdy recess in the earth, lined with stone. It rests where a grave would be. Any Templar fortune would be safe there. Even the Inquisitors, unholy as they are, would never think to desecrate burial ground. In fact, after hearing of the arrests in France, I took all monies and valuables from the preceptory's main house and secured them in that very spot."

Richard paused, his arms crossed over his chest. As much as he wished he could refute it, Brother Thomas might have a point. And the man was surely harmless, as far as the actual safety of the valuables went; many Templars were deeply concerned with matters of goods and finance, Richard knew. The holding and transferring of secular property for any who wished to partake of the service—for a fee, of course—was a mainstay of the Brotherhood.

"I would only need to know how much space is required," Brother Thomas went on, apparently assuming Richard was in agreement though he hadn't spoken his decision yet. Brother Thomas tapped his finger to his lips as if mentally calculating the amount of treasure to be secreted.

"You needn't fear on that account," Richard said, feeling somewhat bemused at the man's continued preoccupation.

"There is but one small sack to concern ourselves with at the moment."

Brother Thomas seemed startled. "There were others, then?"

Richard nodded, rocking back on his heels. "Aye, there were. I and two of the knights with whom I escaped France divided the whole between us when we were forced to separate. I have but one sack with me now. My comrades agreed to make their way here to Hawksley with the goods entrusted to them, if they are able. I anticipate their arrival, God willing, within the next week."

Silence fell then, Brother Thomas's lips pressed tightly together. Finally he spoke. "I see. It seems that in the meantime we can do naught but pray they are safely delivered."

Whether the "they" Brother Thomas referred to was the men or the bags of goods they carried was impossible to tell, and Richard cleared his throat, preparing to find out. But before he could speak further, there was a scratch on the door, followed by its swinging open, though no call for entry had been made. He twisted to see what person would be so bold.

It was Meg, of course.

"I regret the intrusion, my lord," she murmured to him, looking down, though her voice and expression showed that she felt little if any such reluctance, "but I thought it best that you be told that Eleanor has awakened, should you desire to commence your reunion with her."

When he didn't answer immediately, Meg's gaze lifted for a brief instant to his, and he could have sworn he saw a glimmer of softness—sympathy, perhaps?—in her eyes, accented by the deepening pink of her cheeks. But then Brother Thomas stepped forward to speak, and any vision of softness disappeared.

"Greetings, Lady Margaret," the preceptor murmured, his voice tight with thinly veiled disapproval. "While it is good to see you prior to our prescribed time of meeting each week, I cannot help wondering at your interruption. Surely the news you brought could have held until Sir Richard and I were finished?"

Meg flushed more deeply, but whether her discomfiture was the result of embarrassment or anger, Richard couldn't discern at first. In the next moment he decided it was the latter. She lifted her gaze, defiance crackling from every graceful inch of her; he watched, possessed suddenly by an urge to smooth with his thumb the tightened line of her lush mouth. Heat of a very inappropriate kind shot through him, and the realization of it shocked him into motion, causing him to step forward as an instinctive buffer between her and the cleric. But that didn't stop her from beginning to deliver a biting response.

Richard cut off her rejoinder by saying, "I welcome the interruption, Brother, to be sure, for it is news I am very grateful to receive." In the same moment, he lightly touched her arm to coax her toward the door, steeling himself against the pleasure that slight caress afforded him. He had been without a woman for too long, he thought ruefully. Far too long, to take notice of such a simple touch—and one he had no right to enjoy.

She seemed as if she would resist him, her rigidity belying her continuing anger. But then she shifted her weight to walk stiffly with Richard, approaching the portal first as he stepped aside to let her pass.

He paused long enough to look back to Brother Thomas. "We can conclude the details of our discussion later, if you're willing. As you cautioned earlier, it would not be seemly to tarry longer in apprising my wife of my return to Hawksley. Perhaps you can partake of some warmed ale while you wait."

Unable to refute his own warning, Brother Thomas nodded once, curtly, and Richard followed Meg through the door, pulling the heavy slab of wood shut behind them as they left. She still looked wound tight, as if it were taking all her strength not to let a stream of curses fall from her lips.

They hadn't proceeded far down the hall before Richard cast a sidelong glance at her. "While I am observant enough to realize that there is no love lost between you and Brother Thomas, you were nevertheless quite sharp with him in there. Why?"

"Because he pretended ignorance about something he knows full well, and it irritated me," she answered, keeping her gaze trained in front of her as they rounded the corner toward the second chamber.

"Concerning Eleanor?" Richard asked, acknowledging the swell of pain that rose with the question, even as he nodded to Hugh, who was still standing guard outside Eleanor's door.

The blacksmith returned a respectful bow and then gave way, leaving his post to turn toward the stairs. Meg paused with Richard in front of the chamber, giving him a look that was half exasperation, half pity. "Aye, concerning Eleanor," she said. Her voice was soft, yet it apparently echoed louder than she'd expected within the hollow length of the hall, for she winced and lowered her tone even further when she spoke again. "It has been a long time for you, perhaps, and yet before you enter this chamber and see her again, you need to understand something, my lord. Eleanor is not . . ."

She paused, pressing her lips together for an instant and looking away, as if trying to find the right words. She looked back at him again, her fingers threaded tightly in front of her. "Eleanor is lost in a world of her own making much of the time, driven by demons that no one else can see. When she is calm and peaceful, it is but a fleeting moment, sometimes no more than an hour in a day. And even then her emotions are precarious. She—"

"I know, lady," Richard broke in, unable to bear a further recitation of Eleanor's haunted existence. "Far too well, I know." He fisted his hand at his side, his mouth twisting with grief and bitterness as he spoke. "My wife is a weeping child one moment and a stone-faced statue the next. At other times she sits and rocks, humming wordless tunes with no end. It is a pity beyond bearing. I had hoped to find her healed after my time away, but such was not to be."

He saw Meg unsuccessfully try to conceal her surprise. Did it seem so strange to her, then, that he knew—that he *cared*—about Eleanor's loss of peace?

The thought stung. He knew he shouldn't concern himself with anyone's unflattering opinions of him. It affected naught but his pride, and God knew he had little room for that any longer in his life. Still, it rankled nonetheless.

Tamping it down with ruthless force, he directed his energies to the here and now. There was one more question he needed to ask before he could steel himself to face Eleanor again. "Tell me, lady, does Eleanor still cling to her poppet of rags?"

Meg's gaze snapped to his face at that. Something she found there must have satisfied her, for her expression softened, and at last she answered huskily, "Aye, she keeps it with her always and becomes quite distressed if it is misplaced, even for a few minutes."

Richard's jaw tightened, and the sick feeling in his stomach intensified. "Perhaps it is best that I see her now, then, before her mood shifts."

He uttered the statement with finality, but he found that it was difficult to push his voice past the lump that seemed to have settled at the base of his throat. Lifting the latch at the door, he added, "Accompany me inside, if you will. Eleanor may not react well, and you are a familiar face to her."

A slight frown marring her brow, Meg nodded silently, falling into place behind him as he pushed open the portal that had hitherto concealed his wife from his sight.

And then he forgot all else. His gaze took in the small, dimly lit room with its single, barred window; Eleanor was curled in a chair at the far end, facing away from him. She didn't turn to look as he entered—but the haunted shades of his past did. In his mind's eye they seemed to come more alive than ever before, lifting their shapeless heads, fluttering toward him in a dark, swarming mass . . . fixing their burning stares on him as he stood there in the doorway.

He gritted his teeth, his chest burning as the guilt began to twist deeper, deeper inside him. Goaded by the pain, he stepped resolutely across the threshold . . .

And straight on a path to his own personal hell.

Chapter 3

She was so thin. Richard saw her only in profile, but he could tell that much from the way her gown hung in folds and from the sight of the fragile, clawlike hand that clutched the poppet as she rocked soundlessly in her chair. A pang went through him, cutting him with a kind of ferocity. He forced himself to take another step toward her. And another. Her head was bent, her blond hair hanging in limp strands to shield her face from him as he approached.

He reached her side at last, and going down to one knee beside her, he reached out his hand to gently touch her shoulder. She stilled her rocking but didn't turn to look at him. Not yet. The thing she held was tipped toward him, the deformed, pushed-in mass of linen and yarn that was its face sending a new wave of nausea through him, followed by the pummeling force of grief so strong that it nearly stole his breath.

Do not think on it. Now not, not now, not yet . . .

Closing his eyes against the assault, he brought himself

into control, pushing those thoughts, those memories to the back of his mind. They weren't gone, only subdued for the moment, but it was enough for now. He knew he couldn't manage them and her all at once; they'd need to lock *him* in a guarded room somewhere if he tried.

"Eleanor," he said softly. "Lady, it is me, Richard. I've come home at long last."

She didn't react for a moment, remaining motionless, the only sound in the room the hollow rasp of her breathing and an occasional faint popping of a log on the fire.

"Ella," he said, lightly touching her shoulder again. "I—"

His voice fell silent as she finally lifted her head, turning her face to look at him, and then the breath did freeze in his throat, so strong was the anguish that flooded him. She was still beautiful. Aye, hauntingly, ethereally beautiful. But her eyes pierced him to the soul. They were vacant, almost as if she had lost her sight. She stared at him—through him—for a moment. Then her brow furrowed slightly, her teeth worrying her lower lip. She blinked several times, before she suddenly squeezed her eyes shut and threw her head back.

A low, keening moan came from her throat, subdued behind clenched teeth, as if she was trying not to cry out. The grimace was awful to see, accentuated as it was by her pallor and the sharp-boned features of her thin face. Then her mouth worked, and she shook her head back and forth. She was trying to tell him something, he realized, and he leaned in, straining to hear. Her fingers clasped convulsively on the poppet, distorting its torso even more. And that was when he finally made out what she was saying.

"Isabel . . . Isabel . . . Isabel . . ."

The sound of her voice was hollow and eerie, sending a shiver up Richard's back, and in the next instant he felt as if the floor had crumbled beneath him; Eleanor's face suddenly brightened, the wrenching anguish that had shadowed it dissipating like clouds blown away by the sun. "Oh!" she said half aloud, shifting her tear-streaked gaze to the thing on her lap. "Here she is!" With a little cry of joy and a watery smile, she lifted the poppet into her embrace and cradled it gently, rocking it and beginning to hum the same wordless tune she'd once sung to their flesh-and-blood child.

The sight curdled Richard's blood, the sound of that melody raking his soul, ripping more deeply into the painful wound of five years ago. It had never truly healed, and the pain that encompassed him now scorched like fire. Though he didn't want to remember, the other times came flooding back. He remembered the angelic beauty of their child's smile, heard her sweet singsong voice as she used her chubby fingers to tuck a flower, taken from Eleanor's golden hair, into her own soft brown curls. His stomach heaved. Eyes burning, he lurched to his feet and turned away, unable to bear the sight any longer.

Desperately he looked for the door, holding himself as still as he might for fear that he might shatter if he even breathed. It was too much. He couldn't bear it, though he knew he deserved to feel this agony. He couldn't stay here; he had to get away. And then he saw Meg. Her eyes were filled with tears too. So sad . . . and yet full of understanding and sympathy. Sympathy for *him*. That realization edged its way past the horrible swell of emotion flooding him, and he felt the stiff mask he'd made of his face begin to crack.

Nay! He couldn't allow himself to feel any of this. He shook his head, and forcing his feet to move at last, he took a step toward the door. But he never took a second one, for at that moment a chilling shriek rang out behind him, and he felt the slash of nails along his neck, followed by a hurtling weight dropping on his back. Everything seemed to slow, drawn out in a maddening stream of sensations and images that was somehow beyond his power to comprehend. An arm snaked round his throat, cutting off his air, and long tendrils of hair swung into his face, obscuring his vision.

He heard Meg shout something, and his instincts finally caught up with the befuddled mass of his thoughts. He twisted, gripping Eleanor's arm and unwinding it from his neck even as he shifted his weight to press her to the floor. She went limp in his grasp, sinking to the stones with a moan. Hugh came hurrying into the chamber, followed by Brother Thomas. Though the cleric shrank back against the wall at the sight that greeted them, the smithy stood by prepared to help as Richard lifted Eleanor to her bed.

Once Richard released her atop the mattress, Eleanor pulled away, whimpering, and began to grope and grasp at the coverings, continuing until Meg hurried to the bedside to deliver the poppet into her hands. Then Eleanor quieted abruptly; her eyes squeezed shut as she pressed the bundle of rags to her chest, rolled to her side, and pulled her knees up.

In the aftermath, Richard stood very still, just looking at her. His fists were clenched and his chest heaved, the turmoil inside him barely beginning to ebb to a semblance of sanity. Eleanor was motionless now, but not peaceful. Nay, not that. She lay rigid, her whole body wound tight as a bow, clutching the ragged poppet as if it were her link to salvation.

This was his wife, heaven help him. His *wife*. It did not matter that he could summon nothing to fill the raw, aching hole of darkness that yawned wide whenever he thought of her. She was his responsibility, his duty to protect—and it was clear by what had happened today just how well he'd served her. *My God, no wonder that everyone at Hawksley despises me . . . that I despise myself.*

"I should leave now," he finally managed to say in a low voice, his jaw tight with all he was suppressing inside.

He caught Meg's gaze for an instant before he turned to the door, feeling another start of surprise as he did. No longer filled with tears, her eyes were somber and clear, her face revealing a kind of calm strength. Though she must have been disturbed by what had transpired, her expression was not condemning of him as he'd expected it would be. She simply watched him, as if she was trying to learn the inner workings of his heart and mind.

Well, she could keep looking, he thought with a latent burst of animosity, because he'd be damned if she'd find anything there. How could she, when he didn't even know the full extent of the shadows that lurked inside himself?

With the bitter taste of loss filling his throat, he offered her and the two men a curt nod, then turned on his heel and strode out of the chamber into the welcoming emptiness of the corridor.

Less than an hour later, Meg prepared to enter Richard's solar, having been summoned there shortly after Brother Thomas's departure. Considering that Hawksley's lord could choose to dismiss her from service at any time, Meg knew she should make haste in obeying. Even so, she found herself hesitating in the shadows of the doorway.

Truth be told, she was still trying to make sense of what she'd witnessed in Ella's bedchamber. Richard had behaved in a way that had startled her, to say the least. After all she had heard about his careless, grasping—and if the stories of his feats of arms for the late king were true, his quite *violent* nature—the last thing she had expected to see when he met with his mad wife again was tenderness. A man such as he, lodged in the bosom of the arrogant Templar Brotherhood, should have reacted to Eleanor's behavior with nothing less than repugnance and disgust. Yet clearly their reunion had been devastating to him.

The end of it had been horrible; there was no doubt about it. Sweet heaven, to see Eleanor drift into delusion and then bodily attack him, to watch the grief and pain that had consumed him afterward, had been wrenching. His emotions had been tightly reined in, perhaps, but they were apparent to any who chose to look. Aye, she'd have sworn on her life that he'd played no pretense in his reaction to Ella.

And so it seemed that the gossips had been mistaken on one account, at least. He truly cared about Eleanor. And that meant that everything else she'd been told about this powerful warrior might be suspect as well. *Might be*, she reminded herself, for she had little other proof of his nature besides what she'd witnessed an hour ago, along with his decision to let her remain at Hawksley Manor for now. The rest remained to be seen.

"Are you planning to come in, lady, or shall we conduct our discussion in the shadows near the door?"

Meg jumped a little. By the saints, she'd done it again. She seemed to be making a habit of losing herself in thought whenever she was called to speak in private with Sir Richard.

"Nay, I will come in," she called softly, taking the remaining few steps into the chamber, and hoping that her unfortunate tendency around him wouldn't lead him to think her dim-witted.

"For what did you request to see me, Sir Ri—"

His raised brow, reminding her of their agreed-upon informality, brought her up short, but no less than the sight of the man himself, now that she was in full view of him. It was clear that he had begun preparations to retire for the evening; he'd removed his over-tunic and mantle, so that he wore naught now but boots, breeches, and shirt. The neck opening of the linen garment was untied, and she caught glimpses of smooth, hard chest when he stood up from where he'd been sitting, behind a large table where piles of parchment and ink pots were scattered.

As he moved she was struck anew by the realization that he was a man of compelling physical beauty; in this casual setting, more than ever, he exuded a sense of masculine grace . . . a leashed power blended with a comfortable elegance that was nothing less than intoxicating.

Swallowing, Meg paused, her reaction to him inspiring both mortification and alarm. She could not allow this to happen; she lived as a servant on his demesne, and though it rankled that anyone could hold such power over her, he was by right of law and society the one man at the moment most in control of her future, barring the king himself. Just as damning, he was a Templar Knight, and Eleanor's husband— forbidden in every way. That he was vigorous, strong, and undeniably handsome should have no bearing on the matter; she'd known dozens of men who fit that description, and none of them had had this effect on her.

None but Alexander, and look where that got you.

The sly words slid into her heart like poison, stabbing deep. Setting her jaw, she met Richard's gaze. "Well, then. For what reason did you wish to see me?" she asked, leaving off the personal aspect of address entirely.

She thought she saw a glimmer of humor in his eyes before it disappeared under the old, somber weight once more. He leaned back to half sit against the table, motioning for her to take her ease on the stool close to where she stood.

"It concerns Eleanor," he answered, a muscle in his temple jumping, though his face remained unreadable as he seemed to study her own, "and what happened in her chamber today. I imagine it must have been very difficult for you to see."

Though he might be disciplined enough to keep his face composed, the stricken expression in the green-brown depths of his eyes loosed another unbidden rush of sympathy in her. It caught her off guard, and she shifted uneasily on the bench.

"However, while I regret the pain it must have caused you," he continued, "I would have you know something further from me, as well as learn something more from you, regarding her and that unfortunate scene."

Not trusting herself to speak, Meg simply nodded.

"For the first," Richard went on firmly, "I have been made aware that there are certain . . . tales abounding both here and at the village concerning my care—or lack of it—for my wife." No longer as impassive, his face showed a determined cast that made Meg realize suddenly, just how formidable an opponent this man might be on the field.

"Have *you* heard any of these tales?" he asked.

Meg felt herself flush, especially considering that she'd been thinking of them just prior to entering this chamber. "Aye, some of the stories have reached me," she admitted.

"And you have believed them, no doubt."

"Well, I—that is, I—I may have thought they held some truth . . ." Her voice trailed off. But her discomfiture was quickly followed by a flare of irritation. Squaring her shoulders, she tried to refute the heat burning in her cheeks. She would not be ashamed of this. Sir Richard de Cantor had no grounds to blame her for believing what she'd heard; it was he who had abandoned Ella, leaving her to grieve for their child alone. Guilt over that had plagued him—was plaguing him still—if what she'd seen today was true. Why should she feel embarrassment in admitting the doubts she'd harbored?

"It is not that I bear you ill will for that," he said, as if he'd read her thoughts. "Considering Eleanor's condition, I would have been surprised if you had felt otherwise." His lips pressed together. "In truth, what you heard about me was correct. At least to an extent."

His unexpected admission filled her with exasperation. He was forever doing or saying something unexpected and causing her to soften toward him in the process.

"You consider yourself a monster, then?" she asked after a moment. Her voice sounded clipped, as she tried desperately to forge an emotional distance from this man with whom she was beginning to feel a dangerous sense of empathy. "You admit to being selfish, greedy, bloodthirsty, and utterly reckless with the feelings of others?"

To her amazement, his expression shifted, but not to the anger she'd hoped he'd show. Instead she saw a flash of teeth as he suddenly threw back his head with rumble of laughter that threatened to topple him from his perch against the side of the table. When it had passed, he looked at her through eyes still crinkled at the corners. "By the Rood, I had heard they'd crafted tales at my expense, but this exceeds even what I had imagined. So it is as bad as all that, is it?"

Against her will, she felt a smile tugging her own lips. "I am afraid so."

"If that is the case, I suppose I shall have to do a better job of behaving like the ogre I am supposed to be."

"I think I prefer the man I've observed these past hours," Meg murmured, still smiling, though in the next instant she wished she'd kept her renegade words to herself. Her response had called his gaze to her face again, his stare warm and somehow penetrating, as if he was trying to discern whether she was in earnest.

Finally, with a tip of his head, he acknowledged her comment. "Be that as it may, lady, I would have you know the truth beneath the talk. Eleanor's welfare has never been far from my thoughts, regardless of my distance from her and Hawksley Manor. It was for her sake, most of all, that I joined the Templars when I did."

The Templars.

Suddenly it wasn't so difficult for Meg to summon the chill into her heart once more. She raised one brow. "I may be far from a scholar, my lord, but throwing oneself into the ranks of power-hungry men who operate under a veil of secrecy and hidden rituals, who profess to swing a holy blade in one hand while committing crimes of hypocrisy with the other, seems an odd way of showing care for someone. How, pray tell, could that help Eleanor in her affliction?"

He didn't answer at first, his expression darkening. When at last he spoke, his voice was hard. "It is a complicated matter, lady, with reasons and circumstances that fall beyond the scope of your knowledge—though I have been told that you are well familiar with the practice of offering up one's body to suffering for the purpose of redressing sin," he added with a pointed look.

He spoke of her penitential beatings, she knew. The very

thought of them, and of the duplicitous cleric and vicious abbess before him who had dispensed them on her, filled her with a sense of rage that drained the blood from her face. She sucked in her breath, her hands fisting at her sides. How dare he bring that up, as if it had anything to do with what she'd asked him? His had been a voluntary action taken, while her so-called penance had been enacted *upon* her without so much as a—

"And as long as we are in the midst of a seeming interrogation, I have a question of my own for you," he continued, still clearly angry. "Why do you disparage the Templar order so thoroughly and at every opportunity? I have never claimed to be a saint or even a man of inherent goodness, but the Order is a holy one, overseen by the pope himself. The rite of entrance is a secret, well-guarded ceremony, it is true, but admission into the Order is achieved only through rigorous testing of body and spirit. What right have you to mock it?"

"That of my own experience," she retorted hotly. "The Templar Brotherhood is flawed and corrupt, serving as naught but an instrument of death to far too many innocent souls. Men are sent off against their wills to suffer through godforsaken deserts, dying in battles over which they had no say. I beg your pardon, my lord, but I find it difficult to believe that God condones such carnage, whether under the auspices of the Holy Mother Church or nay."

"I see," Richard answered, gripping the edge of the table he leaned against until she could see the whites of his knuckles. "So it is the *fighting* Templar Knights must do to which you object, then? What of the protection we provide to pilgrims and holy places? I agree that it would be far easier to have continual peace and goodwill among men, lady, but the real world is far more violent than that, I am afraid."

Meg made a sound of annoyance in her throat, shaking her head and getting up from her chair to pace toward the solar's window. Her hand rose to press the silver pendant hidden beneath the bodice of her gown, heat stinging her eyes as it always did when she allowed herself to think on this subject overmuch . . . to let her thoughts drift even the tiniest bit into memories of those horrible weeks so long ago when, heart in her throat, she'd waited for word of Alexander.

And when it had finally come, so awful, bloody, and hateful, delivered with cold precision by the man who called himself her sire, it had set off the pains. She'd been confined to her bed. And then thirteen agonizing hours later, her life as she'd known it, with all her hopes and dreams of the future, had ended forever . . .

Turning to face Richard from her position at the window, Meg tried to blink back the heat, schooling her face into even lines. "Nay, my lord. It is not the fighting that Templars engage in to which I object. Even I, pampered and cosseted as I was for most of my life, know better than to think this world may be traversed without near-constant violence. It seems to be the way of mankind, and in that regard the Brotherhood is no different from the rest." She looked away again, staring out to the blackness of the yard beyond the pane, and feeling the cool air seep through the cracks to bathe her skin.

"What I do not accept about your beloved order, however," she continued more quietly, "is the corruption and abuse it allows, wherein a man may be *forced* into service with them. If enough gold crosses the right palms, men can be compelled to join, whether they will it or nay. Such a thing flies in the face of Templar law, so far as I know, for though the proceedings are notably secret, you yourself have confirmed that the Brotherhood is supposed to be very selective in its decision of who may join the ranks." A satirical smile tilted her lips. "But then again, many other forbidden lines are crossed every day by devoted Templar Knights, clerics, and sergeants, are they not? Vows of poverty, chastity, obedience . . . all broken at will or as the time suits. You cannot deny the truth in that, my lord, no matter how dedicated you have been to the Brotherhood. Not if you have eyes."

"Perhaps some break their oaths, lady," Richard answered darkly, "but not all. Not I, nor most of the men with whom I served and trusted my life."

He sounded subdued now. Serious. But she couldn't look back into the chamber yet to meet his gaze. She remained too close to tears to risk it. She swallowed, trying to keep them at bay. That tremulous smile still in place, she murmured huskily, "Would, then, that you and your friends had been comrades to the knight of whom I speak, and perhaps he would not have died."

He was silent for a beat before he said, "This man who died in Templar service—he is the one you loved before you came to Hawksley. The one for whom you sacrificed your honor and were sent away in disgrace."

She couldn't stop herself from turning to him then, her gaze widening, even as a hot tear escaped to slip down her cheek.

He nodded gravely. "I have heard something of your past through Brother Thomas."

A bitter laugh escaped her, and she blinked back the remaining moisture. "Aye, well, perhaps you have not also heard that Brother Thomas is filled with half truths. Concerning me, he was told only what my father wished known by the world, and he repeats that much as if it were all. That my scandal deprived my sire of a lucrative match for me at court

I do not deny, but there is far more to the tale that no one at Hawksley or elsewhere has been privy to hear, praise God."

Richard didn't respond to that, and a silence, thick with what remained unspoken, settled over them. She looked down at her tightly clasped hands, wondering if he was waiting for her to tell him more. But even if he commanded her to relate the whole truth, she could not. It was too painful to think on, no less to discuss.

And in that pain she and Eleanor shared a bond. She'd recognized it immediately after her arrival at Hawksley. In truth, she and her anguished cousin were separated in their experience by little more than a span of time and the thin veil of the twilight world behind which Eleanor had retreated. At certain moments, Meg herself had yearned to find that place of blessed unknowing . . . had wished she too could disappear into a safer realm of her own making, rather than continue to bear the hurt and memories that would swell to consume her. Yet such was not her path, it seemed. Cold, hard remembrance was her lot in life, fortitude in the face of distress a skill at which she was becoming quite adept.

"I am sorry that you have suffered, lady," Richard said gently at last, "and that the one you loved was killed in unwilling service with the Templars. But you must understand that such a thing is a rarity. The Brotherhood as I have known it is composed of good and honorable men who take their duty to God as a holy calling, worth the risk of death."

"And yet there is corruption," she argued. "Rules are broken and bribes accepted."

"Aye, it is an unfortunate truth. Corruption is inherent in any group, though only because mankind itself is corrupt. It is as unavoidable as sin, but I tell you that the Brotherhood strives hard to overcome such elements."

"King Philip of France does not seem to think so," she answered, still incensed and therefore reckless in her daring. "His action against the Templars less than a fortnight past speaks volumes."

She hazarded a glance at Richard as she spoke and saw his face tighten. He paused as if absorbing the blow of her words. When he directed his gaze to her, she felt the weight of his anger—and his pain as well—burning into her, and it set off a flare of guilt in her breast.

"The king of France," he said lowly, "will have his own burdens to bear when he comes to final judgment. But hear you this: Within the ranks of Templars it is well known that prior to the day of mass arrests, King Philip the Fair applied on no less than two separate occasions for acceptance into the order. Both times he was refused, due to suspicion that he showed more interest in gaining control of Templar coffers than a desire to do holy work. It is *that* which is likely behind the arrests, more than any supposed corruption or heretical practices."

Meg felt a twisting sensation as the import of his words sank in. That monarchs could be corrupt as well as Templars was no great surprise, but she'd heard nothing of this particular scandal before. "I—I did not know," she murmured, looking down again.

"Nay, lady, you didn't—nor did the rest of the world, thanks to pressure exerted by King Philip to keep it so. Like you, I possess knowledge and truths that I cannot or will not divulge. And so, while I respect your feelings and their source, I will ask that you refrain from openly denigrating the Brotherhood in my hearing. Will you grant that, at least?"

She gave a short nod.

But her concession could go only so far, she knew; in the

next moment she raised both her gaze and her chin, adding, "I will agree as long as you do not require that I attempt to alter my thinking on the matter as well."

A wry smile lifted one corner of Richard's mouth. "Far be it from me to attempt to control your thoughts, or the thoughts of any woman, for that matter. You are free as always to think as you will."

"Very well, then."

He looked at her, his expression softer now that his anger had abated. "We are not all so terrible, you know. The knights with whom I rode and fought are good men, none without flaw, but with honest hearts and a desire to see right done. Such qualities can be rare in this world, it is true— and yet they do exist, if you will but allow yourself to see them."

Heat filled Meg's cheeks and she frowned, glancing down to her hands again. "I will consider what you have said about the Templars, Richard. But please do not expect me to simply recant all I've felt and believed . . . all that I and those whom I have loved have suffered. I cannot."

"I understand."

A sense of calm seemed to settle over them with that—a feeling almost of camaraderie that took Meg by surprise. It was . . . *pleasant*, she realized, the warmth of the shared empathy shimmering between them and connecting them. Richard seemed to feel it too, his expression enigmatic and his gaze alive with the play of emotion.

Too soon, it dissipated; as if to hurry it along, Richard cleared his throat and pushed away from the table's edge, moving back around behind it to sit in the chair there, as he clearly prepared to conclude their conversation. He glanced away and then met her gaze once more. "There is one thing more I must ask of you before I return to my correspondence and you retire for the evening," he said.

"What is it?"

"It concerns Eleanor. Willa seemed worried, earlier, at the thought of you sleeping in the same chamber with her, and after this afternoon's incident, I too am questioning the wisdom of you staying unattended in her company."

Meg nodded, glancing away herself now. Her fingers ached from how tightly she clenched them in her lap. She knew his query was well-founded; Ella had become violent before, though never so uncontrolled as what she'd witnessed today. Still, what choice did she have but to share a room with her mad cousin? The hard truth remained that such an arrangement was far better than being sent home or, God forbid, back to the abbey.

"I do not know what to say," she answered quietly, "other than that I have had experience dealing with Ella's outbursts. I—I can always summon help if it is needed."

"She behaves often in this way, then?"

"Her actions have become more unpredictable recently, aye, and she has sometimes become violent with those of us who care for her, but I promise you that never in all the time I have been here has she lashed out as wildly and as fiercely as she did toward you this after—"

Meg cut herself off, the stillness that followed her statement deafening. She glanced up at him even as she felt the damning bloom of heat again in her cheeks. "I am sorry. I did not mean to wound in saying so."

"It is but the truth as you know it, lady," Richard replied. "There is no need to apologize."

Looking down at his table, he shuffled the parchments,

straightening the ink pot and aligning the quills as if he craved something to do while traversing through this awkward moment. Despite his assurance, Meg knew that her words had stung him, and she was possessed of a sudden urge to comfort him. To banish the shades of self-recrimination filling his eyes.

"So," he said, looking up from the papers at last and seemingly in control once more, "you are content in the arrangement as it stands?"

"Aye, it will suit."

He nodded. "We shall give it trial, then, but only if you give your word to apprise me should anything change, either in Eleanor's actions or your feelings of safety in her presence."

"I will." Meg stood then, feeling somehow discomfited as she'd been earlier, though she had no reason for it that she could see. If anything, Sir Richard de Cantor had been surprisingly accommodating to her, speaking with her as if she were of some importance, rather than merely a disgraced woman who served in his household, distant kinship with his wife notwithstanding.

"I will leave you to your correspondence, then," she murmured, backing toward the door. "Good night."

Richard paused in the act of dipping a sharpened quill into the ink, fixing her with a gaze that was both penetrating and thoughtful. "Aye, lady, I hope that you will sleep well. But if aught goes amiss, simply call out, and I will come, I promise you."

Meg felt a catch in her throat as he said that, choking her so that she was compelled to nod her answer, so untrustworthy did she deem her voice at that moment. No man had concerned himself with her safety in so long that the sweetness of the care being offered to her now both startled her and touched her deeply.

But why from this man and at this moment, when I have only just begun to regain a sense of balance in my life?

Holding herself rigidly, she took the remaining steps to the door. She could not test the question further in her mind. She *would* not. Nay, she would hold it—and Richard de Cantor—at arm's length. In time, doing so would aid in resolving the muddled mess that had become her feelings. She would see to it.

With a last, long look at the man who sat in dignified silence at the sturdy table, she ducked through the door and hurried down the corridor to the second best chamber and the company of the troubled, lost woman who slept fitfully there.

Richard watched Meg go, trying to crush his constant reaction to her by force of pure will. Heaven help him, but Lady Margaret Newcomb was proving a torment the likes of which he'd never endured. It wasn't just her clear disapproval of him and the Templars or her cutting tongue that tested him, though such things were a trial, no doubt. Nay, it was worse than that. She represented something far more dangerous to him—the embodiment of pure feminine temptation. His body rose in response to her as if he were a green lad, and he, who had prided himself on his self-control, was helpless under the onslaught of aching desire.

It mattered not that she was as little like the polished beauties he'd known at court as a gentle breeze was to a raging tempest; in fact it was that about her which drew him more strongly. There was something about her . . . something that lingered inside him like the teasing lilt of a long-forgotten song. Even the gentle scent of her as she'd crossed the room a few moments ago had been enough to ignite a smoldering fire inside him, the sight of her dark hair, glossy in the candlelight, making him yearn for nothing more than to loose it from its confines and drag his fingers through its silky weight.

To even consider the act of touching her, to feel the smoothness of her skin beneath his palm . . . Sweet Jesu, but it was an image he knew he must do all in his power to banish from his mind.

He tried to slow his breathing, struggled to forcibly calm the heated coursing of blood in his veins. Blessed heaven, but when he was near her he felt so alive—more alive than he had in five long years. And yet he knew she was beyond his reach, a pleasure he could not touch, for many reasons. He was married, damn it, whether or not his union was a loveless one to a woman who had long ago lost her link to sanity. And though no longer a Templar in office, he remained so in spirit, bound in his heart to the saving vows of poverty, obedience, and chastity that had given him strength and comfort when he had needed them most.

Besides, he reminded himself once again, even were those obstacles not aligned against him, he still could not escape the knowledge that every time he allowed himself to feel tenderness toward a woman, it led to naught but disaster. He was not meant to be a husband or a lover . . . or perhaps even a friend to any woman—especially one as beautiful and unattainable as Lady Margaret Newcomb.

He twirled the quill in his fingers, staring at the light reflecting off the wispy edges, before swallowing hard and trying to focus on the parchment in front of him. But the few words he'd scrawled blurred before his eyes. He shook his head, struggling to regain his self-control.

If nothing else, service in the Brotherhood had secluded him and every other Templar from females for good reason. The monastic life he'd led for the past five years had helped him to remain focused on the spiritual. Carnal yearnings were easily suppressed when one was surrounded by sweaty, battle-weary men intent on serving God and staying alive to do it.

But now all buffers were gone. When he looked at Meg, he felt stirrings that were . . . disturbing, to say the least. And forbidden.

Gritting his teeth, he looked down at the parchment once more, reading over the words he'd written and reminding himself again of their purpose. It was a message to Braedan, his older brother and only remaining family. He lived less than two days' ride hence, serving as sheriff of the region just north of Sussex—and therefore having the ear of the king, just as their father and his father before him had done; Braedan would be anxious to learn of Richard's homecoming . . . and Richard was eager to know what, if anything, Braedan had heard at court regarding the imminent fate of England's Templars.

With a sigh, he scratched the remaining few phrases on the parchment, folded it, and prepared to drip wax over the break to seal it with a de Cantor signet ring, one of which both he and Braedan possessed. Next would be a missive to the new king himself. Brother Thomas had spoken of the forthcoming nuptials of the king's favorite, Piers Gaveston, taking place at Tunbridge Castle in Kent, which stood little more than three days' ride from Hawksley.

If anything that Richard had heard about the continued bond between the young king and Gaveston held true, such an event was sure to be elaborate, including days' and per-

haps weeks' worth of games and tournaments in way of celebration. That young King Edward himself would be in attendance seemed a foregone conclusion, considering the close
relationship the two men shared. Richard had witnessed their
attachment himself while serving at court under Edward's
sire, though the adolescent friendship had been discouraged
by the elder monarch while he was still alive.

But since his father's death this past summer, Edward II
had by all accounts set Gaveston up in an elevated position at
court, even going so far as to name him Earl of Cornwall, and
culminating in arranging this lucrative marriage for him to
the king's own cousin, Margaret de Clare. Regardless of the
reason for his being at Tunbridge, Richard planned to use the
occasion to press King Edward with the suit of the English
Templars, in hopes that the new monarch would be strong
enough to resist the pressure that France's king—Edward's
future father-in-law—might bring to bear on him.

Dipping the quill into ink, Richard leaned over a fresh
parchment and began the missive . . . glad for the focus it
gave him, so that, for a short time at least, he might put the
tormenting image of soft brown eyes and full, ripe lips from
the forefront of his mind.

Chapter 4

Meg hurried from the back entrance to the manor house, sucking in her breath at the chill that enveloped her. As unpleasant as the bite of morning cold felt, she was thankful for it too; it would help to clear her head and perhaps allow her to seem alert, even if her body knew better. She was bone-tired, Eleanor's fitful sleep during the past four nights having left her exhausted, body and soul.

Last night had been the worst thus far, though she'd not dared to call for Richard. To do so would have been tempting fate and the security of her place at the manor, not to mention the disturbing feelings she could not seem to curb whenever she was near Hawksley's lord. Besides, Ella hadn't become unmanageable yet. It had been simply arduous trying to help her cousin through her constant, seemingly tormenting dreams. Usually Ella would flail and call out, nothing more, but last night she'd gotten out of bed to run toward the window, clutching at the iron bars that had been placed there for her safety, pulling at them desperately and weeping.

When Meg had reached out a hand to her in the dark, she had turned with a sob, muttering, "Don't touch me; no one must touch me!" before she ran back across the chamber and rolled into a silent ball on her bed. It had been enough to send a chill up Meg's back, and she'd kept a wary eye on her cousin's still form for at least an hour after that. But nothing more had come of it. Only this feeling of crushing fatigue that was left behind.

Ella had been sleeping this morning, though, when Meg slipped from the chamber and locked it behind her to come to the village. Meg hoped she'd rest peacefully until Willa brought up warm bread and sweet milk later, as was their custom each day. Meg would spend time with her again in the afternoon . . . perhaps Ella would allow her hair to be brushed, or she'd agree to bathe if Meg called for her tub.

At least she didn't have to worry about seeing Richard through what would come today, she thought as she hurried to the western limits of the village. With the exception of morning Mass, he had been notably absent from the manor and village during daylight hours since his return home, occupied in conferring with Brother Thomas at the preceptory over Hawksley's accounts and records. She planned to use his absence to her advantage, slipping away from the household to fulfill the promise she'd made to William Carpenter's widow in the village.

Although nearly all the villagers had faced draining struggles in the past year, Joan Carpenter had suffered more than most as a result of her husband William's untimely death. She and their four young children were in imminent danger of losing even more today, for this morn the village began the

annual grape harvest for making wine. It was an event for
which Joan, who was nursing infant twins, would struggle to
complete her share of mandatory labor owed to the manor.

By law, everyone in the village must toil on the lord's behalf before any work could be done for personal gain, and as
head of the household now that William was dead, Joan was
responsible for providing the standard three days' labor in
grape harvesting and wine making; if she didn't, she would
be assessed a monetary fine that she would have no hope of
paying.

Meg strode a little faster through the nearly deserted ham-
let, her jaw as tight as was the hand she clenched around the
rope handle of the bucket she carried. The infuriating truth
was that long before today, Brother Thomas had brought
Joan and several other village families into desperate straits
through his management of the manor in Richard's absence.
When William had collapsed and died during the threshing
this past summer, Brother Thomas had insisted on collecting
heriot, or death tax, for him. The law allowed Brother
Thomas to claim the deceased man's best beast, which happened to be a rather thin cow. Paying the debt had been a terrible burden for William's widow and children to bear.

Yet that hadn't been the worst of it. Nay, Meg thought, grimacing as she rounded the corner and headed toward the
grape arbor that had been cultivated in the sunny, western-
most field. In his pursuit of gain, Brother Thomas had
stooped so low as to invoke the other half of the age-old
death custom, mortuary, claiming the family's second best
beast as well—in this case their only remaining animal—for
the benefit of the Holy Mother Church. As village curate,
Brother Thomas had been within his rights to make demand

for the animal, she couldn't deny it—but in cases of hardship such as this, it was a custom more often overlooked by the Church than not.

Now, left with little other than a small plot of ground barren but for a crop of water-soaked oats, Joan and the children would face a nigh on impossible task of keeping body and soul together this winter. And so it came to be that, though she courted trouble in doing so, Meg felt compelled to ease their burden in what way she could—which today meant picking grapes enough to fulfill their work obligation to the manor harvest.

The fence that enclosed the vineyard loomed ahead, and Meg readied to open the gate and enter the area, seeing a cluster of villagers already gathered there for the morning's work.

"The harvest is half rotted already, thanks to the past month's rain," she heard Matthew Graves say as she traversed the remaining distance. He was the wealthiest of the free villeins and the estate's reeve as well. "An early freeze will spell disaster. We must pick today. There will be nothing left if we do not," he finished, shaking his head.

"God help us all, then," echoed one of the women, tugging her shawl closer beneath her chin with chapped and reddened fingers.

"Aye, God will *need* to help us, if we're to survive—all but His Lordship, that is, the great Templar Knight, returned after these five years," answered one of the cotters, Thomas Chofton, twisting his mouth as if he'd tasted something sour. "Sir Richard will get his due of the harvest, never fear, even though we be left with naught but rotted chaff after he's collected it. All we have gained with his return is the trading of one falsely holy tyrant for another, if you ask me."

Suddenly several of those gathered caught sight of her, and talk quieted. One villager coughed, and Tom looked away and spat on the ground, as if to hide his shame in realizing that she'd heard him disparaging their lord.

Meg paused, a tiny ache unfurling in her chest; she felt the gulf that once more yawned between herself and the common people of this demesne. It was a separation of blood—the weight of centuries of class division—though she'd tried her best to shake off her title and melt into the fabric of village life.

"Has the entire crop been ruined, then?" she asked matter-of-factly, trying to push through the awkward moment by nodding to them all as she walked into their midst as if nothing was amiss.

"Too soon to tell about that or about how much of a harvest we'll get. We'll have to pick and press as usual, even barrel the juice to ferment, if it will, before we'll be able to tell if 'twill turn out to be a passing wine," Matthew said, uncrossing his arms to come and stand near her.

She nodded. "Well, then. We'd best get to work, hadn't we?"

"Beggin' pardon, Meg," Thomas called out, pulling his hat off and nodding in deference, "but with His Lordship returned home and all, do you think 'tis wise to be coming down to the village to help us like this?" He colored slightly, crushing his cap in his meaty hands. "Make no mistake—we're mightily grateful for all you've done for us in the past," he added, backed by a chorus of assenting murmurs. "But that was when 'twas only Brother Thomas watchin' over things—and we could tell pretty well when he'd be around, to be sure you'd be back up to the manor house in time so there'd be no trouble."

"Aye, Meg," Matthew finished, frowning, his voice a low

rumble. "Sir Richard is another matter altogether. None of us knows what he might think—or do—if he found you down here with us."

Meg stiffened. It looked as if there would be no glossing over any of it, then. But oh, how she hated the fear tinging the men's voices. It was a tone she'd heard far too often in her life—a tone reserved for dealings with the members of her class. She had done her best to escape reminders of her past, and yet it seemed she would never quite escape the accident of birth that had made her an earl's daughter.

"Sir Richard is an unknown factor, I'll grant you that," she settled for saying. "He might indeed react as Brother Thomas has, in regard to me working in the field alongside you—and yet I have spoken with Sir Richard myself through my position caring for Lady de Cantor; I do not think that he is the kind of man to protest my assisting you. Truly, it is worth the risk, and I will bear the burden of any trouble that comes of it, if it does, I promise you."

No one spoke, though a few nodded in agreement, while others looked down at their feet or shook their heads. Meg pursed her lips; she had to do more to convince them to let her help. None of these people had any extra bodies to spare in helping any family but their own to accomplish their manor fee with the grape harvest. If she didn't set them at ease, Joan and her children would suffer for her failure.

"Consider this," she added, loudly enough for them all to hear her, "just like most of you, Sir Richard was startled when I requested that he use my given name in dealings with me. But in the end he agreed, unlike Brother Thomas, who has continued to address me by my title, even after these two years. Does that not show the tolerance of Hawksley's lord in these matters?"

Several of the men mumbled agreement, seeming to lean at last in her favor. She decided to add one final argument to seal their acceptance. "Besides, even if Sir Richard proves to be more rigid in his outlook of this, he isn't here in the village this day to pass judgment—nor is he likely to show himself, spending his daylight hours as he has at the Templar precep-tory. It is safe for me to work alongside you this day, and I do it gladly."

With a few remaining murmurs and a few more nods of as-sent, the twenty or so villagers welcomed her and set about their work. She nodded her appreciation as she joined in, helping them to partition off the portion of vineyard to be picked for the lord's share first. Then they all fell to their task in earnest.

It was difficult work, and before an hour had passed, Meg's hands felt stiff from cold and the repetitive motion of reaching into the vines to pick off sometimes half-rotting clusters of grapes. Nary a word was spoken among the villeins, except for a few comments about the condition of the fruits.

After several hours of picking, Meg's basket was finally full, and she left the row to add what she'd gathered to the cart that was standing a little ways away from the manor's bailiff, James Osgood. He'd arrived shortly after work be-gan, and now he sat in what seemed to be bored silence, every now and then glancing up to the clouds thickening the sky, as he marked a parchment with the amount collected by each family in accordance with their duty to Hawksley's lord.

Several of those working glanced up frequently too, worry apparent in their expressions. When a rumble of thunder sounded in the distance, a few villagers gasped, all activity coming to a halt as everyone turned to look at Matthew, who, as reeve, had been in charge of organizing the work for the day. He exchanged a glance with the bailiff before making his way over to him.

The people waited while the two men conferred, Meg standing a little apart from the rest, near the cart as they did; Matthew made a few harsh-sounding comments under his breath, too low for Meg to hear, but it was clear that he was in favor of gathering together their things and heading for shelter with what had been picked already. A few times, he jerked his head in the direction of the children who had been pressed into work for their fathers, to aid in making up their share of goods to the lord. The fact that they were working with the rest wasn't unusual in and of itself, Meg knew, but several of them were so thin and frail that they chattered in the cold, even with the activity that was keeping everyone else fairly warm; a hard wind would be difficult for them to bear.

The bailiff sat stiffly, his expression tight. He pointed several times to the parchment log he was keeping; Meg could hear enough of what he said as he raised his voice while conversing with Matthew to know that not enough fruit had been gathered to fulfill the villeins' obligation to the manor. If everyone took to shelter now and a storm did sweep through, it could destroy what remained of their already meager crop.

But before anyone could come to a decision, a strange silence settled over the area, a hush that felt charged, somehow, and made the hairs on the back of Meg's neck rise. The stiff breeze quieted, and a thick feeling hung in the air.

Tom Chofton suddenly raised his arm, pointing to the horizon. "Sweet Mother of Mercy, will you look at that? It's comin' right for us!"

Meg's gaze snapped to follow Tom's outstretched hand; she stumbled ahead into the row of vines to get a better view, and an involuntary gasp burst from her. The sky at the horizon roiled with angry clouds, seeming black as pitch in places. The storm was so virulent that arcs of lightning and slashing rain could be seen with the naked eye, though the front wall of the deluge was beyond the farthest reaches of the village's fallow field.

As if responding to an unspoken cue, everyone scrambled into action, working feverishly to throw half-full baskets of grapes into the cart and to gather the harvesting implements; Meg hurried with several of the other women over to the children, several of whom were beginning to cry, and helped them in carrying their baskets from the rows of vines, while the bailiff reached to pile up his parchments. Others grabbed hold of the old mule harnessed to the cart, trying to entice the beast toward the nearest cottage having a door large enough to fit through. But the mule felt the unnatural atmosphere surrounding them as well as any—perhaps more—and it brayed in panic, pulling at its tether and kicking frantically to run as its instinct prompted.

Without further warning, the wind picked up in force, and Meg paused in what she'd been doing, struggling with stiff fingers to unknot her shawl and pull it over her head. But a gust seemed to yank the fabric from her hand, and it flew to the ground several yards away before whipping out of sight with the rest of the debris, branches, and leaves that swirled with the descending storm. Then the rain began in earnest, icy and strong, stinging her head, face, shoulders, and arms like hundreds of biting insects.

Confusion swelled, people crying out in a discordant sound that battled with the storm. Someone shouted Meg's name, and squinting through the rain, she raised her hand to shield her eyes, trying to gain her bearings. It was Matthew;

he gestured for her and the rest to come in his direction, even as he turned toward the cluster of cottages nearest the vineyard, followed by many of the other villagers. They continued their attempts to coax the carted mule forward, though in their haste now, some actually pushed along the sides of the grape-laden vehicle to force the beast forward from behind.

Setting her jaw and battling the slashing force of the wind, Meg tried to follow the reeve and cotters, intent on lending her weight to the cart and ducking into shelter with the rest until the worst of the weather passed. But through the tumult, she suddenly heard what sounded like a child crying. Her breath caught in her throat as the noise became recognizable, a repeated cry of "Mama!" cutting through her and bringing her to a standstill at the edge of the vineyard.

Twisting around violently, Meg tried to find the source of the noise. Her breath rasped painfully in her throat as she stumbled toward the spot. At last she found the child, a boy of no more than two, huddled beneath a tangle of vines that had blown over on top of him and a woman who was lying senseless next to him; she had some kind of gash on her brow, the blood visible even through the tempest unleashing itself around them. As Meg got closer, she could see that it was little Nathaniel Parish and his mother, Sarah, another poor woman of the village who made ends meet by taking in sewing and occasional lacework.

Scooping up the boy, Meg knelt to try to rouse his mother. But Sarah didn't respond. Mother Mary, protect us all, Meg prayed silently as she stood to call for help. She heard a loud crack from the wooded area that stood beyond the vineyard and just managed to twist around to protect Nate before a thick branch slammed into the back of her shoulder and scratched her cheek. It hit hard enough to make her see stars, the pain of the blow making her lose her breath for a moment. Desperately she clutched Nate closer and turned the rest of the way, ignoring the white-hot agony that shot down her neck as she shouted for help.

There was no response, and panic gripped her; no one could hear her.

There would be no aid.

Choking back a sob of fear and frustration, Meg set Nate down next to her, leaning over to say loudly, "Come Nate! You must hold on to my skirts and walk with me while I try to pull your mother to shelter."

"No! I scared . . . Mama!" Nate yelled, eyes squeezed shut and his face twisted in agony. He swung his head back and forth with his dirt-streaked hands pressed to his ears, as if he could block out what was happening around him by will alone.

"I know you're frightened, but you must do as I say," Meg shouted over the wind. "We have to get you and your mother inside!" As if to punctuate her words, the rain, now mixed with sleet, began to fall even harder, the force of it more painful with each passing moment.

Finally Meg pried one of his hands free and got him to clutch at her skirt, while she leaned over and grasped Sarah beneath the arms. Her own eyes squinted shut against the raging elements, and she tried to keep her face down and upper body hunched over the senseless woman to protect her and Nate as best as she could, while she began to drag her out of the vineyard and toward the cottages where some of the others had taken refuge.

Their progress seemed agonizingly slow, but then, blessedly, before they'd traversed half the distance to the crofters' huts, she realized that someone was stepping up next to her to take hold of Sarah. A shock went through her, even amid the wildness of the storm. It was Richard. Where he had come from or why he was even nearby would need to be answered later; right now she just praised heaven that he was here. Matthew hurried up behind him to help with Sarah, all of them remaining silent by necessity. Words of gratitude would have to wait. Meg bent to scoop up Nate in her arms again, hurrying much faster now as she followed the men and their burden into the cottage.

With a gasp she finally stumbled across the threshold of one of the rough dwellings and released the frightened little boy. He immediately scrambled to his mother's side, his whimpers quieter now, and in those few seconds, Meg's eyes adjusted to the dim atmosphere inside the hut. It was one of the larger cottages in the village, she realized, narrow and long enough to house a few pigs, a goat, and several chickens at the end farthest away from the villeins' living quarters. She tried to gain her bearings, her senses feeling strangely muddled after the bombardment of the elements; her ears were ringing, while her back and cheek throbbed from the blow she'd taken.

The women's voices rose in worried murmurs and words that continued to sound far away to Meg's ears; they clustered around Sarah, guiding the men to lay her on a pallet away from the door's draft. She could see Richard directing their progress, and she sensed the villagers' reluctant acceptance of his low-voiced orders concerning Sarah, but she felt too exhausted to utter a word herself.

Looking away in what felt like numbed slow motion, Meg suddenly realized that a small fire sputtered and smoked near the center of the crowded dwelling; it seemed in danger of being put out by the sleet coming in through the hole directly above it in the roof, but it was still viable enough to cast some heat, and she lurched toward it, trying to keep her hands from shaking too violently as she held them out to the blessed warmth.

Her knees felt shaky, and sinking down to the packed dirt floor, she tried to stop her teeth from chattering as she reached one hand up to assess the scrape on her cheek. Her fingertips came away dry, though their saltiness stung the area she'd touched. Not so bad, then.

"You've been hurt. How did it happen?"

The low, masculine voice sounded close to her, surprising her with its hint of worry. She turned to look and winced at the pain that shot down her neck. "A branch was tossed by the wind, and it struck me as I knelt to help Nate and Sarah."

Richard crouched down next to her, his brow furrowed and his gaze searching. He touched a finger beneath her chin, and though he tilted her face just slightly more to look at the scrape on her cheek, she still couldn't stop herself from stiffening with the further discomfort.

"Does it pain you so much, then?" he asked gently.

"Nay," she managed to say. "Not there. But the branch hit my shoulder first, and now it is difficult to turn my head."

"Let me see."

Richard's gentle command brooked no room for argument. Though she'd have been hard-pressed to recall a time when she'd entertained the idea of allowing a near stranger—and a man at that—to loosen the lacing of her bliaud, she did so now, giving herself up to Richard's ministrations. Something about his manner brooked no nonsense, and as he moved around behind her to better see the injured area, she tried to relax. His cool, strong fingers slipped beneath her under-tunic, easing it open in preparation for sliding both it and the bliaud off her shoulder. If she hadn't been in such pain, she'd likely have felt mortified at the prospect; as it stood, she knew naught but relief.

"You seem adept at this," she murmured, wincing again as the tunic caught. "Have you been trained as a physician?"

"Not exactly." Though she couldn't' see his face, she could tell that his gaze was trained on her battered shoulder as he answered. "But I served in the most elite division of Templar Knights, and through them I was taught much about healing, to supplement my proclivity with the sword. Such knowledge is useful in the aftermath of battle."

In the next moment, any other attention to his response was lost in sickening throbs of pain, as he gently pressed and explored the affected area with his fingertips. She couldn't stop her harsh intake of breath in response then, or the soft moan of agony that slid from her throat afterward.

"There, now, it is all right," he murmured, his lips almost at her ear from his position behind her. "I will be as swift as I can, but I have to see if the bone is broken. Try to breathe deeply. It will help with the pain."

She did as he instructed and found that it did make his prodding easier to bear. Before long, he was finished, but rather than pull away, he began to stroke his fingertips in a feather-light, repetitive pattern from the top of her shoulder downward, lifting his hand and breaking contact with her flesh each time. Confusion filled her, and she thought to turn her head to question him but was stilled in the act by first a memory of the agony it would cause her, and then, more gradually, by a realization that deep aching lessened with each full stroke of his hand.

"What are you doing?" she finally managed to ask him.

"It is a method for drawing away the pain."

Perhaps because the hurt had indeed eased somewhat, this time she felt the warmth of his breath caressing the spot just below her ear as he spoke, sending delicate—and, she was sure, entirely inappropriate—tingles up the back of her neck in time with his stroking fingers. She kept her face averted, hoping the flush she felt wasn't spreading to the flesh exposed to his gaze.

"You've sustained a deep and likely quite painful bruise, but nothing appears to be broken," he went on, as though he was oblivious to the sensations he was inspiring in her. "This action will help, as will the application of some special oils I have among my possessions at the manor house; I brought them with me from Cyprus, and they are widely known in the Holy Land for their healing properties. But we cannot wait so long as that to begin treatment, and so I will needs apply some common liniment to your injury right now."

"You carry liniment with you?" she asked, more than a little bewildered at the idea of such foresight.

"Nay," he answered, and she could have sworn she heard the smile in his voice. "Even I am not that prepared. The salve I'm thinking of is made easily enough. I'd wager the goodwife of this dwelling has what is necessary to mix it right here in this cottage."

With that, he ceased the stroking movement of his hand, stood, and walked toward the villagers, who were still clustered at the end of the narrow hovel. To her discomfiture, Meg realized that she was acutely aware of his absence, the air around her seeming somehow colder and far less comforting.

Richard exchanged a few words with Catherine, the wife of the villein who rented this domicile from the manor; Catherine looked none too happy—nor did many of the others who huddled together, some around Sarah, whose bleeding wound had by now been staunched, or any of those who sat together near the larger cook-hearth, every so often casting baleful glances at him before surreptitiously looking away again.

But in the next moment Catherine wrung her hands one last time and shuffled off to a corner of the cottage, rattling some pots before she returned with what looked like two handfuls of dried weeds of some sort, a small stone pestle and mortar, and a folded bit of cloth. She jerked her chin toward the shadows at the other end of the cottage and mumbled something that Meg couldn't make out.

It soon became clear what she'd indicated to Richard. He took the plants and tools Catherine offered and walked by Meg with a nod and an encouraging smile toward the animals that were lowing and fidgeting behind a wooden half wall that separated them from the family's living quarters. The storm continued to boom outside, causing the animals to react with fear, but Richard spoke in a low, firm voice to them as he approached, and they seemed to quiet a bit. He disappeared behind the wall, and except for the sound of the goat *baaa*ing and a few liquid, swishing sounds, all was quiet. Before long he returned to her side, working the pestle on a greenish-gold mash.

"Milfoil mixed with goat's milk?" Meg asked, casting him a dubious glance, as she caught a whiff of the herb's unmistakably pungent odor. "I've only ever seen milfoil used for broken bones, or perhaps hanging in a doorway to dissuade insects. Why do you use it in the liniment if my bone is not broken?"

"I'm blending it with comfrey. The milfoil cannot hurt, and the comfrey will help the flesh to recover from deep bruising more quickly," he said, grinding the mass a few more times before he tested the consistency with his finger.

"I've never heard of comfrey," she said, frowning. She turned to present her injured shoulder again at his gestured command. "What is it, and how did a simple goodwife come to have some in her supply?"

"It is also known as bruisewort," he answered, setting down the mortar and pestle and unwinding the strip of cloth just behind her and off to the side a bit. "Does that sound more familiar?"

"Aye, I have heard that name."

As he continued his preparations, Meg asked, "How did you come to be near the vineyard when the storm struck?"

"I was returning from the preceptory, where I had been studying the accounts with Brother Thomas."

Meg stiffened again as he readied to spread some of the mixture on her, but then she sensed him pausing. He shifted behind her, sitting back on his heels as he apparently considered some problem.

"What is it?" she asked, turning her neck as much as her discomfort would allow.

"I must confess that I've never dressed a woman's wounds before," he said, a bemused expression on his face, "and so while I can apply the liniment easily enough, so long as your clothing is in place, it will be nearly impossible to affix the bandage that must needs cover it."

Meg dared to glance again at Richard, to see if any part of what he'd said was in jest. His green-gold eyes held a hint of lightness in them, and his sensual mouth was quirked up on one side, but it was clear he was in earnest.

"What do you propose we do, then?" she asked hotly, "for I cannot very well remove my garments in front of all these people—nor would I if it were only you and I in private," she added, with embarrassment creeping heated fingers down her neck, "for you are not a true physician, nor am I so badly wounded as to wish to suffer that immodesty."

"And yet I would not leave your injury untreated in waiting for the storm to ease enough for your return to the manor. I will ask for the aid of one of the village women."

Meg nodded slightly in agreement, and he stood again to make his way again toward the gathering of villagers near the main hearth. He remained there while Catherine, the good-wife who had provided him with the ingredients for the liniment earlier, broke away from the others to approach her. Catherine frowned as she knelt down next to Meg, though whether in sympathy or from some other concern, Meg couldn't discern.

"His Lordship says I'm to wrap a bandage on your shoulder, Meg."

"Aye, it would be a great help if you would. I did not think it proper for Sir Richard to do himself."

Catherine gave a soft snort as she set to the task, and though Meg couldn't see her face, she knew instinctively that the woman was scowling. "I'm fair surprised that he was willin' to dirty 'is 'ands as much as he did," Catherine muttered. "We all were, I'll tell you."

Meg looked over to the knot of villagers to whom Catherine referred, noting that they'd all ceased speaking completely, now that Richard stood in their midst. He tried to begin conversation, offering a few words to Matthew, but he was answered cursorily before he fell silent and glanced over to her. She winced as Catherine tightened the bandage the first time, using that as an excuse to look away from his searching gaze. But it remained on her nonetheless. She could feel it.

"You were hurt like this helping Sarah and her boy, weren't you, lady?"

Meg nodded in silence, still trying her best not to look over at Richard again. Catherine moved around in front of her then, and blessedly it gave her something other than Richard and his stare to focus upon.

" 'Twas a goodly thing for you to do," Catherine continued, her lips pressed together in conviction. "Far more Christian than His High-and-Mighty, if ye ask me. For all his aid with Sarah and seeming concern for you, 'tis he who has allowed Brother Thomas to drain us of our life's blood."

"Sir Richard has only just returned home after a five-year absence, Catherine," Meg chided gently, surprising herself again in her defense of the man that not long ago she herself had been mentally berating. "We cannot know if he even knows the true extent of Brother Thomas's iniquity yet."

"Aye, well, if he is like any other noble lord or lady, 'twill not matter in the end. Brother Thomas will not suffer for what he's done. Them in the nobility always protect their own—or where Brother Thomas is concerned, them that they've placed in positions of authority over the rest of us."

Catherine's words, delivered with such unexpected matter-of-factness, stabbed deeply into Meg . . . more deeply than the pain that bloomed in her shoulder. But before she could gather her emotions enough to speak, Catherine froze with sudden remembrance of Meg's true breeding. A strangled sound escaped the woman's throat.

"Beggin' pardon, Meg," she said, grabbing her hand and squeezing. "I didn't mean to say that you were—that is, I know that you be a lady true-born, but neither I nor any of the others think of you as anythin' but one of us—I—I mean, not that you're a villein, but just that you're not like them, is all I meant to say . . ." Catherine sputtered, her voice trailing off in despair.

Meg tried to force a smile, not wanting to make Catherine feel worse than she already did. "It is all right. I understand and take no offense. In truth, I appreciate your care of me today," Meg said, beginning to try to slip her tunic and bliaud back over her bandaged shoulder.

"It—it's just that Sir Richard . . ." Catherine continued, trying hard to make amends, "well, I fear he be like all the rest of the high and mighties who have no care for those who sweat and bleed into the ground they trod as their right, and—"

She broke off suddenly again, her lips clamping shut at the same moment that a shadow fell across Meg. Though she didn't expect it, she felt unaccountable warmth uncurl inside her as Richard came close and nodded to Catherine, who had rocked back on her heels, gathering up the remaining strips of linen before she stood. Immediately Meg chastised herself for her bold thought. Richard was Eleanor's husband, whether or not the two shared a close or loving relationship. She herself had no right to indulge any kind of response to him, especially one that involved noticing him as a man. It could lead to naught—and she was quite contented with that truth, she added to herself, lifting her chin rebelliously.

"Thank you, mistress, for your aid with the bandaging," Richard said to Catherine, inclining his head in polite acknowledgment.

The goodwife didn't answer, her mouth still tight, but her cheeks colored a bit, and she jerked her head in an answering nod before hurrying back to the main hearth.

Sitting down next to Meg again on the dirt-packed floor, Richard inspected what he could see of the binding on her shoulder, making a small sound of approval.

"How does it feel?" he asked.

"Better, thank you," Meg answered, pulling at her laces

with one hand and then gingerly raising her injured arm to complete tying them. "I will be back to lifting and carrying in no time, I think."

"Not too quickly. You will need to rest your arm for a week, at least. At the manor house, you must apply the ointment I spoke of twice daily until I deem your shoulder fit for service again."

"Until *you* deem it fit?" Meg gave him a sharp look. "Forgive me, my lord, but I do not think that is your decision to make; the tasks that I undertake each day will not wait for my ease to complete them."

"And yet I command it," Richard said, scowling. "You cannot use that limb too quickly or the injury will not heal properly."

"And what of the work that must be done in the meantime?" Meg asked, cocking her head as much as her injury would allow, and fixing him with a look of consternation. "Willa has more than enough of her own to complete, as do Agnes and Mary, who can be paid for only a few hours each week. We are stretched as thinly as possible at the main house."

"Perhaps one of the village women, then," Richard said, glancing over to those of whom he spoke, who were once more talking quietly while some of the others peered out the cracks in the door to check the severity of the storm. "Wouldn't one of them find it to their advantage to come up to the main house and work with you for a week's time?"

"Oh, aye—if they could divide themselves into two, it might be possible," she retorted. "Why do you think I was in the village this morn, helping with the grape harvest? No one can be spared; it is beyond the ability of many poor families to even see to their own obligations after contributing their manor share."

Richard looked surprised. In the next moment he just shook his head and reached out for more peat moss to throw on the small fire in front of them, though she thought it foolish to try to combat the icy sprinkles of rain that kept coming through the smoke hole in the roof in seeming effort to douse it. "It must be even worse than I suspected, then," he said.

"What do you mean?"

"In going over the manor accounts with Brother Thomas, I noticed certain unusual . . . trends. He is clearly benefiting from his position as Hawksley's steward, and the Templar priory is flourishing with what it has gained from this estate yearly since I bequeathed half of its worth to the Brotherhood upon joining the ranks. Yet the records still show an increase of goods for my benefit as lord of the manor as well. So either this simple estate has miraculously become the most prosperous in the land, or else unfair practices have been brought to bear in order to drive the profit toward those in charge."

"Of course Brother Thomas sees the decisions he has made very differently, you can be sure." Meg looked down at her hands, her jaw feeling tight, as it did whenever she allowed herself to think about the Templar cleric and his ruthless tactics of acquisition.

Sighing, Richard ran his hand through his still-damp hair and raised one knee from where he was sitting, cross-legged, on the floor, propping his elbow atop it. "Naturally, I believed the glares the villagers have been giving me since my return to Hawksley were based upon their view of me as an errant husband. It appears that I have far more to atone for with the people of this demesne than I'd realized."

Meg was silent for a long moment before she nodded. "It will be a daunting task, to be sure, should you decide to undertake it. One which will likely impact your own level of comfort and prosperity; you will be forced to do with less, perhaps in some areas *much* less, if the scales are to be evenly balanced once more."

"That is not a concern," Richard said, unfolding himself from his seated position to begin to stand, "though just how I will accomplish it remains to be seen. I do know, however, the solution to the problem we spoke of earlier, concerning your injury. Until I deem your shoulder fit to resume normal activity, I myself will assist you in any work that must needs be done at the manor."

"*You?*" Meg exclaimed, drawing the attention of most of the villagers in the process. Matthew scowled and muttered something to Tom, though by the way he kept looking over at Meg and Richard, it was clear that he wished to keep an eye out in the event that she needed someone to come to her aid, lord of the manor or nay.

"Truly, you cannot be in earnest," Meg continued more quietly, though she was still incensed, standing now herself, though her progress to that position was not nearly as smooth or graceful as Richard's had been.

"I am. I have finished examining the manor records to my satisfaction; there is no reason that I cannot assist you in whatever tasks you require at the main house until you are fit to resume them yourself."

"But . . . but the work I do is not the kind that a man, no less a knight, is accustomed to performing. Much of it involves menial labor, and as lord of this estate you cannot—"

"Tell me, *Lady Margaret*," Richard broke in, deliberately using her title, she realized with a flush of pique, to make his point. "Do you believe me incapable of performing humble work simply because I bear the title of sir before my name?

You seem to forget that, unlike you, I am of common birth, the youngest son in a family whose only mark of honor came in serving as loyal justices to the king; yet I carried that modest charge proudly, long before I was a celebrated knight at Edward's court—and as a Templar I again learned to mortify my pride by performing the lowest of tasks. There is nothing you could ask me to do that would be beneath me. I wish you to understand that, for I will have my way in this for both our sakes."

Meg swallowed back the retort that had risen to her lips, realizing as she'd listened to his heartfelt statement that continuing to argue would be both petty and self-serving. He was sincere. Utterly and completely. Though ten thousand men in his position might have scoffed at the idea of undertaking the kind of labor to which she referred, she knew without a doubt that Sir Richard de Cantor meant every word he'd said, and it humbled her.

"Very well," she said quietly. "I will accept your offer of help without further resistance, then, and—"

A loud noise of banging and shouting outside made everyone jump, and Meg's final words were swallowed in the tumult that followed. The cottage door crashed open, bringing in with it a sweep of icy wind, rain . . . and a very distraught Hugh.

"Is Sir Richard here? By the Holy Mother, I must find him," Hugh gasped, staggering to a stop and pushing back his sodden hair to clear his eyes as he squinted to peer around the smoky chamber.

Over the wind still gusting through the door and the startled cries of those inside, it was difficult to hear anything; quickly, someone moved behind Hugh to shut the slab of wood against the ebbing storm, even as Richard called out, "Aye, man, I am here. What is the matter?"

Hugh swung his head in Richard's direction, his face a pale mask of shock and distress as he spoke the words that dropped like hammer blows on everyone within the shelter.

"It is your wife, my lord. Lady de Cantor has injured Willa and run away, fleeing out into the storm with nary a cloak nor a shawl to protect her from the elements . . . and God help us all, but we cannot find her."

Chapter 5

❧∽◦◦◦∽❧

Richard's muscles bunched in shock as he prepared to mount the steed that had been readied for him outside the stables; though the rain had stopped in the few minutes it had taken to get from the cottage in the village back to the manor house, the air still felt damp. Mist rose in cool swirls to blanket the saturated earth. In response to it, the men milling around in preparation to aid him in the search for Eleanor stamped their feet or tucked their hands under their arms for warmth, but they otherwise seemed to pay little heed to the conditions, except perhaps for the way it increased the feeling of urgency among them.

Meg stood stiffly, not far from Richard. Though he could not—would not—waste an instant more than was necessary before setting off, he turned to her briefly after swinging astride his steed, feeling as ever swept up in the play of emotions and empathy in her warm gaze. A pang went through him at the depth of understanding that shone there, and when he spoke he found that he had to push his voice past a thickness in his throat.

"I would ask that you have warmed water and several good blankets ready for our return," he said to her quietly, "though with Willa injured as she is, you will need to ask someone else to help you prepare. I'll not have you wounding your shoulder further while I am riding in search of Eleanor."

Meg nodded, her arms clutched around herself at the chill and tears welling in her eyes. "Richard," she breathed, her voice cracking on his name, "Please—I know this will be difficult for you, more difficult than you should have to bear, being so near to what happened here five years ago. But please, you must . . ." Her voice faded as she closed her eyes and breathed in, trying to regain her control.

The wrenching sensation inside him intensified, and he tightened his fists on the reins, the tension he felt apparently transferring to his mount and making it paw the earth in eagerness to run. Meg knew the whole truth, then, of what had happened on that awful day he'd lost everything that truly mattered. *Of course she knew*, he chided himself. *How could she be living at Hawksley for the past two years without someone conveying the entire, sordid tale of my irredeemable sin for her edification?*

Holding his steed in tight control, he glanced one more time to her, seeing that she looked at him again, now with worry clear in her expressive face.

"Do not fear, lady, I will find Eleanor," he said in a voice gone even huskier than before. "I will find her and bring her home as I did then. Pray God the ending of it will be different, though. Pray God . . ."

His voice trailed off to a choked rasp, the emotions, the

memories, and the pain of having to relive them now too raw to let him continue. Clenching his jaw in a welcoming burn and blinking back the heat that stung his eyes, he gave Meg a last, curt nod, then wheeled his mount around. With a call to motion, he led the men who would join the search through the gates out of Hawksley, feeling his heart thudding with the beat of his steed's hooves—and trying without success to block out the ghosts that clawed at him more deeply with every breath he took.

Meg moved away from Willa's pallet once more after checking the dressing that wrapped her head and covered the wound that Ella had dealt her when she escaped. Ella had become violent before, had scratched and sometimes even tried to bite those who cared for her, but it was still difficult to imagine her wielding an actual weapon of any kind—in this case, apparently a small but weighty iron used for the hearth fire—against anyone. And yet she had; of that there was no doubt. And now she'd gone missing, run off into the thick of the storm, just as Meg had been told she'd done more than five years ago on that terrible day that had marked her complete descent into madness.

The only thing different this time was that she'd fled into the tempest alone.

It had been several hours since Richard and the men had begun their search for her, and the shock of hearing the news had faded somewhat, but Meg's anxiety had intensified. Dusk was beginning to settle over the land, with no sign of their return.

Willa slept peacefully now, though she'd regained her senses for only a brief time since the attack on her. At least she seemed free from pain for the moment, Meg thought; her skin still felt cool and free from fever. This waiting, however, would drive the rest of them mad. Agnes had taken to ripping out hems and restitching them, while Mary, Hugh, and any of the villagers who came up to the house every now and again to see if there was any news, went around with hushed voices and steps, as if making too much noise would cast a bad omen on the search.

A commotion outside caught Meg's attention at nearly the same moment that Mary looked into the little chamber off the kitchen where Willa slept.

"Some of the men have returned, Meg," she said in a whisper fraught with anxious excitement, "and they say Sir Richard is close behind, with Lady Eleanor!"

"How is she? Did any say if she was hurt or how she fared?"

"Nay, only that she was found at the base of the narrow ravine to the north of Hawksley. She is being carried home by the master atop his steed."

With that Mary hurried out to ready the blankets that were warming near the ovens at the back of the house. Meg wiped suddenly damp palms along her skirt and checked Willa one last time before following Mary to perform her own part of readying the heated ale and water.

It only took a minute to prepare the things Richard had requested, and when they were set aside in jugs and pitchers near the blankets, she hurried to the front of the manor house. Wrapping a thick shawl around her shoulders, she used her good arm to push open the door and descend the three steps into the yard, noticing that many of the villagers were also gathered, huddled in groups on both sides of the path that led to the manor's gates. They looked toward that portal anxiously, some of the men who had gone on the search mumbling and pointing at something just beyond the curve of roadway, barely visible in the rapidly descending darkness.

Meg followed their direction and felt a start of relief and fear blending to produce a sharp, stabbing sensation in her stomach. It was the remaining village men, followed by Richard. He rode at a moderate pace—as quickly as he could go, considering the burden he carried in front of him. Eleanor looked as boneless as the poppet she liked to cling to, and though Richard held her closely to his chest, jarring her as little as possible in the ride, Meg couldn't help gasping and raising her hand to her lips as they finally entered the gates, wondering if perhaps he had found Ella too late, and life had indeed fled from her weakened frame.

Someone grasped his steed's bridle as he dismounted with careful attention to the woman in his arms, but as he approached, Meg's voice froze in her throat. She found that she couldn't ask him outright, though the need burned in her to know the truth; she didn't know if she could bear to hear her fears were confirmed.

But then Richard freed her from her struggle, meeting her glance for an instant. His own face was a mask of stony pain and dark emotion, as, in answer to the question he read in her eyes, he briefly shook his head, saying in a low voice as he passed by, "She still lives, praise God. She has been badly hurt, but she lives."

The flood of relief she felt was tempered as she watched him look forward, his jaw set so that she could see the ripple of muscle on the side of his face; he strode the remaining steps to the entrance, sweeping sideways with his fragile burden through the open door of Hawksley Manor . . .

And leaving Meg, along with everyone else who stood in witness, to grapple with the chilling uncertainty of whether, when all was said and done, he had brought Eleanor home to heal or simply to die.

The three days following their return vanished in a blur of activity and sleeplessness, interspersed with moments of agonizing clarity that etched themselves into Meg's heart and mind. Eleanor had roused from oblivion only once, just after Richard carried her inside the manor house. She'd regained her senses enough to struggle and cry out, feebly striking at him, before whimpering to be brought into the first chamber instead of to her accustomed bed. The outburst had been wretchedly painful for any within view to witness. Many had turned away, blinking back tears, but Meg, even through her own horror-struck empathy, had kept her gaze trained on Richard and Eleanor, as if that might somehow help to support them both through the ordeal.

That her cousin wanted to be carried to the first chamber, a room she'd had great difficulty tolerating for even a short while since the tragedy of five years earlier, had shocked Meg—and Richard too, if the expression on his face had been any indication. But to try to keep her peaceful, Richard had seen to her wishes, carrying her to the room he himself had only recently reclaimed, and having the warmed blankets, ale, and water brought in from the second chamber, where they'd been placed in readiness.

And that was where she had remained, hovering between life and death, for three days.

It took some persistence, but just before noon on the third day, Meg finally convinced Richard to leave the chamber for an hour or two; it would be at least long enough to get some fresh air, something to eat, and a warm bath, she'd reasoned. Ella had taken sick after the storm, and so in addition to her

injuries from the fall, she'd become feverish and had struggled to breathe at times. But for now she was resting peacefully; in fact, an hour after she'd sent Richard down, Ella
remained calm enough that Meg decided it would be oppor-
tune to go below stairs for a bit herself, leaving Agnes in
charge within the chamber and Hugh watching at the door.

She would need to wait to take a full bath as Richard had,
she knew, but she had time at least to slip into the second
best chamber, wash up, and change into fresh clothing. And
though the pain in her shoulder had all but vanished, thanks
to Richard's poultice on the day of her injury, she realized,
of a sudden, that she was hungry; her stomach rumbled
loudly as she tried to tame her unruly hair into some semblance of propriety within the confines of a circlet and
braid.

Her toilet complete, Meg prepared to go and find some
bread and perhaps a slice of cheese or an apple in the larder.
Peeking into the first chamber once more before heading to
the stairs, Meg met Agnes's gaze and received an encouraging nod, and so she descended to the main hall and made her
way down the corridor to the kitchen.

The house was strangely quiet. Nothing had followed rou-
tine since Eleanor had been injured, which accounted for the
uncommon hush all around. Many of those who might usually be occupied here or on the grounds preparing food, re-
pairing tools, or bending over steaming vats of laundry, were
instead stealing a few moments of precious rest or else down
in the village tending to work there. Even Richard was
nowhere to be found, and Meg thought it more than likely
that he'd decided to go outside for a while, as the weather had
been so uncharacteristically bright since the passing of the
storm.

Aye, she would be on her own to do as she wished, she thought, suppressing a shudder of delicious anticipation.

In the years since the painful outcome of her own transgressions with Alexander, she'd had almost no independence to speak of, lest it was time spent in the seclusion of her chamber, or locked in one of the nun's cells at the abbey where she'd been confined at the beginning of her penance. Traversing Hawksley Manor like this with none to watch and judge whether she was working as diligently as one in her shameful position ought to would be an indulgence, a throwback to her girlish fantasies, when she was not the lowly servant she had become, but rather the lady of her own fine estate, as she'd been born to be. In her reverie, she was beholden to none but her lord husband—and he would be a man who was wise enough to recognize her abilities and intelligence, and to encourage her individuality.

A man as Alexander had been . . .

The bittersweet twisting in her heart jerked her from the reverie, stifling it with a pain that still cut deep. Such imaginings were never to be. Alexander was dead—though even when he was alive, her father the earl had snuffed out the idea of their union. To see his youngest daughter, who was destined to fetch a powerful, influential husband at court, wed to a mere knight without even a fifth of the land that her dower would bring? Never. And so in the heat of her passion and love she had defied her sire, entering into her scandalous relationship with Alexander . . . and ensuring in the process that she'd never be fit to marry any of her father's prospects in the future.

Most damning of all to society had been the fact that she had given herself to Alexander willingly. A woman who had been used by force prior to her wedding night was difficult enough to foist off, but no man of noble birth and title would easily overlook the kind of open, immodest behavior she had shown, regardless of the wealth to be gained.

She gritted her teeth and strode onward. That she had *loved* Alexander hadn't mattered at all. She had learned the bitter lesson that love never counted when money was to be made or connections forged in powerful marriage alliances.

But it was in the past now, however, and unchangeable. The headstrong girl she had been had vanished forever under the painful weight of heartbreak, grief, and domination. It did no good to remember other times, or to dream other dreams.

Mentally chiding herself for allowing her silly reveries to hold sway over her for even a moment, Meg crossed the remaining steps into the kitchen in search of something to eat.

And instead found Richard.

He was sitting in a roughly hewn chair near the sturdy, knife-scarred worktable that Willa used for cutting vegetables. It stood near enough to the kitchen fire that it would be an attractive spot for avoiding the chill that seeped through any house in England, it seemed, from autumn to spring.

A ripped loaf of bread was lying on the table near his elbow, and his arm was slanted at an angle so that his chin could prop in his hand; a golden-skinned pear with one slice taken from it seeped its sweet juice into a tiny puddle next to the bread.

Meg's mouth quirked into a half smile. It was clear that exhaustion had taken over long before he was able to eat much. He looked almost boyish in sleep, his hair waving damply from his bath, the usually serious set of his face relaxed and . . .

Very, very handsome.

That realization sent a shock through her, and she felt herself flush as she took an instinctive step back. What by all the holy saints was wrong with her? She was behaving like a lovesick girl again, swooning over the sight of an attractive man. And not just any man, she reminded herself, but one who was a Templar Knight and pledged body and soul to someone else . . . to Eleanor—her tormented cousin, who even now fought to maintain her tenuous hold on life.

Shame suffused her. Such reactions weren't like the solemn, contemplative woman she'd become these past years. But something about Richard—some sense that thrilled to sweet, hot life whenever she was near him—made her remember feelings and longings better left in the past.

It is only because you were thinking about Alexander again.

The voice in the back of her mind didn't sound very confident, but she latched on to its reasoning like a drowning person clinging to a rope.

That is why you noticed Richard, nothing more.

Pursing her lips, she glanced to the side of the fire and the folded blanket that had been left there after the preparations for Eleanor's rescue; she took it up, determined to put anything from her mind but the tasks at hand. Serving others' needs was her only concern now and had been since she'd arrived at Hawksley. The pleasures of romantic love—of a husband, hearth, or home—weren't for tarnished women like her. That truth had been drummed into her relentlessly at the abbey, and she found to her surprise that she took some comfort and strength in it now, as she bent over Richard in preparation for arranging the blanket over his stretched-out legs while he slept.

But all her good intentions exploded in a burst of surprise when at that very moment, Richard made a low sound in his throat, reached up, and pulled her toward him. Before she could even gasp, his palm slid swiftly and gently past her cheek to delve into the loose braid at her nape and bring her mouth to his in a kiss that was so thorough and passionate that it took her breath away.

When she tried to protest, he gave a little tug, and she toppled forward on him. Her words were smothered under the pressure of his mouth, and a soft moan broke from her as he deepened the caress, tasting and seeking. Instinctively she responded in kind. It had been so long since she'd been kissed like this, and it felt . . . wonderful.

The sensation of his lips playing over her own sent liquid heat spiraling through her, reducing her to boneless jelly in his arms. Fortunately for her, Richard was quite capable of supporting her weight, even in his nearly prone position; he held her closer, his warmth seeping through her clothing to pitch her senses higher with the intimate contact of her breasts and belly pressed against his muscular body.

Somewhere in the depths of her buried consciousness, the voice inside her sprang back to life, announcing that what they were doing simply wasn't right. Under the rush of sensation, its call was even more muted than before, but she heard it nonetheless, and it commanded her in no uncertain terms to cease this delicious torment. Valiantly, Meg tried to obey, but it was more difficult than she would have ever imagined.

It took her a few moments longer than it should have to finally pull away from Richard. At the same time that she pushed up in an effort to stand, he stiffened abruptly, seemingly brought to full awareness by her movement. His eyes snapped open, and he scrambled to his feet as he tried to assist her in regaining her balance as well.

One of his hands still clasped hers warmly after they stood; the other lingered on her waist. With a murmured curse, he let go of her as if her touch burned him.

"Lady, I pray you forgive me," he murmured, frowning and pushing his fingers through his hair as he looked away. "I do not know what possessed me to do that just now. I—I can only say that I am—I mean, I hope you can—"

"It is all right," Meg broke in, her voice sounding calmer by far than she was feeling. Kissing him had been both wonderful and disquieting for her. That it was a forbidden kiss was difficult enough to bear; the only thing worse would be to have to endure listening to him confess what a terrible mistake it was, one that he regretted with every fiber of his being.

"I—I am not offended," she added, somewhat more huskily. "I am at fault as well, for not finding means to awaken you sooner. Please think no more of it."

He remained silent for a moment, continuing to look off-balance and troubled, though the slight darkening of his complexion revealed a level of embarrassment as well. But then, clearing his throat, Richard met her gaze again, obviously preparing to say something further.

He never had the chance. Before he could voice the words, Hugh looked in at the door, his expression pained and his voice somber as he said, "Pardon, my lord, but it is Lady Eleanor. You must come quickly. Agnes says she has taken a turn, and it does not look good."

When they reached the chamber, Agnes was leaning over Eleanor, murmuring soothing words and bathing her brow with a dampened cloth. The room was dim but for a slant of sun that shone through one of the shutters, and yet no light was needed to know that Agnes had called for them with good reason; Eleanor's breath came in frequent, shallow gasps, the effort to take them wracking her thin body so that she seemed to struggle with each tortured inhalation.

Meg stood a little to the side of Richard, and she could see his face in profile; his expression was controlled, but a muscle in his jaw jumped, before he closed his eyes for an instant, his mouth tightening.

When he opened them again, it was to glance at Hugh and murmur, "Call for Brother Thomas."

Meg's heart sank; Brother Thomas had administered Last Rites shortly after Eleanor was brought home, but she seemed to have rallied since. That Richard wanted the cleric to return only confirmed what Meg knew to be true and unavoidable now. On leaden legs, she approached her cousin's bedside, kneeling beside it to take Eleanor's frail hand in her own for what might well be the last time.

"Hush, Ella," Meg murmured, trying to keep her voice steady as she raised her other hand to gently stroke Eleanor's cheek. "All will be well. Rest, now. Try to rest."

The growing lump in Meg's throat prevented her from speaking further. But something she said, or the gentleness of her touch, perhaps, must have seeped through Ella's torment, for she did seem to calm a little, and her breath, while still labored, did not seem to pain her as much.

Richard had approached the other side of Ella's bed as Meg spoke, and now he knelt, meeting Meg's gaze, his own filled with sadness as he clasped his hands and bent his head over Ella in prayer. Meg felt as if the three of them were poised over a great chasm, waiting . . . waiting for something to break the heavy spell that held them in thrall.

For a moment more, the chamber remained still, but for the rasp of Eleanor's breathing. Then Richard finished his prayer and reached out to take her other thin hand in the sheltering warmth of his own. As if in reaction to his movement, her eyes fluttered open, and she turned her head to look at him . . . and most startling of all, to offer him a faint smile of recognition.

Richard stiffened in response; his own breathing caught as he stared down at her. "Eleanor?" he asked softly, and Meg's heart contracted at the cautious, desperate hope she heard in his voice.

"Aye, Richard, truly it is . . ." Ella answered. Her lips were pale, and she began gasping again as the exertion of saying those few words took its toll, leaving its mark in the spasm of pain that brought her delicate features into a grimacing frown. Richard tried to support her, lifting her shoulders off the bolster a bit, and she seemed to breathe easier.

"I—I need you to know," she continued haltingly, her voice still hoarse, "I never meant for it to be—for you to—" but before she could finish, her voice was cut off with another choking inhalation, succeeded by wracking coughs. Meg lurched forward as well to help prop her up this time, biting her lip as she and Richard worked together to try to alleviate Ella's suffering.

Once the coughing stopped, Eleanor attempted to take another breath. Nothing happened. She gasped and struggled for air, but it was in vain, and Meg and Richard were left with little they could do but look on, horrified by their inability to help her.

Shaking her head from side to side and arching back in

their arms, Eleanor squeezed her eyes shut. A trickle of wetness seeped from the corners, and after a few more agonizing moments, her lips began to take on a bluish cast, her cheeks looking sunken. Desperately Meg stroked Ella's back to try to soothe her, all the while stifling tears herself, as she murmured, "Sweet heaven, Richard, what can we do to ease this?"

"I do not know," he said. His own voice was low and close to cracking with the torment of witnessing Eleanor's suffering.

Finally the spasm passed. The tension in Ella's body ebbed, and she was able to take in some air. She lay very still, gasping in shallow breaths for several minutes. When she opened her eyes once more, it was to look first at Meg, then at Richard, struggling to say in a scratchy whisper, "You need to know, it was not your fault . . . not yours—"

"It is all right, lady. Do not speak," Richard murmured. "Please, you must conserve your strength."

She shook her head slowly but remained silent as he'd asked. Meg saw her swallow once, twice . . . and then abruptly, she stiffened and gazed straight ahead, her breath coming in short and shallow pants as before. A kind of light filled her expression, and her body tightened, only this time with what seemed like anticipation.

"Isabel," Eleanor gasped on an exhalation.

Richard went completely still in response, though Meg wasn't entirely sure she'd heard anything at all, Eleanor's voice was so tenuous. But then Eleanor gripped Richard's hand tightly and began shaking it back and forth, her knuckles showing white; she seemed to be trying to get his attention, though she did not shift her stare. Suddenly, a smile of pure joy broke over her face, and another swell of tears rose and seeped from the corners of her eyes.

"It is Isabel," she cried, her voice still hushed with her weakness. "Do you see her? Oh, blessed angels . . . tell me you see her, Richard—please, tell me! Look—you must *look*!"

Richard flinched as if he'd been struck; he was keeping himself so tightly in control that Meg could almost feel the strain of it rolling off of him, but still he forced himself to do as Eleanor asked. In slow, measured, movements, he turned his head rigidly to the side; his eyes glistened with what he was holding back as he stared into the air where she gazed, a grief so deep and biting that he was barely managing to restrain it contorting his face.

"Aye, Eleanor, I see," he choked out at last, the words sounding as if they had been ripped from his throat. "I see . . ."

The chamber remained silent then but for Agnes's soft crying in the background, as Eleanor, who had calmed with Richard's assertion, took a last few ragged breaths.

"Isabel," she said softly again, the word indistinct, her pants for air slower now, with longer space between. A serene expression settled over her ravaged features, and she began to sink back into Meg and Richard's arms, going limp. She blinked once more, that same, gentle smile curving her lips as before, as she murmured, "Sweet Isabel . . ."

Then, with one last exhalation, her grip on their hands relaxed, and she fell completely still.

Meg's cheeks felt wet from the tears that spilled down them now, hot and unheeded. She stared at her cousin, a swell of grief filling her.

"Her suffering is over, at least," she whispered, the words grating past the thick and aching path of her throat.

"Aye," Richard said hoarsely, his face set with resignation.

Meg let go of Ella as he made the sign of the cross and eased her back onto the bolster with tender care, finally resting one of her hands atop the other before closing her eyes with a gentle touch. "May God grant her peace."

Meg could only lurch to her feet, stumbling back a few steps. It was all too much. Feelings she'd struggled so hard to keep hidden from the eyes of the world rose up, choking her. She could hold them back no longer.

The chamber swam before her eyes. She felt Agnes's and Hugh's stares on her, saw through the blurring heat Richard's concerned gaze as he turned toward her—but she could not speak in reply. Shaking her head again in a silent plea for she knew not what, she dragged open the door, fleeing into the dark of the corridor.

And then she ran. She didn't know where she was going; she only knew that she needed to seek out a place where she might find a measure of peace . . . a sanctuary where she might deaden the memories that had come back with a vengeance to tear at the already frayed edges of her soul.

Chapter 6

❧

Jaw tight, Richard made his way down the path that approached the narrow chapel at the outer limits of the village. After the proper prayers had been said over Eleanor and the preparations begun for her burial ceremony, he'd gone searching for Meg, but so far he'd had little luck in finding her. She had seemingly disappeared.

He was glad for the distraction of seeking her, he told himself, consciously avoiding recognition of the pang of desire he felt simply to be near her; nay, this search would keep him from dwelling too deeply on his own painful thoughts, which did not stem from Eleanor's death but rather from all that remained unresolved, all that had not been redeemed and perhaps never would be.

In truth, these last few days had been like passing through a level of hell. Eleanor's attempt to absolve him of his guilt on her deathbed had been a tiny blessing, delivering the first crack to the thick cloak of blame and regret he bore—but it hadn't been enough to banish it. The fact was that he hadn't forgiven himself for what happened more than five years ago; returning to Hawksley, facing Eleanor, and then watching her suffer so had been like scraping at the old wounds of his sins. He was left feeling more bloodied and raw than ever.

Grimacing against his tormenting thoughts, Richard strode more quickly, determined to concentrate instead on finding Meg. The angular shadows of the stone chapel loomed directly ahead of him in the late afternoon sun, and he stopped and raised his hand to his brow to shade the glare and assess the area around it, including the fenced-in burial ground. All seemed quiet, with not a living soul in sight.

It was to be expected. As a simple village church, the place would probably be deserted from now until morning, when daily Mass would be offered, but it still would not hurt anything to check inside the chapel. Meg was not what he would consider conventional in her view of the Church or its teachings—the nature of her own transgressions and her antipathy toward the holy Templar order and its members made that abundantly clear. But witnessing death could drive people to seek out comfort from a higher source, and a chapel was as likely a place as any to find that kind of solace.

He covered the remaining distance to the arched entrance; the door creaked open at his touch, and he crossed the threshold, stopping a few paces inside. The cool darkness of the nave swallowed fingers of sunlight that stretched to illuminate the motes of dust swirling about. As was customary, Richard genuflected toward the altar and made the sign of the cross as he waited for his eyes to adjust to the dim interior. Upon standing again, he breathed in deeply of the spicy, smoky scent of incense that lingered in the air, remembering other times. Happier times. He'd forgotten how quiet and peaceful it could be here with no one else about. He took a step forward down the center aisle, and another.

Just as he reached halfway to the altar, he glanced ahead to the right, and saw Meg. To his surprise, she was asleep at the very front of the nave, having been apparently praying before the statue of the Blessed Mother and Child that stood positioned near the door to the sacristy; whether from weeping or pure exhaustion, she'd curled up there after laying her head on the kneeling panel of one of the prie-dieux at either side of the statue.

Carefully he approached, not wanting to startle her. Her lashes were still clumped wetly from crying, and a tiny frown marked the space between her brows. He came closer still, and she began to stir as his boots sounded on the stone flagging of the aisle. In another moment she'd stood up and was brushing the backs of her hands over her eyes.

"I am sorry to disturb you, lady," he said as she stood. He noticed that her cheeks seemed flushed, and what was likely embarrassment prevented her from meeting his gaze directly. "It is only that I was concerned for your welfare."

"I—I am sorry to have caused you worry; it seems that I was more tired than I realized." She looked down at the floor, and then lifted her gaze. "I must also apologize for disappearing from Ella's chamber without explanation as I did."

"Think no more on it," he murmured, stepping closer to her. "It is never easy to lose someone, and we cannot know how we will react until it happens."

"But her passing is not the reason I felt the need to leave."

She looked away from him, staring at the statue of the mother and child. When she continued, her voice was more hushed than before. "It was something else. Something I have never told anyone here at Hawksley—but it was why I was so affected when Ella . . . when she—"

Meg stopped, her mouth tightening as if she didn't know if she should—or could—continue; they paused in awkward silence, until Richard took an action that he hoped would distract her from the discomfort she seemed to be feeling, stepping up right next to her to look at the statue. It was a beautiful rendition of the Christ Child and His mother, carved from marble of an unusual hue. Rather than the gray or whitish stone that was used for many religious figures he'd seen in village churches throughout England, this one had a pinkish cast, with darker lines and swirls throughout the marble.

"Has anyone ever told you of this statue or whence it came?" he asked, breaking the uneasy quiet that had surrounded them.

Meg pulled her gaze from it to glance at him and shake her head.

"It was purchased at much cost from a Christian craftsman in the Holy Land," Richard continued. "Brother Thomas made the arrangements at my request. The carpenter from the village created the pedestal in time for its arrival and blessing—and there it has stood, looking calmly out over the chapel for almost six years."

"You ordered its purchase before you joined the Templars?"

"Aye. But I sought it out for the same reason that I eventually petitioned for entry into the Brotherhood."

Richard imagined he felt a slight burning sensation in his chest as he spoke, but he forced himself to go on when he sensed Meg's uncertainty about asking him to explain further.

"It was my first attempt to buy forgiveness, you see," he continued, swallowing against the now stronger lance of pain, "purchased just after the accident that took my daughter's life."

By the Rood, but he was beginning to sound self-pitying, he thought, staving off a grimace; he'd come here to comfort Meg, not elicit her sympathy. In an effort to lighten the moment for her sake, he gave a dismal try at a smile and added, "I do not need to tell you, of all people, that my plan to find absolution failed miserably."

"But . . . absolution for what?" Meg asked, frowning as she'd been from the first words of his explanation. "I do not understand. You were grieving, certainly, but you had not yet abandoned Eleanor or cast off your position as lord of this demesne. Why would you need pardon then?"

Richard looked at her in disbelief. There was no mistaking her question, yet it did not seem possible. Could it be that she didn't know the whole, sordid tale . . . that she thought his only sin was in leaving his wife in the wake of their child's death? Bitter laughter welled up in him, but he managed to hold it back to no more than a choking sound, contained behind a sardonic half smile.

Shaking his head, he looked away, lest he find himself unable to keep his response in check longer.

"Forgive me," she murmured, a flush rising to her cheeks. "I have overstepped my bounds. It is not my place to question you."

"Nay, there is no fault in it," Richard answered; he was finding it difficult to swallow the irony of this new development. Clenching his jaw again, he stepped away from her, approaching the statue to touch the cool, smooth texture of the stone that comprised the hem of the Blessed Virgin's garment.

"I would like to know, however," he asked evenly, so that

she wouldn't see how important her answer was to him, "just what you were told about the accident and how it transpired."

"Nothing more but that Eleanor took a carriage out into a storm and that she was gravely injured in a mishap on the road, while the only other passenger—your young child— was killed." A shadow flickered in Meg's eyes. "I was also told that shortly afterward, overcome by your own grief, you joined the Brotherhood of the Templars, leaving Eleanor behind to mourn alone."

"That is all?" Richard asked, steeling himself against the waves of hurt and memory that were rising up in him in response to all this; he felt as if someone were ripping away the last of the thin bandage he'd managed to keep over the raw and aching wound of his soul. "Nothing about why Eleanor had gone out that day, for example?"

"Nay, nothing," Meg said, frowning slightly. "What I'd heard seemed enough to explain why Ella had drifted into a world of her own making, clinging to her poppet as if it were all that kept her in body."

"And enough to make you despise me as a thoughtless, unfeeling husband who had abandoned his wife in her greatest time of need, as well, wouldn't you say?"

Meg flinched the slightest bit, but then straightened her back and clasped her fingers in front of herself. "I will not pretend that I thought highly of you in the two years that I served here before your return. But I confess that my beliefs about you have altered in the days since; you are different, in many ways, from the heartless man I had envisioned."

"Do not be too quick to cast away those harsher thoughts, Meg," Richard answered darkly, "for the truth—that which is above and beyond what you were told—is perhaps worse than what you may have imagined."

She paled a bit, he thought, though it could have been a trick of the dim light inside the chapel. But then her face took on that resolute cast he was coming to recognize, her full, lush lips pressed together, her jaw lifted, and her brown eyes glinting with challenge.

Beautiful, he realized.

Not in the expected way, like the fair dainties of court, but he found her stunning nonetheless. And that would make what was about to happen all the more excruciating and apt for a man as sinful as he was.

By heaven, when he'd thought of the grand and awful penance he'd find in returning to Hawksley Manor after all these years, he hadn't realized it would include another painful declaration of guilt as well. Just after the tragedy, he'd bared his soul to God in the confessional; that had been difficult enough. But being forced to reveal the agonizing truth of his sin to this woman, a lady who would have every right to despise him when he was through, was quite another. And yet it had been ordained for him to endure it, for here they were.

He ran his thumb back and forth over the polished edge of the sculpture, only turning back to Meg when he'd harnessed his feelings into some semblance of control. He swallowed again before he spoke.

"What you haven't been told is that long before I left Hawksley Manor to join the Templars I was not physically present here. I served the king and was away for long spans of time in the two years preceding the accident. Eleanor did not react well to my absence."

"You fought in the Scottish wars, then?"

"Aye, at first," Richard murmured, "but the king soon realized that he had a better use for me. My elder brother,

Braedan, had trained me in the sword skills he had learned while on Crusade, and when I reached my majority, I continued that work, perfecting my swordsmanship to a high level of proficiency. The king decided that it would be a waste of my abilities to keep me in combat on the field, so he ordered me back to England to help in training his son—the man who now sits on the throne as Edward II."

Meg looked startled, taking a few steps back and sinking to sit in the front pew. "I—I had no idea that you'd lived so closely with members of the royal family," she said. "That might explain, then, why you looked so familiar when I first saw you upon your return here."

"How so?" Richard asked, frowning.

"I too spent some time at the court in my youth, when my sire was called to attendance there," Meg tried to explain. "Often my family would make the journey and stay for a month or more in whatever place the king had chosen to convene his nobles. It—it is quite possible that I saw you at one of those sessions without knowing, then, who you were."

The thrill of surprise he'd first felt in response to her comment deepened, spreading through Richard as he struggled to think back, to make a placement in his mind of any time he might have seen this woman in that other life he'd lived. It seemed improbable that someone like Meg would have gone unnoticed by him, different as she was from many of the other noble ladies he'd known. And yet he himself had been a different man then, distracted by the pursuit of his ambition—younger, more foolish . . . and most decidedly married. Whatever his faults had been, straying from his vows had not been one of them.

"It is possible that our paths crossed," he settled for saying, "though I fear I cannot claim clear memory of it. I was blind to anything other than the path toward increasing my own wealth and my family's position in society. The king found my skills both entertaining and useful—and I was only too happy to oblige him, in exhibitions and personal combats, along with the training I developed for his son."

"With what part of that arrangement could Eleanor find fault? Absences such as those you've described are not so uncommon among men in noble families," Meg chided gently.

"Perhaps . . . but unlike most men, I allowed that hunger to hold sway over nearly all else. And yet that is not the worst of it." Richard paused for a moment, the bitterness of what still needed to be said difficult to bear. Guilt pushed him forward, refusing to give him any quarter. Gritting his teeth against the assault from within, he closed his eyes and tilted his head up for a moment, looking away before bringing his gaze back to lock with Meg's.

"The rest of the ugly truth," he said in a voice grating with self-loathing, "is that on the day of the accident, Eleanor begged me to remain at Hawksley Manor with her. I tried not to be unkind in resisting her pleas, but I was angry, for Eleanor had become increasingly unreasonable in her demands after the birth of our child, suffering as she did under the wild shifts of temperament that continued to plague her until her death."

Meg looked startled. "I did not realize that she had her spells even before the accident."

"Aye. They worsened afterward, it is true, but they had appeared far earlier, even before we wed. I was blind to such things, then—naive perhaps, and enamored of Eleanor's great beauty." Resignation suffocated him, and his body felt tight, strung like the bow he had carried around as a lad. "On that day she was more shrill and discontented than usual, which allowed me to feel justified in ignoring her outburst and going forward with my plans to return to court. But she was tenacious. She followed me room by room through the manor house—even out to the stables, insisting that I decline the king's summons. And I refused to listen."

Richard sucked in his breath, his throat tightening in a grip so painful that at first he wasn't certain he would be able to complete the awful tale. "God help me," he said hoarsely, pushing on, "but I refused her. I uttered words I regretted almost immediately, yet I was too proud to beg pardon for them and left without looking back. Later, the servants told me that she became enraged and ordered a carriage readied. She bundled up Isabel, set off in pursuit of me, and—"

Losing his breath for a moment, Richard shook his head, wanting to shut his eyes at the horrible images replaying themselves in his mind. But they would not be stilled. Until it was all out, they would just keep coming.

"Not far from the ravine," he continued quietly, "where the road slopes steeply to the right, the carriage tipped, and Isabel fell. I found my little girl, not far from the rock that had . . . that she'd . . ."

Richard's voice disappeared then, squeezed into oblivion, the heat that had been pricking behind his eyes rising to a haze. He swallowed convulsively against the aching knot in his throat, needing to finish, needing Meg to understand. She had to know the full truth, to be able to see once and for all the kind of sinful man he was, guilty and irredeemable.

He shook his head once and forced the words out. "I ordered this statue carved at an exorbitant cost in an attempt to help expunge my sins, donated most of my material gains to the Church . . . and eventually, pledged my body and soul to God in service with the Templars, all to try to find some way to redeem what I had wrought with my selfishness and pride. I would have cast myself beneath the wheels of that carriage a thousand times if it would have saved Isabel, but it matters not. For in the end I cannot escape that it was *I* who killed my child and led my wife to sink into her final madness. And I did it with the cursed hammer of my own ambition."

The silence that blanketed the chapel in the wake of his confession was so profound that a raindrop might have resounded like an enormous drum, had one fallen just then. As it stood, all Richard could hear was the rasp of his own breathing in his ears; he swallowed several more times, closing his eyes and trying to stem the tide of hot, aching emotion that had swept over him as he spoke.

The truth he had just shared was horrible, black, and unalterable. That was the hell of it. He could never change any of it. No matter how many times he confessed or how deep a regret he felt, Isabel was still dead . . . and now Eleanor was too.

And so when he felt the first, cool stroke of Meg's fingers on his own, he was startled into looking up, meeting the warm empathy of her gaze even as he felt her strength seeping into him through her touch. Hot, sharp stabs of sensation shot through him as she lifted his hand to her lips in silence, her expression grave as she brushed a kiss over his fingers before turning her head to close her eyes and gently press his palm to her cheek. The embrace was artless and innocent, yet it set off ripples of longing through his body, making him yearn for something he could not name, but that he ached for with every fiber of his being.

"Ah, Richard de Cantor," she murmured softly as she looked at him once more, "how you have suffered in this. You must forgive me for judging you so harshly in my own mind, without knowing the full truth. And then you must forgive yourself."

For the second time that afternoon, Richard realized that he had lost his power of speech. If Meg's physical action had startled him, the possibility of her understanding and acceptance overwhelmed him, unleashing another flood of emotion that was almost painful in its power. In the next breath she lowered their entwined hands slowly, still maintaining her link with him, and he closed his eyes, relishing her touch even as the weight of his shame pressed in on him.

"How can—why do you believe that I deserve such forgiveness?" he asked at last, his voice rough with all that he was feeling. "Even to think upon that day is to tempt my own sanity, for it is beyond bearing to know that my child is gone. I cannot bring her back. *Nothing* can bring her back, and that is what I cannot escape. I cannot—"

"I know," Meg answered huskily, and he lifted his gaze to her again to see that her eyes glistened with tears she had not shed. "You feel naught but a raw wound left in the place your daughter once lived."

"You cannot truly know, lady—not the bitter truth of it. And I pray God will keep you from feeling the pain of it ever in your life."

"It is too late for that."

Her fingers tightened on his own as surprise swept through him. Both of her hands clasped his now, as if she needed *his* strength, *his* understanding; she blinked through a feeble attempt at a smile. The motion released the sheen of tears in her eyes, causing them to spill over.

"You see, I *do* know, Richard," she said, her voice catching on a tiny, hitched breath, "for I too lost a child of my own."

The import of what she'd said sunk in like a leaden fist; Richard knew he must have appeared stunned, for she nodded weakly and continued.

"I carried a babe without the sanction of marriage; her father was the knight I spoke of earlier—the man who was sold into the Brotherhood. She was all that was left to me of him, and I cherished every movement, every flutter of life as she grew inside me. Like yours, my daughter was precious to me. But she did not live long past her birth," she said, her voice cracking with emotion again. "I named her Madeline, and I held her tightly even after she'd gone, until they came and took her away from me."

Richard was silent for a long moment before he spoke, the shock of her admission sitting like a stone on his chest, to steal his breath.

"I did not know, lady," he murmured finally, "and I am sorry for your loss."

Meg nodded stiffly. "Until now, I have spoken of her to no one—including Brother Thomas. But that is why I could not stay longer at Eleanor's deathbed today; her last moments called up all the pain of Madeline's death once more—and when she called out for Isabel, I—"

Meg swallowed hard, clearly unable to finish what she'd begun to say, and Richard stared at her, his throat tight as well. He shook his head. "I understand, lady. All too well, I understand the pain of it."

She met his gaze with an open, wounded expression that made him ache; she was a strong woman, thank heaven—strong in mind, body, and heart—but this kind of agony would test even the most faithful. Right now her soul sought a comfort that he knew could never be found in this world. And though he wished the anguish they'd lived through upon no one, he could not deny that their shared pain brought with it a sense of intimacy that he'd never known with another . . . as well as a fierce desire to ease the hurt she'd endured.

"I am truly sorry, lady, for all you have suffered," he said gently, lifting his hand to brush the lingering wetness from her cheek.

She nodded once more, quickly and in silence before closing her eyes, clearly suppressing new tears that threatened to swell. But in the next moment she breathed in and looked at him again, forcing a watery smile. Stepping back, she approached the statue and ran her fingers along the square base near the Holy Mother's feet.

"What is important now is that I keep the secret of my babe from all at Hawksley—and from Brother Thomas in particular."

"You think that he would judge you more harshly if he learned of her?"

She gave a hollow-sounding laugh. "His outrage would know no bounds, I am certain. In his eyes my sin would be compounded tenfold with the knowledge that a child was born of it."

"But why was he not told about her when you first came to Hawksley?"

"That I do not know. Perhaps it was a divine blessing— one small concession granted me from God, to give back some of what He took." She turned from the statue, her face resolute and her eyes fierce. "My child," she said in a tight, passionate voice, "was *not* a sin, and I will never again allow her called so by anyone in their efforts to instruct me. Never again."

"They used her against you before, then," Richard said in a low voice, not as a question, but as a statement of dark certainty. And with that utterance he felt the first churnings of a long latent urge to do violence building inside him.

She didn't answer him, instead turning back to gaze at the statue and seeming as if she even now tasted the bitterness of what she had experienced. At last she said hoarsely, "I would have withstood the penitential beatings, or the bread and water and enforced hours of prayer I was made to accept at the onset of my penance while at Bayham Abbey, remaining steadfast in the face of it all. But my sire and the spiritual keepers he chose for me delved beyond that; for every day of those eleven months, my daughter's death was held up and delivered to me in sermon after sermon as just payment, earned by the blackness of my sin."

Richard's heart lurched with the thought of how agonizing that must have been for her; after Isabel's death he had subjected himself to endless guilt and self-loathing—he continued to do so now—but he had never had to endure the open taunts or accusations of others as well. He did not think he would have survived if he had.

"And yet they were not finished with the instruction they claimed would save my soul."

"Nay?" he asked, his voice gone husky with imagining what other diabolical torment she had been made to suffer.

She shook her head, the difficulty of what she was saying clear in her rigid posture and strained expression. "In truth, I suppose that I should be grateful to my father, for it was because of him that I was sent to Hawksley at all. It was another form of penance, you see, thought to be a more apt atonement—only it did not prove as edifying as they had planned."

"I am not sure I understand."

"The circumstances were ripe for a lesson in the flesh; Eleanor had lost a child and disappeared into her world of grief so deeply that she needed a nurse to care for her in every way. I, the formerly pampered and cosseted daughter to an earl, would be put in that menial position, not only to mortify my earthly pride, but to provide a painful, constant reminder of what I too had lost and could never mourn openly without ignominy."

"My God," Richard muttered. "How you must have loathed your place here and all that came with it."

"Nay," Meg answered, twisting to look at him with a sad smile. "That is what I meant a moment ago. It has not been as horrible a penance as they had hoped it would be, for I grew to care for Eleanor as a sister, and to ache for her sufferings even more than for my own. At least my sanity had been left to me—and the dignity to be found in none here knowing the whole truth behind my position as her companion."

She clasped her hands together and looked down, the solemnity of her demeanor conveying the gravity of what she was saying. "That is why I must beg you once more not to tell anyone at Hawksley Manor about Madeline. I do not know if I could bear it, should Brother Thomas decide to do as the abbess did and employ my babe's memory as another whip to wield against me."

"I swear to keep silent about it," Richard answered forcefully. "None shall learn of your past from me, you have my word."

He stepped closer to her as he spoke, wanting her to see the sincerity of his assertion, even as he held back the hot emotions that flowed through him with startling virulence, making his fists clench at his sides. By heaven, but the urge to seek revenge against those who hurt her in that way rose up in him strong and full, though he'd spent the last five years suppressing the instinct in his service of God.

"Thank you, Richard," she said quietly. She glanced away, as if weighing how—or if—she should say something further. At last she met his gaze again, her expression open and vulnerable as she added, "I—I do not know what compelled me to share all of this now, but somehow in your presence I am comforted as I cannot remember having felt before."

The delicate hue in her cheeks rose, and she bit down into the lush and tender fullness of her lower lip, sending a pang of sharp desire through him. "I pray you do not find offense with my saying so," she almost whispered into the sacred hush that surrounded them, "but I wished to tell you how grateful I am for your understanding."

The slight twisting sensation inside Richard intensified. "Nay, lady," he answered huskily, shaking his head, "there is no offense to be found in your words, for it is nothing more than the same comfort I feel when I am with you."

She nodded once, in shy acknowledgment of his compliment, and he felt the overwhelming urge to reach out and stroke his fingers along her cheek again . . . to sweep them in a gentle caress through the silken waves of her upswept hair. But such would not be proper, he knew, or perhaps even welcomed by her. It was enough for now to simply revel in the sweetness of her company for as long as it might last, and to enjoy the unexpected gift of their shared understanding.

Holding out his hand, he said, "Come. Let me walk you back to the house. Then, if you wish, you can retire until supper, without fear of disturbance."

Gratefully she nodded, and Richard waited while she crossed the remaining distance between them, before slipping her hand into his. The brush of her palm against his sent another thrill of longing through him, the innocent joining at once tender and yet somehow charged with something more.

But the heightened feelings that were sweeping through him could come to naught, he knew, whether or not he might yearn for more. Such thoughts were dangerous for a man like him. Even were he free of all vows, he had no right to flirt with the disaster of involvement with any woman. Besides, in all likelihood, Meg would leave Hawksley before the week was out, her task in caring for Eleanor now finished. She would return home, or to court, to resume her life as the daughter of an earl. Only time would tell.

In the meantime there was much necessary work to be done that would surely distract him from the dangers to be found in the swirling of his own thoughts. Eleanor's funeral Mass would come tomorrow, followed within a week by the village's traditional All Saints' feast and what promised to be a difficult, yet gratifying moment, when he made his first steps toward rectifying Brother Thomas's abuses of power as steward of Hawksley Manor.

Resolute in that truth, Richard tightened his jaw, forcing his thoughts away from how good it felt to walk next to this woman and hold her hand in his. He simply directed his gaze forward, leading Meg from the cool recess of the chapel into the bright sun of the path, moving inexorably toward the manor house and the completion of the difficult tasks that awaited them.

Chapter 7

When they reached Hawksley's yard again, they both pulled up short at what they saw. Someone had arrived in their absence, as was evidenced by the activity near the stables where stood a carriage being unloaded. Meg looked to Richard expectantly, already knowing that it could not be someone unwelcome by his expression of pleasure.

"Braedan," he murmured to himself before glancing toward her with a grin that seemed to light his face. "It seems my brother has arrived at last, and from the looks of it, he's brought Fiona and their children along as well."

The effect of that smile on her was powerful—devastating, in fact—making her knees go weak and her pulse quicken; as with the first time she'd seen him smile in the privacy of his solar, Meg was struck by just how attractive a man Richard de Cantor was. The vague thought made its way through her mind then that he should smile more often, but it was fol-

lowed fast by the intuitive realization that if he did, she would
be hard-pressed to do aught but sit and stare at him.

She was still coping with her renegade musings when he
tugged at her hand, saying, "Come!" as he quickened their
pace toward the manor house. Fortunately, he was a gentleman in the truest sense, for even in his enthusiasm he accom-
modated her stumbling steps. His excitement, however, was
contagious, and she too was laughing and breathless by the
time they reached the approach to the main door. Once there,
she told him to go ahead, and he strode ahead of her to cover
the remaining distance, just as the portal opened and a man
came out.

From the moment she caught sight of the stranger, Meg
knew that there could be no mistaking that he was Richard's
brother; she watched the two men reach out to clasp forearms, before Braedan pulled Richard into a hug that she was
sure would have cracked the ribs of a lesser man. Out of respect she remained back a bit, wanting to give them some
privacy in their long overdue reunion. But it didn't mean that
she couldn't use the time to her advantage, to study them
where they stood together.

Dark-haired like his brother, Braedan stood of a height
with Richard, though he was clearly the elder by some ten or
dozen years perhaps. They shared certain features—the same
strong jawline, sensual mouth, and slant of brow, though
Braedan's eyes were not green-gold as Richard's were, but
rather a startling blue. In fact, they appeared different enough
on the whole that Meg thought it likely that one brother had
favored their mother, while the other had taken after their sire.

"It is good to see you again, Richard," she heard Braedan
murmur, as he gripped his brother's shoulder affectionately.
"Though the timing of our arrival could have been better, it

seems. Your man Hugh told us about Eleanor, and we have paid our respects to her already. I am sorry, little brother, to hear of what happened here since your return home."

"As am I," said a feminine voice just inside the half-opened door. As the words were spoken, a slender, auburn-haired woman of a similar age to Braedan stepped outside to join them, her movements graceful and smooth. She was lovely, Meg noticed at once, with distinctive, tawny-hued eyes that at the moment were filled with gentle sadness. She approached Richard to give him a warm embrace and kiss on the cheek, then stepped back to slip her hand into Braedan's as she added softly, "Eleanor was always so delicate of health. We had all prayed for her return to vigor, but it seems we must take comfort that she is at peace at long last."

"Aye. It was a blessing, difficult as it is to accept," Richard murmured before twisting to look back at Meg in response to the other woman's polite glance in her direction. "Ah, yes—you must pardon my horrible manners. I lived for five years in the company of fighting men, and I am afraid some of the higher graces I once possessed are rather rusty."

Stepping back so that Braedan and his wife could have a clear view, he held out his hand in invitation for Meg to approach, saying as he did, "Braedan, Fiona, allow me to introduce Eleanor's distant cousin Meg. She cared for Eleanor in the two years prior to my return, and she has been a great help to me and everyone else at Hawksley this past week."

"We are pleased to make your acquaintance," Braedan said with a slight bow to her. "Is your surname . . . Spencer perhaps?" he added as he straightened again, nodding toward her with a quirk of his lips that gave her a start, it reminded her so of Richard. "It was the name Eleanor carried before her marriage, and so I presume you share it, since my doltish brother has failed to give us yours in full?"

"Nay," Meg almost choked, flashing Richard a look of apology and trying to will the flood of heat from her cheeks. By the Rood, but she must have blushed more times in the past seven days than she had in the entire twenty-six years that preceded this moment. Forcing herself to meet Braedan's puzzled gaze again, she managed to add, "My family name is Newcomb."

"Newcomb?" Now Braedan looked truly startled, as much from her cultured way of speaking, Meg expected, as from the fact that Newcomb was not a common name except within the ranks of the higher nobility—specifically her sire's prominent and powerful family.

"From the Berkshire region," she murmured, knowing where this was going and wishing there was a polite way to avoid the rest.

"Those at Hawksley know her simply as Meg, however," Richard broke in. It was obvious that he was making a gallant attempt to brush over the awkward moment for her, and she felt a burst of gratitude followed quickly by the swell of guilt brought on by Braedan and Fiona's reactions.

"Ah . . ." Braedan said, looking as though he wished to inquire further about her presence here but was too polite to do so in the face of his younger brother's clear avoidance of that track of conversation.

Fiona too, who had offered Meg a smile of acknowledgment upon first introductions, shifted a little in self-conscious silence. A rebellious flare surged up in Meg's breast; it was not fair to make them feel awkward, she thought. Not when it mattered naught but to her own pride that they learn of her true parentage. Even if she did not speak of it, they would draw their own conclusions or ask Richard to clarify her identity and reasons for being at Hawksley. It would be less painful, perhaps, to simply get it over with and tell them herself.

Tilting her chin up, she took a deep breath and turned her gaze back to Fiona and Braedan. "Richard is being kind in keeping silent, but it is no real hardship for me to tell you. My full name, given to me at birth, is Lady Margaret Priscilla Elizabeth Newcomb. I am the youngest daughter to the Earl of Welton and his wife, Anne, and I was placed here as Eleanor's nurse two years ago after I committed an . . . indiscretion. Because of the close working relationship it was necessary to cultivate with the villagers in caring for Eleanor, I asked from the beginning that everyone call me simply Meg. It has worked well in that time, and so I continue to request the boon of forgoing my title while I am at Hawksley."

A beat of uncomfortable silence passed, and Meg thought she was doomed to endure another intensifying flood of heat in her face, but at the last moment she was saved from overt humiliation by Braedan's wife, Fiona, who had been studying her intently as she spoke.

Fiona stepped forward, linked her arm with Meg's, and patted her hand, saying, "It has been my experience that one's past, or at least society's judgment of it, can be a difficult burden to carry. Believe me when I say that you shall have nothing to fear from me or Braedan questioning you further on yours. I, for one, will be glad to call you Meg."

"As will I," offered Braedan.

"Thank you," Meg murmured, startled by their gracious response. Most people in their position might have recoiled in disapproval; that Richard's brother and sister by marriage had done just the opposite made her feel humbled and fortunate indeed to have stumbled upon such a kind and accepting family.

"It is settled, then," Fiona announced happily, beginning to lead Meg toward the house. "Though I need to beg a favor of you, dear, in helping me to sort out the foodstuffs we brought with us as gifts for Hawksley's larder. Perhaps if the cook does not mind some assistance, we can even cobble together a quick supper to feed my noisy brood—who have run off to explore the orchard and stables, if I am not mistaken," she trailed off under her breath, craning her neck to look in that direction in vain, before shaking her head and making a soft clucking sound with her tongue.

"You will have to see them later, it seems. You too Richard," Fiona called lightly over her shoulder to the two men, who were still standing apart from the main door. "It is entirely possible that you will not recognize them after all this time, they've grown so. But it will give you and Braedan a chance to talk before they descend on the house like locusts in search of sustenance."

Set at ease by Fiona's matter-of-fact manner, Meg allowed herself to smile in response to Fiona's jest about the children's ravenous tendencies. It would be good to have another woman to talk to, she decided, as she listened to Fiona's pleasant voice. She answered her questions as well as asking some of her own—about the family's trip to Hawksley, the names and ages of their children, and how long it had been since any of them had seen Richard.

Aye, Braedan and Fiona's visit would be a welcome, happy distraction to the gloom they'd lived under at Hawksley for so long, Meg thought as they made their way to the kitchen. Very welcome indeed.

* * *

Richard refilled Braedan's cup where they sat at the table that served as a desk in his solar, and they both drank in companionable silence for a moment, with naught to disturb them but the crackling of the fire in the hearth. Braedan had already told him all the news of home, and Richard had heard about the newest addition to their family, as well as the exploits of the older children since he'd seen them all last. And though the estranged state of Richard's marriage had been no secret between them for many years, they had even discussed the bittersweet, final moments of Eleanor's life and the arrangements for the Mass in her honor on the morrow.

But there was more that hadn't been said, he knew. More that hadn't been asked—about his return home and what had precipitated it, and about the dangers the Templars in England might be facing in the coming weeks. The other talk had all been a prelude to it, but it was there nonetheless, waiting to be acknowledged, like some great, dark beast in the corner of the room.

Ah well, Richard thought. No time like the present.

"So . . . why don't you ask what you wish to know about the arrests in France? Once that is out of the way, it likely will be time to rejoin the others—and with the air cleared between us, we may actually be able to enjoy the supper your wife and Meg are preparing for us."

His brother grimaced slightly and shook his head. "That transparent, am I? I must be getting old to not find means of keeping my thoughts better hidden from you."

"Nay, not old, brother," Richard answered, grinning broadly. "Just . . . well-worn."

The comment earned him a bone-jarring punch to the arm, even as Braedan flashed an answering grin. "Aye, well, at least I care about your reckless hide." He tossed back the rest of his drink and set the cup back on the table. "Was it as bad as I've heard, then?"

Richard nodded; his lighter expression faded and his jaw tightened with the bitter memory of that harrowing, rain-swept night. "We were blindsided, Braedan. Why the pope has not stepped up and demanded an accounting for King Philip's actions, I do not know—nor is it certain that the men with whom I rode even made it out alive. For all I know they could be suffering in some hellhole across the Channel while the Inquisition tries to make them confess to falsehoods and abominations."

"You are fortunate to have escaped at all. Word spread throughout London that thousands were taken in France, and all in a single day."

Richard couldn't answer this time, just jerking his head in acknowledgment before draining his own cup and push-ing it away.

"Know this, brother," Braedan added after a moment. "Come what may, I'll take your back on this one. Fiona and I have already discussed it, and she is in agreement with me. Whatever it takes, we are prepared to do it, even should it mean my giving up my role as chief justice to aid you in get-ting to safe haven."

The extraordinary offer took Richard by surprise, making his throat ache even more; to mask the reaction he shook his head and gave a slight smile, still staring at his empty cup. "You have always watched out for me, Braedan, even when I didn't deserve it." He wondered if the wine was muddling his brain and adding to his unfortunate tendency lately to look back, or if it was something he wouldn't be able to keep him-self from doing anyway. "I will not have you or your family put at risk for me again."

Braedan's expression sobered. "What is happening now—what *may* happen in the coming weeks—is not a matter of your allowing, Richard; it is a matter of me telling you the way it will be." At that he cast Richard a big-brother look that told Richard he would brook no further argument.

Richard shook his head again and looked away, kneading the back of his neck with his hand to try to loosen some of the tension that had been building there. In truth he couldn't deny that he was grateful for his brother's backing. The bond between him and Braedan was strong, unbroken by the years or their long physical separations. Family loyalty, honor in the pursuit of justice . . . all were part of the de Cantor name and legacy, something from which Richard had once felt distanced but was now grateful to possess in the struggle that was to come.

"You know I cannot flee England, even should the Inquisition cross the Channel," he said to Braedan quietly, staring down once more at his cup as he turned it back and forth in the stretching light of the smoky tapers that lit the chamber. "I will not. The Templars have committed no crime, at least none of those with which King Philip has charged them. To run would be the same as admitting guilt."

"I was afraid you'd say that."

"How could I say otherwise?" Richard asked, getting up at last and moving to the hearth to throw another log on the fire. "It is a matter of what is right."

"It could be a matter of your life, should they begin arresting the Templars here as they did those in France," Braedan countered.

"Aye, it is possible. But it was also possible every time I rode onto a field of battle in the past ten years. The same is true for you with every year you serve as chief justice of the roads and forests outside of London."

"Perhaps," Braedan argued, "yet those are calculated risks, based upon the necessity of maintaining order and justice in the kingdom."

"Fighting the persecution of the Templars *is* justice, Braedan. By God, they are being tortured—killed by the dozens in an effort to make them confess to falsehoods," he said, his voice hoarse and passionate, "and for no greater reason than that the king of France felt threatened by the order's wealth and autonomy from his authority."

Braedan leaned back in his chair, releasing a long sigh before shifting his gaze to Richard in reluctant acceptance. "I cannot argue with you, Richard. And yet one man alone cannot halt a rising tide. I just do not want to see you swept away and drowned by it."

"I am not going to face the Inquisition single-handed, do not fear."

Braedan made a scoffing sound. "Aye, well, I know I've offered to stand with you little brother, and two de Cantors side by side are a formidable force, it is true. But I fear that even our combined skill will not be enough to keep a corrupt horde of French prelates at bay."

An answering laugh burst from Richard before he could keep it back, and he looked at his brother in wry amusement. "As inviting as is the idea of taking on enemies with none but you beside me, Braedan, it is not what I had in mind."

"What, then, is your plan?" Braedan demanded. "You have said you will not leave England. Will you take to the underground and wait it out?"

"Nay." Richard clipped off the answer and cast his gaze to

his brother, adding fiercely, "I will not be hunted like an animal again. I endured it once, on that first day, in order to spare the lives of the men with me and to protect the goods entrusted to me by the grand master. But I will stand my ground should I be confronted with arrest again."

"And how, pray tell, do you think *that* will be successful?" Braedan demanded. "This is no small matter, Richard. The Inquisition is powerful, known for crushing all in its path to oblivion. That they have not yet reached England matters little; it is only a question of time." He jabbed his hand through his hair, looking both ferocious and worried all at once. "Christ's blood, it would be suicide to try to stand against their might without a damned army of supporters."

"Do not fear. I have sent an appeal to a higher power—higher even than you, big brother."

Braedan went still for one shocked and aghast moment before growling, "You're going to rely on *prayer*? God-a-mercy, Richard, have you lost your mind?"

"Not quite yet, I am happy to confess," Richard countered, scowling now himself and adding, "Not to mention the fact that praying would do me no good at all, I'm afraid."

"What, then?"

"I have sent a missive to King Edward himself, based upon our former connection as pupil and master, asking his help in keeping the Inquisition behind French borders."

That information set Braedan back on his heels. Finally he shook his head and sighed. "It is a bold move, I grant you. But it will be difficult to get the king to do *anything* against the French, considering that his future wife is King Philip's own daughter."

"I know. And yet their wedding will not take place for several more months. In the meantime, it is well recognized that

Edward, like his father before him, is sympathetic and supportive of the Templar Brotherhood." Richard tapped his finger rhythmically on the table next to his empty cup. "It is a gamble, I admit, but if anyone might find means to mitigate King Philip's greed and power, it would be his equal on English soil."

Uneasy silence held sway between them again after he'd spoken, with Braedan obviously weighing Richard's plan in his mind. After a few moments he shook his head once more, appearing resigned. "I cannot say that I like the idea of all this. The king is young and untested in the ways of politics. But at the same time I understand your reasons for holding your ground. Hell, in your place I'd likely do the same thing," he allowed reluctantly.

"Thank you for admitting that."

"That doesn't mean I am going to let you off so easily," his brother grumbled. "You must ready yourself for the coming conflict, Richard, for with or without the king's help, it will nonetheless find you."

"Aye, I know. And I will do what I can to be prepared; I will train—with you, if you care to," he said, shooting Braedan a glance, "to keep my fighting skills honed, and I will keep abreast of any news. But first I need to tend to the arrangements for Eleanor's funeral Mass and the feast in her honor tomorrow, as well as make preparation for the All Saints' Day feast next week. When all of the crofters are gathered here for that, I will be naming a new steward of the manor."

"Why a new steward? From what I could see, Hawksley looks to be in fine form, considering the length of time you've been away already."

Richard got up and made his way to the solar's window.

"Aye, that is just the problem. It seems that Brother Thomas took *very* good care of the manor in my absence, securing a high profit for me—and almost as much for himself. Unfortunately, it was at the expense of the crofters. He perpetrated many injustices on the people in my absence."

"I never could abide hypocritical men of the cloth," Braedan muttered. "How did you learn of his negligence?"

"Meg hinted at it, and the villeins certainly seemed none too pleased to see me, though I initially thought that due to Eleanor's illness and their perception that I had abandoned her five years ago in the midst of her need." He rubbed the back of his neck again. "But when I went over the past years' records with Brother Thomas, I finally saw the truth. I will need to rectify it, if I can, for the circumstances are shameful under which the crofters have been living. During the feast, I will address it publicly. Aside from that, however, I must needs stay put unless the king summons me, for I am expecting word or the arrival of those men with whom I rode on the day of the arrests—though with each hour that passes, my hope that they escaped the Inquisition's clutches grows dimmer."

"How many are there?"

"Three. Two brothers, Alex and Damien de Ashby, and a third named John de Clifton. Alex is a scrapper—a bit of a rogue knight . . . we were in France, in fact, to bring him to face charges for breaking his vow of chastity with the order. Of all of us, I thought him most likely to reach England unscathed." Glancing away, Richard added lowly, "And yet here I stand, safe at Hawksley, with no sign of him or the others thus far."

"Do not despair yet, brother. It could be that they make their way more slowly, thanks to injury or for the simple reason of being unfamiliar with the region—"

"Or it could mean that they were taken by the French before they made it to England," Richard finished, the thought like a fist to his belly.

"It is possible, aye, but we will continue to hope for the best. God willing, you will learn something soon."

Then Braedan fell quiet. So quiet that Richard at last glanced up at him to assess the reason behind it. *Damn*. His brother was brewing something else in his mind, and Lord knew he wouldn't stop until all his questions were satisfied.

"All right," Richard said, settling in for what promised to be a bit longer; he leaned back against the wall between the window and mantel and crossed his arms over his chest. "What else? You're sitting there looking like a hound ready to corner a fox . . . and I suspect I'm the fox."

"When did you become so testy?" Braedan drawled, leaning back, even as he twisted to face his brother. He lifted one arm and draped it over the back of his chair, stretching the other out onto the table and keeping his gaze shuttered all the while. Richard felt a little shock as he realized that Braedan had unconsciously taken up the same pose their sire had used time and again in those months before Braedan went on Crusade, when Richard was but a lad and Braedan an impatient young man in the habit of flirting with danger.

Finally Braedan murmured in a deceptively bland voice, "So—tell me about Meg."

If Richard had still been at the table, drinking, he would have choked on his ale. "What do you wish to know?" he managed to say, struggling to sound as nonchalant as Braedan had done, though in truth he was surprised at the flare of protectiveness he felt toward Meg even in response to his brother's seemingly innocent query.

"Well, for one, an earl's daughter is the last person I would have expected to see serving as a nursemaid at a country manor. Her wrongdoing must have been quite serious to have warranted such a placement. Yet she seems to be a lovely woman, from the little I've seen." He raised his brows, pinning Richard with his gaze. "What is your opinion of her?"

"I haven't thought much about it," Richard lied.

Braedan didn't look convinced. "Well, then, do you know aught about the details of the—what did she call it?—the *indiscretion* that brought her here?"

Richard felt his mouth tighten. By God but Braedan was like a dog with a bone. "From what I have been able to gather," he answered levelly, "her transgression involved an unsanctioned affair of the heart, with her position here imposed upon her as a form of penance. She seems to have found a measure of peace since then, but it is clear that she has suffered greatly for her mistakes—that she still suffers, in fact."

"Ah . . ." Braedan said, lifting his chin just a bit, though never removing his gaze from Richard, as he added quietly, "Would it be fair to say, then, that she is a woman in need of rescue?"

A beat of silence passed as Richard absorbed the sting of that question. He didn't truly blame Braedan for it, not considering his history with women, but it hurt nonetheless. Taking in a breath and mustering a smile that felt more like a grimace, he said, "Is she like Elizabeth and Eleanor . . . that is what you are truly asking, is it not?"

Braedan did not shift his stare, its weight on him both penetrating and tinged with concern as he murmured, "Aye, little brother, I suppose that is what I want to know. For your sake, though, not mine."

Richard did not answer at first, his tight smile still in place as he swung his gaze to the shuttered window, seeing shades of the past in his mind's eye . . . recalling Elizabeth's sweetly innocent smile and remembering the way they'd laughed together, caught in a springtime shower while in the first flush of young love. He relived the emptiness he'd felt when she'd disappeared, taken into his corrupt uncle's clutches, followed by the grief of learning she'd died in childbirth—a miserable ignominy wrought by Draven himself.

It had been so long ago, but Braedan was right. He had wanted to—nay, he had felt *compelled* to try to save Elizabeth, through whatever means was open to him. Even after she was gone, that hunger had burned in him, manifesting itself into a rage that had only been satisfied by dealing death to the one who had ruined her.

And yet Elizabeth hadn't been the only woman to hold that position in his life. Nay, he had cast himself into the role of rescuer to a lady's need again, even after that, with Eleanor. Aye, slight, fragile Eleanor, with her sunshine and her shadows, her quick smile and even swifter tears . . .

"I am sorry to raise old ghosts, Richard," Braedan broke into his musings, dispersing the memories into blessed darkness again. "I only question you about Meg in the hope of preventing you from taking on another burden in your desire to help those in need, especially those of the gentler sex."

"I understand." Richard's voice was low with restrained emotion as he swung his gaze to his brother. "And I do not blame you for it. But you need not fear. Meg is strong—resilient in a way that perhaps even I am not."

Braedan kept his gaze upon him, searching, and Richard attempted an encouraging smile, forcing the next words he spoke, though they were unaccountably difficult for him to say. "Besides, even if I am wrong about her, it will not matter.

She will likely be leaving Hawksley soon, now that her work here is done."

"Has she said as much?"

"Nay. But then again there hasn't been much time to discuss those details. She will tell me of her plans after Eleanor's funeral feast is concluded, I suspect."

Without saying more, he turned back to the window, pushing open the shutter in his sudden, almost desperate need to feel the chill of the air on his face. It creaked open, letting in a ribbon of frostiness that rushed over him, winding through the chamber and dancing with the flames in the hearth.

"I will trust in your judgment, then, Richard."

He heard Braedan's voice coming from behind him, and though he could not bring himself to turn from the bracing cold just yet, he called in answer, "Once again, I thank you."

"Having said that, however," his brother continued, "you should know that it would be a great relief for us all if someday you would try to find a woman who could truly share the burdens of life with you."

"Someone like Fiona?" Richard asked quietly, at last twisting to meet his gaze.

"Aye, just like her."

Braedan's smile as he spoke those few words revealed the depth of love he felt for his wife as much as if he'd launched into a lengthy account of her virtues. "I would be truly glad for it if you did—though thinking of her reminds me that perhaps we'd be wise to go down soon, else she will be coming up to see what is keeping us. And trust me when I tell you that you do not want to witness that."

Pushing himself to his feet with a low groan, Braedan suddenly grimaced, mumbling, "Ah, but it is a terrible thing to become stiff and sore from nothing greater than sitting for too long."

"I can arrange a better reason for your aches, if you're so inclined," Richard offered in lilting challenge, turning fully and pushing away from the wall. "We can undertake the exercise with our blades that I mentioned earlier—day after next, if you'd like. What say you, old man?"

"I say that I still have a few moves that will force you to keep your biting tongue to yourself, sapling." Braedan laughed, making his way to the door.

"We shall see," Richard called after him, smiling and shaking his head as he watched his brother work out the kinks in his limbs. "Go on ahead and give my regards to your wife. Tell her that I'll be down shortly, eager to sample her cooking."

"All right," Braedan called over his shoulder as he went into the corridor. "But do not tarry too long, little brother, for she is a regular virago when it comes to serving meals while they're still hot."

"Duly noted."

As Braedan had left, Richard felt his smile fade; he breathed in deep, letting the air spend slowly before he stepped to the window to close the shutter and ready himself to join the others. But something made him pause before he pulled it shut. He looked out over the yard and village below, noticing how serene it all looked in the waning light. Autumn shadows stretched long fingers over the earth, calm and peaceful, and he found himself lingering over the sight, turning over in his mind all that he and Braedan had discussed.

For all of his pretenses otherwise, his brother's question about Meg sat heavy on his heart. Yet he had spoken true when he'd answered him; he would wager his honor that she was strong in her heart and soul, the very opposite of the women in his past to whom he had usually found himself bound in some way. And though he would probably go to hell for it, he realized suddenly that he wanted nothing more right now than simply to be near her, basking in the warmth and light that she somehow managed to bring to his battered heart.

The feeling swept through him, strong and deep, filling him with a yearning that would not abate. It was wrong, it was dangerous, but it stretched to life, as if a part of him was awakening after a long sleep. He wanted to be near her, by God, even if that meant nothing more than to breathe the same air or to sit next to her in silence.

She was warmth and life, a heady breeze to blow away the darkness that had crouched over him, shadowing his heart for so long. Aye, for even through all the misery she had endured, something inside Meg still managed to burn brightly, and it beckoned him, drawing him close in a way he couldn't re-member ever feeling before. In a way that helped him battle the guilt and pain that warred inside him with every breath.

But it could not be, even without Eleanor or his commit-ment to the Templars. Yet trying to stem the tide of what he was feeling was like trying to contain the ocean in a thimble.

Defiant, eager, and teetering on the edge of something larger than he cared to admit even to himself, Richard leaned out and yanked the shutter closed with a snap. Then he blew out the taper on the table and made his way out of the cham-ber, in determined search of the woman who, by her very presence, had managed to do something he hadn't thought would be possible for him in this lifetime . . .

For somehow, Meg had made him feel hope again.

Chapter 8

❧

Meg sat at the table in the main hall, somewhat over-whelmed at the happy commotion going on around her. She couldn't remember the last time she'd witnessed such joyful chaos. Fiona and Braedan's children had been straggling in from outdoors one by one, most having come from the stables, where they'd gone immediately upon their arrival at Hawksley to see the mama cat that had taken up residence there with her new kittens.

The laughing, jostling, and washing up that had begun in the kitchen had now spilled into the main hall where supper would be, and Meg and Fiona were helping Willa set the last of the bowls of steaming chicken stew, buttered cabbage, and pease pudding on the center of the long table. All that remained was for the rest of the children to sit and the men to come downstairs, so that the meal could begin.

"All right, children, find a place now, those of you who have washed your hands!" Fiona called out over the furor, stopping with her hands on her hips to silently count the number of her brood who had made it to their seats. "Two, three, four . . ." she mouthed as she pointed to each head. Looking up with brow knitted, she murmured, "Where is Elspeth? And Adam?"

Meg looked around her at the four children already sitting—two girls and two boys, who, if she remembered Fiona's hastily delivered recitation of introductions in the kitchen, ranged in age from three and a half to fourteen—and realized that indeed nine-year-old Elspeth and the oldest, sixteen-year-old Adam, were missing. "I will go and see if they linger in the kitchen," she said to Fiona, pushing away from the table in preparation to look.

"Nay, you should not need to do that, for they know—"

Fiona ceased speaking as Elspeth suddenly bounded into the main hall, windblown and rosy, her red-gold hair tousled about her head. The girl stopped short when she saw her mother's expression, clamping her mouth shut and wiping her freshly washed hands none too decorously on her over-skirt. Elspeth's bid at acting contrite was hampered just a bit, Meg thought as she suppressed a grin of her own, by the hint of an incorrigible smile that remained firmly in the curve of her lips.

"And where is your brother, young miss?" Fiona asked Elspeth, arching her brow for emphasis. "I called for *all* of my children to come wash for the meal nigh on a quarter hour ago, so how is it that you are so late in heeding my request?"

"Beg pardon, Mama," the girl said, sidling into her place on the bench, where her jostling earned a pinch from seven-year-old Robert, to which she responded by yanking a tendril of his red hair.

When he yelped aloud, Fiona stared at them both in exasperation, hardly glancing down as she tried to keep the youngest, little Henry, from sticking his hand into the bowl of the pease pudding. "Well?" she said to Elspeth, keeping her gaze fixed on her errant daughter even as she wiped Henry's hand. "Do you know where Adam has gone off to, then?"

"We were out near the orchard," Elspeth admitted, "and Adam dared me to climb into one of the trees to reach a perfectly luscious-looking apple. But I couldn't get higher than the second branch because of this—this silly *dress* I was made to wear today," she said with a dramatic, pouting flourish, "and so he gave in and climbed up to get it for me. But then you called, and he told me to go on, and . . . well, I expect he'll be coming along shortly."

Fiona just shook her head and started to sit down, interrupted from the act once again by Braedan and then in a moment more by Richard, who came one after the other from the stairway that led to the manor house's family quarters.

"Well, love, what delectable dishes have you prepared, then?" Braedan teased, coming close to Fiona to brush a kiss over her cheek. And though she knew she wasn't supposed to hear it, Meg nonetheless caught his added murmur of "None that could be more delectable than you, however, my love," whispered in his wife's ear before she laughingly batted at him and directed him toward his seat.

"I confess that the meal is not my doing," she answered. "Willa and I were too busy chasing down your unruly children to manage much in the way of helping Meg, for it is she who deserves the thanks for the dishes before you."

"Then a hearty cheer for Meg, for whatever awaits us on the table smells delicious," Braedan answered with a swiveling bow, making her blush before he turned back to Fiona and offered his hand to assist her to her place.

Fiona's eyes had taken on an added twinkle from the moment Braedan had entered the room, Meg noticed, the air itself feeling charged somehow with husband and wife together again; the realization made Meg's heart twist just a little. The affection, respect, and very real attraction the two clearly shared set off a kind of wistful yearning inside her.

That fluttery feeling intensified all of a sudden when Richard approached, shaking his head and smiling at the crowded table. She had hardly managed to calm her reaction when he turned to her, meeting her gaze with that devastating smile still tilting his mouth as he said quietly, "Aye, a hearty thanks to you, Meg. It seems you've prepared a repast fit for royalty."

"We aren't royal, Uncle Richard—we're just hungry!" called out Anna, who was five and seemed even more enamored with having a boy's freedom of dress and behavior than Elspeth was. Meg sent up a silent prayer of thanks for the distraction that ensued, with a tumult of scolding from the adults and bubbling laughter from the younger children. In quick order everyone settled, and Meg found herself sitting next to Richard at the end of one side of the table, directly across from Braedan and Fiona, who had placed themselves nearest the little ones to assist them with their meal.

"Well, then," Richard said, lifting his cup to the table, "let us begin this wonderful supper while we commence the welcomes, so that we may see the starving Anna fed. You may all have grown several inches since last I saw you, but I'd wager I can still name each of you correctly—though I don't believe I've ever met this young chap," he added as nodded toward the youngest de Cantor, seated at the other side of the table.

"That's Henry. He's the baby," piped up Anna again as she

reached for the bowl of buttered cabbage her mother offered her. "And naming us should be easy, Uncle Richard, since Mama always makes us sit in order to keep track of us."

"I'm not a baby!" Henry hollered, his fingers curling into chubby fists.

"Are too!"

"Anna, that's enough," Fiona chided her dark-haired daughter, while Braedan flashed a stern fatherly look, meant to subdue. But it had a much lesser effect when he added a wink at the end of it.

"Henry is indeed the youngest," Fiona added, scooping some of the pease pudding onto his trencher, "but as he said, he is hardly a baby anymore, at nearly four years old."

"And a fine young gentleman he is already," Richard commented, earning a brilliant smile from the lad in question. He took a bite of chicken stew, then shifted his gaze to the little girl next to Henry, drawing a blush from her as he said, "And next we have the lovely Anna, who was but newly born when I saw her last, but who has grown into a beautiful young lady." Looking a bit farther down the table, he nodded, "And Robert is next to her, if I remember correctly. You must be . . ." He paused dramatically, squinting his eyes. "Let me think on it a moment—seven years old now, is it? Almost ready to go off and serve as page, then, eh lad?"

Robert nodded enthusiastically, his mouth too full to answer right away. At last he finished chewing, took a breath, and said, "Aye, it is true, sir—I leave for Lord Exton's estate come spring, to begin my training."

"Excellent; we can always use another strong de Cantor arm in the family."

Meg felt that fluttery sensation inside her once again as

she observed Richard's interactions with the children, watching silently as he spoke next with Elspeth and finally with fourteen-year-old Rebecca, who was the very image of Braedan, only with her mother's eyes.

Richard's ease with them all was astonishing, really. She remembered all too well what stern indifference from the adults around her had felt like when she was a child, and she would have thought Richard himself would be of that ilk—not only as a man who had been immersed for so long in a life of fighting and violence, but also as a father who had lost his own daughter so early and tragically. Yet he was just the opposite.

In truth, Richard continued to surprise her at every turn, and it was becoming all she could do to keep reminding herself that he was a man who would not—could not—ever be anything to her but someone who had been kind enough to understand rather than to judge her earlier transgressions.

The table was much quieter than before, now that all the children were focused on eating. But with the silence came a heightened awareness of her proximity to Richard, which Meg had been better able to suppress when surrounded by the clamor. Forcing herself to try to ignore the warmth spread through her with each accidental touch of their arms or brush of their fingers, Meg deliberately lifted her head and directed her gaze across to Braedan and Fiona, asking, "Your other son who did not travel with you—William, I believe you said . . . is he away training at Lord Exton's as well, then?"

"Aye," Braedan answered, pausing mid-motion as he prepared to eat a piece of the bread he'd torn from his trencher. "And a strong, determined lad he is. We named him for Fiona's own brother," he added, glancing to her with a grin, "and an apt name it is, for the two of them share many of the same qualities, not to mention their bright red hair."

"He has just turned eleven," Fiona continued, smiling at her husband's comments about their son and her brother, "but he has done so well in his training that the weapons master has asked for him to squire a bit earlier than is usual. He will be home for a short time after St. Catherine's Day before returning to Lord Exton's care following Twelfth Night."

"And what of Adam?" Richard asked. "He was little more than a skinny lad of eleven the last time I saw him. He must be nearly a man by now, ready to get his spurs. Did he not arrive with—"

"Here I am, Uncle," broke in a deep and melodic voice from behind them, "and I must beg your pardon for being so tardy to supper—and your pardon as well, Mother, Father . . ."

Meg twisted around toward the door to the kitchen at the same time that Richard did—only Richard stiffened abruptly upon sight of the person who'd spoken. Startled by his reaction to the young man, Meg glanced at Richard, surprised to see that she could read nothing in his expression, though his complexion had paled.

"Adam," he said in a voice that sounded somewhat hoarse to her. He cleared his throat and rose to face his eldest nephew, extending his hand almost woodenly, as Adam set down the basket of apples he was carrying to stride forward and clasp it with a wide smile lighting his face.

Though just sixteen, the lean boy he must once have been was no more, for standing before them was an exceedingly handsome young man. Adam was tall for his age, with shoulder-length ebony hair several shades darker than either Richard's or Braedan's and features so fine they bordered on elegant. He was saved from over-prettiness, however, by a firm jawline, dark, slashing brows, and a mouth that for all its sensuality was unmistakably male.

But it was his eyes that arrested her attention more fully, once her initial response to his startling attractiveness had passed. Meg shifted her gaze quickly to Richard, then to Braedan and Fiona before looking back at Adam again. It was clear that this lad took after none of the other members of his family, for his eyes were as dark as obsidian, with long, sooty lashes that accented an expressiveness of gaze that would make any number of young maidens at court swoon.

Aye, Meg needed no more than a single glance to realize that, though he had not yet attained full manhood, Adam de Cantor was growing into what her mother would have called the embodiment of a fallen angel, sinfully attractive in a way that made it difficult to pull one's gaze from him.

That didn't explain, however, why Richard was reacting to him as if he were seeing a ghost.

"You look well, Uncle," Adam said, giving Richard's hand a hearty shake, his expression shifting to one of gravity as he added, "though I must add my condolences to those I am sure have already been offered by my parents, at Aunt Eleanor's passing."

"She is at peace now, so it is for the best. But thank you."

Richard was doing his best to sound natural, Meg decided, though as Adam took his place on the bench, she saw Richard catch Braedan's gaze with an unmistakably sharp glance. The uneasiness inside her intensified at the exchange between the brothers; there was clearly something more to all this than met the eye.

After his nephew had taken his place next to Rebecca, Richard added—without looking at him again, Meg noted— "Before you settle into your meal, I must introduce you to Eleanor's cousin Meg, who has been living at Hawksley Manor for the past two years."

Richard leaned back and nodded to her, and she was swept up as always in the ease of his warm regard. To her, he said, "You have made acquaintance with the other members of Fiona and Braedan's brood, Meg, and now it is time to meet their eldest. Adam . . . de Cantor."

"It is an honor," Adam murmured, nodding to her in a manner quite worthy of the most polished court swain. "Please accept my sympathy to you as well, on the loss of your relative."

"Thank you," Meg answered, nodding back; she felt the pull of Richard's stare on her, and so she met his gaze again, wondering at the conflicting shadows at play in the hazel depths of his eyes.

"Hawksley's orchard is one of the finest of any manor I've seen, Uncle," Adam commented in the next moment, seemingly unaware of the rippling tension at play around him. He took hearty portions from the bowls of still-steaming victuals everyone passed, saying, "I beg pardon if it was untoward of me, but I couldn't resist picking enough to fill one of the small baskets I saw stacked near the gates of the fruit grove."

"It is no trouble, Adam," Richard answered, finally glancing again at the young man. "They were out in preparation for the cotters to begin picking this week. You are welcome to what you like."

"Perhaps the children could assist in the harvest," Fiona suggested, wiping at Henry's mouth again. "They do all enjoy being outdoors. Even the girls, though I know it is not fashionable for them to take too much sun. Still, there will be no harm done, I think," she added with a smile, "as we are not expecting to make any grand appearances at court any time soon."

"I am, Mother," Adam asserted, pausing in the act of sopping up some gravy with his bread. "I'd like to serve the king as Father has done. But first I must be knighted and prove myself worthy on the field. What better place to do so than at the royal court?"

"You know full well that attending summer court is not a foregone conclusion, young man," Braedan said sternly. "We said we would discuss it; that is all."

"But Father," Adam protested, sitting straighter and directing the full power of his persuasive, dark gaze on Braedan, "I have completed my training as a knight. I can hold my own in sword combat, even with you"—Richard's gaze snapped to Braedan again at that—"and I am ready to make my way in the world! You were no different. Nor was Uncle Richard, from what you have told me. It is time for me to—"

"Beggin' pardon, sirs and ladies," a high-pitched voice broke in from the doorway, cracking on the last word. It was James, the tanner's younger son and unofficial village watchman. He swallowed hard enough to set his throat bobbing, staring around and crushing his hat in his hand, as he sought his master somewhere around the overflowing table of people.

"What is it, lad?" Richard called, drawing his grateful gaze.

"We—we thought it important enough to disturb your meal to tell you that there are riders, sir, comin' at a goodly pace down the road from Kent."

"How many men?"

"Only two, sir." James paused to swallow hard again, his blue eyes wide and his fingers twisting convulsively in the fabric of his hat. "But sir, they bear a royal banner. The red and yellow lion of young King Edward himself!"

* * *

An hour later, Richard stood at the edge of the orchard Adam had praised so heartily, watching the sun beginning to stretch flame and gold fingers across the sky—and reviewing in his mind all that had happened in the time since James's pronouncement had thrown the household into a tumult. Supper had been hurriedly finished and the table cleared so that the king's messengers might be received and fed. Richard had retired to his solar with Braedan to read the contents of the royal parchment that had been delivered, while Fiona and Meg supervised the children and tried to arrange where everyone would sleep.

But Richard had vacated the manor house shortly after finishing his conversation with Braedan, needing to clear his mind and think over what might be the next steps of this process he had pushed into motion with his own missive to King Edward. Now all that remained was to speak with Meg about the portion of the royal missive that affected her. Ironically, the only way to accomplish that with some level of privacy had been to send for her to join him here, away from the furor inside the house.

Alone.

She would heed his summons in short order, he knew, and they would be alone again. The thought of that sent a strangely pleasurable tingle through Richard that was offset by his ever-present guilt—compounded by the knowledge that he likely had no business feeling this way about any woman so soon after his estranged wife's death. But he did feel something for Meg; he couldn't deny it. Something powerful and good.

Something that could never come to fruition, especially now that the king was commanding her to attend court again after all these years. She would surely leap at the chance to

*leave behind the dull and dismal world of Hawksley Manor
in favor of the glittering excitement she'd known before.*

She was a lady born, and he was but a humble knight
whose history with women was dismal at best. He could not
risk caring so deeply again. He could not . . .

"You wished to speak with me, Richard?" her soft voice
came from behind him, and he turned, steeling himself for
the inevitable conversation, even as he tried to quell the
warm flood of sensation that her presence evoked in him.

"Aye," he murmured, "I did. Though I hope I did not disturb
any necessary activity at the house by summoning you now."

"Nay; it was near chaos for a while, but the children have
begun to settle now that night approaches."

He stepped aside so that she could also have a place
against the fence bordering the orchard, and as she moved to
the spot, he drank in her beauty, the understated elegance of
her set off in the gilding sunset, the sweet and spice fragrance
of her that teased him. She made him want to reach out and
bury his fingers into the silken weight of her hair, pulling her
close and taking her lips with his so that she might taste the
passion that burned him from the inside out. But of course he
did nothing except to nod in polite welcome.

Innocent to the unrest at play within him, she leaned
against the fence and took a deep breath, making his catch in
the process. By the Rood, but she was beautiful—even more
so for not realizing that truth about herself. He cleared his
throat, trying to appear unaffected.

"I must confess that I am grateful for the reprieve of your
request to see me," Meg added, catching him off guard even
further with an impish smile. "Not that your nieces and
nephews aren't thoroughly delightful, of course," she added.

"But unlike your brother and sister-by-marriage, I am simply not used to having so many children about."

"Has everyone found a place to sleep, then?" he asked a bit hoarsely, half astonished that he could find his voice at all.

She nodded. "It will be a tight fit for a few days, but it will work, I think. The first chamber and its bed have been completely aired and refreshed; your brother, Fiona, and the two youngest children will sleep there. Elspeth and Rebecca will sleep with me in the second chamber, while Adam and Robert will take pallets into the main hall."

She frowned slightly, looking away and pausing for a weighty moment before saying, "Speaking of Adam, Richard, I could not help noticing that you reacted rather strongly to his appearance in the hall this evening. I do not wish to contribute unwittingly in any way to some difficult situation, and so I must needs ask, is there aught I should know about him—aught of which I should be aware that has happened between the two of you?"

Now it was Richard's turn to pause, her innocent question bringing up the same flood of dark and difficult memories that Adam's arrival had inspired but an hour past. His nephew's physical appearance had startled him—shocked him, even—so much so that he had pulled Braedan aside after the royal messengers had delivered their news, to chide him for not warning of the changes time had wrought in the lad. It was uncanny, the likeness between Adam and their despised late uncle-by-marriage, Kendrick de Lacy, Viscount Draven; the realization of why had shaken Richard to his core.

But Meg didn't need to know all the sordid details. Not today, with all else he needed to tell her . . . not to mention that it was not his place to share such things about a boy who was not his own.

Struggling to offer her a smile, bitter as it was, Richard settled for saying, "There is naught about Adam to worry you, Meg. By all accounts, he is a fine young man. I was simply startled by how closely Adam resembles a distant relative of mine and Braedan's."

Meg nodded. "I can see how that would have been a shock."

"Aye, it was. For more reasons than I can explain just now. Someday, perhaps . . ." He called up another smile, this one more genuine. "But that is neither here nor there. What is important now is that you've managed to find sleeping quarters for everyone, as I am certain it could not have been easy, considering this small manor's limited accommodations."

Meg flushed, in pleasure, he hoped, at his compliment. "I was a bit concerned that your nephews might take cold on the floor," she murmured, "but Fiona assured me that they will be quite comfortable, and being near to the fire will keep them warm."

"It seems that it is all arranged, then," he said with a nod, finding some humor—and welcome distraction, at least—in the single, glaring fact that Meg seemed to have forgotten.

"Mm-hhmmm." She nodded. "All is ready for nightfall."

"Except for one bit," he said with a wry smile edging his lips.

"What is that?"

His comment had pulled her soft gaze to him again, just as he'd hoped it would. "You haven't yet told me where *I* am to sleep."

Meg's answering expression was priceless, made even

more delightful by the crimson flush that spread over her cheeks. "Oh, my," she breathed. "You're right. That is, I— well, I and Fiona . . . we spoke of it briefly, but I thought you had discussed the particulars already, with your brother in the solar."

"I am afraid not," he murmured in feigned seriousness. Where he would sleep tonight was in truth of little matter to him—but teasing her like this was proving far more enjoyable than he'd have ever anticipated, and so he resolved to keep it going for as long as he possibly could. "My brother and I discussed the business of the royal missive, but nothing was mentioned regarding tonight's accommodations," he added, careful to keep his tone bland enough to be considered in earnest.

"Well, then." She seemed quite at a loss. After a moment, she took another deep breath, clearly fortifying herself for delivering news that she believed would be less than popular. "I suppose it is up to me to tell you, then, that you will be . . . that is, that you . . ."

She seemed to be struggling with what to say to explain this obvious gaffe when she stopped short, having caught him, he was fairly certain, in suppressing his smile. She looked startled for a moment, but then pressed her quite kissable lips together and raised her brows, accenting velvety brown eyes that held a sudden, entrancing twinkle. Aye, she was definitely on to him. The effect of her expression was utterly disarming, and Richard struggled to maintain his unruffled demeanor in the face of it.

"The truth," Meg finished at last, her lips curving slightly, and with a pointed stare that dared him to refute her, "is that as lord of the manor, *you*, sir, unlike the rest of Hawksley's lowly inhabitants this evening, may claim an actual choice over where you will sleep."

"Is that so?" Richard managed to say, though he needed to cough before he could get himself under control again. He crossed his arms and tried to look suitably impressed. "Certainly I am unworthy of such privilege, though I am honored at the tender care and foresight you have obviously employed for my comfort."

Now it was Meg's turn to choke back a laugh. "Aye." She nodded. "Every possibility was explored to exhaustion, and I assure you that each option rivals the others for pure luxury. Would you like to hear them?"

"I can barely stand the suspense."

It took her a moment to respond, and now it was she who needed to clear her throat, biting her lips, he was convinced, because of her own struggle not to laugh aloud. Finally she offered in a somewhat ragged voice, "I shall tell you straight away, then, that your first choice comprises the storeroom abutting the first chamber; as a sleeping chamber, it is what many might describe as . . . efficient in size. The floor has been cleared and swept clean, and so you will have room for a pallet and—well—not much else."

Her dry tone as she finished her description almost made him burst into laughter then and there.

"The second choice?"

She nodded in mock seriousness. "Your second option involves joining your nephews on the chilled, rather hard, and yet quite invigorating stone floor of the main hall."

"And the third . . . ?" he prompted, giving up all pretense of seriousness now as she paused in her recitation of his notably sparse accommodations.

"Your third choice would be to sleep in the conversely warm—but quite *fragrant*, I am afraid—empty stall in the stables," she barely managed to get out, crossing her arms in a matching posture to his, and giving him what was clearly meant to be a decisive nod, before she simply could hold back no longer; and when she dissolved into laughter, he joined her, reminded in a deliciously wonderful way how good it felt to share such innocent merriment with someone.

Within a few moments their humor began to ebb, and Richard wiped his eyes, still chuckling, before meeting her smiling gaze. But he was struck with the realization that he had never really seen her laugh before—never seen her so carefree—and he knew then that he wanted more than anything to make her feel that way again and again.

"Thank you for that," Meg said breathlessly, when she was able to speak again. She rubbed her cheeks as if they ached from the unaccustomed grinning. "It has been a very long time since I have laughed so . . ."

"I know what you mean," he said gently, his own face feeling stiff as well. "It is far too long for me also, and yet while I am standing here with you, I cannot seem to come up with one good reason why."

She glanced away, then, and he couldn't tell if she was more pleased or embarrassed, from the way the hint of scarlet in her cheeks blended with the ever-deepening rays of the setting sun.

"It is getting late," she murmured at last, her gaze lifting for the briefest instant to his again in a way that was somehow both demure and utterly tantalizing. "Perhaps you should tell me what it is you wished to discuss with me, before darkness drives us into the house again."

"You're right, of course." He held on to the lighter feeling for as long as he could before he finally let it go and sighed, running his hand through his hair and peering off into the darkening orchard. "I sent for you concerning the missive I received from the king during supper. It was in answer to a message I had dispatched to him upon returning to Hawksley, asking his aid in protecting England's Templars from the French Inquisition."

"And what did he reply?"

He thought she might have stiffened a bit in response to his mention of the Templars, but in the rapidly spreading shadows, it was difficult to tell for sure.

"I do not know for sure yet how much support he will offer. He has summoned me to the court he has gathered at Tunbridge Castle in Kent, in honor of his favorite, Piers Gaveston's, marriage to Margaret de Clare, so that we may discuss the issue. The wedding will take place in the coming week, and I am expected to attend—if not in time for the ceremony itself, then at least for part of the weeks of festivities following."

"I see . . ." Meg sounded somewhat breathless again, though this time it was clear her reaction wasn't from laughter. "So, you have been called to court. And you have brought me here to be sure I understand that I must—I must now . . ." Her voice trailed off, and she reacted as if she were recovering from a blow of some sort.

"Are you unwell, lady?" Richard asked, stepping forward to place a steadying hand to her shoulder.

"Nay, I am fine," she answered, though she sounded anything but. She shook her head, all merriment gone from her expression, and her beautiful eyes grave. She paused for a long moment as if gathering her thoughts, then tipped her chin to gaze up at him, adding solemnly, "And I understand completely, do not fear. There will be no uncomfortable scene before your family. I will take but a few days to put my affairs in order, and I will be gone from Hawksley long before you return from Tunbridge."

"What?" Richard gazed down at her, stunned. She looked so lost, so stricken, that he couldn't stop himself from reaching up with his other hand to cup her cheek, his fingertips brushing away the wetness that had begun to well in her eyes. "What are you talking about?"

"Leaving Hawksley, of course," she exclaimed, and he was relieved to see that level of passionate response, indignant as it might be, replace the empty sorrow she had displayed a moment past. "That is what you brought me out here to tell me, isn't it? Now that Eleanor is beyond the need for earthly care, I no longer have a place here. I must move on."

"Nay, lady—nay," Richard said, shaking his head with a soft and exasperated laugh, before leaning forward to rest his brow against hers. He closed his eyes. "Good God, that is not why I summoned you out here—though I confess that I thought you would indeed tell me that you yourself wished to leave Hawksley in the coming days, once the observances for Eleanor were complete."

She had gone very still beneath his touch, and he pulled back to look at her again, though continuing to cup her face in his palm, adding, "Is that not what you intended—to return to the life you left behind at the commencement of your penance?"

"Nay, it is most assuredly not."

She looked away from him—though she did not extract herself from his touch, he noticed. Instead she reached up and took hold of the hand cradling her cheek, capturing it between the warm strength of her own palms before finally releasing him and stepping away. She shook her head. "Do not even you understand, Richard? I would not forsake this or any place, even the cursed abbey where I was placed before coming here, in order to return to my former home in Berkshire. I *hated* my life as Lady Margaret. I thought you of all people would understand the reasons why."

"But you cannot deny that living within the world of the nobility yields many benefits," he countered, surprised at her vehemence, even as he secretly rejoiced in learning that she did not wish to leave. Still, there had to be something to remind her that it wasn't all bad—something she could hold on to after he found the words to tell her about her own summons back to the fold of court. "The past is finished and your future awaits you. To most, a life of relative luxury would be far preferable to days of toil at a modest country manor."

She laughed, though the sound caught in her throat. "Then perhaps I am foolish, but I do not find it so. I despise it all, now more than ever—the posturing and falsity, with each family vying for a stronger measure of power through any means open to them . . . including that of dangling their daughters like so much sweet bait to be snapped up by the highest bidder."

She broke off, her voice catching, and Richard made a move as if he would offer her comfort, but she shook her head, forcing a pained smile.

"I—I am sorry, Meg," he murmured, fisting his hands in a futile effort to hold back what he realized he could not change with any amount of pretty words—to be the deliverer of tidings that would likely cause her even more distress atop that which she had already endured.

"Do not be. As I have already confessed to you, I committed a grave transgression in the eyes of those who owned my future—a sticking point in my father's plans for me—but through it I found honest love with a simple man who cared for me for who I was, not for what an alliance with my family would bring to him. Indulging in that forbidden union eventually brought me pain, I cannot deny it, but it saved me too. And if I can help it I will never go back to that false world I left. Never."

Crackling silence settled over them for an instant, broken when she added, "But that brings me to my current dilemma, does it not? I will not return to my former home, and yet I cannot remain here."

"Nay, Meg," Richard said fervently, locking his gaze with hers, "you may remain here for as long as you wish, make no mistake on that. It . . ." He paused for a moment, his voice husky with the feeling buried beneath the simple thought he wished to convey. "It would be my most fervent hope, in fact."

"What?" The word slipped from her on a gasp, and now it was she who took a few stiff steps forward, her posture rigid with surprise, to face him—to peer into his face in an attempt to read his expression beneath the cooling blanket of dark that had slipped over the world.

"Aye," he murmured, still hoarse. He did not want to offend her, but he needed her to understand the sincerity of his offer, and that it came with no further obligation from her. As he took her hands once more in his, he reacted to the jolt of pure, sensual heat that rippled up from the friction of their bare palms. She apparently felt it as well, for she uttered a breathy gasp that echoed the groan he himself had bitten back. Struggling to keep himself under control, he lifted his gaze to hers again, barely managing to say, "You did a great service in caring for Eleanor; one that can never properly be repaid. I would be honored if you would consider Hawksley Manor your home for as long as you wish it . . . and a place to return to between your travels, when you make them."

Her eyes glistened in the pale dusk of moonlight and the first few stars that were winking to life above their heads, while their breath hung between them, smoky puffs in the rapidly chilling air. "I—I am overwhelmed, Richard," she said at last, faintly, her voice as husky as his had been moments ago. Her fingers shifted in his, the simple stroke of them against his palm sending another erotic jolt tingling through him, to settle low in his groin.

"Do not be," he said gruffly. "It is but a small thing."

"It is as immense to me as if you had given me keys to a kingdom."

The kingdom of my heart, perhaps.

The thought slipped into Richard's mind before he could forestall it, though thank God he managed to keep from uttering it aloud.

"And yet there is something more, is there not?" she continued quietly. "I can see the weight of it in your expression."

"You are, as always, more than perceptive, lady," he murmured as he released her hand, a self-deprecating smile quirking his lips. But a spark of relief lit in his breast at her question, for though he despised the discomfort he was about to inflict on her with his news, he was also grateful for it, for providing him with a distraction—one that had nothing to do with his renegade heart, praise be—away from the tormenting, sensual images that were crowding his mind so relentlessly.

"What is it?"

"It is why I called you out here, to speak with you in private," he murmured, doing his best to break it to her as gently as possible. "I have received a command that I was instructed to relay to you personally; it was included in the parchment I received this evening from the royal messengers."

"*I* was mentioned in the king's missive?" she asked, her brows knit together.

"Aye, lady, you were," Richard said quietly. "And that is why I do not seem as light of heart as I might be otherwise, knowing as I do now the distress this information will cause you."

She went very still, her face seeming more pale, even, than it already was in the pearly light of the newly risen moon—but she did not crumble as realization dawned full. Nay, that strength of hers that he had asserted so vehemently to Braedan shone through, making her posture stiffen and her expression take on a resolute cast that made him long to kiss it back to softness again.

"I have been summoned back to court along with you, haven't I?" she asked calmly, almost without emotion.

"Aye, lady, and sorry I am to be the bearer of such unwelcome tidings. But it is true. In his missive, King Edward decreed that I should escort you with me when I return to his royal court."

"I suppose there is little chance that the king might have mentioned his purpose in bidding me come after all this time."

"I am afraid he did not."

Richard watched the desolation sweep across her delicate features as the full import of the news sank in. Despising himself for having brought this pain to her, he delivered the final blow as quickly as he could, adding in what she must have considered the voice of her doom, "We have some time, Meg—but we are required to arrive within the next sennight . . . in time to celebrate his favorite's marriage at Tunbridge Castle."

Chapter 9

~~~~∽○○∽~~~~

The moon was just beginning to wane, though dawn wasn't yet imminent enough to spread color over the dark slate of the sky by the time Meg gave up on sleep. She made her way as quietly as she could from the second chamber down to the kitchen, driven by thoughts that had been swirling endlessly, shadows stretching and old memories coming back to sting her ever since Richard had told her of the royal command.

She was being summoned back to court. God help her, but it could mean nothing good.

Perhaps it was simply the new sovereign's way of asserting his authority to do as he wished, a voice of false courage asserted deep inside her. *Or it might be an effort to show benevolence at the start of his reign, calling back some of those who had been banished, to thereby win the hitherto tenuous regard of his subjects.*

Or more likely Father has found a new way to make use of me, and has used his influence to arrange the summons.

That thought made her shudder far more than the chill that invaded the thin shawl she'd hastily thrown over her shoulders as she made her way through the still-darkened manor house. She hadn't bothered to dress fully for the day yet; no one would be about for another half hour or more, and so rather than awaken Elspeth and Rebecca with scuffling around for the more elegant garments she planned to wear for Eleanor's funeral Mass, she'd simply belted a plain wool bliaud of dusky blue over her loose-fitting, long-sleeved chemise.

These were the kind of garments she most often wore when she was digging in the manor garden or working alongside the villagers in the field, and she'd become accustomed to them; in truth, though there had been a time when she had coveted only clothing of the highest fashion, she felt far more comfortable and *real* in these sturdy garments than in the frivolous concoctions of her youth at court.

Clenching her fingers in the heavy fabric of her skirts now as if it would somehow anchor her, she made her way carefully past the sleeping boys in the great hall; Adam was curled to the right of the large, circular fire pit in the floor, while Robert rested to the left, his arm outflung and his head tipped back, though neither lad was snoring. All was as she'd expected, still and dim. She was glad for it—and glad for the chance to escape if even for a few moments from the dark twisting of thoughts that had tormented her in the loneliness of her bed.

Almost holding her breath as she stepped through the kitchen, she glanced toward the tiny curtained alcove, behind which Willa still slept; it wouldn't be long before the day's light would rouse the older woman from sleep, Meg knew, to begin her customary tasks for the day, and that would include stirring the fires in the kitchen and adding fresh wood.

So although the wooden chair that Richard had dozed in yesterday still perched near the hearth—the one that had held them when he'd kissed her so boldly, she remembered with a burst of delicious heat—she knew she could not remain here to indulge her need to distract herself from her own thoughts. Willa would surely question her sleeplessness if she spotted her, and Meg was in no mood to field any pointed questions. If those questions concerned aught about Richard or her summons to court, she had no idea if she'd be able to answer anyway.

Nay, she would need to push on farther to find a place that would grant her diversion for a few moments . . . that and perhaps a bit of fresh air to help clear her muddled thoughts.

With her object in mind, Meg unlatched the bar of the door leading from the kitchen to the gardens and stable area, resolving to gather a handful of the fragrant herbs for use in the day's meals; it was pleasant to work in that small garden any time, with the spicy scent of the plants around her, but it would be especially welcome this morn, as she watched the sun rise and tried to calm her thoughts.

She'd reached within a few paces of the garden when she stopped, and a prickle went up her spine. Someone was there, standing against the wall abutting the garden fence.

Blast that she couldn't see enough yet in this predawn light to identify the person, though she feared it wouldn't matter. It had to be a stranger, for it was far too early for any of the village men to have made their way up to the manor house garden, not to mention that she couldn't recall any of them working this particular plot, as it was small and yielded only enough for the manor's use; nay, if anyone helped her here, it was Willa or the occasional young lad who earned a half-penny by helping dig the carrots or weed the strips of thyme and mint.

The person standing there in the shadows was too large and broad to be a lad.

She'd gone stiff at the sight of the stranger, and now, trying to calm her racing heart, she reached as quietly as she could for one of the wooden spades left leaning on the fence en-closing the flower beds yestermorn. The house was a good twenty paces behind her, not so far that she couldn't outrun the intruder, but if he took up chase of her, it would be close; she wanted to be prepared to defend herself if need be—and she wouldn't be above screaming bloody murder to summon help either.

In the dim, rising light, Meg took one step back, and then another, keeping her gaze trained on the shadow-man where he stood, unmoving. To keep him in her sights, she traced her path backward a little wider than she had in her approach, not daring to look where she was going, but just stepping slowly and carefully in the direction of the house. And so it was that she placed her foot directly into a pile of twigs and leaves that someone had left scooped in a pile of rakings, the force of her weight on the mass setting off a series of cracklings and snapping that would be sure to wake the dead.

Frozen in alarm, Meg held back a shriek, her gaze pinned to the man and her breath held with panic while the seconds that followed played out like hours. She swung the spade up, brandishing it for a weapon, even as she leaned her weight back onto the offending foot for better balance as she waited for him to come leaping toward her, now that he had been dis-covered. At the same time she sucked in a huge breath of air, preparing to shout at the top of her lungs to rouse those sleeping in the house to come to her aid . . .

But as quickly, she snapped shut her gaping mouth and stared in awestruck wonder at the figure near the wall.

He hadn't moved. Not a hairbreadth.

Squinting, Meg took a cautious step closer, then another, the gathering light making it easier to see with every passing instant. One final step and the image of the stranger came clear before her astonished gaze, followed swiftly by a flood of hot embarrassment.

"Ready to hack him to death, are you?"

The softly drawled question came from just behind her, and she whirled to face the owner of the voice, knowing even before she completed her turn that it was Richard. He stood halfway between her and the house, having apparently come out into the yard within the past few moments.

"How long have you been standing there?" she managed to ask, ignoring the warmth in her cheeks as she struggled to gather her dignity enough to appear nonchalant. Surreptitiously she lowered the gardening implement, hoping he wouldn't be able to see the whitened knuckles of her death grip in the still-dusky light.

"Long enough to realize you meant to do deadly harm to that poor chap yonder," Richard answered, following his comment with a chuckle and a nod in the direction of the scarecrow that leaned on the wall. "It seems a harsh ending for a simple hodmedod who has ne'er had a chance to do his duty. I finished putting him together last night, after we retired from the orchard, but it was too dark to bring him to his appointed post by then."

"It seems an odd task to have undertaken at that late hour," Meg groused, still smarting at having been caught looking so foolish. She held on to the spade as she watched Richard's slow approach.

He shrugged when he came up alongside her, taking the tool from her and nodding her toward the garden with him. "Matthew spoke with me several days ago about the trouble they've been having in the southern field. I thought this fellow might help a bit . . ."

He let his voice trail off as they reached the "fellow" in question, and Meg saw up close the handiwork that had tricked her into thinking a stranger had made his way into the garden. The scarecrow was well-done, she had to admit, though she wouldn't say so aloud to Richard—her pride still stung too much for that—but he'd built the old-style hodmedod as full and large as himself, and he was of imposing stature compared to most men she'd known.

"I daresay it will be very successful in its intended assignment," she finally settled on saying dryly, "for it certainly did a tremendous job at frightening me."

"That I regret most heartily," Richard commented, setting the spade next to his creation, "but then again, I did not expect anyone to be up and about early enough to be startled by him." He leveled a warm gaze on her that as usual penetrated all her defenses and made something inside her come to life with sudden, sharp awareness. "Couldn't sleep, I take it?"

She shook her head, unable to respond in voice for the unexpected lump in her throat. He was concerned for her. And she realized suddenly that she wanted nothing more than to curl up against his chest and hear him tell her it would be all right. But of course that could not be. It could not be, and that was the wretchedness of it all.

"Nor could I, as I am sure is apparent by my presence here with you," Richard answered in that delicious timbre of his that managed to convey humor, understanding, and concern for her all at once. "However, I'd have to say that my sleeplessness proved to be fortunate for this musty chap," he finished, gesturing to the scarecrow with a smile, and drawing a laugh from her after all.

But the feeling was bittersweet, followed quickly by another wave of desolation that blended with a pang of yearning, of tender, aching desire—she could not deny it. For some reason she could not fathom, Richard de Cantor had found a way to tease her back to a world of feeling again, bringing all her senses to startling, sometimes painful awareness, even when she knew it would be far easier to remain numb.

But the truth remained that with every moment she spent with him, it became ever more clear to her that he was a man of many facets and much depth—a kindred spirit from whose company she derived great comfort and, sinful as it likely was, great pleasure as well . . . and that realization disturbed her more by far than any confrontation she could have had with the man he'd crafted of straw.

Richard seemed to discern her turmoil as well, and perhaps he even felt something of the same himself, she couldn't help secretly hoping, for he sighed and then wordlessly tipped his head back to gaze at the lightening heavens.

Sensing that anything she might say aloud now could never come out as she intended, Meg simply followed his lead and glanced up herself at the canopy of sky above them; it was still filled with stars, though they were rapidly winking out under the force of the rising sun. Pink and gold bloomed in the clouds at the horizon, gilding their edges as if with strokes of magic, and the effect was lovely . . . magnificent, even. A slight shiver went through her, whether from the cold or the wash of conflicting emotions at play within her, she did not know, and she pulled her shawl closer about her.

"It is beautiful," Richard murmured huskily, "but you are chilled."

He uttered this at the same time that he looked away from the heavens to focus on her. There was something measured in his gaze, and another chill swept through her, this time mostly assuredly in reaction to that look in his eyes. It was a look for her. For *her*, she realized in astonishment. There was no mistaking it.

Silent now, he lifted his arms slowly and held them wide, inviting her to share the warmth beneath his cloak. But she hesitated, the part of her that yearned for nothing more than to be near him warring with a different aspect of her nature—the part of her that had been honed to sharpened steel in the crucible of pain she'd experienced during the past three years.

Again, Richard seemed to read her thoughts. He nodded, gesturing her closer again. "I am warm and you are not. Joining me under the shelter of this cloak will be a very simple solution—and innocent too, if that is what you fear." But then something shifted in his gaze, flaring to dangerous life as he added in a murmur, "I promise to make an effort to behave myself, as I was not able to do in the kitchen yestermorn when I kissed you."

"What if I did not want you to?" The bold question escaped her before she had time to hold it back, and she saw the heat in his gaze flicker higher.

"Did not want me to what?"

"Behave." She licked lips that seemed to have gone dry, her reckless longing intensifying as she continued, without allowing herself to really think about what she was saying, "What if I *wanted* you to kiss me again?"

"Do you?" His question was simple, but it resonated with a sensual promise that made her knees go weak.

"I—I do not know."

"Why not?"

"Because I am afraid. Because I fear that it may not be proper to desire such a thing from you, even though I know that you and Eleanor—that you were—"

"That Eleanor and I were married in name only for the past six years?" he finished for her quietly, never taking the intensity of his gaze from her. "Aye, in that you are correct."

He lowered his arms then and took a step closer to her, and another, until she could feel the heat of him searing through her clothing, though they did not touch. "And it is entirely possible that what I am feeling for you right now may not be considered proper by society at large, lady." He tipped his head forward now, his lips almost touching hers before brushing past and along her cheek, only to pause near the delicate shell of her ear. "But it fills me nonetheless," he ended in a whisper that sent tingles up her neck, spreading through her as the moist warmth of his breath teased her in the cold.

His scent—smoky spice laced with the cool breath of approaching winter—tantalized her, the silken brush of his hair along her cheek heightening her senses to almost unbearable tautness. But somehow she forced herself to remain still under this erotic assault, though her heart hammered in her chest, and her breathing came shallow. She knew she only had to turn her head and her lips would graze along the smooth warmth of his skin, along the strong and sensual line of his jaw, until she reached his mouth and tasted the pleasure of his lips . . .

But then suddenly he stepped back, and cold rushed to fill the gap between them once more, almost making her gasp.

She dragged her gaze to Richard; he looked strung as tightly as a bow before its arrow is unleashed. His eyes were shuttered, and his own breathing seemed labored, while the muscle at the side of his face twitched with what he was apparently holding back.

"I wish you to understand something, lady," he murmured huskily, fisting his hands at his sides, "I have become adept these many years at restraining my desires, both as a Templar Knight and as a husband . . . but I am neither of those things any longer. And God help me, but I have never been tested as I have been with you. Know you this, but also know that you have nothing to fear from me. What happens between us will be only as you wish it. You have my word of honor on that."

She could not answer at first, and the only sound between them was that of the faint rasp of their breathing and the occasional rattle of dry leaves, skittering before the puffs of chill dawn air that wove in and around the manor house and outbuildings.

"Thank you," she whispered at last, surprised she could muster any sound at all from behind the knot that seemed to have formed in her throat. "I—I do not know what to say . . ."

"You need not say anything," he answered, reaching out and gently rubbing the pad of his thumb over her bottom lip, sending another rush of sensation through her, as he added, "What has been said between us is enough for now."

She nodded, and he brought his arm back to his side, leaving her feeling instantly bereft and wishing she had the courage to do what emotion rather than fear commanded. But she could not. Not yet.

"Eleanor's Mass will take place within these three hours, followed by her funeral feast," he continued, "and in no more than one week hence, we will need to leave for Tunbridge Castle to satisfy the king's command. So ready yourself for the journey, Meg, and know I will be there beside you should you need me." His gaze sent heat spiraling through her as he added huskily, "For anything."

Before she could bring herself to utter a response, he took her hand and lifted it to his lips, brushing a kiss over the backs of her fingers that was all the more searing for its chaste sweetness. Then giving her a soft smile, he straightened, turned, and walked back to the house, leaving her with the muddle of her feelings, and the beauty of morning unfurling all around her.

Richard stood in the shadows just beyond the door to the kitchen and looked back toward Meg, watching her. She hadn't moved since he'd walked away; from his position he could see her in profile, elegant and bathed in the pearly dawn light. At least she did not appear as tense as she had in those moments after he first came upon her in the garden, when she'd thought his hodmedod was actually a stranger skulking around the house.

Oh, very good, he thought ruefully; his confession of feelings hadn't unleashed in her the same kind of fear that the thought of an imminent attack had.

God help him, but he must be desperate to take hope in such trifles. A wry smile pulled at his lips. Aye, he was in a bad way, all right. For a moment there he hadn't even been sure he could walk away from her. It had, in truth, been one of the most difficult things he could remember doing in recent memory. They had stood so close that he had felt her warmth, teasing him through the breath of distance between them. Like a honeybee besotted in a field full of blossoms, he'd drawn in the gentle, sweet fragrance that seemed woven into the silk of her hair; and when he'd leaned in even closer to her, wanting to taste her, yearning to pull her into his arms . . .

Stifling a groan, he shifted in the cool dark of the kitchen, cursing his thoughts for the way they affected the part of him that still burned and ached, heavy with need for her. It was humiliating to react so to Meg's nearness, but much as he tried to remain in control of his baser yearnings, he was nearly helpless to keep his desire for her hidden.

He hadn't lied to her; never in all his years as a Templar had he been tempted in this way, and it wasn't for lack of opportunity. In truth, he'd been approached by countless women in his travels for the Brotherhood, most offering themselves freely, drawn to his group of elite warriors without care for whether they were supposed to be men dedicated to God's service. But he'd never wavered from his vows. Oh, he'd felt the stirrings of desire—aye, he was a man like any other, and his body had yearned for the kind of intimacy and physical completion that had been denied him so long. But he had always been able to suppress his need with meditation or the rigors of training and battle.

With Meg, such diversion wasn't possible. He thought about her constantly, relived each moment they spent privately together until he believed he would go mad from the play of images in his mind.

And today he'd finally told her something of what he was

feeling, his pride be damned. Though he'd had to use every ounce of his will to keep from kissing her again at that moment, he knew he would eventually, and sooner rather than later if he could manage it.

But he wanted it to be right. Not an accident, as had happened that first time, or something uncertain in any way for either of them. Nay, when they kissed next, he wanted it to be something special and good, undertaken with a freedom of knowledge that what they were doing was right for both of them.

He could be patient until then. Training and living as a Templar had taught him that much about himself—and the reward would be all the sweeter because of it.

Yet that didn't solve his dilemma right now. Gritting his teeth against the uncomfortable, heavy ache of his erection, Richard took one last look out at Meg where she stood in the garden, swathed in the pink and lavender light of morning. Then he backed away from the door, intending to return to his tiny storeroom and a bath of the coldest water he could find.

Chapter 10

By the time the sun peaked in the sky over the All Saints' Day gathering a few days later, Richard had decided that he was a complete and absolute fool. There could be no other explanation for it.

What in heaven's name had he been thinking to take a vow of patience with Meg?

Ever since, he could think of little else *but* kissing her, embracing her . . . making love to her. His mind was besieged with the endless, tantalizing images that slipped without warning into his thoughts. Of her mouth, the color of new cherries, full and sweet . . . of the delicate floral of her hair and the scent of her skin . . . of the way she'd felt in his arms—and thoughts of how she'd feel there without a barrier of velvet and linen between them . . . all of it spinning around him in silken bonds until he thought he would go mad with the delicious torment of it.

Oh, they had come near to kissing again, several times

since that morn in the garden. The looks passing between them had gone from fleeting glances, to more lingering looks of flirtation, to locked stares so scorching that he'd been surprised the grass or floor or yard spanning the distance between them hadn't ignited in flames.

But still they had not actually kissed again.

That first day it had not been so difficult to maintain his usual demeanor of gravity; throughout Eleanor's funeral Mass, the needs of the occasion had allowed him to resume his cloak of shadows easily enough. But in the time that had followed—in the hours and days that had slowly stacked themselves atop each other to bring him to this moment—he'd realized that he had become tired, simply and utterly tired of guilt and melancholy. It was as if he were a man who had been confined to a dark box for too long; when the lid was finally lifted a crack and a breath of cool, fresh air swept in, all he could think of was greedily sucking in more of it, not retreating back to the darkness again.

Aye, he would not deny that he felt deep and resonating sadness for Eleanor's suffering and her death at such a young age, but the truth was that he'd done his real grieving for her years ago, after the tragedy that had stolen Isabel from them, and when the Eleanor he'd thought he knew had vanished, never to return. Over time he'd managed to come to terms with that reality, even though he still harbored a sense of personal responsibility over it.

With the day of official mourning finally past, he'd realized that he felt empty more than anything else.

Empty and impatient to feel again, the way that Meg inspired him to—a fierce yearning to taste happiness and that fire that had so long been quenched in his life.

And that brought him to today. Today, when he felt as if

there were a caged beast stalking around inside him, waiting for any excuse to break free. The sensation was as unsettling as it was unacceptable, and so as the villagers all gathered for the onset of the All Saints' Day feast in the manor yard and outbuildings, he'd done his best to harness the feeling, mingling with the people, trying to strike up conversation and offer thanks for their hard work on behalf of the manor during the years that he had been absent. But he'd been met with little more than halfhearted responses. Even those were mostly being offered, he decided, out of fearful deference to his title as lord of the manor, rather than out of any real respect.

But that would change, he hoped, as soon as he made his expected speech for the occasion, for it would include some unexpected information.

"Have you thought this through fully, little brother?" Braedan asked, referring to the announcement Richard was preparing to make. They had been discussing it moments ago, and to keep anyone else from hearing what more they would say on the matter, Braedan tilted in a bit toward Richard as he spoke. However, he kept his gaze fixed on the throng of people milling around the courtyard; the feast had been set up here to accommodate everyone from the village, as well as any who chose to attend from the nearby Templar Preceptory.

Right now, Braedan and Richard sat alone at the long table that served as the focus of the outdoor "chamber," with seating for the manor's lord and family. Richard had asked that it be set up here at one end of the yard, for though the air was chilly, he preferred to be among the people, rather than indoors, away from the festivities, as was the fashion with many nobles.

"I have thought it through, Braedan," Richard answered,

leaning back in his chair as he watched the way the villagers skirted wide around the cluster of Templar brothers. None of these Templars were knights; they were rather farmers, retired sergeants, or clerics like Brother Thomas, who had conducted the feast day Mass and was now standing at the center of the group from the preceptory—but they nevertheless seemed to warrant a level of fearful unease from the village folk.

Richard pulled his gaze away to look at Braedan again. "It is the only way to restore the people's trust in me, not to mention that it is my responsibility to see that the cotters on my land are at least self-supporting, if not prosperous. I will not be able to deliver recompense for five years of the abuses delivered at their expense, but I can at least make a move in the right direction before I must needs leave for Tunbridge on the morrow."

Richard took a drink from the cup of French wine that had been placed before him and then nodded to Matthew, the reeve, as the man was forced to walk close to the head table to make his way around a knot of villagers who were dancing.

"Does he know yet that you plan to name him acting steward of the estate upon your return to court?" Braedan asked, the flick of his gaze indicating that he referred to Matthew.

"Nay. I only made my final decision last night. But he will fill the role well, I think."

"And what of Brother Thomas?" Braedan asked more quietly. "Is he aware that he is about to be removed from his position of influence?"

Richard's jaw felt tight. "Nay. And yet it is no less than he deserves, though I will call him over in a few moments to tell him in private before I make the announcement to the entire village." He tossed back the remainder of his wine, setting the cup down carefully and shaking his head. "After learning of what he did and watching his interactions with the people, I cannot blame Meg for continuing to harbor such innate distrust of Templars."

"She does not seem to distrust *you*," Braedan offered smoothly, his gaze shifting to the object of their conversation as she slipped outside from the door that led from the buttery, with Fiona close behind her. Both carried baskets of bread, brought, it seemed, to replenish the food table. They emptied their baskets, talking as they worked—and pausing to break into laughter over something known only to them—before they turned and disappeared into the storeroom once more.

Richard tried to keep his expression neutral, though the lance of heat that shot through him at the mere sight of Meg caught him, as always, off guard. He cleared his throat. "Aye," he said evenly, "although that may be because I am not officially a Templar any longer."

Braedan gave him a knowing look. "I don't believe that has anything to do with it. You are as much a Templar in your heart now as you were the day you first donned the crimson cross."

Richard tried to look nonchalant as he shrugged. All of what he had finally acknowledged to himself—and Meg— about what he was feeling was far too new for him to converse about it as glibly as he might the weather, even with his brother. "She has suffered, Braedan," he settled for saying, "and much of that suffering is tied to the Brotherhood."

A trickle of laughter drew their gazes, and Richard felt an unbidden smile pull at his lips, as he watched the game of hoodman's bluff undertaken in the far end of the courtyard by the village children. At nearly the same moment, though, some of the villagers cast anxious looks in his direction, as if he would disapprove of the jesting and play; such games were traditional at any feast, and for a moment he was taken aback at their assumption—until he glanced over to Brother Thomas's group again, and saw the sour expression on the cleric's face.

"By God, he cannot leave these people in peace, even on this day," he muttered, pushing himself to standing.

"Will you approach him now, then, and prepare him for your forthcoming announcement?"

"Aye. Though a part of me would like nothing better than to simply let him learn of it unwarned, before the eyes of those he bled for his own profit. But that would likely be a sin of sorts, stooping to self-indulgence as he has these years with the fruits of this estate, and I want no further comparison between him and me, even in my own mind."

"The satisfaction of making the change of stewardship will still be there," Braedan reminded him, standing himself now and grinning as he added, "and taking pleasure in accomplishing that won't be a sin as long as you don't enjoy it too much."

"I will make the effort to maintain a sober outlook in the next few moments, but it will not be easy," Richard answered dryly.

"Good luck." Braedan walked from behind the table in preparation to head toward the manor house. "After I manage to locate my children, I am going to go and find my wife, to see if I can entice her away from her work long enough to sit and eat something, with any luck before you make your announcement to the villagers. Otherwise, I will simply have to hear about it from you, once I manage to get her to the table."

Richard nodded and waved him off, watching him make his way toward the place he himself would much rather be at the moment—in Fiona and Meg's company—before he steeled himself to turn and make his way toward Brother Thomas and the comeuppance which his soon-to-be-former steward was long overdue in receiving.

"The man looks like he's been eating something sour," Willa commented, peering out the open door from the kitchen at Brother Thomas where he stood apart from the other Templar brothers, apparently talking to Richard. She was taking a break from the work she, Fiona, and Meg were doing, readying another pot of stewed apples to add to the repast for the feast; during the temporary lull, she took the opportunity to wipe her hands on a cloth before fanning her reddened face with it.

"From the little I've seen of Brother Thomas, I would say that he always wears that expression," Fiona said, wiping some parings into a bowl.

"He is not someone I would describe as lighthearted," Meg added, pausing in the act of peeling some of the fruits. "In more than two years, I think I have seen him truly smile but twice, and that was upon collecting his share of what proved to be remarkably good harvests."

"Perhaps he simply wishes he was at court, for the excitement to be had there."

That final remark was offered lightly, almost jestingly, by Fiona's eldest son, Adam, who had slid his elegant, lean frame into one of the chairs flanking the worktable; Meg couldn't help but admire the young man's aplomb, and she bit back a smile at his continued attempts to persuade his mother to let him attend the festivities at Tunbridge Castle.

Fiona, however, only cast him a look of blatant exasperation. She was about to unleash what would surely be her third or fourth diatribe of the week on the futility of his efforts to cajole her, when he held up his hand, unfolding himself from his chair as he laughed and said, "I know, I know, Mother . . . and I shall cease my pleas"—he flashed her a brilliant grin that lit his face with stunning results—"for now, at least."

"You are incorrigible, Adam de Cantor," Fiona muttered, but she too seemed unable to keep from smiling at him.

"Perhaps. But I have to keep trying—and I will, you know, until you concede to my wishes." Without warning, he tipped his head forward, lifting his brow in an exaggerated but nonetheless devastating expression that revealed a hint of the sensual power he would wield as a grown man. "It is a fine skill for a man to possess, do you not think . . . that of charming a woman into doing his will?"

As with Richard's noticeable disquiet upon his first sight of Adam, Fiona reacted abruptly to her son's teasing—and to his expression, Meg realized with surprise—the color leaving her cheeks before her eyes suddenly welled with tears. In the next instant Fiona forced a wan smile, but the entirety of her reaction was enough to bring Adam to her side immediately.

"Mother, forgive me for upsetting you—I meant it only as a jest," he murmured, worry sharpening the lines of his perfect features. He took her arm to comfort her. "Do you wish to sit down?"

"Nay, I am fine. Don't be silly." Fiona shooed him away, and though she brought herself into control again, it was clear that she had been shaken. "But enough of this prattling. Here." She handed him a pestle and mortar with several deliciously scented spices. "As long as you're here, we might as well put you to work so that we can finish this replenishing and go back outside."

Contrite now, he nodded and began the task to which he had been set.

Willa met Meg's gaze, the same question Meg had felt at the table last night simmering in her eyes. What was behind these mysterious reactions to Adam de Cantor? When Richard had appeared so visibly shaken, Meg had been able to explain it to herself by reasoning that it had been several years since he'd seen his nephew, and perhaps the lad's growth to near adulthood had startled him. But for Adam's own mother to respond so? It defied any logic Meg could provide, though she intended to seek answers when the time was right.

For now, to smooth over the awkward moment, Willa leaned in, took a finished bowl of apples, and tossed them into one of the pots on the fire before saying, "Back to Brother Thomas . . . if you could not tell, there be no love lost between me and him. I cannot tell you how pleased I am to see Sir Richard home and taking authority of the manor back from that man." She said the whole of her speech with a conspiratorial air, and again Meg smiled, knowing as she did how much Willa enjoyed a good gossip every now and again.

"Five years ago, when he was named Hawksley's steward upon Richard's departure, I thought him a reasonable choice," Fiona admitted, "though it appears that my judgment was flawed."

"You were here when Richard left Hawksley?" Meg asked quietly. It should not have surprised her to learn of it, she knew, and yet she hadn't realized that Fiona and Braedan had visited the manor at that time.

Fiona nodded. "We arrived shortly after Eleanor's accident and sweet Isabel's death, God rest her. It was difficult to see him off to join the Templars so soon after all that had happened, but his mind was set. In other circumstances, I am certain that granting management of an estate to the Templar Brotherhood would be tolerable, if not beneficial, but in this instance . . ."

She shook her head and her voice trailed off, as if she didn't wish to say anything further that might sound disloyal to her brother-by-marriage.

"In this instance," Meg finished for her, still unable to keep back her bitterness for the Brotherhood, her feelings for Richard not withstanding, "the Templars demanded what they always do at such times: They assumed possession of half Hawksley's worth and then took over management of the estate in the lord's absence. It is all part of their grasping nature, I think, with the added insult of placing a hypocrite like Brother Thomas in a position of power over innocents with no defense against his corruption."

Complete silence followed her pronouncement, and she pressed her lips tightly together, knowing that she had over-stepped bounds of propriety in stating her feelings, but not re-pentant for having done so. She sensed Fiona's gaze level on her, studying her, and felt Adam's discomfort at having wit-nessed her outburst. The poor lad didn't quite know what to say—or do, since he had already ground the spices fair to dust.

And so Willa, stepping once more into the role of distract-ing conversation away from a difficult topic, heaved her am-ple frame from her chair and motioned to Adam. "Well, now. I could use your help, young sir, if you'd be willing to give it. This pot of apples"—she nodded toward the vessel closest to the fire—"is ready to be taken to the folks out of doors, and I cannot carry it meself. Would you be so kind—?"

"Certainly," Adam answered, leaping forward in the way only strapping lads eager to serve as grown men can do; he used the towel Willa offered him to keep from burning himself as he grasped the hot handle, and with Adam taking the greater part of the burden in lifting it, they made their way to the door and out into the cloud-cast yard.

"We'll be back for another when this one is spent, which won't take long, I'll warrant, from the appetites we've seen so far," Willa called out as they went. "Just give that last pot a stir every now and again, will you, ladies?"

Fiona nodded, while Meg gave her assurance, and then they found themselves alone in the sweet-smelling kitchen.

All was silent for a few moments inside, though the sounds of the feasting and dancing outside provided muffled background. Fiona was back to slicing the last of the apples, but Meg felt the weight of her gaze on her every now and again. At last Fiona spoke.

"May I speak frankly with you, Meg? I will not be offended if you would rather not. But in the short time we have known each other, I have felt a kind of . . . kinship between us, I suppose, and I would be glad for the opportunity to discuss something with you."

Meg felt herself flush with pleasure at Fiona's compliment, and she nodded, gratified to know that she hadn't been alone in feeling this sense of developing friendship with Richard's sister-by-marriage. "Of course—I would be glad to hear anything you'd like to say," she answered liltingly, striving for a light tone.

"Thank you." Fiona smiled too as she put the last of the sliced apples in the pot, and then turned to direct her full attention on Meg.

"You seem to have made the best of the painful situations you have faced in your life," Fiona offered. "And while I am sorry for what you have suffered, it has clearly helped in making you strong." Her demeanor was straightforward, as she added, "Such trials by fire are the way of it for many women, I think, myself included—though I thought I would offer you my advice, that it is one of life's unexpected boons that men like Braedan and Richard can make our harsh realities far more bearable."

Meg found herself unable to speak in reply, and Fiona smiled softly, directing a more knowing glance at her. "Of course, I am certain that I am not telling you aught that you do not know already, but Richard is a fine man, both loyal and fierce regarding those he loves and what he believes to be right and true. And I have noticed in the time we have been at Hawksley that he seems quite loyal to you."

Meg shifted, slightly discomfited by Fiona's observation. To mask her reaction, she stood and leaned over to give the apples a stir herself, admitting aloud as she did, "I do not know about that, but it is true that we have come to an understanding. However, it is no secret that before his return home, I criticized him in my own thoughts. I considered him selfish, dominating, and cruel for the choices he'd made. I realize now that he is actually . . . that I feel he is—"

Setting the spoon down, she stiffened.

I feel that he is kind and good and truly honorable, and—

God help her, it couldn't be true, and yet it swept through her again, startling in its power.

Sweet Mother Mary . . . she was falling in love with Richard.

She hadn't really known it herself until this very moment, but there it was. And yet she couldn't let on about it to Fiona, or there would be no place to hide from the woman's perceptive gazes, no way to disguise the pleasurable, maddening tingle that shot through her whenever Richard was near. As broad-minded as Fiona appeared to be, Meg feared that she, like the rest of society, might condemn her for her wayward heart.

In the end, she glanced over at Richard's sister-by-marriage, losing her breath when Fiona continued to fix her with that observant stare, simply nodding in that practical way of hers as she murmured, "Well, go on, then . . . what *do* you truly think of Richard?"

Meg hoped the steamy warmth of the chamber, fueled by the bubbling pot of apples, would disguise the heat that was building with increasing intensity in her face, "I—that is, I am sure that—" She stumbled over the words before sputtering to a stop. Breathing in, she coughed, feeling unbearably self-conscious.

"It is all right, you know," Fiona said, and somehow the way she offered those words seemed to soothe. "I am not in the habit of being judgmental; in fact, I value sincerity highly, having once lived my entire life under the pall of a grand and horrible deceit."

At Meg's startled look, Fiona waved her hand in self-deprecation, making a squinty face that was intended to draw a smile from Meg, which it did.

"Not to worry," Fiona went on, "it is a long and complicated tale, but one with a most happy ending, thanks to Braedan—and Richard too. And yet that is neither here nor there, at the moment, except to assure you that I will not be critical of anything you choose to share with me now, or ever."

Humbled, Meg glanced away, feeling ever more of a connection to this extraordinary woman who had happened into her life, and a poignant sense that knowing her years earlier might have given Meg the strength to fight more tenaciously for what she'd known to be right and true back then.

Lifting her gaze to Fiona again, Meg settled for answering her as honestly as she could right now. "In truth, I do not know exactly how I feel about Richard, except to believe that it is . . . good somehow. I—I feel *gladdened* when I am near him," she added shyly, smothering another smile at the girlish sentiment of that admission. "And I have come to realize that he is not what I'd assumed him to be."

"I am relieved to see that you are able to recognize the burdens he bears—and I hope of course that perhaps, thanks to your own trials, you may find means to help him along the way," Fiona murmured, patting Meg's hand comfortingly.

"If I can, it would be no more than what he has done for me," Meg answered, the newness of speaking about these feelings sending the flush into her cheeks again.

Fiona didn't seem to notice, adding, "Aye, he is a good man, with a true heart. In fact, all of the de Cantors that I have known have been good men. Richard and Braedan come from a long line of justices to the king, you know. They believe in doing what is right at all costs."

"I had heard of their family name in connection with that role during my time at court," Meg said. "And I can see the markings of that quality in Richard. It is something I find . . ." She paused again, struggling for the words before she murmured, "I have not known many men in my life who consider what is right to be more important than how they are perceived by those influential to society."

Fiona nodded. "Even more so than Braedan, Richard takes nothing lightly. From the day I first met him as a lad of fifteen, he has done nothing without doing it fully, with his whole heart."

Meg bit down hard on the inside of her cheek to keep from letting her thoughts drift again to the way Richard had looked at her last week in the garden at dawn, when he'd vowed to be patient in waiting for her kiss. Sensuous warmth uncoiled deep in her belly at the memory of the days that had followed, with all the meaningful glances and innocent yet unmistakable occasions when their hands would make fleeting contact or they'd brush into each other in the corridor.

But Richard had kept to his word; they had not kissed again—nor would they until she made it clear that she was ready.

At the moment she couldn't help wondering why she had not, yet.

Just barely managing to overcome the flood of maddening thoughts, Meg murmured huskily, "Aye. I have noticed that Richard seems to feel things deeply . . ."

Nodding, Fiona offered, "That is one reason Braedan and I regretted our lack of foresight in cautioning him about Adam." Fiona frowned. "It was thoughtless of us, after all that happened those years ago, and all he did for us—"

She broke off as she noticed the look that Meg tried—and failed—to conceal.

"Ah . . ." Fiona murmured, her beautiful mouth twisting ruefully. "It seems that Richard did not supply you with the details behind his reaction to my eldest son."

"He did not," Meg affirmed softly, "though he alluded to the reasons and suggested that they might be more easily discussed at another time." She flushed. "I will confess to being curious about the whole story, however."

Fiona nodded. "It is a dark tale, to be sure, and complicated, but one that you likely should know if you wish to understand the events that shaped Richard into the man he is."

Meg flushed more deeply.

"I am afraid I cannot relate it to you at this very moment, unless we want the ravenous crowd out there to suffer through eating scorched apples. Perhaps tonight, though, after the children are to bed, we can continue where we—"

"Can continue with what?"

The question boomed from the doorway, which in the next instant was filled by Braedan, who poked his head in and breathed deeply. "Mmmmmm," he added, closing his eyes in blissful reaction. "Whatever you're cooking in here smells delicious enough to devour whole."

"That is fortunate, love," Fiona said, laughing and swatting at him with one of the cloths used to wrap the hot metal handles on the pots, "because aside from the chewing part, that is exactly what we hope will happen with these apples."

Braedan chuckled as well, stepping fully into the kitchen chamber and nodding to Meg, who'd stood now as well, making her way over to the hearth in preparation to help Fiona lift the steaming vessel from the fire.

"Nay, let me take that," Braedan said quickly, reaching out to lift the burden from both the women's hands. "I came looking for you, wife, to entice you out of this kitchen to eat with the rest of us." He nodded to Meg, adding, "And you as well, lady. You have both been slaving here for far too long. It is time to cease the work and rest for a while."

"But darling," Fiona began, even as she began to shoo him out the door with his burden, "I must stay inside long enough to help clean up this—"

She was interrupted by a collective cheer that rang out in the yard, and they all turned to the opened door to see what had inspired the noise. A moment later, James came running by, poking his head in, his face wreathed with smiles as he

shouted, "Sir Richard has named Matthew steward of Hawksley, to replace Brother Thomas, and he's promised to divide
the manor's stores from the last three years' harvests with
every cotter before he leaves!"

Surprise and happy disbelief swept through Meg; she went
still for an instant before breaking into an answering laugh of
pure pleasure, as James grinned and tipped his hand to his
forehead in salute, then took off with a whooping run
through the yard, to rejoin the revelry that had erupted among
the villagers.

"I cannot believe he actually did it," Meg murmured. "He
will have made an enemy of Brother Thomas in this—
perhaps of the entire Brotherhood at the preceptory, even—
but he went through with his promise to help the cotters."

"Aye, that brother of mine . . ." Braedan shook his head in
admiration. "From the time he was a lad, he never backed
down from what needed to be done, even if he knew that he
risked everything to do it." Shifting the steaming pot into his
other hand, Braedan gestured to her and Fiona. "Come, then,
and we shall hear all about it from the man himself—what
say you?"

"I think it is a wonderful idea." Fiona laughed. "But first I
must clean up this mess we've made preparing the apples."

"Nay, you two go on ahead," Meg said, still smiling. "It
will take but a few minutes, and there is no use in having both
of us stay behind. Go with your husband, and I will be out
shortly, I promise."

"Are you certain?" Fiona asked, her happy expression
dimming a bit with concern.

"Of course. Go out and enjoy yourselves." She grinned
then, the happiness bubbling through her thanks to Richard's
announcement making her feel uncommonly lighthearted.

"All I ask is that you save a spoonful of the apples for me to sample."

"We'll do our best," Braedan called with an answering grin as he and Fiona made their way out the door, "but from the spirited looks of this crowd, it will not be an easy task!"

Shaking her head and laughing again, Meg turned from the doorway and set about the work of cleaning up the implements they'd used in preparing the feast dishes this day. It wouldn't take long, and in all honesty she was glad for the few moments of solitude it would give her, as she tried to reconcile in her thoughts and her heart all the changes that had taken place there over the past few weeks. Changes concerning Richard in particular, or at least her view of him. And now this latest surprise . . .

With warmth filling her at the thought of Richard's willingness to sacrifice his own gains to see justice done, Meg finished clearing the rest of the table and set to dipping her cloth into soapy water to scrub the scarred old tabletop. Once that was completed, she could finally rejoin the others outside and let Richard know face-to-face just how much she esteemed his action on behalf of the village. She imagined how she would approach him, pausing in her scrubbing as she did and standing up to close her eyes for a moment, considering what she might say.

Why, perhaps she would—

But suddenly a harsh voice rasped into her thoughts, pulling her from her reverie and smothering her with loathsome, grasping malevolence.

"I should have known you would have something to do with all this, Jezebel—and you're going to mend what you've broken or you shall answer to me for it."

Chapter 11

❧ ⌒◯◯⌒ ❧

Meg spun to face the owner of that hate-filled voice, lifting her hand to her throat and nearly gasping in fear until she realized who it was that had spoken. And then nothing but revulsion and animosity filled her.

Brother Thomas.

The hypocritical Templar cleric had pulled closed the door to the yard, and now he approached her with slow, even steps, his face a pale mask of bitterness and suppressed rage.

"What are you doing here?" Meg asked, taking an involuntary step back, even so, though she stopped herself, refusing to budge another inch once she realized she'd given ground before him. "I have had no dealings with you these past weeks, nor do I wish to have any further."

"Aye, but you have had dealings with Sir Richard, haven't you?" he asked in a tone thick with insinuation. "You have flaunted yourself before his eyes, offering yourself up to him as you did before with the man who first used you those years ago—only this time you've whored yourself in truth, for the satisfaction you made Sir Richard crave clearly came with a price."

"I do not know of what you speak," Meg said in a low voice, feeling the blood drain from her face at Brother Thomas's accusations. He was twisted of mind and had long been obsessed with the carnal aspect of her earlier sin; anyone with eyes could see it. However, this time he'd struck a mark with his insinuations, considering her newfound feelings for Richard.

And yet Brother Thomas couldn't know of that. She herself hadn't truly recognized it until today.

"Ah, but I think you *do* know, sinful temptress," he murmured, having approached near enough now to use his body as a force of intimidation against her. He was not exceedingly tall or well-built, but he was still young enough to be firm of muscle, and tall enough to stand almost a head over her. Shades of the many penitential beatings she'd received at his hands swept through her with a sickening lurch; his scent, stale sweat and garlic, enveloped her, the entire effect of his nearness filling her senses so foully that it was all she could do not to wrinkle her nose in disgust at him.

But though she refused to give further ground at his attempt to menace her, she also was not stupid. Regardless of all else, he was still a man, and as such he was physically more powerful than she was, not to mention that he held no qualms about offering her personal violence, especially if he convinced himself it was in the name of her spiritual correction.

And at the moment she was alone here with him, and no match for his greater size.

"I think you do know," he repeated, his voice dark with anger. "And you are going to use your considerable charms to make him reinstate my stewardship, or it will go very badly for you."

Defiant in her helplessness, she lifted her face. Her jaw was tight as she decided that, though she might not be able to take physical action against him right now, she could at least attempt to shame him into standing down.

"I have neither tempted Sir Richard deliberately, nor offered myself to him for any reason, and I have no say in the decisions he makes concerning Hawksley Manor," she ground out, never taking her heated stare from Brother Thomas. "Once again I will say that I have no knowledge of what you speak."

To her surprise, Brother Thomas did not refute her again. Instead his expression shifted, sharpened perhaps, and his eyes half closed as he raised his hand—she thought at first to strike her—but instead he lifted it to her hair, to the length of tresses that spilled from the pearl clasp securing it at her nape.

She did gasp then, jerking away from his touch. But he gripped her, holding her hair firm, and she was forced to remain still to avoid another smarting yank, the first of which had brought tears to her eyes. And so she just stood there, unmoving but for the panting rise and fall of her breast, driven by the frantic beating of her heart.

Good Lord in heaven. Shock spun through her, icy cold. This was something she had never considered before. It seemed too impossible, too unnatural to entertain, even for an instant. Yet here it was, staring her in the face with greedy eyes and stale breath.

Brother Thomas wanted her in the way a man wants a woman; he wanted to use her body, not heal her soul.

Nausea rose up full in her throat, and her breath came harsher as she tried to prevent herself from giving in to the urge to vomit in his face. His gaze dipped to her chest, then, and she cursed her own inability to stop breathing, knowing that she was giving him more reason to stare, to fantasize, perhaps, with her gasping breaths. Even now his gaze was caressing her there as clearly as if he'd brought his hands up to cup and squeeze her flesh.

Involuntarily, a panicky sound slipped from her throat, fear at what he might try to do—something that would be far worse than a penitential beating—finally suppressing her defiance. But it would take only one touch, just one move, and she would fight him for all she was worth, even if it seemed certain that his superior strength and size would prove him the ultimate victor.

Yet there was one other way, perhaps, to end this now, before sinking into violence.

"Back away from me, and I will pretend that we never spoke about this or aught else this day," she said, almost choking on the words, and shrinking from him as much as his grip on her would allow.

"Nay, lady," he said, his breath hot against her cheek, "for we *have* spoken, and I will have my satisfaction."

Her stomach plummeted, and desperation took firmer hold, making her cry out, "If you will not let me go, Brother Thomas, I shall be forced to scream for help."

"If you try to scream, I shall have to prevent you," he whispered back mockingly, rubbing the silken strands of her hair as he did and leaning in to inhale its delicate scent before gripping her chin painfully in his other palm; then he jerked her face toward him, forcing her to meet his gaze, presumably to ensure she would make no mistake about his seriousness. "And that will not be pleasant, I can assure you. Only do as I wish . . . share with me the lush bounty of the treasure

God has given you . . . and I promise that experience will be far more gratifying."

"Never," Meg rasped, blinking back the stinging heat that panic brought to her eyes. She felt cornered and trapped, but dread flooded her with strength of will she didn't know she still possessed. Her hands tingled as she surreptitiously reached back toward the table, searching with her fingers for something, anything she might have left out while she was cleaning that she could use against him, whether to force him back or strike him aside the head. But she found nothing.

"Do not toy with me, woman," Brother Thomas said more harshly now, grappling with her to pin her hand to her side. "I have been tested mightily by you these two years, and this day's news has sealed your fate. I will not be made the fool now as well!"

He was leaning over her as he grunted those words, bowing her back against the table, and Meg endured a moment of revolting clarity when she believed he might actually consider pressing her the rest of the way down to the boards here in the middle of the kitchen, and taking her by force.

"Let me go!" she said more loudly, pushing back against him and struggling to raise her knee in her determination to free herself. "You cannot do this—someone will come in. Think then how you will appear—"

A guttural growl sounded behind them and with a sudden rush of motion, Meg felt Brother Thomas lifted bodily off her. She scrambled to right herself, feeling a wave of dizziness wash over her as she heard the metallic rasp of a blade clearing its sheath; almost simultaneously, she saw that it was Richard, brandishing the weapon like an avenging angel, even as he grasped Brother Thomas by the back of his robes and threw him against the wall opposite her.

The cleric grunted audibly at the impact, but he did not try to get up, instead cowering on the floor there; he raised one hand as Richard swung into position over him, holding his blade pointed toward the man's black heart.

Meg watched them in silence, reeling from shock and powerless to tear her gaze from Richard, who for the first time appeared as the fierce and relentless warrior about whom she had heard so much upon her arrival at Hawksley. He stood before her, the perfect incarnation of leashed rage, his physical might undeniable and his expression brutally intense as he honed in upon the object of his fury.

"Mercy! Mercy!" Brother Thomas called, his voice cracking with terror. He gazed frantically up at Richard and then at Meg, holding both hands before his face now as if that might forestall the shining steel doom poised to impale him.

"Why should I grant you mercy?" Richard said, his voice echoing low and dangerous. "You deserve none. Not after what I saw."

"But you are a Templar; you cannot take arms against me! It is forbidden by our laws!"

"So is fornication," Richard growled, "And yet you were about to attempt that sin against an unwilling woman."

"Nay—nay, you mistake me, Sir Richard," Brother Thomas implored, slowly rising to his knees. "I was only, that is, I—I—"

"What say you, Meg," Richard broke in to Brother Thomas's babbling, though he never shifted his gaze from the trembling cleric. "Was I mistaken in what I saw?"

Meg's heart lurched, right along with her stomach. She glanced from Brother Thomas's pleading face to Richard's resolute one, knowing without a doubt that she should consider how she answered him very carefully, for a man's life, as vile as that man might be, was likely in her hands.

"Will you kill him if I say you were not?" she asked shakily, needing to confirm her suspicions.

"Aye."

That one word, delivered in a deep, clipped voice that held no hint of pity, was enough to draw an audible cry from Brother Thomas, like that of an animal that had been wounded. But then his mouth gaped open and closed several times without sound, and Meg stared, disbelieving, as he suddenly stiffened, his hands still outstretched, while his face took on a grayish cast; in the next moment, still without his uttering another sound, his eyes rolled up in his head, and he fell over onto the floor.

"Good heavens, is he dead?" she gasped.

"Nay, we are not that fortunate," Richard muttered, loosening his stance. With a sigh, he sheathed his sword and took a step forward to nudge the toe of his boot against the Templar cleric where he lay, gape-mouthed on the stone floor, though his breath rasped loudly. "The coward has simply fainted dead away."

"Oh." Meg pressed her fingers to her lips—trembling still—and her eyes were wide. Brother Thomas had become senseless with fright. He was not dead. That was good, wasn't it? She despised him, it was true, but to cause his death . . . she knew she would not have liked to live with that horrible knowledge.

In the midst of her still-scattered musings, she heard Richard mutter a mild curse followed by a guttural sound of disgust.

"Saints preserve us—he's gone and soiled himself."

Meg felt another hiccupping gasp rise in her throat as she

considered that latest humiliation, glancing down to where Brother Thomas was sprawled, a puddle of pale liquid seeping from beneath him.

Oh, my. When he came to, he would be truly mortified.

As well he should be.

The phrase rang through Meg's thoughts as she watched Richard drag Brother Thomas out into the yard, but it was followed hard by another bout of shaking. The ludicrousness of it all stood starkly before her dazed mind until she seemed unable to focus on aught else but that. And so it was that her trembling soon led to a kind of quaking that had little to do, it seemed, with great danger nearly avoided. The shaking spread up from her belly, up and up, into her throat . . . manifesting itself in an uncontrollable fit of giggles that were barely audible—so high-pitched they verged on madness.

They seized her so completely that she realized she could not breathe, and tears sprang to her eyes, forcing her to lift both hands to her face to try to contain herself. But it was no use. They shook her and shook her until suddenly something changed and then they weren't giggles anymore, but huge, gulping sobs.

The sounds wrenched from her throat, harsh and painful, and she knew then that she was crying, feeling so lost and empty . . .

Richard's arms came around her from nowhere, it seemed, pulling her to him and cradling her against his chest, holding her and rocking her in the fullness of his solid warmth. He was strength and magic and light, and somehow he made the hurt recede, bringing the world back into focus so that she could open her eyes again.

They felt scratchy and hot, so she shut them once more,

just needing to feel the steady beat of his heart beneath her ear, and clinging to him as she breathed in his comforting, clean scent while he held her close.

"It will be all right," he murmured into her hair, stroking her cheek gently, so tenderly that she thought her heart might break from the sweetness of it. "It is all over now, and there is nothing more to fear."

"I—I am so sorry," she said through the last of the hitched sobs. "I do not know what came over me. What happened to Brother Thomas was not amusing in any way—"

"Well, perhaps it was a *bit* amusing," he offered, a hint of laughter in his voice. She looked up sharply, still tucked against him, to see the sparkle of it in his beautiful, green-gold eyes.

"How can you say that?" She frowned through her tears and pushed away from him a bit, blinking, everything about her feeling raw and exposed. "I despise him, but I do not wish him dead. And—and for a moment I thought you might truly kill him, and then I thought he had gone and died on his own, and—"

"Hush now, lady," Richard murmured, pulling her back to him with another low chuckle; he tried to soothe her with his touch as he was with his voice, stroking gently along the back of his head and down her spine. "I know what you are feeling, and I was only trying to help ease your thoughts a bit."

She remained silent for a long moment, just letting herself be still in his arms. But at last the question that had been burning inside her could be quieted no longer, and though she was half afraid to hear the answer to it, she asked softly, "Would you have truly killed him, Richard, if I had told you there was no mistake in what you saw?"

He didn't answer at first; instead he breathed in and out

twice more before she felt him stiffen and cease the hypnotic motions of his hand.

"When I found him treating you so vilely," he finally ground out, "I was ready to gut him without question." He took in another deep breath, and she felt it leave him on a sigh. "It is to his good fortune, however," he continued, "that my training has stressed the use of logic in moments of conflict, not emotion. Besides that, he was unarmed. So nay, I probably would not have actually killed him. But he did not need to know that."

She nodded, closing her eyes in relief. "Thank you for telling me."

But at that he leaned back enough to cup her face with his warm palms, gently tipping her gaze up to his, and she felt breathless again with the intensity of feeling that shone from his gaze.

"Make no mistake, though, Meg," Richard said, his voice low and intense. "Had Brother Thomas truly violated you—had he even gone one step beyond what he had done when I interrupted his foulness, it would not matter that he was unarmed, or a Templar, or a cleric . . . he would be a stiffening corpse right now."

"I—I understand," she murmured with a tiny nod, sobered by the force of his care for her.

"As it stands"—he gave her a soft smile and brushed his thumbs to catch the last trace of wetness beneath her eyes—"the wretch is alive and well, being tended to out in the yard by some of the other Templar brothers, and serving as the grist for this week's gossip in the village as well. So in a way I suppose that a kind of justice has been served."

Meg pressed her fingers to her mouth again, still overwhelmed with it all. It was the perfect punishment for a man as vain as Brother Thomas, and far more fitting, considering what *hadn't* happened, thank God, than tossing him into the cold clutches of death.

"What will become of him now?" she murmured.

"The other brothers will report his misdeeds to England's grand master, William de la More, and he will be punished according to Templar law. As for today, they are readying to escort him back to the preceptory, where he will be kept in seclusion until he is questioned by the higher Templar authority."

Meg nodded in relief, feeling exhausted and so, so grateful for Richard right now, and the fact that he was . . . well, simply *Richard*, that she blew out a deep breath and struggled not to lose her composure again.

"I—I do not know what I would have done if you hadn't come in when you did," she murmured, looking up at him again and seeing his handsome face wavering under the force of her welling tears. "I wish to thank you—for that . . . and for everything."

"You do not need to thank me," Richard answered, his lips quirked up slightly, his voice a husky timbre that slid across her senses and set her heart to dancing. "I only wish I had come seeking you sooner, so that I might have prevented Brother Thomas from his foul deed altogether. It was ugly, lady, and it was wrong, for if I had my way, you should never know aught but goodness and beauty around you."

His gaze stayed on her, warm and intense, and Meg felt herself slipping into it, wanting to drown in the feelings he was bringing to hot and heady life inside her with that look. There were no words to explain it, and so in the end she simply tipped up her chin, knowing that it was time at last. The interminable wait of the past few days was over.

She felt his fingers brush with tantalizing heat along the side of her neck, up to thread in her hair . . . hearing his low growl of pleasure as her own hands lifted to tangle in the soft waves at his nape. With a quiet moan, she met his gaze, catching a glimpse of the erotic intensity that flared in his eyes just before his sooty lashes swept down, and he tilted his head to take possession of her mouth with his own.

Leaning more fully into him, she reveled in the sensations, in the need that swelled inside her as his lips slanted down hungrily across hers once more. The delicious tension in her belly wound tighter, causing a pooling, languid heat to tingle between her thighs . . . spiraling higher with the soft, guttural sound he made as he shifted to allow his other hand to slide down her back. Suddenly she felt his palm curving warmly over her buttocks, and with a firm tug, he pulled her closer, the motion causing the part of her that was so sweetly aching to press against the hard, jutting heat of him.

"By God, is everyone all right?"

Braedan's voice rocked through the stillness of the kitchen, making Meg jerk back in startled reaction, while Richard uttered a groan of pure frustration.

"Meg—oh, my dear, I am so sorry to have left you alone! Have you been hurt?" Fiona called in echo of her husband's question, and Meg looked over at Richard's brother and sister-by-marriage somewhat stupidly, feeling disheveled all at once in a way she had not noticed until now. Self-consciously, she smoothed her hand over her hair, hoping that she could appear more calm and collected than she truly felt with the whirlwind going on inside her.

Richard too had stiffened and turned to face Braedan and

Fiona, and now she felt his quiet movement, the way he placed his hand on the small of her back in gentle support. And at that moment she knew that she would not have to pretend to be strong with him beside her.

"All is well," he answered, his voice sounding a bit strangled as he pressed forward with his palm to encourage her to accept Fiona's worried embrace. "And no one sustained any lasting hurt, thank God."

"Except to their pride perhaps," Braedan murmured, jerking his head in the direction of the open door and the sight just beyond it of Brother Thomas being carried away by the other Templar brothers. The villagers had gathered in a makeshift circle around them, many whispering behind their hands, the news of the hated preceptor's humiliation already spreading like wildfire among the people.

"He deserved that knock to his pride and more, if Richard felt the need to throw him out of doors," Fiona asserted hotly, still fluttering around Meg like a mother hen over an injured chick.

"And yet Richard is right," Meg finally said, her own voice a bit raspy, "in that all turned out well in the end."

Braedan was slapping him on the back, as Adam and then Elspeth came running hell-bent into the chamber, agog with curiosity over the hubbub in the yard, only to be followed in short order by Robert and the rest of the children, all but for little Henry, who was napping and being watched over by Willa. The bailiff and several of the villagers also poked their heads in over the course of the next few minutes, to assure themselves that all was well and that no help was needed.

Before long, the furor began to die down, and Fiona managed to herd away most of her children, at the same time finding tactful means to tell everyone that they needed to go about their business. The remaining villeins filed out shortly after, leaving only Meg, Richard, Braedan, and Matthew, the estate's reeve and now its new steward.

"Are you sure there's nothin' we can get for you, then, Meg?" Matthew asked, crushing his cap in his hands. "The missus would be glad to bring over a posset or something to help, if you'd like."

"Nay, Matthew, I will be fine, truly. I had a fright, but thanks to Sir Richard, no real harm was done."

Matthew slid an admiring gaze in Richard's direction, nodding in deference. His chin tipped again as he added, "It is a fine thing you've done this day, milord, not only for Meg here, but for all of us. I vow my allegiance to serve honorably as your steward."

"I have no doubt of that, Matthew," Richard answered, walking over to the door to clap his hand to the reeve's shoulder in acknowledgment. "And I know I have chosen a far better man for the task than I did five years ago. We have much to discuss before I leave for Tunbridge Castle, so you may expect me to call on you tonight, to make our final arrangements."

"Very good, sir," Matthew murmured, offering another nod as he backed to the door. "I'll be going back with the others to the village now, to leave you to your peace. Thank you again, milord," he added finally, backing out the door.

Richard nodded once more in acknowledgment. Then Matthew was gone, and Richard pushed his hand through his hair, letting go of what sounded like a long-held breath as he twisted to face Meg and Braedan. "I for one am ready for a bit less excitement . . . long overdue for it, in fact. It seems as though we've seen little these past weeks but one gripping event followed by another."

"It will be good to have at least one quiet evening to finish your preparations for your trip to Tunbridge," Braedan agreed.

Meg leaned back in her chair, closing her eyes for a moment as she added quietly, "I too never thought I would crave an evening of complete monotony, but I can honestly say now that such a thing would be a blessing."

Their conversation was interrupted suddenly by the sound of footsteps on the small wooden stairs leading from the yard to the kitchen door, followed by a voice that called out, "I could not help hearing your sentiment, milady, and now it is my unhappy duty to tell you that you may need to wait a bit longer for the quiet you desire."

It was Adam who had offered the comment somberly from where he stood in the doorway. Richard stepped closer to Meg, placing his hand on her shoulder, and Adam offered a slight bow of greeting to him as well before he straightened, clearly bearing the weight of some news he'd been sent to deliver.

"What is it, son?" Braedan asked him, frowning.

"A man has been discovered, Father, lying wounded and senseless in the southernmost field—a large man, bearded and pale."

Adam's gaze flicked again to Richard's then, his dark eyes shadowed with concern as he added, "But crumpled beneath his cloak he wore a surcoat, Uncle . . . and it was of white linen, emblazoned with the crimson cross of the Templars."

Chapter 12

Richard ordered that the wounded man be carried into his solar and made as comfortable as possible on a makeshift pallet Willa provided for his use. It was soon discovered that he was none other than one of Richard's comrades—one of those knights with whom he had struggled to escape France on the day of the arrests. John de Clifton had been through an ordeal, that much was clear, whether or not he could speak about it much yet.

Meg left Richard to help John change out of his tattered clothing in preparation for washing the wounds on his leg and side, while she went downstairs to help Willa gather the herbs Richard had requested, as well as some steaming water and a bowl of broth that Willa scooped from the ever-cooking vegetable pottage over the kitchen fire. If John could drink a little of it, he might find the strength to tell Richard what had happened.

When she returned to the chamber, bearing the basin of

herb-scented wash-water, she saw that John already looked stronger. Though his eyes were still closed, he was half-sitting on a pallet near the fire, leaning back against a thick bolster with a blanket wrapped around him; at the sight of him now, Meg couldn't help but hope that his injuries were not as deep or as serious as she'd thought upon first glance.

As she waited for direction from Richard about how she might assist him, she allowed herself the opportunity to study the man who had been one of his nearest friends.

John, like Richard, was tall compared to many men, and he was clearly a practicing knight, with the finely honed build of a man whose livelihood relied on his ability to wield his sword. But he was of fairer complexion than Richard, with a plentiful dusting of curling, sandy-hued hair across his chest that was only a few shades darker than the reddish-gold hair upon his head and along his arms.

And also unlike Richard, John sported a matted, full beard that seemed desperately in need of a good trim.

Her musings were interrupted when Willa hurried into the chamber, bearing the pottage broth and handful of dried herbs Richard had requested. Her face reddened a bit when she realized the unclothed state of their new visitor, but she stood by with stalwart readiness, in case the master needed her aid.

"This is fine, Willa, thank you. You may go, if Meg is willing to stay and assist me," Richard murmured, taking the proffered items. Meg nodded, and Willa backed out the door gratefully. But it was apparent that Richard's voice had caused John to stir, teasing him to awareness, for he made a groaning sound and moved as if he was attempting to get up off the pallet.

"Steady now, man," Richard said, and Meg came down on

her knees at the other side of John, helping Richard to ease
him back onto the bolster. "You've no need to move from this
spot for a good long time. Until I say so, in fact."

"Richard."

John uttered his name on a raspy exhale through parched
lips, and his eyes slit open a crack to look first at him, then to
Meg. "I have reached Hawksley at last, it seems," he whispered, his voice echoing with exhaustion and perhaps pain.
He swallowed, the action clearly difficult, and so Richard
lifted a cup of cool water to his lips, urging him to take a few
sips, before he set it down again and went to work preparing
the poultice and bandages.

"No need to talk yet, John. You have reached Hawksley indeed, and had a devil of a time doing it from the looks of you.
But we'll discuss what you've been through later, after I've
dressed these injuries," Richard commented as he began to
grind the herbs, murmuring a request for Meg to hand him
the pitcher of wine as he worked and pouring in a few dollops
until the contents of the bowl began to form a paste.

"Would you like another drink?" Meg asked John quietly,
when she saw him labor to swallow again, and he nodded
weakly, reaching up to grip her hand as she held the cup to
his lips.

"Thank you, lady," he rasped when he was through, his
gaze shifting to her again, though his head remained still on
the bolster. "I am happy to see you well recovered from the
illness that Richard had spoken of to me . . . the one that had
in part prompted him to join the Brotherhood."

"Nay, I am not—that is . . ."

Meg felt the old knot clench in her stomach as she struggled to explain that she was not Eleanor.

"The name of the woman tending to you is Meg—she is a

cousin-by-marriage, and you are in very good hands with her," Richard said firmly, and she glanced at him as he took the wine again, feeling her face flood with heat when the brush of his fingers sent her pulse racing despite herself.

"As for Eleanor," Richard continued, "she is no longer with us, John. She entered her final peace and suffers no more."

"I am sorry," he croaked, his eyes closing again with the effort.

"Quiet now, man, and try to save your strength for the work that is to come," Richard chided, at last peeling back the makeshift covering he had pressed onto a six-inch gash near the top of John's ribs. "I need to gather some other herbs for these wounds if I am to be able to bring you to fighting shape again."

"I believe I have had enough of fighting for a while," John rasped, giving him a weak smile, "so please, you have my blessing to take your time."

Richard shook his head with a muted chuckle at that, and Meg found herself almost smiling with him. That his friend could jest boded well for his physical state and ultimate chances of recovery.

But that little ray of light faded quickly again under the onslaught of doubt that had been awakened inside her when John had mistaken her for Eleanor. She pushed herself to her feet and stepped back from the pallet, her emotions unaccountably in chaos.

Something had crystallized, in that single, unexpected moment, something that she had managed to bury, hiding it from her own conscious mind in the time that she'd known Richard. But the truth hit her now in full, agonizing force, and she realized that she wanted nothing more than to flee this chamber and the ringing death-knell of it through her heart.

Falling in love with Richard was quite likely the worst possible thing she could have done.

She had indulged her burgeoning feelings, even knowing that they came without benefit of marriage or a sanctioned betrothal. Once again, she'd chosen a path that went against all the mores of society, which would expect a mourning period for Eleanor and almost certainly disapprove of any relationship between Richard and another woman before that time had elapsed—not to mention a link with an earl's daughter who had been so completely disgraced by polite society and disowned by her own family.

Worse even was that in her own mind, she'd begun to accustom herself to the idea of Richard as . . . *hers.* He was a man to whom she was desperately attracted, and she'd allowed herself to weaken, to desire him in ways more than foolish for a woman with no family, dowry, or right to hope for a marriage of any kind, with anyone.

The thought stabbed deep, followed by a burst of bone-numbing fear.

Heaven help her, but she'd been ready to enter with Richard into the same kind of relationship she'd had with Alexander.

An illicit love affair.

To expose herself to the same heartache and pain . . . to make the same mistakes, with possibly the same tragic results.

Her breath caught, and stinging heat rose behind her eyes, making it all she could do not to cry out with the sudden rush of pain that realization brought her. Somewhere deep inside she'd known the truth of it all along, but she'd chosen to suppress the warnings of her conscience, stupidly moving ahead into the forbidden, because it had felt so good to be admired again by a man as wonderful as Richard, and to give that admiration back in return.

"Now, then," Richard said aloud, breaking into her thoughts as he rocked back on his heels next to John's pallet. "We've made a fine start, but I want you to lie back and rest while I gather the last of what I need to finish."

Blissfully unaware of her turmoil, he stood and motioned for Meg to join him out of John's earshot; they walked together, away from the fire, to pause within the shadowed arch near the door.

"His wounds are not overly deep," Richard said, "but they have begun to fester and will require stitching. I need some sturdy thread and a needle to sew up the gashes as soon as is possible after I finish washing them out."

"Of course—I have items that will suit in my mending basket," Meg managed to say, though her voice sounded strangely hoarse despite her best efforts.

Richard's gaze slipped to her face then, his brows knit with concern, and she found herself looking at the floor to avoid meeting his stare. "The basket is in my chamber," she added in what she hoped was a more normal tone, "and will take me but a moment to fetch."

Again, Richard said nothing in answer. The silence stretched between them . . . and it was then that it happened. She felt the subtle change in him and sensed the heavier weight of his gaze upon her, though she continued to keep her eyes downcast. But she could not shield herself from the powerful force of his physical presence; he stood so close to her that, as during their interlude in the garden, she could feel

his warmth, breathe in his delicious scent . . . and she shifted
uncomfortably, realizing how difficult it was to be so near
without reaching out to touch him.

It was torturous, the ache of it driving her to near madness,
and she knew that she was either going to give in to her weakness and slide into his arms or force herself to put enough
distance between them to regain her clarity of mind.

She took a step back.

"Meg . . . ?" The way he uttered her name cut through her,
the questioning and hurt in his tone slicing to her soul.

He knew.

She understood that with sudden, startling clarity. Even
without her speaking, he knew what she was doing, felt how
she was trying to pull away from him.

But how could he?

The question resonated through her very soul, it seemed,
bringing her near to hysteria, for the answer was achingly
clear to her own heart. Richard de Cantor knew what she
was about right now, because he had taken the time to truly
know *her*. Not one man in a thousand might have done the
same; that she had only just realized how impossible it
would be to see that promise between them brought to
fruition carried with it an ache so relentless that she had to
take several breaths before she was able to find her voice
again.

"I will go and fetch the needle and thread straight away,"
she repeated, speaking the words as calmly, as evenly as she
could. Then she breathed in once more, stiffened her back,
and turned to leave the chamber, gasping aloud when he
reached out to her, laying his hand just above her elbow in a
touch of velvet and steel that sent tiny, charged waves of sensation rippling through her.

"Meg . . ."

His voice trailed off this time, a thousand meanings embedded in that one word, uttered in his low, urgent tone. She lifted her gaze to his then, unable to keep from doing so, even though she knew that staring into his beautiful eyes again might well undo her.

And it did.

The sweet, melting sensation inside her swirled to buttered honey, weakening her legs and stealing her breath.

He said nothing more.

Nothing more was needed. She saw it in his gaze, felt it in the touch of his hand upon her arm.

"Richard, I . . . I wish that we . . . that I . . ." She breathed the words, none of them seeming worthy of what she was feeling, none possible to explain the yearning and anguish that were gripping her and eating her alive. She wanted to kiss him, right now, thoroughly and passionately. She wanted to pull him into her arms and lavish on him all that she was feeling, to show him all that she desired.

She wanted to make love with him.

The thought rocked through her, violent and bittersweet. For it warred against the part of her that knew with all logic how mad it was to pursue further what had begun to blossom between them. Aye, it was true that he was no longer bound by his honor as a husband; Eleanor was gone now—she'd been gone in every real sense for more than five years already—and by rights he was no longer in service as a Templar, constrained by his vows of chastity.

But it didn't matter. Not really.

For what was between them could come to naught. She could not be his wife or even his betrothed, now or ever. She had no right to expect anything of him but a passionate attraction, a dalliance of fire without benefit of sanction, unless he was willing to bear the devastating scandal that could result. And she feared that even Richard de Cantor wasn't so good that such disgrace attached to his name would mean nothing to him.

It was heartbreakingly simple.

She just hadn't wanted to accept it.

"I will go to fetch the thread and needle now, Richard," she said, her voice husky and almost cracking now with the effort it took her to say the words with finality, to pull away from the intoxication of his nearness. "I will have Willa bring them to you forthwith."

She allowed herself one more glance at him, feeling the knife of loss twist more deeply at the wounded look she saw in his eyes.

And then without a breath, without another sound, she stepped away from him, opened the door, and left.

Richard watched the door close behind her, shaken to the core by the sense of desolation she left in her wake.

What the hell had just happened here?

Sickness twisted his belly, and he dragged his hand through his hair, still stunned by it all. She had retreated from him, and in far more than just a physical sense. She was running from *them*—or at least what he thought they'd been becoming together. But why? God help him, didn't she know? She was light and joy to him; she made him feel whole again. He'd thought he meant something to her too, but now she was casting him off as if it was nothing but a figment of his imagination.

Maybe she did feel nothing. Perhaps she only just realized it and decided to act now to spare you any further embarrassment in losing your heart to her.

The subversive voice echoed inside him, dull and cold, and he hammered it down with ruthless force.

Nay. He knew better than that. He might be a sinner, but he was no fool. Meg cared about him; she felt the same simmering heat. She felt as well as he the sense of extraordinary understanding that flowed between them. But something had frightened her enough to send her running.

Unfortunately he couldn't find out what that was or how to remedy it from in here.

Half turning, he glanced at John, who lay quiet, still, by the fire. Blood seeped from even the new bandage that had been applied to the wound on his ribs but a few minutes ago, and Richard knew he couldn't wait much longer to complete the procedure of closing this gash or the one on his friend's thigh, else his life might be endangered.

That knowledge was the only thing keeping Richard here in the solar right now, instead of barreling after Meg to find out what in God's name had caused this sudden rift between them. He wracked his brains, trying to think of something—anything—that might have happened or been said between Adam's announcement about John's discovery and this moment. Something to give him a clue. But there was nothing.

He sighed, jamming his fingers through his hair again. Now was not the time to demand answers from her. Much as he wanted to, it couldn't be. But as soon as he'd stitched his friend and ensured that all had been done to support his recovery, he planned to get to the bottom of this . . .

Whether the Lady Margaret Newcomb wanted him to or not.

It was one of the few times Meg could remember being grateful that Hawksley's rounded stone dovecote was situated so far from the main buildings. Normally she cursed the task of helping the village lads collect eggs or whatever number of birds were needed for Willa's stew, but today she didn't mind the walk.

She'd come out here after arranging for Willa to bring Richard the things he'd asked for; she hadn't been able to face seeing him again right now, needing solitude more than anything. The autumn air was crisp, but the late afternoon sun shone warm still, thank goodness, so she felt comfortable with only the wool shawl she'd thrown over her shoulders as she'd left the main house as quietly as she could, to avoid attracting notice.

Now she'd reached the dovecote with its comforting rounded walls and the fluttering, musical sounds of the birds all around—from the outside, anyway, which was where she intended to stay. It was bright, the air was fresh.

And best of all, it was completely private.

She sank to the ground with her back to the stones and buried her head in her knees, grateful that it was secluded enough here to indulge in the tears that had been aching for release for the past half hour. They'd been burning the backs of her eyes ever since she'd left Richard in the solar, looking as if she'd just plunged a dagger through his heart. And so now she let go, and they came, fast and hot and not at all in a way her mother would have described as feminine, she was sure, but she felt better when they had passed.

For the most part.

Sniffing and dragging her sleeve across her eyes, Meg looked up, squinting at the view spread out in stunning display before her. As chance would have it, she sat facing the southern field. The field where the boys had found John, lying senseless. The field where Richard's hodmedod still stood sentinel, protecting the recently planted winter rye from rooks and daws.

The sight of that straw-stuffed man sent a renewed ache of loss and memory through her, and she bit back the rush of fresh tears that threatened to overflow, refusing them quarter. Enough was enough. A bit of self-pity every now and again was good for the soul; wallowing in it was not.

Instead she forced herself to study the beauty of the land surrounding her. The clouds of this morn had mostly blown away, leaving in their place a sky so blue it almost made her teeth ache. The pigeons and doves flew in and around the dovecote, swooping above and around the field in search of errant rye-corns, then flying back in a graceful dance through the air. It was awe-inspiring, really. She hadn't taken the time to truly notice it before; she'd always been so busy with the household tasks or caring for Ella. But she was grateful for this tiny stretch of time before she'd have to leave this place for the glittering halls of court.

Never to return, after today's terrible epiphany.

Much as she wished to refute that mocking reminder, it would not be quelled. She frowned, indulging in another moment of self-pity, before she was shaken from it by the sight of an elongated shadow coming around the curve of the dovecote to her right.

She stiffened and stood up, suddenly wary. The dark shape stretched and shifted as its owner walked closer, and Meg realized that it had to be a woman, for the bottom of the shadow appeared to be a solid mass, as if a skirt was casting off the sun.

In the next moment, her suspicion was confirmed. Fiona rounded the building and then stopped short, jumping back a little, at the same time that she raised her hand to her throat.

"Oh, my gracious, *there* you are," Fiona said, her voice lilting with both humor and exasperation. She shook her head. "I have been searching all over for you, and was despairing to find you anywhere on the manor proper. In truth, the dovecote was my last possibility, before I'd decided that you might have taken a walk down to the village or chapel."

"I am sorry to have caused you worry," Meg said by way of apology, hoping that the traces of her earlier crying had faded enough not to be too noticeable. A tiny spear of anxiety prodded her. "Is something the matter that you came seeking me? Am I needed up at the house?"

"Nay, all is well there," Fiona said, waving in dismissal. She came closer to Meg then, however, entering the sunny patch where she'd been sitting, and studied her face as she approached. "It is whether or not all is well out here that I came seeking to know," she added gently.

"I cannot imagine why you would think it was not." Meg forced a little laugh and touched her fingers to her hair, tucking into her circlet a tendril that had come loose in the breeze.

"Only because Willa suggested that you seemed out of sorts. She seems very motherly toward you, I've noticed." Fiona smiled. "She sent me away from her preparations for the evening meal, insisting that I look for you to see if aught was amiss."

With her emotions so near the surface just now, Meg felt tender enough that even mention of Willa's concern made her swallow back another lump in her throat. However, resolving to adopt a cheerful tone, false as it was, she answered, "Willa is a dear to worry, but it is nothing. I just needed some air after the difficulty with Brother Thomas and the stuffiness of the sick chamber. And Richard seemed perfectly capable of completing the ministrations for his friend on his own, so I thought to take a few moments to simply do nothing out in the fresh air."

Trying not to wince at the strained, high pitch of her voice, Meg instead tipped her face to the sun as she finished speaking, holding out her arms and blocking out Fiona's perceptive stare for a moment by closing her eyes, as she added, "It is beautiful out here, is it not? I must confess that I will regret the need to leave on the morrow."

"Well, at least you know you will be coming back here when your appearance at court is finished. That is a boon, is it not?"

Fiona's unintentionally painful comment set Meg to coughing, though she pretended that it and the tears that sprang to her eyes were the result of a bit of dust in her throat and nothing more.

"Perhaps we'd better go back to the house now," she said, once she'd gotten herself under control again. Anything was better, she decided, than continuing to try to hide her tormented thoughts from Richard's far too perceptive sister-by-marriage.

But to her chagrin, Fiona wouldn't be dissuaded.

"Oh, there is no need to rush back," she said, linking her arm with Meg's and leading her back toward the dovecote. "To be truthful, I'm relishing this interlude away from the hubbub of the house—and my own children, I must admit." She gave Meg a conspiratorial wink. "Besides, Willa assured me that she has preparations in the kitchen under control, and as you said, Richard needs no help, for he is truly gifted in all matters of wounds and healing."

Meg nodded, and Fiona slid into place next to her, and they both sank down to sit, leaning up against the dovecote wall as she kept talking softly, going on about Richard and his training. Telling her about the name he had made for himself as an elite warrior knight even before he joined the Brotherhood, and about his heroic victories and the battles he entered into, in the name of the king.

Meg let it all wash over her, knowing that she couldn't have spoken right now even if she'd wanted to. Not with the thread of thoughts flooding her tormented mind . . . memories of Richard tending to her after the storm, mixing the liniment and rubbing it gently into her shoulder. Of Richard coming so near to kissing her in the garden at dawn . . . of the charged glances that had passed between them . . . of him holding her close and stroking her with his tender, soothing hands after Brother Thomas attempted his vile aggression toward her . . .

The thoughts went whirling around in her mind until she thought she might go mad from them—so much so that in desperation she sought for any distraction she could find, finally blurting out during a lull in Fiona's recitation, "Pardon me, Fiona, but if time permits, might you be willing to tell me the story you began to address in the kitchen before we were prevented from it—the tale behind Richard and his reaction to Adam?"

Fiona went utterly silent then, and Meg hoped that she hadn't overstepped her bounds. What she had asked to hear involved Richard, to be sure, but at least a conversation about his deceased relative might distract her from dwelling on Richard's own wonderful qualities and reliving her tender memories of their time together.

Sighing, Fiona lifted one graceful hand to rub her brow. She turned her head, and Meg felt the gravity of her stare, as if Richard's sister-by-marriage was trying to determine whether Meg could be trusted with something of great importance. At last she nodded once, reaching out to take Meg's hand.

"I believe you to be good of heart, Meg, and it is clear that Richard holds you in great esteem. Therefore, I will ask you this, before I can answer your question in full: Can you keep a confidence?"

"Aye," Meg answered, squeezing back when she felt the encouraging pressure of Fiona's palm in hers. "But I can only agree to do so if whatever it is you are about to tell me proves to be of no danger to anyone."

"Of course. I would expect no less—and you can rest assured that the only danger to be had from this information would be in the spilling of it prematurely. It concerns Adam, and he cannot know of it until Braedan and I deem it the right time, for his sake."

Meg nodded. "I understand and give my word to keep your confidence."

"Thank you," Fiona murmured, releasing Meg's hand and leaning back with a deep breath. "I imagine it will be easiest to begin with what happened at supper our first night at Hawksley. You remember, I am sure, how Richard responded to seeing Adam for the first time."

"Aye. He looked as though he was seeing a ghost," Meg responded.

Fiona nodded. "Perhaps it was because in a way, he had."

At Meg's troubled expression, Fiona continued, "You see in the five years since Richard and Adam last met, Adam has grown into a young man who looks almost the exact replica of his father."

Meg frowned openly now and glanced at Fiona. "I am afraid I do not understand."

"You have also noticed that Adam does not resemble Braedan, I gather," Fiona said wryly.

Meg let out her breath in an awkward laugh. "I do not see a great likeness, it is true."

"That is because Braedan is not Adam's father. Nor am I his mother."

At that admission, Meg was struck into dumb silence. She could only shift her gaze to Fiona in disbelief, seeing the tight lines of remembered pain edging Fiona's mouth and shadowing her eyes; Meg felt a tiny burst of guilt unfurl inside her for having brought forth this clearly difficult subject for a woman she'd quickly come to admire and respect.

"It is all right, truly," Fiona murmured, as if sensing her discomfort. "It is a tale that precedes Adam's birth, though the year of that event marked the first chapter in the story of my and Braedan's life together." She cast a sidelong look at Meg. "Are you sure you wish to hear the rest of it? It will needs be abbreviated, naturally, unless you relish the thought of being here still with the sunrise tomorrow morn."

Meg felt a smile pull on her lips at that comment, setting her at ease. But before she could answer, Fiona added, "Not all of what I will tell you is pretty, and I pray that, should you decide to hear all, you will choose to hear with an open heart, for it would be a great loss to me if you were to change your perception of any of us who are involved because of it."

A knot formed in Meg's throat again at the thought that this woman could worry for one moment that anything she could say would cause Meg to judge her harshly—she, who had been publicly disgraced for an illicit affair and illegitimate child, and sent to endure years of penance for her sins. The thought humbled her, and she murmured, "Nay, Fiona, have no worry on that account. I would be grateful to hear what you wish to tell me and will do so without judgment, just as you did when you heard of my difficult past."

Nodding with a short, decisive motion, Fiona glanced at her, the corners of her eyes crinkling as she tried to smile. "Very well, then. In the name of our developing friendship I will share with you what remains. In short, it is this: Before I knew Braedan, I had not lived my entire life as the respectable woman you've come to know. Rather, for many years I survived as a common woman of the *stewes*, known not by my true name, but rather as Giselle de Coeur, the Crimson Lady."

The Crimson Lady?

Meg's mouth might have gone slack had she not caught herself in time to stop it from falling open. Though spoken of only in tantalizing whispers among the men at court, and because of that eventually by the gossiping, randy lads, that name had been infamous even when Meg was a girl. The Crimson Lady had been known as a courtesan of the highest skill, sought far and wide by noblemen and kings for her auburn-haired beauty and her ability to bring men to their knees with desire.

Meg swallowed now and looked at Fiona, recalling how she'd noted her uncommon loveliness from the very first, with her hair like muted flame and her eyes such an unusual, tawny hue.

"I wondered, considering your youth," Fiona said, sounding strained, though she kept her gaze steady upon Meg, "if that name would have any meaning to you, but I can see by your expression that it does. Was it when you lived at court?"

Meg questioned her ability to answer aloud, so great was her shock at Fiona's revelation, but she managed to offer in soft response, "Aye. I first heard bits of the tales when I was but nine or ten."

Fiona nodded, but she had to press her lips tightly together for a moment before she could continue. "Well, then," she said, trying to seem matter-of-fact, though her voice caught just a bit, "It saves me some of the painful details." She struggled to smile again, but it was clear that the effort proved great.

"Needless to say," Fiona continued, "it was a horrible life I led, fashioned for me by the man who had first purchased me from my mother—a man who was known as much for his perfection of face and form as he was for his depravity. Draven used his appearance to his benefit in acquiring the girls he needed to sustain his wicked trade." Her mouth twisted as if with remembered bitterness. "He was like a dark angel, tall, powerful, and physically stunning, and I hated him with every part of my being."

Meg swallowed. *Tall, dark, stunning . . . with a face like an angel . . . Sweet heaven . . .*

Fiona nodded in confirmation. "Anyone who knew Draven would only need glance at Adam now to realize that he is Draven's son. That is why Richard reacted so strangely when he saw him again, for those five years he was away had wrought changes in Adam—startling elements of similarity to the man who sired him."

"But how did Richard even know Draven, to be disturbed by any likeness in Adam?" Meg asked after a moment, confused. "Surely Richard would have been too young to have had dealings with anyone involved in such . . . unsavory business." She flushed. "Besides, even had he been full-grown, I cannot imagine Richard drawn to any aspect of trade in the *stewes*."

Before Fiona could answer, a few pigeons fluttered in to

land on the tiny ledge built onto the cupola far above their heads, chased there by a crow who squawked indignantly at them from the field. The birds cooed and jostled one another in their efforts to enter the dark interior of the dovecote, and Meg and Fiona both looked up at the minor commotion. When all was quiet again, Fiona's gaze fell on Meg once more.

"You are as perceptive as Richard suggested," she complimented softly, and Meg felt herself flushing again, not only with Fiona's praise, but because Richard had thought it too.

"And you are correct," Fiona continued, pretending not to notice her blush. "Richard never would have dealings willingly in the *stewes*. He came to know Draven as a result of finding himself orphaned as a youth of fifteen, while Braedan was away on Crusade. Richard was sent to live with his only remaining relative, an uncle-by-marriage, named Kendrick de Lacy—Viscount Draven."

"How awful," Meg breathed, her heart twisting anew for what it must have been like for someone as driven by justice and right as Richard to be forced to live with such a miscreant.

"I am sorry to say, however, that even that was not the worst of it."

Meg turned an expectant gaze on Fiona.

"Richard and Braedan had a foster sister," Fiona explained, "a delicate girl nearly three years older than Richard. Her name was Elizabeth, and when Draven assumed control of the de Cantor holdings in Braedan's absence, he took her by trickery into his foul possession to work in the *stewes*. At Richard's tender age, there was naught that he could do to stop his uncle. Worse still, he had become enamored of Elizabeth in the years she had fostered with their family, and her loss nearly destroyed him."

Fiona kept her gaze steady, "Elizabeth conceived Adam as a result of her foul misuse by Draven, and she died shortly after giving birth in a hovel somewhere in the *stewes*."

Meg's stomach lurched with the thought, realizing for the first time why the sight of Adam had been so difficult for Richard. Adam was the child of the man he'd hated and the woman who had been his first love . . . a woman his uncle had destroyed in a wicked, heinous manner. It was no wonder Richard could not look at Adam without being reminded of that painful truth.

"What became of Draven?" Meg asked huskily, as much to keep her thoughts away from Richard's suffering as to see her curiosity on the matter satisfied. "Was he punished for his evil?"

"Aye, he paid for his crimes with his life."

"He was executed?" Meg felt a tiny jolt of surprise at the idea.

"After a fashion. The de Cantor code of justice was brought to bear on him; he was killed during a scuffle with a group of outlaws led by Braedan, who had by then returned home and was attempting to right the wrongs Draven had perpetrated upon us all."

"I see," Meg murmured. "It must have been difficult, considering that they were near relations, but I imagine that stopping a man as evil as Draven must have provided your husband with a certain level of satisfaction."

Fiona simply kept her gaze level, and Meg sensed the gravity in her expression, similar to when she had asked about her ability to keep a confidence. When at last she spoke, it was to murmur, "But it was not Braedan who killed Draven, Meg. It was Richard."

The shock of that spilled through Meg, adding a new layer to all to which she'd been made privy already. "How . . . ?" she asked in disbelief. "He must have been little more than a boy! How could he have undertaken such an act?"

"He was determined, and at the time it appeared as though Draven would get away with his crimes." Fiona pursed her lips. "As I mentioned earlier, Richard feels things deeply and does naught but with his whole heart. Bringing Draven to justice was one of those things, but it did not come without great price. He bears deep scars and the weight of guilt from that time; the first over not being able to save Elizabeth, and the second at killing his own uncle, whether or not that death was deserved."

Meg was still reeling from all that she'd heard when Fiona shook her head and glanced away before finally finishing, "Braedan and I had so hoped that Richard's marriage to Eleanor and Isabel's birth would help to heal some of those old wounds. But as you know too well, it did naught but create more sorrow for him."

The full realization of what Richard had truly suffered, above and beyond what she'd already known about, ripped through Meg, breaking open the wounds of her own heart. She could not escape it; what Fiona had told her only made her love Richard all the more—and made her feel more deeply the pain that keeping herself distanced from him was going to cause her.

"There is a happy ending to all this, however," Fiona said, clearly trying to lighten the moment and succeeding in distracting Meg from her misery, even if it was just for a little while.

"And what is that?" Meg croaked.

"Everything could have ended on a far darker note," Fiona offered, squeezing her hand again, "but as it stands, it is quite miraculous. Braedan and I found each other. We were fortunate enough to have located Adam shortly after his first birthday, and we have raised him as our own since that day." She gave a nod then, acknowledging, "We need to tell him of his real parentage, it is true, and very soon—most definitely before he attends court and is forced by his appearance to take on the burden of Draven's sins—but it will help that, though he may look like his sire, he possesses the light and soul of his mother."

Pausing, Fiona flashed Meg an enigmatic look. "And as for Richard . . ."

Meg cursed herself for rising to the bait, but try as she might, she could not stop herself. "Aye?" she echoed hoarsely.

"Braedan and I are relieved to see him home from his service with the Templars, and our greatest hope is that he will find at long last a strong woman who has weathered storms of her own . . . one who is kind of heart and capable of loving deeply. A lady with whom he can build a new life, free from the darkness and guilt that have plagued him for so long."

Meg suddenly felt very sick.

"You wouldn't happen to know anyone who might match that description, would you?" Fiona said, grinning and pulling on Meg's hand in a playful gesture.

Fiona's question was well-intentioned, Meg knew, offered in the spirit of a sister teasing her younger sibling. But Meg felt nothing except overwhelmed and heartbroken in the face of it.

In short, Meg could not find words to respond to her banter in any polite fashion.

And so she quite simply burst into tears.

Chapter 13

Richard thought about pacing back and forth across the width of the main hall, to rid himself of some of the pent-up energy inside him. He considered getting up, going out of door, and hacking at a quintain with his training sword until his mood was spent—or taking his gelding on a jaunt through the countryside that was fast and hard enough to leave them both in a lather.

But in the end he simply leaned back in the great, armed chair before the fire in the main hall, with his legs stretched out in front of him and his hands laced across his belly, watching the flames dance and listening to them crackle with almost fiendish fervor. His black mood shifted and swelled. He felt pensive, unable to keep his mind from churning on two problems that were plaguing him: the news that John had shared with him about the French Inquisition and Meg's sudden change of heart.

Neither was making him very happy at the moment.

Only an hour ago, Meg had run back into the house and straight up to her chamber, her face streaked with tears, followed closely after by Fiona, who seemed near tears herself as she apologized to him repeatedly for having "made matters worse." And this just after John had gathered his strength enough to tell him of the Inquisition's inexorable approach on England. He had made a near escape after being captured, he'd said, on the coast near Montivilliers, but he'd been in a good position because of it to overhear their plans.

After what John had related, it seemed clear to Richard that his time to appeal to King Edward for aid in keeping France from the English Templars might well be up, before he even had the opportunity to make it.

Aye, in the black mood he was in, it was to the benefit of his nieces and nephews that Willa was occupying them out of doors with picking the last of the apples. But Fiona and Braedan were not so fortunate, having chosen places of purgatory near him; they had ceased all conversation quite some time ago, and now he glanced over to where they sat, positioned exactly as they had been for the past quarter hour, sharing in his gloom.

Braedan stared at an empty cup in front of him, rocking it back and forth in an absentminded way atop the table, and ending the motion only in response to Fiona's dropping her hand on his arm in a silent plea to desist. Glancing up first to her, and then over to Richard, he finally broke the hush surrounding them to murmur once more, "Richard, I wish you would reconsider. Mayhap now is the time to strike out to the north. With the Inquisition so near, you risk too much to make an appearance at court."

Scowling, Richard stared more deeply into the flames; they matched his emotions well enough that for an instant, he allowed himself the fanciful notion that they writhed with some kind of innate sympathy to him. Ridiculous, he knew, and yet it pleased him to think of it.

But he also knew that Braedan would not be put off for too long in getting an answer to his suggestion.

Sighing, Richard turned his head from his perusal of the fire, experiencing a tiny jolt of remorse at the anxiety he saw couched in his brother's blue gaze. "I cannot deny the king's summons, Braedan, as well you know—I refuse to be deemed a traitor, running to Scotland and hiding from what might come, when I still have a chance to do some good. I will gain an audience with King Edward. What comes after that is in God's hands."

"You may need God's hands to protect you, if those hypocrites make it across the Channel and demand the arrest of English Templars," Braedan muttered, and Richard saw Fiona's expression tighten with worry at the thought.

"It will go as it is meant to be," Richard answered just as forcefully, feeling the weight of his choice bearing down on him as well, but knowing it could be no other way. "I could not live with myself if I took a path based on my personal safety over the greater good—nor could you, if you were in my place, as well you know."

Braedan just shook his head and made a grumbling sound, but the fact that he did not offer any further argument meant that he could not refute Richard's claim.

"This is all so terrible," Fiona murmured, clenching her fingers. "And to have this . . . this awkwardness with Meg added to your worries, in addition to everything else . . ." She made a sound of distress, her hands fluttering to her throat, then onto the table, and then back to clench in her lap again. "I am sorry, Richard. I feel so horribly about it all. I only thought to encourage Meg when I spoke to her of the possibility that you might be suited for each other."

"It was not your fault, Fiona, truly. You must believe me," Richard answered in an even voice, standing and walking over to place a hand on her shoulder. He meant it too, and if nothing else, he hoped to end this day with the knowledge that he had succeeded in relieving his kind sister-by-marriage of her misplaced guilt at the unhappy turn of events that seemed to have taken place with Meg. "You did nothing wrong, believe me."

"He is right, love," Braedan said, picking up where Richard had left off. "It is my fault as much as anyone's. I was the one who assured you that Richard was carrying a torch for the lass—"

"You *what*?" Richard swiveled to glare at his brother.

"—and anyone with eyes could see that she thought tenderly of him as well," Braedan continued without missing a beat.

"My head is spinning with all of this," Richard muttered, jabbing his fingers through his hair in exasperation, "It truly is."

"I am only trying to explain," Braedan continued in that older-brother tone that made Richard want to punch something, "so you will understand why Fiona tried to get Meg to talk more openly about her feelings for you."

"It is unfortunate, then," Richard grated back, in a bid to keep his itching fists at bay, "for I cannot imagine any worse response than to have a woman begin sobbing at the mere suggestion that she might be well suited to me."

He felt another jab of conscience when Fiona flinched at his complaint, and so he bit back the next little tidbit, which had included a curse, keeping it confined to his thoughts.

Hellfire and damnation.

Tilting his head back, he inhaled a great lungful of air, studying the whitewashed ceiling and running both hands through his hair again, before letting his breath out slowly.

This was getting nowhere quickly, and he feared he'd just managed to undo any good he might have accomplished in convincing Fiona that she bore no responsibility in the rift that had materialized without warning between him and Meg.

He had to resolve this and soon—and that meant he would have to take the most expedient course, which also happened to be the most painful one.

"Fiona," he said gently to his sister-by-marriage, sitting down next to her and taking her hand in his, "please tell me once more, if you will, exactly what you said to Meg, and she to you, in the moments before she ran back to the house."

"But *why*, Richard?" Fiona looked at him with both pleading and sympathy in her gaze. "I have told you most of it already, and it does no good to torment yourself with it—it cannot be changed . . ."

"I know, Fiona, truly, and yet I must needs hear it again if I hope to make any sense of this." He gave her hand a warm squeeze. "Please. Do as I ask."

Fiona's eyes were dark with concern, and she swallowed, looking to Braedan for support, clearing her throat when he also gave her an encouraging nod. "I—I simply said that your brother and I would like nothing better than to see you find happiness at long last with a woman of strength and sympathy—one who is kind of heart and capable of loving deeply, as you deserve. As you so *richly* deserve, dear Richard," she repeated fervently, her brow furrowed with the emotion she was holding back as she gripped both of his hands in hers.

"Ah, lady," Richard murmured, lifting one of her hands to his lips to brush a kiss over the back of it, "as always, you honor me with your care, far more than is warranted by my oafish behavior."

"Nay." Fiona pressed her palm to Richard's cheek, shaking her head and smiling through the tears glistening in her eyes. "It is never too much, Richard. It never will be—and I shall never let you forget that."

Richard felt a stab of heartfelt gratitude strike deep in his chest before spreading to fill him with comforting warmth. "Thank you, lady," he murmured, smiling back at her and tipping his head in acknowledgment. He met her gaze directly once more, pausing for an instant before he asked, "What did Meg say in response to you, then?"

"First I jestingly asked her if she knew of any woman who would fit the description I had made, and it was then that she burst into tears. She mumbled that it was impossible. 'It simply cannot be' . . . those were her exact words, I believe," Fiona explained, frowning. "I tried to comfort her in her obvious distress, but she only murmured an apology, jumped up, and ran back to the house."

"That is all?"

"Aye. That was the extent of it. It was baffling to me then, and it is still so now."

"Did she say aught about exactly what was impossible—or why?"

Fiona frowned more deeply before shaking her head. "Nay. She said nothing else, though the clear implication was that she found the idea of a developing affection with you to be the thing she found so hopeless."

"Hmm."

Richard considered that—and knowing Meg as well as he thought he did, he also tried to contemplate the possible reasons that she might have decided to end what had been happening between them without any real warning.

He reviewed for what seemed the hundredth time everything that had been said in the solar, thought over each word he could remember having spoken—or that had been said to Meg by anyone, for that matter. And suddenly an idea took nebulous shape. It wasn't a foregone conclusion by any means, but perhaps . . .

"Thank you, Fiona; I am grateful for your help with this," Richard said, giving her a quick embrace before pushing himself to his feet again and turning toward the corridor leading to the second chamber.

"What will you do now?" Braedan called, moving in to take his place near Fiona.

Richard paused at the portal, twisting to look at the two of them, who were dearer to him than any other couple he'd ever known.

"With John recovering and out of danger, I will leave for Tunbridge Castle on the morrow, as planned," he answered before glancing to Fiona, his mouth quirking in a half smile as he added, "but right now I am off to find Meg. For my curiosity has been piqued, and before I escort her to King Edward's court, I must know if my suspicions about her sudden change of heart hold any merit at all."

"Good luck to you, Richard," Fiona offered, blowing him a kiss.

"Aye, best of fortune, brother," Braedan added, giving him a little half smile of his own as he draped his arm over Fiona's shoulders and pulled her close. "And remember that the way of the heart rarely runs smoothly; we can attest to that from experience."

"Thank you both—I am grateful for the encouragement," Richard called out in answer, a bemused smile tugging at his own lips now as he turned to take the stairs three at a time, adding under his breath, "for in this instance I do believe that I am going to need it."

A scratching sounded on her door just moments after Meg had heard someone pounding up the stairway at a headlong pace. Assuming that it was one of the children, who seemed to run everywhere they went, she took a second to brush her fingers over her hair and try to discern if she was tidy before she made her way across the chamber to open the door.

Her eyes were swollen and her skin surely looked mottled—she hoped it wasn't one of the smaller de Cantors or she might give him or her a fright, with the way she looked—but she wasn't about to be so rude as to ignore the summons. This wasn't her chamber alone now, after all.

And so when she pulled open the door and saw Richard standing there, she nearly stumbled, aghast with surprise and trying to stem the lancing ache that swept through her just from looking at him.

This wasn't fair. She hadn't prepared herself to face him yet.

"What are you doing here?" she asked, trying not to sound accusatory and failing at it miserably.

At first Richard looked as though he was going to say something clever, but then he glanced down and let out his breath in a long, low exhalation, before lifting his devastatingly beautiful gaze to her face.

"I came to ask you something, lady. Three questions, in fact, if you will answer them."

"I—I do not know," she choked, stiffening and refusing to step from the doorway, as it might be construed as an invitation for him to come inside—and that would have been far more than she could bear, she knew. "It depends on what they are."

"They are questions that demand your honesty, nothing more, nothing less." As he spoke, he offered her that look that always sent a thrilling jolt of heat spiraling through her—the one that made her feel as if, somehow, she was the loveliest woman in the world. Never releasing her from his gaze, he added softly, "It is not so much to ask, is it, after all we have confided in each other?"

She almost crumbled, then. The memory of all they had confided, of all she'd felt and all they'd almost shared, swept through her with startling force, making her want to sink to the floor, or cry out, or worse, even throw herself into Richard's arms. But she couldn't do that. She couldn't.

"I—I—"

She could not get anything out. Knowing she must look wide-eyed and frantic, like a doe cornered by a hunter, she took a step back, then another, raising her hand to the door and intending to close it tightly, to block him out so he couldn't see the hurt pitching through her. She shook her head, mumbling, "Nay, I am sorry—so sorry, Richard."

His hand shot out, stopping the door in its progress as effectively as if it had been little more than a wall of air.

"By the Rood, woman, if you are to cut me from your heart without a by-your-leave, the least you could do is to toss me the bone of your honesty for comfort."

He'd said it. Oh, God, he'd said it aloud and now it was real. He knew she was pushing him away, and it made the desolation that was throbbing in her heart swell to a new level.

She searched his face, aching at his haunted expression and his shadowed eyes, and she clenched her fists against her side, feeling the half moons of her nails cutting into the flesh of her palms. She had drawn blood, it seemed, from the stinging she felt . . . but it was better than reaching out to him in comfort as she longed to do right now.

"I do not know if I can bear it, Richard," she whispered, though whether she meant the torment of answering him or just standing here face-to-face with him, she wasn't entirely sure herself.

"I swear to make no effort to persuade you to think or believe anything differently than you do right now, if that is what you fear," he said, still pinning her with his gaze. "Only be honest in answer to my questions; it is all I ask."

The battle raged within her, won at last with the single, softly spoken phrase he uttered, that snapped the last remaining thread of her broken heart.

"Please, Meg."

Overcome, she nodded only once, knowing she couldn't speak without crying and wanting to save what little strength she had remaining for the effort ahead of her.

"Thank you," he murmured. "Now answer if you will: Is there aught concerning my actions that has repelled you—or have I said anything that has caused you the distress you so clearly feel this day?"

Meg felt sick with the agony of knowing he might consider anything of that kind as a reason for her change toward him. Shaking her head, she managed to say hoarsely, "Nay,

Richard, you have been nothing but gallant in all of your dealings with me. You are—"

You are kind, tender, caring, and the most wonderful man I have ever known.

The statement finished itself in her mind, unspoken, for though she had promised to be honest, it hurt too much to say it. And so she just shook her head and choked out, "I hold absolutely nothing against you from either the past or now—but you must understand, Richard. What is between us—it—it simply cannot go further without the threat of scandal . . . do you not see that? Because of *me*, Richard, not you. Because of me."

He did not respond, and so she took in an uneven breath, wondering how she would find strength to go on. "Please do not make this more difficult for either of us than it is already," she implored. "Try to understand that we cannot change what is, as much as we might like to."

He nodded gravely, not looking dismayed, as she'd thought he might, or even overly concerned. In fact, it seemed that he was not finished with her questioning, even now.

"My second question, then, is this," he went on, as if she had not just spilled her heart and soul at his feet. "Do you care for me as I have come to believe you do, in a way that goes . . . deeper than friendship, perhaps?"

Even through her shock, the sound of his words, uttered low and with such vulnerability behind them, caressed her into another paroxysm of agony. She pressed her lips together, the pain of his asking her to admit this aloud too much to bear. She had tried to explain what she was feeling; she had humbled herself to try to help him understand, so why was he doing this to her? Shaking her head, she blinked away the stinging in her eyes, her voice a near whisper as she rasped, "You are not fair, Richard . . . it is not fair to ask such a thing of me now—"

He forestalled her protests, murmuring simply, "You promised honesty, lady, remember?"

She made a small, wounded sound, and he smoothly finished, "You must answer, Meg, before I can go on to the third and final question."

She felt her back go rigid. He was going to push through with this, by heaven, and yet he seemed strangely unperturbed by it all, while she—well, she was sinking lower and lower into the depths of desolation with every moment that passed.

"Will you answer, then?" he demanded softly, never taking his eyes from her face. "Do you feel more for me than simple friendship, lady?"

The pressure inside built to an unbearable level. He would not be satisfied—would not leave her alone until she'd spoken the truth on it. Rebelliousness rose up in her, to her relief driving away some of the pain, enough that she was able to offer a clipped "Aye, then, if you must know. You are correct in supposing that."

Once more he nodded, this time with an expression that was the farthest thing from miserable that she could imagine; she stared at him in surprise, wondering what kind of extraordinary thoughts were allowing him to feel so jubilant in the face of such a harsh reality as knowing that she cared for him so, while at the same time being forced to confront the inexorable truth that she was putting a halt to anything further developing between them.

"Give me your hand now, Meg."

"What?"

The thought of that was so disturbing that she actually hid both of her hands behind her back, covering them with the folds of her skirts. "You never said anything about needing to touch me, Richard, nor did I agree to that condition. A third question is all you are entitled to," she said, once again grateful for the tiny flare of defiance that rose up, helping her to push aside her more difficult feelings.

"Ah, but it is within the context of my question that I need your hand in mine—I cannot do one without first gaining the other."

When she still hesitated, he murmured, "Come, lady, have courage. I will do no more than hold the tips of your fingers in mine, if you so wish it. Is the thought of that so odious that you cannot grant me such a small request, even now and after all that has passed between us?"

He knew her too well. Her heart skipped a beat with his plea, and she was contemplating the possibility of denying him again, when, as if in mutiny to her own will, her right hand slipped from its hiding place and jutted forward; it poised suspended in the space between them, with her palm down and her fingers outstretched. His for the taking.

And take it he did.

In a way she would never have thought possible.

He turned his hand up and lifted it to hers, just barely brushing across the sensitive pads of her fingertips. He moved against her with a gentle friction that was unbearably erotic . . . cool and searing all at once. At last his own fingers stroked in one, sweet movement down the center of her palm, before he took full possession of her hand in the warm strength of his own.

She inhaled on a ragged gasp, aware for the first time that she had stopped breathing.

Now she simply continued to stare at their joined hands, using every ounce of her will not to move, not to snatch her fingers back to safety again . . . not to let her legs, which felt suddenly weak and shaky with the waves of desire that simple caress had sent shooting through her, give way beneath her.

"You are trembling, lady," he whispered.

"Aye," she breathed, incapable of anything more eloquent. She felt his gaze fixed hard upon her, though she could not seem to look away from his hand holding hers.

"But not in fear or loathing?"

"Oh, nay . . ."

To her horror, her answer seemed to slip out on a moan, even as realization slowly blossomed. *The third question*, her mind dimly supplied. *He's asked his third question*.

"That is all I needed to know," he murmured in that same low, husky tone as earlier.

Her gaze snapped up to his then, and the sensual force of his expression, the searing desire flaming in his eyes washed into her with the strength of an enormous wave; she would have likely staggered back, even, had she not been anchored by his touch still upon her. He held her gaze as he bent over her hand, and she braced herself for the thrill of his lips brushing the backs of her fingers as he had done once before . . .

But he stopped short of that connection with her flesh, shifting past the mark and leaving just a whisper of air to convey the tantalizing warmth of how near he'd come. Then straightening, he released her hand with a final, hushed "Thank you for your honesty, Meg. We leave for Tunbridge Castle tomorrow at dawn."

And then with a half smile that turned her insides to jelly, he nodded and walked away, leaving her standing there in shock, as confused and miserable as she'd been before he arrived.

And much less composed, thanks to the sensual spell he'd woven with his heated glances and skillful touch.

* * *

Meg felt no better three nights later, when they finally ceased riding on the last leg of their journey to Tunbridge Castle. They'd stopped to take shelter in two rooms provided by a tavern called the Bull and Hen, according to the raucously painted sign swinging out front, and as she'd climbed from the carriage and tried to ignore the protests of her stiffened and bruised muscles, she'd been forced to acknowledge that her discomfort now had more to do with hurt over Richard's seemingly relaxed demeanor around her than the yearning for him that continued to plague her.

He had been a complete gentleman, solicitous and concerned for her comfort ever since they'd parted at her door on that horrid afternoon. And though she had caught him staring at her on occasion, his gaze sometimes filled with simmering heat or layered with emotions she wasn't quite able to read for the swiftness with which he hid them, he'd never attempted to speak with her or take action of any kind regarding the sudden change she'd wrought in their relationship.

It was maddening and more than a bit depressing to think that he had made peace with it all so quickly, when she was suffering with every breath she took and every moment she spent in the glorious agony of his company.

It had helped a bit to have the buffer of her new lady's maid, Jane Cleary; Jane was a young woman from the village who had been more than happy to serve in that elevated role, and Meg's initial protests had gone by the wayside when she'd seen how excited and proud Jane and her family were that she had been chosen for the position. Meg hadn't had the heart to tell them that her aversion to the idea of a lady's maid had naught to do with Jane and everything to do with bitterness at being made to resume her old habits as the daughter of an earl. In truth it nauseated her to think on it.

But Richard had pointed out that, regardless of her desire or not for a lady's maid once she returned to court, she needed a chaperone to make the journey at all with a man who was still considered young, vigorous, and irrefutably un-married by society at large.

And so it had been decided. The three of them had de-parted for Tunbridge, with Braedan set to meet them there some days later, after he'd seen Fiona and the children settled back home.

And now here she was, lying on a lumpy pallet in a dark-ened chamber above the Bull and Hen, with naught but Jane's soft snores and her own twisting thoughts to keep her com-pany as she struggled to find sleep for the third night in a row.

She imagined Richard in his bed on the other side of the thin wall, though she had heard nary a sound to know if he was there or not. It was late enough that she could not imag-ine he would be elsewhere, however, and so she wondered what he was thinking of, if he was awake, as she was—or of whom he was dreaming, if he had been fortunate enough to attain slumber.

Considering the brave and composed face he had shown throughout each day of travel with her, the idea that he slept seemed more probable; aye, if she could see past the knotted wood between them, she imagined she'd find him curled up, as undisturbed and contented as a babe.

It was just as well, she thought, for she was doing enough worrying for the both of them.

Through Willa, who had taken over most of the nursing duties after Meg found it too painful to be in such close proximity to Richard, Meg had learned that Richard had pressed from John a promise to stay at Hawksley until he was fully healed, by which time Richard would have sent word from court. That way, if aught was amiss at Tunbridge with either the king or a sudden arrival of the French Inquisition, John could retrieve Richard's portion of the Templar treasure from the preceptory's burial ground, before fleeing with it to the safety of Scotland. John's own portion was still in France, having been confiscated by the gendarmes upon his capture near Montivilliers.

The whole idea of Richard facing danger or arrest upon his arrival to Tunbridge had filled Meg with more dread even than the thought of what she herself would face when she reentered the unforgiving realm of noble society—but she'd been compelled to keep silent about her worries. She could do naught else, thanks to the distance she herself had dictated would needs exist between them.

And she was miserable.

Miserable about Richard and his seeming composure, even after what had happened between them.

Miserable with worry over the perils that might lay ahead for him.

Miserable in her own heart over the loss of him, the man she loved, and the strain of needing to be strong through it anyway . . . knowing that she would never, *could* never put him in a position of having to choose between the honor of his reputation and loving her.

She had thought it would be easier to simply cut it short—to end it as she had, back at Hawksley when she had first realized the trap they were falling into.

She had been wrong.

The pain of it kept worsening with every hour, every minute that had passed since, until at long last she had come to a point of decision, on this, the eve of her return to court after three long years. Upon gaining her audience with the king, she planned to throw herself at his mercy and beg permission to take the veil. Then she could disappear into the cool, silent halls of a nunnery and live out her life in religious seclusion, working and praying until the end of her days.

It was the only possibility open to her, she had decided—the only life she would be able to bear. For she had come to the realization that she simply did not wish to live as she had anymore, in a world filled with beauty and light, shadows and suffering. Without Richard it meant nothing to her; his loss was a blow from which she would never recover.

And so in the wee hours of the morning, when human souls find most sympathy with the dark of night, Meg finally fell into exhausted, fitful slumber; but her eyes were dry and her heart was barren, except for the bitter emptiness that, after the short span of fierce, impossible joy she'd known with Richard, had returned again with angry vengeance . . .

Nevermore, she feared, to leave.

King Edward's Court

Chapter 14

Tunbridge Castle stood proudly in the west of Kent, a towering motte and bailey fortress with curved stone towers that jutted to the sky, and graceful arched doorways that called to mind the gates of heaven; it was no surprise, then, Richard thought as he prepared to enter the royal reception chamber with Meg, that young King Edward had chosen it as the site for the wedding of his favorite, Gascon knight Piers Gaveston.

Edward and Piers had been raised as boon companions, though Edward's sire soon had cause to regret his choice of the grasping and arrogant Gaveston for his son's confidant. By the time Richard first served at court to aid in young Prince Edward's weapons training seven years go, it was clear to everyone that the prince had become overly enamored of his dashing friend; the king had been forced to take matters into his own hands, banishing Piers to France for a time.

Now, with his father gone and unable to interfere longer,

Edward clearly relished his position as king, exulting in his ability to do as he wished where Piers was concerned, even when his choices angered his own barons. For though Richard and Meg had arrived at Tunbridge less than an hour ago, Richard had already felt the ripples of tension and heard some of the gossip afloat regarding the barons' universal dislike of Gaveston, who had been showered with so many gifts and titles in the months since Edward had ascended the throne, that most of the nobles considered it nothing less than shameful.

As a crowning insult, Richard had heard that the king had recently conferred upon Piers the earldom of Cornwall, one of the most sought after holdings in the land.

But even without that affront, the nobles would have found much about which to grouse, for it was clear that King Edward had spared no expense in seeing Tunbridge dressed out in extravagant splendor as a backdrop for the wedding festivities that were still raging strong. Richard's head spun with what such opulence must be costing the royal coffers. The noble families of England, it appeared, were not amused.

However, except for the way the king's mood might impact what Richard hoped to see happen in the next half hour, none of the upheavals or jealousies of court held any real meaning for him. The nobles' backbiting did not concern him, nor did their subversive strategies for obtaining positions of power, or the prospect of taxation, or deprivation, or even the struggle that might come in keeping the French Inquisition at bay.

Nothing held much meaning for him right now, in fact, except for the woman who was standing so still and quiet by his side.

He glanced over at Meg where they waited in the silk-hung

corridor outside the royal reception chamber and allowed himself a brief moment of unabashed feeling. He had been forced to hide his true emotion, in deference to her, but that did not change that she was breath and air and sunshine to him . . . she was everything good in a world of struggle and darkness. Even as tired and drawn as she had seemed during the last few days, she remained achingly beautiful to him in every way, and he reveled in the rush of emotion that spilled through him now, filling him as a blessed spring feeds the parched earth.

It was almost time, thank God. Only a few more moments of suffering for them both, and it would be over, he hoped, in the most glorious of ways.

It had been one of the most difficult things he had ever had to do, pretending to be composed in the face of the emotional distance she had placed between them. But once he'd realized why she was doing it—that she was trying to protect him . . . *him*, of all people, from the shame of an association with her and the scandal that would surely result from it so soon after Eleanor's passing—he had found the strength to do it for her sake.

She did not know, it seemed; she could not see what she meant to him, and he had not been able to tell her in any way she would have believed. Nay, even had he not promised to forgo any attempts to persuade her to a different view, he did not think he could have found the words to do justice to what he was feeling for her. Not then. And he knew her well enough to have realized that, at that point, it would not have done any good had he tried.

Talk was an important and often necessary skill for cultivating a meaningful relationship with any woman—he had learned that lesson early on in his life—but it was not everything. Deeds, he had found, often spoke more eloquently than words, and he hoped that truth would work to his advantage as soon as this interminable wait was over and they were admitted for their welcoming audience with the king.

"Richard . . . ?"

The unexpected sound of Meg's voice broke into his impatient thoughts, and he met her gaze, both gladdened and surprised. He knew that whatever she wished to say must be important, for this was the first time she had initiated conversation with him in more than three days. Now, as he took in her wan complexion and her wide, dark eyes, so clearly troubled, it was all he could do not to reach out and enfold her in his embrace, to hell with his vows to leave her be until they were before the king.

"What is it, Meg?" he asked carefully, keeping his hands at his sides.

"When we enter that chamber," she continued, her voice sounding stronger now than he had expected, "we will both be confronting the futures that await us."

"That is true," he murmured. His heart twisted to think how apt her words might prove to be, though even he could not be entirely sure that the outcome would be as favorable as he hoped.

Nodding, she stood before him with her spine straight and her chin tilted up slightly. "This may be, then, the final opportunity that we will have to talk in relative privacy."

My God, I hope not.

The thought shot through Richard's mind, though he could not say it aloud. Not yet.

Meg glanced to the sentries standing guard at the massive, closed doors to the chamber before looking at him again, her voice lowered to add, "I feel compelled, therefore, to tell you that I pray for your deliverance from any danger that may come because of your service as a Templar. It is no secret that I have not always held the Brotherhood in the highest regard, but before we are parted I want you to know that my thoughts have . . . changed in many ways, and—and it is because of you."

She seemed to struggle with something more, and a delicate frown marred the perfect sweep of her brows. "Richard, I—"

But then she stopped, her lashes sweeping down to shield the rich brown hue of her eyes from him before she glanced up at him with such a direct, endearing honesty that he felt as if he would explode from the need to tell her how he truly felt. Her voice took on a husky note when she finally finished, "I want you to know that I hope only for the best for you, Richard. Now and always."

Richard's heart swelled with love for her. Even now she was worried for his feelings and his safety. Not for herself and the ordeal of facing her sire and a future unknown to her, but for him.

Something seemed to break within him at that moment, as if a dam had burst, allowing all his pent-up feelings to spill forth in a blinding rush.

"Ah, Meg," he said hoarsely, "I must tell you . . . I know that I promised to keep silent on it, and I had planned to wait until our audience with the king, but I can hold back no longer." He lifted his hand to cup her face then, seeing her start at his sensation of his touch, the first between them after these many days. She gasped and her eyes welled as he continued, "I need you to know that there is nothing in the world that could make me—"

With a banging of staffs, the sentries at the door of the chamber in front of them stepped aside, and the giant wooden portals swung open with a groan. The sudden flurry of activity cut Richard off in the midst of his declaration, and before he could finish what he'd been trying to say to her, one of the royal guards called out in a booming voice, "His Majesty, King Edward welcomes to his court the honorable Sir Richard de Cantor, in the company of the Lady Margaret Newcomb, daughter to the Earl of Welton. You may both enter."

With that the sentry stepped back, releasing a spill of golden light that washed into the corridor. His movement also revealed a length of polished stone floor within the chamber, a span filled with scores of curious noblemen and ladies, most of whom seemed to be craning their necks to look in their direction, likely in hopes of catching a glimpse of the renowned Templar Knight who had once trained with the king, and the disgraced earl's daughter about whom gossip had run rich and fervent with scandal for several years already.

They were eager in their attention, Richard realized, because they secretly hoped for some new morsel about which to talk. Something sensational. Aye, he remembered well from the time he'd spent among them so long ago. Gossip was the order of the day, rumor and intrigue all part of what kept the wheels at court grinding. It was what the noble elite craved.

And so, he decided resolutely, as he tucked Meg's hand into the crook of his elbow and stepped with her into the glittering light, he was going to do his best to give it to them.

Richard tugged Meg along with him, following the tactful glances of the guards near the door to see in what direction he should go to find the king. He and Meg did not speak further, but he felt the stiffness in her limbs and her hesitancy as they made their way through the throng.

He didn't blame her; it seemed that the weight of a hundred stares pressed upon them with greedy curiosity, not to mention that many of these people were likely kin or near acquaintances of hers from her life as a lady of the realm. This was her first time back among them since the indiscretion and tragedy that had banished her from their presence, and though he could not regret the circumstance that had brought her into his life, he knew too well how difficult it must be for her to face these ghosts of her past again.

After another three steps, Richard spotted King Edward; he was standing at the end of the massive hall surrounded by a retinue of courtiers, watching an exhibition of archery. Richard took Meg in that direction, but when they reached halfway to the king's position, she suddenly jerked to a stop. He glanced to her quickly, noting that what little color she'd had in her cheeks had drained away, and her breathing was more shallow than before.

"What is it, lady?" he murmured, leaning into her and folding her hand against him more securely.

"My father," she breathed, her stony gaze fixed on a small gathering of people ahead of them and to their left—in the opposite direction from the royal party, thank heaven—but within just twenty-five paces of where they themselves stood right now.

Richard followed the line of her stare to take in the sight of the man he knew at first glance must be the Earl of Welton. He was richly robed, and he stood scowling at them from the front of a group playing at dice on a small table nearby. Standing behind him, almost eclipsed by his girth, stood a well-dressed but timid-looking woman with chestnut hair; she startled at sight of them, her red-rimmed eyes welling with tears, and Richard felt Meg's hand clench more tightly on his arm.

"Your mother?" he asked softly, and Meg nodded, though he had not truly needed confirmation of the fact; the resemblance between mother and daughter was clear, though Meg clearly possessed a vibrancy her mother either had never known or had lost in the course of the life she had lived.

In the moments just after spotting Meg, the earl had turned to a large, dark-haired man who was in the midst of the dicing, and now the two of them fell into motion with clear intent to intercept Richard and Meg.

"Do you wish to speak with him?" Richard asked, his voice low and tight, though his gaze never left the two men.

"Nay, I do not."

"Come then," Richard said to her, turning with her and resuming their path toward the king. "Even should he manage to cover the distance to reach us, propriety dictates that your sire will not be able to interrupt our greeting to King Edward, once it begins."

Again Meg nodded, her arm still tense against his and her spine rigid as he steered them through the remaining groups of people that stood between them and their goal. When they finally reached the archery area, Richard saw that the king stood less than ten paces away, with his back to them, though they could see him in profile as he turned and laughed at something said by the man standing next to him.

At three and twenty, King Edward was tall, and as handsome as his father had been, though only time would tell if he would prove as effective a monarch. None could deny, however, that he was athletically gifted, and at the moment he was clearly enjoying the display of archery skill being put forth for his entertainment.

"Well done, Preston!" he called, rocking back on his heels,

his arms folded over his chest as he nodded to a lad who had just nearly hit the center circle of the target with his arrow.

The young man held up his now empty bow in salute, offering a jaunty bob of his head to Edward, and the king nodded back, laughing as he called out, "Who is next, then?"

Richard was about to take that clear opening to announce his and Meg's presence, when he suddenly spotted a flash of colors that made him slow his steps. The man who wore the striking crest turned more fully, and then it was Richard's turn to jerk to a halt, just as Meg had a few moments earlier.

Azure, a semis of fleurs-de-lis.

The motif of France.

Meg noticed at almost the same time that he did, apparently, the awareness eliciting a shallow gasp from her. Her gaze flew to his, troubled and concerned with the same question filling his mind right now.

But he had no sure answer, and so he could only return her uneasy glance and murmur, "I do not know, lady," before he attempted to study the gathering of men and women surrounding the king; he needed to determine how many were French and who they might be—trying not to leap to any undue conclusions out of his own excessive wariness caused by John's warnings back at Hawksley.

Three, four . . . nay, five . . . All told he counted a half dozen Frenchmen interspersed in the group. But then another shock lanced through him. There, to the right of the gathering. A bishop stood in full regalia, with long, flowing robes and distinctive miter cap, looking regal and keeping aloof from the festivities.

There was no reason for any clergy as important and respected as a bishop to be present at such an event. Not unless he had come with others who would need attend, and he had had no real choice in the matter . . . and that would be true only of the Inquisitors from France.

"Richard . . . ?" Meg said, and the note of fear in her tone pulled him from his dark thoughts, making him glance to her in concern. It took but a moment to discern the cause of her distress; her sire and the man who accompanied him were nearly upon them.

French Inquisitors or not, it seemed that he and Meg had run out of time.

Well, then, he thought ruefully, gripping Meg's hand as he finally undertook the remaining steps that would bring them into the king's view, it was a fine thing that his driving purpose for attending court and publicly addressing the sovereign had changed so drastically in the past four days. For at this moment he was quite certain that he could not have chosen a more hostile crowd before which to raise the plight of England's Templars, even had he planned the moment for the full of a lifetime.

Slipping past the last of the young king's retainers and outpacing Meg's father just enough to cut him off at the turn, Richard escorted Meg with great satisfaction to a spot directly in front of the king, where she promptly sank into a deep curtsy and he bent to a full bow.

Edward looked down at them in surprise, seeming younger than his years, somehow—more a spirited lad than a powerful monarch. But his face lit with pleasure as he recognized the favorite weapons trainer from his youth, in the company of a lady who had been disgraced and banished from court years ago, but whom he had called back to usefulness in society by his God-given grace.

"Stand, Sir Richard de Cantor, Lady Margaret Newcomb,"

he called out, smiling broadly. "Stand and greet your sovereign, who welcomes you with great delight to this celebration in honor of Our dearest Piers Gaveston, Lord Cornwall, on occasion of his marriage to Our esteemed cousin, the Lady Margaret de Clare."

Reaching out, he clasped Richard's forearm, and then turned to Meg and gently took her hand by the fingertips, nodding over it while she bobbed another, smaller curtsy.

"Sire, we are privileged to have been summoned to your presence," Richard said, feeling a genuine affection as he looked at the former prince who was now his king. Edward had been somewhat difficult to train in arms as a youth, being exuberant only about those pursuits he enjoyed—theatrics, masonry, and athletics—and far less agreeable concerning the weapons work and tactical military instruction that his father had required of him. But Richard had undertaken the task of preparing Edward with determination, and eventually the prince had learned to handle a sword with some level of skill, coming to respect Richard for his efforts and goodwill in the process.

"We cannot tell you how gladdened We were to receive the message of your return to England, Sir Richard," the king said, his expression shadowed a bit as he added, "though We were saddened to receive your latest missive, informing Us of Lady de Cantor's passing. Our condolences to you. It is Our fervent hope that you will find some distraction from your grief here in the bosom of Our royal court."

"Thank you, sire. It has been a difficult time, it is true, and my return to England was rather . . . abrupt, as I noted in my first missive to you."

"Aye," the king murmured, tilting his head in toward Richard to add more quietly, his gaze drifting to the French nobles surrounding them, "and We understand the concern which you raised in that correspondence, though as We are sure you can appreciate by a glance round this gathering, We cannot undertake to address it presently."

As he spoke, King Edward nodded and smiled to one of the French courtiers who was readying to try his hand at the archery target and sought the sovereign's permission first, never taking his gaze from the man as he added, "We shall confer in private about it later, if you like, but in the meantime there is naught to be gained from waving any banners of notice before the eyes of Our guests from across the Channel."

"I understand, Your Majesty, and I thank you for your concern."

"Of course."

Richard paused for just an instant, preparing to introduce the true matter about which he had yearned to approach the king, but before he could speak further, Edward shifted a bright gaze to Meg, who had been standing pale and quiet beside them. She looked as though she had been waiting to say something as well, but of course she could not until the king had first spoken to her directly himself.

"Ah, Lady Margaret," King Edward said pleasantly, "you have not been forgotten, and We will have you know that much has been discussed concerning your future felicity, begun this day with your return to society. Your sire, in fact, has arranged for you what We hope will prove an advantageous marri—"

"Pardon, Your Majesty," Richard broke in suddenly, "but I beg your leave to speak once more."

Dead silence greeted his rather loud interruption, and Richard knew with a sudden, sinking realization that one and all had just heard him do what was never done. Not to a king, anyway.

He resisted the urge to squirm, hoping that his head would remain attached to his neck after this, but in truth he had not had a choice. Not once the king had brought up Meg's father, in clear preparation for telling her what they planned for her future—which by all accounts sounded like an arranged marriage.

Richard glanced at Meg and saw that she was staring at him in alarmed bewilderment; her expression almost matched the sovereign's, he couldn't help thinking idly. Almost, but not quite.

King Edward was scowling like a thundercloud, clearly unaccustomed to suffering such impudence from anyone—perhaps having never experienced the like of it before in his royal life, lest it had been dealt to him by his own late sire, who had been ferocious enough in his manner and actions to be called the Hammer of the Scots.

"What is it, Sir Richard?" the king asked finally in clipped words, his voice high and tight. Displeasure spilled from him in waves, and he fixed a black stare on Richard. "We trust it is a matter of supreme importance for you to have chosen such an unseemly manner of broaching it."

"Aye, it is very important, sire," Richard murmured, bowing his head in acquiescence. "Perhaps the most important of my life, and I beg your pardon for not addressing it sooner or in more courteous form."

"Very well, then." The king's eyes still blazed. "Speak."

After meeting Meg's questioning gaze for the briefest instant, Richard addressed himself to the king, his heart burning with what he had been forced to keep hidden for four painful days and three even more agonizing nights.

"It concerns the Lady Margaret, Your Majesty, as it is she who is responsible for the action I find myself compelled to undertake right now," he said firmly, drawing a low hum of murmurs from some of the onlookers around them, many of whom perhaps were hoping that he would say something to add more juicy scandal to their inventory of gossip.

"For in the midst of darkness," he continued, "I was blessed to find her . . . a woman of great strength, courage, and intelligence, who has become more precious to me, in truth, than my own life."

The hum in the chamber rose as he glanced at Meg and held out his hand to her, seeing her expression of shock and feeling her fingers trembling in his palm. Gazing deeply into her eyes, he smiled—and then exulting in finally speaking the words he had been waiting for so long to say, he looked back to the king and declared, "Your Majesty, I therefore beg your permission to wed the Lady Margaret Newcomb—for there is no greater honor I can imagine than the one I would know in calling her my wife."

Chapter 15

"**W**ill you, Meg?" Richard asked her very softly, though she still managed to hear him, somehow, over the exclamations of surprise erupting all around them. The king, however, remained silent.

His *wife*. Richard had just asked her to marry him.

Meg stood there in stunned silence, each moment seeming like years as she kept her gaze locked with Richard's, trying to ignore the swell of noise and activity. Joy bubbled up from deep within her—cautious, wonderful joy. But she kept it contained, needing to let this all sink in first, struggling to make sense of the enormous shift her emotions were undergoing, turned around completely from what only moments ago she had been steeling herself to accept.

She had been seconds away from begging permission to enter a nunnery.

Seconds away, she suspected, from learning that her sire and the king had other plans for her.

But Richard had intervened. He had asked to marry her despite the scandal attached to her name, or the censure he would surely endure for pursuing a union with her so soon after Eleanor's passing.

He had asked in front of the king. In front of the French contingent. In front of the entire assemblage of English nobles and ladies.

Oh, my.

She suddenly realized that they were still standing there, in the same positions they'd been when Richard had made his proposal, and that he was still gazing down at her, only with an expression that appeared more and more worried with every moment that passed. She frowned, wondering what could be the problem. And then it dawned on her.

She hadn't answered him yet.

But before she could say anything at all in response, a booming voice erupted over the confusion in the assembly, "Pardon, sire, but I must protest and declare that no one will be marrying my daughter unless I give permission for it—and by God, I most certainly do not!"

The increased level of tumult that rose after the earl's vehement declaration was unlike anything Meg had seen before. The king's men rushed in to surround the sovereign, buffering him from some of the shoving and shouting that was breaking out around them, while the king himself barked commands for Richard, Lord Welton, and Meg to be brought to his solar for a private audience. Even as he issued that command, Richard had whisked her from the center of the storm, murmuring words of comfort and ensuring that she was all right, before they were separated momentarily.

After what seemed an endless time of waiting and worrying, they had been reunited in the solar, a large and impressive chamber that the king had chosen as his private refuge during his stay at Tunbridge Castle.

King Edward sat behind a short, polished table near the hearth, flanked by his closest friend and confidante, the newly married Piers Gaveston, who had hurried to join the king upon word of the commotion taking place in the hall. Every now and again the two men would lean into each other, the king conferring with Gaveston on some point, before proceeding again after the consultation was concluded.

Richard and Lord Welton stood in front the table, though only the earl had pressed his case to the king as yet. Meg had been relegated to a place somewhat removed from the men, off to the right, near the gracefully carved entrance to the private chapel that adjoined the solar. Ostensibly, her distance from the proceeding had been arranged to prevent view of her from raising further undue emotions, particularly from her sire, but also under the pretext of offering her a chair in which to sit, next to a tiny table with refreshments she had been invited to sample . . . a courtesy that had not been extended to the men involved.

But she hadn't been able to eat anything. Not unless she relished the idea of choking; her throat was too tight even to entertain the thought, her own emotions barely kept in check every time she had the misfortune of seeing or hearing her sire—which had been continually during the past quarter hour. He had been arguing the case of his rights to her, and it was all she could do not to jump from her chair and shout at him to stop discussing her as if she were a bolt of cloth or a feudal manor to be bartered.

She should not have been surprised by his mercenary view of her, she knew. He had never seen her in any other light, after all.

But it had hurt nonetheless.

Still, rather than wasting her breath, she had forced herself to remain as silent as she could bear to be. To let this play itself out as it would, and to give Richard the freedom to do and say what he must, without worry over her to distract him.

"Your Highness," Lord Welton uttered once again, glowering, "this is highly irregular, and I protest that this . . . this *absurdity* put forth by Sir Richard is being given any consideration at all."

"Tread carefully, Lord Welton," the king cautioned, flashing the irate earl a sharp glance. "It is Our judgment you call into question, for Sir Richard and his family have given many years of loyal service to the crown, and We *are* considering his petition to Us in regard to a union with Lady Margaret. Quite seriously, in fact."

"But sire," Lord Welton continued, his tone far more wheedling, "Our meetings on the matter but a month past were very clear: My daughter would be released from the shame of her banishment for the purpose of providing a suitable bride for Sir Ector Thornton, in exchange for certain . . . assistance he gave to me in the matter of the uprising at the village near my holding at Twyford Crossing—"

Meg's heart rose to her throat, and she only just managed to stifle a gasp.

"—and I know I do not need to remind you, sire, that Sir Ector also served your father well in the Scottish wars. He was promised due payment for his efforts on England's behalf."

"Sir Ector has already received payment for his efforts in Scotland, Welton," the king countered harshly. "The whole, bloody business still turns my stomach. He helped himself to anything he could lay hands on after slaughtering entire *villages*, by God, and he is owed no more for that."

"Sire," Richard finally spoke, his expression cold and tight in reaction to what he had just heard, "I feel compelled to point out that Lady Margaret's wishes—and welfare—seem yet to be considered in all of this." He cast a dark look at Meg's sire before directing his gaze back to the king, adding, "And while it is clear that I have a personal stake in the matter, I cannot help but believe that I would make a far more suitable husband for her than a rogue knight who profits from dealing death to women and children."

"Sir, you are too righteous, considering your own notorious past," Lord Welton interjected scornfully. "But be that as it may, my daughter's tarnished reputation precludes her having any opinion at all in the matter of whom she will wed. It is fortunate for her, in fact, that Sir Ector is willing to overlook how she cast off her virtue so shamefully four years ago, behaving as little better than a common woman with a man unworthy of her status."

Meg's quite vocal gasp then was nearly drowned out by the curse Richard growled at the same moment that he spun to grip the earl by the front of his fur-trimmed robe, muttering, "You do not even deserve the privilege of uttering her name, *my lord*."

"Hold, Sir Richard—restrain yourself!" King Edward exclaimed, as the guards stationed at the doors of the solar rushed to separate them.

Meg had lurched to her feet at the burst of violence, and

now, as the scuffling subsided, she stood rigidly, her hands icy and her heart heavy. She moved forward, intending to go to Richard, but before she could span even half the distance between them, a scratching sounded at the door, followed immediately by the portal swinging open, though the king had not granted leave for it to be done.

Rising to stand, King Edward bellowed, "What is it?"

His demeanor was steely until he realized the identity of the interlopers; then he was forced reluctantly to wave off his guards, who had rushed from their efforts in separating Richard and Lord Welton to attend to the new disturbance near the door.

"Frère de Villeroi," King Edward said more calmly, in acknowledgment of the first of the three Frenchmen who swept into the chamber; it was clear, however, that he still chafed at their presumption of entrance. He nodded to the other two men adorned in the crest of fleur-de-lis, before his gaze slipped more sharply across the fourth and final man to step through the open portal; it was the dark-haired stranger who had accompanied Meg's father in the main hall . . . a man with a powerful build and a face made far less handsome than it might have been by its hawkish expression and the thin veil of cruelty simmering in his dark gaze.

Sir Ector.

Meg's mind echoed with the instinctive knowledge of his identity, even before she heard the king utter his name. Sweet heaven, this was the monstrous knight her sire intended for her husband.

Richard had been standing in barely leashed rage near the end of the table where he had been placed after his clash with Lord Welton, but now he moved swiftly to Meg's side, taking her hand and using his body as a physical buffer between her and the men who had just entered the chamber.

"To what do We owe this pleasure, Frère?" the king intoned, every nuance of his voice and body indicating, however, that he considered their intrusion anything but pleasant.

"We have just learned something quite . . . distressing, Your Highness," the man named de Villeroi offered in heavy, nasal accent. "It troubles us, in that we were not told of it by you, sire, but rather were forced to receive it from another source."

Meg noticed that Sir Ector, who had taken a place near her father upon entering the chamber, exchanged a knowing glance with the earl, and her stomach rolled sickly, even as Richard squeezed her hand in comfort.

"It is our fervent hope that you will rectify this oversight with immediate action," de Villeroi finished, staring expectantly at the king.

"Well, what is it, man? We cannot address your complaint without knowing it first," King Edward groused.

Frère de Villeroi simply gazed at the sovereign, showing little fear in facing the wrath of the young English king, as he added, "We have been made aware that there is a Templar Knight in attendance at your royal court—a man present in this very chamber, in fact. King Philip assured us of your cooperation in the matter of the Templars, for he knows the love you bear him through your betrothal to his daughter, the fair Isabel of France."

King Edward did not answer immediately, and the Inquisitor leveled a weighty gaze on him. "We await your assistance in bringing this Templar into our custody, Your Majesty, so that we may begin our interrogation of him, concerning the profane acts committed in secret by those accepted into the Brotherhood."

With every word de Villeroi spoke, Meg felt as if a suffocating hand were wrapping ever tighter around her throat. She looked up at Richard in desperation, seeing the muscle in his jaw twitch as he stared intently at the man who was plotting to see him arrested and tried for heresy.

Nay! she wanted to shout. *You cannot take him*! But she restrained herself for Richard's sake, responding to the gentle pressure of his hand on hers as he silently encouraged her to be strong. To weather this storm with him, as they had survived the tempests that had come their way already.

As it stood, King Edward stepped to Richard's—and his own—defense before anyone else had a chance to speak to the charges. "We are afraid it is you who are mistaken, Frère. We can assure you that there are none who fit that description in this chamber or elsewhere at court."

De Villeroi seemed taken aback for a moment, before he offered offered smoothly, "I beg your pardon, sire, but I was informed that a Sir Richard de Cantor is present, a man who served with the Templars as recently as three months past, if my source is correct." He shifted a hard stare to Sir Ector, who returned the steely gaze.

"*Served* is the correct term," the king retorted. "Sir Richard de Cantor is no longer a Templar Knight."

"Indeed," de Villeroi intoned blandly. "Yet even past service with the Templars is sufficient cause for interrogation— a point about which I thought you would be quite clear, sire, given the nature of our visit to your fair land. We seek proof of the vile heresies perpetrated by the Brotherhood here in

England along with those we have discovered in France, and questioning the men who are—or *were*—Templars is the best way to achieve that objective."

At that, Richard released Meg's hand and took a step forward, having plainly endured all the hypocrisy he could stand. "The crimes committed are not being perpetrated by Templars, Frère," he grated, his entire body tense with reined fury. "It is you and the rest of the French Inquisition who commit atrocities, by torturing innocent men in order to obtain false confessions."

The Inquisitor shifted his gaze to Richard in a slow and deliberate movement. "Those who are truly innocent would not break under any force of coercion, sir, which is why such methods are applied."

"The methods applied are so horrific that a man would confess anything you asked of him, just to make them stop," Richard countered hotly. "Let us be honest about that, at least. You do not seek proof of innocence or guilt, Frère; you seek to break men in order to gain deceitful support for King Philip's plot to destroy the Templar Brotherhood."

De Villeroi raised his brow at Richard in disdain. "I shall take great pleasure in undertaking the process of proving *your* innocence or guilt, Sir Richard, of that you can be sure."

"Enough," the king snapped, pushing himself to his feet. "We do not believe Sir Richard subject to your examination, Frère, and We will not allow this to continue further."

"Think carefully before you make that judgment, sire, for much rests on your decision, as I am sure you know."

The Inquisitor spoke in calm, even tones, but the weight of what he was truly saying—the threat of political upheaval that a break of betrothal between King Edward and Isabel of France would cause—hung heavy in the balance.

Meg forced herself to take deep, steadying breaths as she struggled not to yield to the feeling of danger that was winding through the silence of the chamber, snaking into every corner, until she felt they would all be paralyzed with its presence. She looked around blindly at the men aligned in their factions of power, each group battling for precedence over the others. And so it was that her gaze fell on Edward's favorite, Piers Gaveston, sitting to the left of the king at the table in front of the room.

Throughout the entire proceeding, she realized, Piers had been watching with mostly silent interest, studying Richard, then shifting his gaze to the Inquisitor, and then to Lord Welton, before letting it fall upon the king. Now he leaned back in his chair and spoke aloud, taking everyone in the chamber by surprise.

"We seem to have reached an impasse, my lords—and lady," he murmured, acknowledging her with a glance, "in regards to both the earlier question of Lady Margaret's marriage and the more recent discussion of Sir Richard's status as a Templar Knight. I pray you will not consider me over bold, but I have a suggestion that may address all grievances satisfactorily."

King Edward looked relieved, slumping back into his chair and giving his favorite a look of clear affection. "By all means, brother, speak on the matter," he said. "We would be elated to hear any thoughts that might bring Us to a suitable resolution in all of this."

"With pleasure," Piers answered, obviously enjoying the consideration being given to him. He sat forward, fairly thrumming with self-importance, and Meg could not help recalling that, even during the few times she had seen Piers in her youth, back when he had first earned Edward's notice and adoration, he had reveled in being the center of attention.

"There is an ancient custom, more recently out of practice among men of war and valor—men like Sir Richard," Piers continued, nodding to him, "that in its outcome delivers a definitive proof of guilt or innocence—such as the kind sought by Frère de Villeroi," he added, nodding to the French Inquisitor. He paused dramatically, but King Edward was obviously in no mood to humor even his favorite at a time such as this.

"Of what custom do you speak, dear one, and how may We use it to solve the dilemmas facing Us?" he asked Piers peevishly, his voice carrying an edge of irritation that served to reveal how thinly his patience had been worn by the events of the afternoon.

"It is the grand custom known as Wager of Battle," Piers offered, his expression glowing with pride and poorly concealed enthusiasm at the prospect of witnessing a martial display of the kind at which he himself excelled. "In the matter facing us, our brethren from France shall provide their best champion to face Sir Richard in a test of proof: Should Sir Richard prevail and win the battle, he shall be deemed innocent, with no need to undergo further questioning, and with the additional boon of the Lady Margaret's hand in marriage. If he is defeated, he shall be given over to the Inquisition, to be questioned as they will, with Lord Welton retaining rights to give his daughter to whom he sees fit."

Nausea swept over Meg, and her entire body tightened, even as Richard slipped his arm protectively around her.

"Nay, sire," Richard protested in a low voice. "You cannot

consider this seriously. Lady Margaret is no spoil of war to be bandied about in this way."

"Are you so fearful of defeat then, Sir Richard, that you will not entertain the idea of entering a Wager of Battle?" Frère de Villeroi asked mockingly.

"It is not the battle itself to which I object, you can rest assured," Richard ground out, snapping his gaze to the man, and had Meg not known the true goodness of his heart, she might have cringed at the murderous look in his eyes at that moment. "I have no doubt in my skill with a blade or my ability to defeat any champion the Inquisition might place before me—but I condemn the suggestion for its use of Lady Margaret as a prize of victory. It is dishonorable. She is a lady, not chattel to be bartered and fought over."

"Would you not fight for her, then, Sir Richard?" Sir Ector challenged, throwing him a look of contempt before flicking a gaze at Meg and adding under his breath, "I certainly would, though not for her honor, I must confess. But to be saved the trouble of breaking her into the sadd—"

He never got to finish, for Richard lunged at him, his fist slamming into Ector's jaw with enough force to send him spinning to the floor; Ector recovered with a growl and rolled to his feet, preparing to launch himself at Richard in retaliation, but he was held back from the action by the guards who had again been directed by the king to leap in to break up the fray.

"Sir Richard, one more such eruption and you will be physically restrained," the king snapped before shifting his gaze to glare at Sir Ector, who was angrily shaking off the guard's hold even as he swiped his hand across his bloodied mouth. "And as for you, sir, such insults are uncalled for and unmannerly. We will not condone it and further caution you that if not for Our esteem of Lord Welton, whose patronage We value most highly, We would have you barred from this chamber and Our court altogether for that boorish outburst."

Wisely, Ector said nothing more, though he glowered at Richard as if he'd like nothing better than to drag him into an outright brawl.

Richard responded not at all, except for the animosity Meg could feel still spilling from him in waves; even his rate of breathing remained steady, and she wondered at his extraordinary self-control . . . at his ability to remain so calm in the face of the kind of threat that seemed to be aligning itself against them right now.

Her own heart raced in the horrid anticipation of it all, but she was given no quarter for respite, for in the next moment, King Edward shook his head. "We cannot debate this further, it is clear, without tempting more violence—and in truth, though it is far from satisfactory, We see no better solution for this tangled state of affairs than the one offered by Our brother, Lord Cornwall."

Face tight with the burden of this decision, King Edward looked to the lead Inquisitor, asking in a clipped tone, "Frère de Villeroi, do you find a Wager of Battle to be an acceptable resolution from the view of the Inquisition, aye or nay?"

"Aye"—the Frenchman nodded after a short pause, contempt for the entire proceedings apparent in his pinched expression—"provided that we are given ample time to procure our selected champion and bring him to this field of battle. To have served as a Templar Knight—one of the most elite within the Brotherhood, I have been told—Sir Richard must possess highly developed combat skills, and a suitable opposite will needs be found. A sennight should suffice."

The king nodded once, sharply, before shifting his gaze to Lord Welton. "What say you, my lord? Will you abide by the terms of the wager, as laid out by Our brother Cornwall, regarding the offer of Lady Margaret into Sir Richard's keeping if he is victorious, and to you if he is not?"

Lord Welton looked none too pleased, blustering for a moment before answering, "It distresses me, sire, for I would have you know that if Sir Richard prevails, I shall be forced to find other means of rewarding Sir Ector for the assistance he has provided me and the crown, I might add, in the aforementioned matter at Twyford Crossing. It will be costly and a burden that I am not happy to bear alone."

"Cease your complaints, man, and simply answer the question: Do you agree to abide by the outcome of the wager or *not*?" King Edward demanded, scowling at Lord Welton's continued attempts to feather his nest with the crown's gold.

"Aye, I will abide by it," Welton finally muttered after a disgruntled pause, but not before giving Richard and Meg another malevolent glare. "And if all goes as I pray it will, then when this is over, the Brotherhood of Templars will have been of great use to me for a second time within these five years," he added cruelly.

Meg felt the blood drain from her face, and Richard tensed next to her, as the implication of her sire's taunt sank home.

"Have a care, my lord," Richard grated, his voice low and all the more dangerous, she knew, for its seeming composure, "or I will undertake to finish the task the guards prevented me from a few moments past. Do not test me on it."

King Edward frowned, plainly unhappy at the continued

volley of insults and flaring tempers. But he let it pass, likely in favor of concluding this discussion as swiftly as was possible. Turning to Richard, he offered the same question he had posed to the others, in a manner making clear that he considered it more a formality than anything else. "And what say you, then, to the matter at hand, Sir Richard—will you submit to the Wager of Battle with the Inquisition's champion to prove your innocence?"

"It depends."

That equivocal response had not been what the king had hoped for, evidently, for he uttered a curse under his breath that sounded anything but regal and directed the full force of his kingly ire at him to bellow, "On *what*, pray tell?"

"On the matter of Lady Margaret," Richard answered, just as forcefully, though with an underpinning of calm that the king had lacked. "I decline to wager her future on the outcome of any battle I must fight, Your Majesty. Barring that condition, I will agree," Richard finished, meeting his sovereign's gaze with his own direct stare.

"Not acceptable!" the king countered in irritation. "The others have agreed to the terms as stated—and We declare that it will be as Our Lord Cornwall has suggested, for We have found no other solution concerning the issue of Lady Margaret's marriage. You seek to marry her, and Welton seeks to give her to someone else. Trust Us when We tell you that you do not wish Us to be forced into making a choice between yourself and the earl. Simply accept the terms so that We may conclude this audience!"

"And if I do not?" Richard said tightly.

King Edward flashed him a look of weary exasperation. "If you do not, Sir Richard, then We will have no choice but to remand you into the custody of Our French brethren for interrogation, in accordance with the wishes of Our future father-by-marriage, King Philip, at which point the Lady Margaret by necessity will be given into the care of her sire, who will arrange for her marriage to Sir Ector posthaste, if We are not mistaken."

The king gazed at Richard, understanding and vexation combining to soften his expression as he finished, "It will gain you nothing, Sir Richard, and might well cost you much that is dear to you. Choose, then, quickly, and let Us get on with this matter."

Meg stood next to Richard in crushing agony, knowing that there was no real choice for him in this—both his life and hers hung in the balance either way. Awash with love for him, she waited for his answer, seeing him look away for a moment, and watching the muscle in his temple jump as he clenched his jaw, as distraught as she was over the trap that seemed to have been laid out for them with no means of escape.

At last he glanced to her, devotion for her shadowed by bitter resignation, and her eyes stung with heat as he turned to the king and said lowly, "Very well, sire; I am compelled to agree."

"It is done, then," King Edward said, though his expression remained troubled.

In the silence that cloaked the chamber following his statement, the men involved all stared at one another, with Richard serving as the common target of hostility for de Villeroi and Lord Welton.

"If this affair is concluded, we shall bid you good night, Your Majesty," de Villeroi called tightly at last, readying to leave the chamber with his countrymen.

"Aye, Frère. But remember, you have one week. I will keep Sir Richard confined to quarters here at Tunbridge Castle until a sennight from today, but if you have not produced his opponent for the wager by that time, I will order him freed, make no mistake."

"There will be no mistake, Your Highness," de Villeroi answered, bowing, stiff with condescension, just before he left the chamber with his comrades in tow. "You can be certain of it."

Then, though they clearly objected to it, Lord Welton and Sir Ector were sent out of the solar as well, having no choice but to obey the king's command that they leave him to his peace. When Piers also took the opportunity to bow out, with the excuse that he had been absent from his new wife for too long already, the king was left with none but Richard and Meg in attendance, which was apparently just as the sovereign had intended, Richard realized with surprise as soon as the door closed behind the man and the king spoke.

"We have privacy now to discuss certain details pertaining to the matter just resolved, Sir Richard, Lady Margaret," King Edward said, walking from behind the table and gesturing for them to follow him into the small chapel. As they entered the cooler, dimmer interior of the holy space, he nodded silently back toward the solar room and the guards still holding their posts near the door. "We wish to put forth those details away from ears that might hear and perhaps gossip of them later."

Bowing his head in acknowledgment, Richard murmured his thanks, with the sentiment echoed by Meg as well. They genuflected before the small altar, as did the king, before moving off to the side of it, where Meg and Richard stood

close together but not touching out of courtesy to the king—
though Richard would have liked nothing better than to enfold her in the comfort of his arms at that moment.

Instead he waited patiently for Edward to speak to them,
noting, as he watched the king gazing silently on the can-
dlelit altar and the crucifix affixed to the wall above it, that
Edward looked drained; it would not have been a far reach to
describe him as a man uneasy with the weight of the monar-
chy on his broad shoulders, though he bore it the best that he
could.

At last, with a sigh that seemed to support Richard's musings, Edward twisted from his perusal of the crucifix and
gazed at them with a bittersweet expression on his face and
gentleness in his eyes.

"You love each other; that much is clear. But love alone
cannot govern a kingdom, unfortunately; if it could, you
would be preparing to exchange vows instead of readying to
enter a Wager of Battle in a sennight." He offered them a wan
smile. "And yet to be king gives some privilege of decision,
beyond the realm of what is politically necessary. Not much,
though sufficient, perchance, to make the next week more
bearable for you both."

"Sire . . . ?" Richard asked quietly, uncertain where the
king was leading with his enigmatic words. Meg shifted just
a bit closer to him, enough so that he was able to surreptitiously take her hand, keeping their embrace hidden behind
his leg and the folds of her skirt.

"As part of the agreement, Sir Richard, We promised that
you would be confined to quarters here at Tunbridge, until
the time of the wager."

"Aye. That is understood, Your Majesty."

"What We did not promise is where those quarters would

be, or what freedoms We would allow you in the course of the week to come." King Edward's expression seemed less pensive now, though still serious, as he added, "It is Our intention to see that you are provided with ample opportunity—as much as you desire—to train for the upcoming contest. You will needs be under the watch of guards, but they will not interfere with your training or allow others to do so."

Richard felt Meg give his hand a warm squeeze, even as a rush of thankfulness filled him at the king's consideration. "I appreciate that, Your Majesty, more than you know."

King Edward nodded, still solemn, as he added, "Also, rather than in the barracks with the guards, you will be housed in a small but well-secluded chamber in the western wing of this castle. It is fit out with all that is available for comfort, so that the week ahead should bring no hardship to you." Edward gazed at them both, the full meaning behind his words sinking in as he finished, "It is furnished, in fact, as a wedding chamber might be, were one to consider it so."

Richard heard Meg's slight intake of breath, and felt a kind of tightness in his own chest for a moment. Glancing to her, he saw her beautiful face bathed in the glow of candles that spilled from the altar, alight with a surprise that reflected his own. Looking back at the king, he was forced to clear his throat to say huskily, "I do not know what to say, sire . . ."

"There is no need to say aught," the king replied. He directed the full of his earnest stare upon them, his eyes revealing once more the sensitive nature that more often than not had condemned him in the eyes of his commanding and distant father. "We could not grant the formal union you wished," he said gently, "and yet We can at least grant you

Our blessing, for We believe that you share a truer union of hearts than many a pair even after the fullness of vows have been spoken. Do as you will in the time you have remaining together, for though We trust that right will prevail, it is beyond our power to know for certain what is to come."

"Thank you, Your Majesty," Meg whispered, swallowing hard before she could continue. "You have given us a great gift."

"Love is always a gift, Lady Margaret," the king admitted, his half smile still in place, pensive and knowing. "To be cherished to one's last breath."

After a pause, he offered them a slight nod, finishing, "We will leave you here now, for a few moments of privacy. Know that, although We will not speak again until the day of the reckoning, Our thoughts will be with you. May God in His infinite wisdom grant you both peace until then."

Richard bowed once more and Meg sank to a deep curtsy as the king exited the chapel; after he pulled the door shut behind him, they could hear his muffled commands that they be given a few moments before they would needs be escorted to their chambers, after which their belongings might be moved to the western wing.

And then it was silent.

The tapers flickered softly, and the thick, sweet scent of incense hung in the air, lending the moment a kind of peaceful sanctity. Pulling their clasped hands in front of them, Richard brushed a kiss over Meg's fingers.

"So, lady, here we are . . . left to ourselves at long last."

"Aye," she murmured, looking down at their intertwined hands for a moment before lifting her gaze to meet his in the mellow candle glow.

"In this quiet, holy place . . ." he continued.

"It is peaceful, to be sure," she answered, her expression flickering in her obvious uncertainty over where he was leading with all this.

Richard smiled. "And yet you still have not answered the question I posed to you more than an hour past."

He felt her stiffen slightly and saw the hint of a shadow in her eyes before her lashes swept down to shade them from his sight. "You asked me to marry you," she said huskily.

"That I did. Without response from you, I might add."

She lifted her gaze then, a tiny flare of heat banishing the flickers of darkness. "I was taken by surprise, Richard, as well you know. If you would have the truth of it, I was readying myself to petition the king for permission to take the veil, just before you spoke."

"The veil?" Richard scowled. "You wish to become a *nun*?"

"Not truly, though it is a pure and holy calling." She fixed him with her stare. "But I felt no other choice open to me. By the Rood, do you not know that I have been living in agony these past few days? I believed myself soon to be separated from you forever, while you seemed none the worse for the knowledge. I had resolved to pledge myself to God rather than go on alone in life—or worse yet be compelled to go on as another man's bride."

Richard looked at her, feeling his heart ache anew at the pain and courage he saw in her beautiful eyes. "I am sorry, lady," he murmured, "for the suffering I caused you by not speaking earlier of my intentions."

"Why did you not, then?" she asked. "Why did you let me believe that you were unmoved by the gulf that was yawning between us?"

"In that *I* had no choice, lady, for when I came to your chamber that night at Hawksley, seeking answers to your sudden and seeming change of heart toward me, I promised to refrain from persuading you from your convictions . . . from attempting to influence you in any manner to a different way of thinking." He rubbed his thumb over the smooth silk of her palm. "Do you remember?"

She nodded with a slight frown. "Aye."

"I could not go back on my word." The corners of his mouth lifted a bit. "Not that you would have allowed me to, anyway. I knew that you would not hear me at that moment, and so I resolved to be patient and ask you before the king himself, so that you would understand the strength of my conviction that we belong together."

She flushed. "But do you not understand? I fear what it will mean for you to be bound to me in scandal. And now this Wager of Battle you must fight . . ." A small, helpless sound escaped her throat. "I dread the danger you will suffer, Richard, and it is the result of championing me . . ."

Her voice trailed to a husky sound, and he could see clearly the tears glistening in her eyes as she turned her face away, struggling to hold back her emotions.

He shook his head, his own emotion thick in his chest as he lifted a gentle touch to her chin, guiding her to look at him. "Ah, lady, do *you* not understand?" he murmured hoarsely. "Death is no worse for me than the thought of your absence from my life. There is naught in this world that could keep me from championing you, to my last breath. You are my life, Meg. Naught else matters."

Her beautiful eyes welled anew, though this time a quavering smile struggled to gain hold over the lush curves of her mouth.

"What say you then, Meg? Will you accept my pledge, here and now, to be your husband in my heart, at least until such time as we are allowed to wed in truth, with all of this darkness finally behind us?"

"Aye, Richard, I will," she murmured at last in answer, "and I will offer my troth to you in kind."

With a solemn nod, he gently tugged her toward the place just before the center of the wooden altar, made all the more beautiful for its polished simplicity. Then, grasping both of her hands in his own, he said firmly, "Here, before God, I affirm my love for you, Lady Margaret Newcomb. With all that I am and all that I may be, I pledge myself to you, from this moment until the day of my death. I do so swear it."

Meg's eyes glistened in the soft and flickering light from the tapers on the altar, that same, gentle smile curving her lips as she answered huskily, "And I avow my love for you, Sir Richard de Cantor. There will never be another in my heart, for I give my whole self to you, all that I am, now and forever. I so swear, and seal my promise . . . with this kiss."

Tilting his head down as she lifted her face to meet him, Richard brushed his lips over hers before coming back to savor more deeply, reveling in the sweet, silken heat of her mouth beneath his as they shared a caress of longing and passion, of hope and redemption that nearly brought him to his knees.

And when they parted at long last, he continued to gaze into her eyes, love for her filling him, along with a deep, aching need to make her his completely, in every way. To lavish upon her all that he was feeling . . . to worship her body as fully as he cherished the beauty of her heart.

And he would. This was but a taste of the paradise to come, for though the gates of hellish uncertainty yawned wide before them, they had been granted this precious moment of time together, and he did not plan to squander a single second of it.

"Until tonight then, my love," he said in a voice gone hoarse with emotion, holding her face tenderly cupped in his palm before he pressed another kiss to the smooth and graceful sweep of her brow.

"Until tonight."

Chapter 16

A s darkness fell over the land, a cool autumn wind whistled around the towers of Tunbridge Castle, audible even from inside the rush-lit corridor where Meg was making her way to the end of the western wing. Her heart beat a swift pace as she approached Richard's door—her door as well, until dawn at least, she reminded herself, the thought of it causing a ripple of warmth to spin through her.

As the king had promised, the chamber he'd granted them was very secluded. So private, in fact, that the sentries assigned to Richard were not posted at his door but rather at the end of the corridor twenty paces away; she could see them standing at attention, faces out toward the main hallway as she looked back to them.

Richard was to be left alone each night until sunrise, one of the guards had informed her respectfully, his gaze downcast, when he had come at dusk to the rooms Meg shared with Jane. And so after bidding Jane a quiet good-night, she had allowed the sentry to escort her to this place, continuing down the corridor at his nod.

Now she stood before the door, her palms damp and her skin feeling flushed, despite the chill of impending rain that had settled over the castle. The wind moaned again, a distant keening, and Meg closed her eyes, imagining Richard standing behind this door, waiting by a warm fire for her to arrive. Waiting to consummate their love in a way that she yearned for as much as he.

But there was one thing left to do first.

Lifting her hands to her breast, she touched the heavy silver pendant that had lain there, close to her heart, for almost four years. It had been Alexander's final gift to her, given at exorbitant cost, when he had had little else to offer her but his heart. At the time, Meg had known for but a fortnight that their baby was growing within her, and Alexander had given her the necklace as a promise of his love for them both.

Within a sennight of that, however, her sire had discovered their forbidden alliance and had sent Alexander away to forced service with the Templars. She had not taken the pendant off since. Not through her confinement or news of Alexander's death in battle, not through Madeline's difficult birth, or the years of penance at Bayham Abbey and Hawksley Manor that followed . . . It had never left her since the moment Alexander had slipped it over her head.

But it was time, now.

With a silent, tender prayer in memory of the man and the love that had shaped so much of her life, Meg released her breath slowly, slid her hands up the linked chain to the back of her neck, and lifted the pendant off. It swung in front of her, heavy and still warm from her body, before she dropped it into her palm; then, closing her fingers over it for a final, brief moment, she let it fall into the pocket of her mantle.

Swallowing hard to dissolve the knot that seemed to have formed in her throat, Meg lifted her chin before scratching on the door in front of her, almost at the same time pushing it open to step across the threshold of the darkened chamber.

"You are here at last."

"Aye, Richard," she answered in response to his husky murmur. "It is where I have longed to be all day."

Her gaze traced the direction of his voice, and she caught sight of him standing, half hidden, in the shadows between the blazing hearth and a tapered window that allowed the light of the moon to spill across the floor in a narrow, milky ribbon.

Neither spoke further for the moment as she let the door swing shut behind her, the action plunging the room into shadows again, except for the glow from the hearth and the wash of light coming through the costly glazed pane.

"Will you come closer, lady?" he invited at last in low entreaty. "Toward the fire, that I may see you . . . and touch you, in time."

His words strummed at Meg's heart, making her shiver with pleasure, and she took a step closer, and another, until she stood directly before the hearth. The heat of the low-burning blaze billowed forth in tantalizing contrast to the slight chill of the rest of the chamber, causing another delicate shiver to sweep over her flesh.

Richard remained off to the side, still hidden, though his gaze seemed to scorch her through the veil of darkness that separated them; he stared at her, heavy-lidded, his eyes more beautiful to her now even than they had been that first day, when she had gazed at him and been lost in their green and gold depths.

Her breath ceased for a moment, then quickened, as he suddenly stepped into the light, walking until he stood a mere palm's breadth away, still looking at her, but not touching. Nay, not yet. The shadows and flickering glow of the fire played off his features, allowing her to see him for an instant before casting his face into shadow again.

As she gazed up at him, the delectable tightness in her belly intensified, anticipation heightening her pleasure. It was the same wonderful tension she'd felt winding through her time and again with him at Hawksley, only with the increased awareness of what they would be doing this night at long last . . . of the tantalizing way he would satisfy the craving that consumed her.

Soon she would feel his arms around her; she would feel his body pressed to hers, her mouth ravished by his; she would know the sweetness of tangling her hands in the thick, silken waves of his hair.

Soon . . .

"Ah, lady, you are so beautiful," he whispered, his gaze caressing her and setting her flesh to tingling by his look alone.

Reaching out at last, he took one of her hands into his own; she tried to will her fingers to stop trembling as he raised her palm to his lips, brushing his mouth over the sensitive flesh there so lightly, so gently, that the tingling began to spread up from her hand, building to a swell of tormenting warmth that pooled low in her belly.

"Do you have any idea what you do to me, Meg?" he said, going quiet and still in the intimate silence that surrounded them. "Do you know how much I want you right now?"

"If it is aught like the way I feel for you, Richard, then,

aye, I do," she managed to breathe, her throat tight with feeling—with passion and overwhelming love for him.

Reaching out with his other hand, he pulled her toward him, at last wrapping her in his embrace; moist heat prickled at the backs of her eyes as she soaked in the sensations flooding her with his touch, feeling the whispering brush of his lips at her temple.

"I love you, lady," he murmured into her hair as his strong, warm hands traveled the length of her spine. "And I wish to show you how much, as fully and completely as I am able . . ."

He shifted, and she felt the hard length of his erection against her belly. Gasping, she swayed against him in response.

". . . and as oft, too—though that may prove easier to accomplish than the first, considering how long it has been for me," he finished on a low note, his words laced with a smile she could not see until he pulled back enough to gaze into her eyes once more. Then he cupped her face in the palms of his hands, tipping his head forward to press soft kisses to her brow, her nose, and her cheeks as she smiled in return and lifted her lips to his, meeting his mouth in slanted, hungry passion that left her breathless.

Another gasp escaped her as he suddenly rocked his hips forward, his hard thigh slipping between her legs in relentless demand against the tender flesh there. Pleasure jolted through her, hot and sweet, and she heard herself calling his name on a breath, felt his whispered murmurs against her throat as he threaded one hand through her hair, loosening it from the jeweled circlet and sheer netting that confined it.

As if in the midst of some sensual dream, she felt her head grow heavy; he cradled it in his palm, tilting to the side and kissing along the exposed length of her neck. At the same time, his other hand slipped down behind her back to curve warmly over her bottom and pull her more fully into him, his leg nudging hers wider apart, both of them still clothed as he stroked her rhythmically against the muscular span of his thigh.

She was powerless to prevent the low moan that escaped her then, her own legs tightening at the shock of erotic friction that pulsed through her. Thick, molten desire spooled in waves so intense that she was compelled to cling to Richard's arms, her fingers digging into his shirt, to keep herself from sinking to the floor. Only a few moments more of this delicious torture, she knew, and he would bring her to completion here and now.

"Richard, I . . . oh, yes . . . oh," her words came out in an incoherent murmur, "please, it is just that . . ."

"Hush, now love," he whispered against the tender spot just below her right ear, still rocking her relentlessly, erotically against him. "Allow yourself to feel the beauty of this . . . to know but a hint of the joy I long to give you."

Her fingers clenched tighter, curling into his shoulders as the sensations swelled, and she moaned again, pulled along helplessly on the tide of it in swift, heated jolts. The lapping waves of pleasure crested higher, coming harder and faster, until they converged in a blinding rush . . .

With a cry, Meg arched back as a powerful release rippled through her, sapping all the power from her limbs. She would have collapsed to the floor but for Richard's hold on her; he whispered words of love, passionate murmurs that penetrated the haze of pleasure enveloping her.

She felt him sweep her up into his arms then, carrying her to the thickly curtained bed before laying her down gently there. When she was able to open her eyes, his face blurred in the rush of emotion overwhelming her. Somehow she smiled at him through her tears, her love for him so great that the ache of it settled in her chest, just at the base of her throat, preventing her from speaking a single word of what she was feeling to him.

But he could see it in her eyes; she knew he could, for he was lying on his side, his head resting on one hand, and he smiled down at her as well—a slow, sensual smile—that sent curls of heat winding through her again, even through the lingering warmth of her completion.

"If you enjoyed that only half as much as I did, then I will have cause to rejoice," he said softly, reaching out to touch the tip of her nose with his finger.

"Oh, aye," she finally managed to say, "and yet I believe I shall enjoy even more giving you the same pleasure in return."

As she spoke, she slid her hand over the taut expanse of his belly, finally letting her palm brush lower to tease the burning, hard length of him that strained beneath his breeches. His entire body tightened at her touch, and he groaned, though he allowed her to caress him so only for a moment before he gripped her wrist, pulling her hand up to his chest as he curled up to a sitting position.

"Why do you wish me to stop?" she asked softly, sitting up next to him.

He jabbed his hand through his hair with a shaky laugh, meeting her gaze. "I do not wish you to stop, believe me, Meg. But it has been six years for me, and your touch felt far too wonderful, I am afraid, for me to endure in my current state without spending."

"And why would that be such a terrible thing?"

Brushing his fingers in a sweeping caress of her cheekbone, he smiled again, softly, tenderly, his gaze never leaving her face as he murmured, "Because I want to be buried deep inside of you, then—and we have far more to experience and enjoy together before I can allow myself that bliss."

"Oh." Meg swallowed hard, unable to pull her stare from him and the pure sensuality of his expression, squirming a bit in response to the pleasure blooming anew inside of her.

"And yet this bed is not the place I would undertake that with you . . . at least not right now. It is too drafty and dark here than is meet for our intents, don't you think?" he asked, even as his smile shifted into something more intense. His gaze skimmed the curve of her mouth before lifting to her eyes again, the heat exuding from his stare almost palpable, she thought, for the way it left delicious little bursts of warmth in its wake.

In the end she could offer only a weak nod of agreement, her power of speech having vanished again under the sweep of desire filling her.

"Come then," he whispered, tugging her to stand; his gaze drifted toward the center of the room, almost midway between the bed and the hearth, and he led her away from the bed in that direction.

"Where are we going?" she managed to ask, though her voice was little more than a husky shadow of itself.

"Not far." He brought her to a gentle stop when she stood directly in the ribbon of moonlight, turning her to face the exquisite glazed window as he took up a position flush behind her. "In fact right here should be perfect," he whispered against her ear, the moist heat of his breath sending another trail of shivers down her arms.

"But I cannot see you like this, Richard—and that does not seem fair in the least."

Her throaty teasing invoked just the response she had hoped for; he chuckled lowly, brushing the scented weight of her hair away from her neck to press several delicious kisses along the tender skin exposed there. She closed her eyes and swayed back against him as he continued that sensual assault, reveling in the strength of his arms as he wrapped them around her from behind.

"Never fear, my love," he said between kisses, "you shall have your satisfaction in that . . . though I confess that I shall have mine first, for I cannot wait a moment longer."

Any response she might have considered making faded under a new rush of sensation as he slid both hands from her shoulders down the length of her arms, his touch warming her skin through the sleeves of her fitted kirtle, leaving a tantalizing trail of heat. When he reached her hands, he threaded his fingers with hers and lifted, guiding her arms up until she was touching the back of his neck, resting the weight of her hands there so that she could feel the silken texture of his hair with her fingertips. She stood in front of him in that position, with her back arched slightly, with her head leaning against his chest . . .

And then he swept his touch down in a gentle stroke to her hips, before gliding back up to her belly and over her ribs, continuing that burning path to slip beneath the edges of the sideless surcoat she wore over her kirtle . . . finally sweeping up to cup her breasts in the warm cradle of his palms. She sucked in her breath, unable to keep herself from arching more fully into his hands as he plucked at the hardened peaks of her nipples through the thin layer of fabric that covered them.

"I would see you now in truth, Meg, as I have seen you in my dreams for so long," he whispered, ceasing his play only to help her slip the surcoat off her shoulders, letting it fall to the floor. Then his long and elegant fingers went to work at undoing the row of tiny, tight buttons down the front of her kirtle, and upon reaching the top of her ribs, tugging open the edges of the garment enough to allow him access to the bounty of flesh beneath.

With a low moan, Meg lowered her hands from behind his neck, helping him to slide the bodice down to the tops of her arms, the act baring her breasts like offerings to him in the pearly moonlight. He pressed kisses along her shoulders and up her neck, creating a new flood of tingles that tightened her exposed nipples to aching buds, making her long for nothing so much as to feel the soothing, erotic warmth of his palms cupping her again, this time with no barrier of cloth between them. But he made her wait, teasing her as he stroked all around them with feather-light caresses, while never actually touching the place that yearned for him most.

"You are exquisite, Meg," he whispered as he shifted around in front of her, casting her into shadow for an instant before he sank to his knees on the floor in front of her.

Then, with the moonlight spilling over her once again, he finally gave her what she craved, his hands coming up to cup and worship her breasts, followed swiftly by the wet heat of his mouth, suckling her, driving her mad with the desire his flicking tongue sent spiraling through her. She threaded her fingers into his hair, arching back helplessly again with another cry of torment and pleasure as he tasted of her, lavishing his full attention first on one nipple, then the other.

His hands slipped down along her ribs as he continued to work the sorcery of his mouth on her, tugging at the bunched cloth of her kirtle in an effort to pull it the rest of the way down her arms and off over her hips. It took Meg a few seconds before that realization managed to pierce the fog of sensation he'd woven around her, but when it did, she stiffened, pulling back a little and tightening her hands so that he stopped his kissing and looked up at her, his eyes shadowed in the moonlight and so achingly beautiful that her breath caught in her throat.

"What is it, love?" he murmured hoarsely, ceasing the gentle, stroking movements of his hands.

Familiar heat rose in her cheeks, winding through her and flooding her with self-conscious anxiety. "I—I think it would be better to move back to the bed now, Richard," she said, glancing away from his gaze in embarrassment.

"Are you chilled, then?" he asked in concern. "I had thought it would be warm enough here before the fire."

"Nay, I am not chilled," she answered, doing her best to offer him a smile of reassurance. "But shadows will be far more forgiving than moonlight, I think."

He continued to look at her, his expression serious but still unknowing, and so she cupped his face in her hands, adding softly, "My body bears all the imperfections of having carried a child, Richard, and I would not have your pleasure marred by that truth, if I can help it."

What she was saying took a moment to sink in, apparently, for Richard remained unmoving in front of her for several breaths, before he suddenly closed his eyes and lowered his face as if absorbing the shock of some kind of blow. Meg stood rooted to the spot, feeling stunned by the possibility that it was so difficult for him to accept the reality of her past after all they had endured together. The hurt of it stabbed through her, throbbing and painful, and gathering her wits, she tried to take a step back, only to be forestalled by Richard tightening his grip on the folds of fabric at her waist.

He lifted his gaze to her again, then, and with an icy-hot jolt, she realized that she had been wrong . . . oh, so wrong to have thought he'd reacted with reproach to her. His eyes were somber and full of such exquisite tenderness and passion— such love for her—that she was forced to blink back the stinging warmth that rose behind her own eyes.

"Ah, lady," he murmured, his voice barely audible for the emotion that roughened it, "do you not know that you are perfection to me in all that you are . . . in *all* that you are, do you understand? Naught could mar my pleasure in loving you, now or ever, sweet Meg, except your absence from me. Naught else," he asserted hoarsely, his gaze piercing hers, "for in that alone would I be destroyed."

As he spoke, he gently tugged at her gown, pulling her arms free and easing the whole of it down past her hips so that it finally fell, pooling at her feet with a swishing sound.

She stood naked before him, her body bathed in the milky moonlight and her vision blurring with silent tears as he lifted his hands, so strong and yet so tender, to the gentle swell of her belly. She closed her eyes then, choking back a muffled sob as he stroked his fingers over the tiny, raised marks that spread outward in a circle from that once smooth expanse . . . clinging to his shoulders under the force of fierce, rushing emotion, as he brushed his lips over those only remaining signs of the babe that she had once loved and sheltered within her body.

"Oh, Richard, I love you so," she whispered raggedly, her hands threaded through his hair, holding him close as he pressed his cheek to the place he had been kissing.

His arms wrapped around her hips, the warm strength of his hand splayed over the small of her back, stroking up her spine in a delicious ascent until he stood to face her again. He

pulled her close in his embrace, his voice nearly breaking as
he murmured, "And I love you, Meg—my God, but I love
you, more than I ever thought it was possible to love anyone."

He lifted his hands to her face, and his fingers trembled as
he tucked a tendril of hair behind her ear, following that caress with another brush of his lips to her temple and cheek
before he took her mouth in the fullness of his passion again.
Need pounded through him, hard and sweet, and he reveled
in the sensation of her hands pulling at his clothing, helping
him to remove his garments as well now, so that they both
stood in the swirling blend of heat and chill, naked in each
other's arms.

Then he simply stood there, holding her for a long moment,
breathing in the lushly floral scent of her hair and allowing
himself to soak in the incredible sensation of her body pressed
to his. All was silent but for the quiet popping of the hearth
logs, that sound intensified with every gust of wind that rattled
at the glazed pane and swept a bracing draft down the chimney. Of a sudden, a light pattering noise began, increasing in
force while the moon dimmed behind clouds blown across it.

"The storm has finally arrived," Meg said softly into his
shoulder, her breath a warm caress against his flesh.

"Aye, but we are safe from it here in our haven from the
world."

"I wish we could remain so forever," she whispered, her
voice catching, and Richard's heart twisted, knowing what
she truly meant with her seemingly simple words.

"As do I, my love," he murmured, stroking his hands over
her hair and pressing a kiss to the top of her head. "And yet
the gift of this night is all we need think of right now . . . the
gift of you here in my arms is all that I see. My love for you
consumes me, blocking out all else, for I will it to be so."

Meg gazed up at him, the unrest in her expression dissipating under the force of a yearning that shone clear in her gentle, dark eyes. "I will it too, then, Richard. Help me to push away my fear." Her beautiful face was vulnerable with the emotions she seemed to be struggling to keep in control. "Make love to me now," she said huskily, "and drive away all else but the knowledge of what is true and sacred between us."

"Aye, lady," he answered on a ragged breath, lifting her into his arms so that her legs opened to cradle his waist; then carrying her the few steps to the bed, he laid her against the coverlet, never breaking contact with her as he shifted his hips and positioned the tip of his hard length against her, quaking with the strength of will it took to hold back for another moment as she arched up, seeking, wanting the completion of their joining.

"Know that I love you, Meg," he whispered, locking his impassioned gaze with hers and seeing all that he felt reflected in the depths of her eyes. "Nothing will ever have the power to change that . . . not even eternity."

And as she uttered a sound of pleasure that was a gasp and a sob all at once, he rocked forward in one swift motion, sheathing himself to the hilt within her sleek, hot embrace, though he was forced in the next instant to awestruck immobility at the sensation, so incredible that his vision dimmed with a flash of stars. Uttering a groan of surrender, he pulled back again, sliding almost free before rocking home once more, loving her with sweet, full, and glorious thrusts, over and over, while she lifted her hips to meet him.

Through the haze of ecstasy mounting inside him, he heard her murmuring his name, saw her face contorting with the power of what he too was feeling; he stiffened, his thrusts growing shorter and more intense, sensing the oncoming rush of completion and yet yearning desperately to hold back until Meg could reach that glorious peak with him.

And then she cried out, her fingers gripping his shoulders as she arched into him, her sheath clenching in strong, rhythmic ripples around him, the sensation tilting him over the edge of bliss himself.

He thrust once more, feeling the almost unbearable rush of release as he spilled into her, uttering her name like a prayer . . . in that blessed act of love finally releasing all the pain and darkness that had been haunting him for more than half his lifetime.

Just before daybreak, Richard eased out of bed, careful not to disturb Meg. She had succumbed to slumber at long last, and he was loath to awaken her. They had made love twice more during the night, each time more slowly and thoroughly, until both were so exhausted and replete with what they had shared that sleep had been the only possibility left to them.

But the peace of that satiety had not lasted long for Richard; he had startled to awareness some half hour ago, his mind twisting with dark thoughts of all that might come to pass once the sweet reprieve of the week ahead had ticked away.

Padding over to the glazed window in the predawn stillness, he looked out, able to see through the mantle of darkness still covering the world that the sun was readying to burst forth at the horizon. A thin line of gold shimmered beneath the duller gray of clouds there, signifying the approach of day—and with that dawning would begin the true test of his will, he knew, leading to the battle he would be compelled to engage in with an as-yet faceless opponent. For though he had managed to keep from showing his apprehension to Meg last night, it churned in his belly nonetheless, a great, caged lion scraping his insides with jagged claws.

It wasn't fear for himself. Nay, he had made peace with the transience of his life as a warrior and Templar Knight long ago. This was rather a bone-deep dread over what would happen to Meg if he was defeated by the Inquisition's champion. He had sent word to Braedan already, informing him of yesterday's events and urging his haste to Tunbridge. But he knew that Braedan's presence, whether in helping him train for the upcoming battle or in serving as a support for Meg, was a temporary solution at best.

The hard truth was that if he failed in the contest to come, there was little Braedan would be able to do to keep Meg safe. The king would give her back into Lord Welton's control, to be gifted in perverse payment to Sir Ector . . . and it was that thought alone that tormented Richard endlessly, depriving him of rest and nearly of reason. He had no desire to lose his life; such a fact was undeniable, and yet the thought of dying held little power over him compared to the panic of knowing that Meg might be abandoned to such a terrible fate in the wake of his defeat.

Glancing back to where she slept, her face peaceful and her beauty of soul and form so vivid that it made his stomach clench, Richard breathed in deeply, resigned to undertake what he needed to do.

He would work harder than he ever had to hone his weaponry skills during this week the king had granted him. He would love Meg with all the passion in his soul, even as he prepared to resume the cloak of brutal instinct—the razor-sharp outlook that would allow him to strike at his opponent as he had done in every battle fought in all his years as an elite Templar Knight: With intent to do nothing less than kill.

He would set his mind to the task with cold-blooded precision, erasing from his heart any shadow of regret or mercy. The man he faced a week hence would need to die at his hand, regardless of all else. With what was hanging in the balance, Richard knew he had no real choice in the matter . . .

Because the alternative for the woman he loved was impossible for him even to contemplate.

Chapter 17

The day of the battle burned clear and cold, in contrast to the heavy rains that had fallen during the entire week prior to it. At dawn, early morning haze had blanketed the golden brown fields and stretches of forest surrounding Tunbridge, clinging to the branches of trees in swaths of lacy mist.

It would have been beautiful, Meg had thought, if it had been any day but this.

She and Richard had not said much in those early morning hours; instead they'd made love, slowly and tenderly, and with so much bittersweet passion that it had been all Meg could do not to weep. She had held back for Richard's sake as much as her own, wanting to make their time last . . . needing to push away the harsh reality of what was to come for as long as was possible.

But no one could stop time, and the day with all its fears had intruded soon enough. As Richard had completed his

316

morning ablutions, she had stood at the delicate leaded glass window that had witnessed their first tender lovemaking, looking out at the misty beauty spread out before her and choking back her dread.

Too soon, it seemed, the guards had come for him. She'd held firm through the final brush of his lips across hers, followed by his murmur of farewell. She had even managed an encouraging smile for him, a vision of bravery to go along with her whispered wish for Godspeed and the promise to be with him in witness of the battle, when it was time.

And then he had been gone.

She had been left standing here in the place that had known the fullness of their passion, feeling lost and alone without him—praying with all she possessed that she wouldn't be left without him forever, when this was all over.

Rising from her knees almost an hour later, she brushed her fingers beneath her eyes. Braedan would be coming soon to be by her side during the span of the wager; she wouldn't have him thinking her too cowardly to endure what lay ahead for Richard's sake. When a scratching sounded at the door, Meg crossed to open it, murmuring one last prayer for strength to see this day through as she prepared to make her way with Richard's brother to the expansive arms chamber of Tunbridge Castle, the place that would provide the backdrop for the trial this day of the man she loved—and because of that, her trial as well.

Richard stood in the middle of the wide, dirt-floored arms and training chamber, facing the line of French Inquisitors and clerics; they were flanked by several English priests and a bishop on one side, and King Edward and Piers Gaveston on the other. He felt calm, somehow—perhaps resigned was a better word for it—as he waited for his Wager of Battle to begin.

By law it needed to be started before the sun reached its zenith and would be over by sunset, with the man left standing proclaimed as victor. However, he doubted it would last even half that time, since the Inquisition had seen fit, at the king's insistence, to forgo the usual quarterstaffs that were traditionally used for weapons in such contests of old; instead, the battle would be fought with the combatants' own swords. Death or injury severe enough to end the wager was far more likely to be delivered with a blade—a prospect far preferable to being bludgeoned to death in a long and bloody match with thick wooden staffs.

He glanced behind himself, toward the large gathering of people who had assembled in witness of the wager. Avoiding any eye contact with Lord Welton or Sir Ector, who stood at the far right of the crowd, Richard instead met Meg's gaze for an instant. Love swept through him at the mere sight of her. She was frightened over what was to come, he knew, but she had not allowed it to show in her efforts to make this more bearable for him; her eyes were dry and her back was straight. She would be strong for his sake, and the realization underscored his resolve to complete what must be done as quickly and effectively as he was able.

Braedan stood next to her, his expression solemn. He offered Richard a nod of encouragement, his presence another boost of strength to get him through this ordeal; Richard remembered another day and another trial, almost fifteen years ago, when Braedan had stood by him as well, awaiting verdict against him in their uncle's death. Not much had changed in all this time, it seemed, Richard thought wryly, as he nodded back in grateful acknowledgment of his brother's support.

Then he turned back to face those who would judge the Wager of Battle, trying to stem his unrest. For though he itched to grip the sword that once more hung with its familiar weight at his hip, yearning to get this over with, he could not take any action until his opponent arrived to face him on this field.

All he could do was to wait.

"What is taking so long?" Meg whispered to Braedan, unable to keep the edge of fear from her voice.

"The Inquisition's champion has not yet made his appearance, it seems—although I was certain that I saw evidence of his arrival at Tunbridge last night. Two of the Inquisitors sitting at the table over there," he continued, jerking his chin in the direction of the French contingent, "were down in the stables with several of the king's guards near dusk; three men had just ridden through the gates—two French guards and a third man, who was cloaked so that I could see little but the fact that he was tall and well-muscled."

"You think the third man is the Inquisition's champion, then?" Meg asked, frowning.

"Perhaps." Braedan nodded, keeping his gaze on Richard where he stood waiting. "Aside from his stature, he was mounted upon a war steed, by all appearances—a fine gelding of the kind I saw more oft than not when I served in the Crusades."

The unsettled feeling that had plagued Meg all week deepened, and she glanced to Richard's brother. "It seems odd that the Inquisitors would send for a champion who needed to be delivered under guard."

"I was thinking the same thing."

Braedan looked to the door at the right of the chamber, where Richard had entered and where the guards stood posted to escort in the Inquisition's man, and Meg followed his gaze. All was quiet there, but it was clear from the dark looks and murmured sounds of argument coming from the front table of judges that something was amiss.

"I wonder . . ." Braedan began, but he could not finish his thought, because at that moment, King Edward pushed himself to his feet, his expression tight with annoyance.

"Let Us begin the formalities, at least, so that we may proceed with the Wager of Battle once the French champion deigns to make his appearance in this chamber."

"Very well," Frère de Villeroi intoned; he was wearing the full robes of his position as head of the French Inquisition, and now he stood, facing the gathering of witnesses, before shifting his stony stare to Richard.

"Sir Richard de Cantor, you are offered one final opportunity to disavow the Templar Brotherhood for the sinful profanations committed by its members . . . spitting on the Cross during secret initiations, engaging in the foul practice of sodomy, and taking oaths against Christ's divinity. Confess to these heresies before us and these witnesses—repent and find yourself released from the Wager of Battle that has been levied against thee. What say you?"

Meg kept her gaze fixed on Richard, seeing the muscles of his powerful back stiffen as the charges were read, and feeling, though she could not see his expression, the smoldering anger that the Inquisitor's words unleashed in him.

His fist clenched at his sides, and she saw him breathe in deeply, before he called out in a strong, clear voice, "I reject the charges brought against me and the entire Templar order,

Frère, refuting in the harshest terms the allegations put forth. The Brotherhood is innocent of heresy, its members suffering the degradation of arrest and foul torture as a result of naught but the fear and greed of your sovereign, Phillipe the Fair, the king of France!"

Richard's pronouncement set off a series of gasps and exclamations in the chamber, and Meg watched, her stomach knotted with anxiety, as Frère de Villeroi paled, his face sharpening with malevolence as he directed his stare at Richard.

"As you wish," de Villeroi ground out, his mouth so tight that his jaw seemed almost not to move as he spoke. "You have consigned your soul to hell this day, of your own free will." Jerking his head toward the entrance to the chamber, he snapped, "Bring forth our champion!"

Meg felt Braedan's arm tighten around her with the pronouncement, and now she reached up, gripping his hand in a rush of dread. The man walking through that door in the next moment would be the embodiment of her worst nightmare, she knew, for his sole purpose in being here was to kill the man she loved.

Her heart pounded, and nausea nearly overwhelmed her as she fought back against the instincts that clamored for her to run out to the fighting arena and pull Richard away. To keep him safe from the danger he was about to face. Sick with terror, she watched him turn toward the entrance, saw his face in profile as he waited for his opponent to enter, his jaw tight with resolve and his posture showing no fear.

Taking a deep breath, Meg tried to stem her hysteria, tried to convince herself that if she could just remain calm and strong, the French defender would appear, and with him the realization that he was only a man like any other—a man that

Richard, with his finely honed skills as one of the most elite of the Templar Knights, had a good chance of defeating.

But in the next instant she realized that she'd been terribly, horribly mistaken.

The unknown champion strode through the door, his cape billowing behind him, and Meg felt as if a dagger had slid with cold precision straight through her own heart.

"Alex?" Richard said in disbelief, his face going slack with shock.

She saw the warrior meet Richard's gaze, watched both men recoil from each other, almost identical expressions of stunned incredulity on their faces. But it all entered her awareness through some kind of hazy distance, her mind numb with the truth that had been placed before her with such painful clarity.

This was no faceless stranger. She *knew* this man. Sweet Jesu in heaven it could not be . . . it could not, it could not, it could not . . .

"Alexander?"

She hardly realized that she'd said his name aloud, until he stiffened and looked toward her, slowly, precisely, like a man turning to face his doom. And then his gaze connected with hers, the force of recognition slamming into her, sucking the air from her lungs. Frantically she wrenched her gaze away to look at Richard, brushing off Braedan's comforting support and stumbling toward the two men, the pain and horror of this all sweeping over her in an overwhelming rush.

Sir Alexander de Ashby stood before her . . . the man for whom she had forsaken her whole life so many years ago. The man who had fathered her child and then vanished into eternity. But he was not dead. Nay, he was very much alive— he was here, prepared to do battle with Richard. To try to *kill* him, by heaven . . . to destroy the wonderful, compassionate, vibrant man she had come to love more than her own breath.

It was too much to bear. For the first time in her life, her strength failed her, and as she took another two steps toward them, the deafening silence in the chamber suddenly filled with a strange buzzing sound, like the approach of a massive swarm of bees, even as thick black shadows began to converge on her vision; she felt her knees giving out beneath her, her last conscious sight that of Richard's face, his beautiful gaze full upon her, his expression crowded with shock, sadness, and the agony of bitter realization.

And then she slipped into sweet, blessed darkness.

Chapter 18

⁓◯◯⁓

When awareness returned some minutes later, Meg had found herself in the small bedchamber she had been given upon her arrival to Tunbridge, with both Jane and Braedan tending to her. But, frantic to see Richard, she had sent Braedan out to plead her case to the king, who, he told her, had called a postponement to the combat and retired to his solar with the French Inquisitors and their champion in an effort to try to sort out what had just happened.

Braedan had returned less than an hour later, his face grim, but with the news that he had managed to use what little influence he had as a king's justice to secure for her a few moments of privacy with Richard.

Now she stood outside the chamber where Richard had been placed under heavy guard to await the king's decision. At her nod, the sentries stepped aside, allowing her access, and she crossed the threshold, hearing them close and bolt the door firmly behind her.

And then all else fled from her thoughts but the yearning to see Richard . . . to touch him and hold him, to tell him how much she loved him. He'd turned at the sound of her entry, and now she ran into his arms, unable to keep back a muffled sob as she buried her face in his neck, hugging him tightly to her.

"Hush, Meg, it is all right," he murmured, pulling back enough to touch her cheek gently. But though it was clear that he tried to conceal it from her, the strain of what had happened weighed heavy in his eyes, grief and worry tightening his expression.

"I—I cannot believe it, Richard," she said.

"Nor I, lady," he answered quietly. "In truth, I am at a loss." His voice was thick with frustration and some other emotion she couldn't quite discern; it called up a flare of unease in her, but she tried to suppress it, attributing it to the upset of what they had endured already.

But her concern swelled again, followed by a wave of hurt, when he suddenly released her, moving away a few paces to the window—not a costly, glazed pane as had graced the chamber the king had granted them use of, but a plain, carved opening, protected by a wooden shutter. It was not like Richard to pull away from her, not for anything. They had always faced trouble together, come what may. But he was pushing her away now, and the knowledge of it was difficult to bear.

Still, loath to add to the burdens he already bore, Meg swallowed her pain to ask, "Do you have any idea what you will do, then?"

He shook his head, still looking out the window as he answered, "I must await the king's decision, that much is clear. Pray God he will choose to postpone the Wager of Battle until another champion can be found. For if he does not . . ."

His words trailed off, and he shook his head again, swallowing hard, she saw, against the force of the emotion gripping him.

"It is a fine mess, is it not, Meg?" he asked her at last, his tone tinged with irony as he turned to look at her again, offering a half smile. "Even were the man I am supposed to kill in proof of my innocence not one of my closest friends—a fellow Templar, for whose sake I spilled blood many times over—he is still the man you first loved, resurrected from seeming death and placed before me now in a perverse mockery of fate." A rusty laugh escaped him, and he gazed at her, agony clear in his expressive eyes. "If Alex and I are forced to do battle against each other, I am doomed, regardless of whether I win or lose."

As he spoke, Meg went very still, what he'd said cutting to the heart of her and making her start in surprise. *He is still the man you first loved . . .*

His comment repeated itself in her mind, and she stepped toward him, realization dawning and making her understand the distance he had been placing between them since she'd come to find him here.

"Richard," she murmured after a long pause, seeking his gaze, "you know, do you not, that there is naught I fear in all of this, except what I have always feared—the possibility that you might be hurt in the conflict to come. That Alexander is the one man out of all the Inquisition could have chosen for you to fight"—she shook her head and exhaled with a shaky sound of disbelief—"that he is *not* dead, and that he was one of the friends with whom you escaped France—all of it is a terrible shock, there is no doubt. But it changes nothing, do you understand? Nothing."

Now it was Richard's turn to go still, what she'd said finally penetrating his thoughts, it seemed, so that he twisted away from the window to meet her gaze, his expression so vulnerable and yet so wary that it wrenched her heart.

"What are you saying, Meg?" he asked quietly. "Alex is the man you first loved, the man for whom you once were willing to give up your whole life. A man you thought was *dead*, by the Rood, returned to you whole and strong. Can you forsake him now, as if naught ever passed between you?"

"Nay," she murmured, never taking her gaze from Richard's. "I cannot pretend that we shared nothing together, and in truth I hope to speak with him in privacy before this day is past, but for no other reason than to close those old doors between us and to ask him to withdraw from this madness of combat. To ask him, for all we once were to each other, to refuse the Inquisition's command that he enter into battle against the man I love. For that man is *you*, Richard. I love you with all that I am, and no one could ever change that."

He seemed stunned for a moment, though his expression was still guarded as he murmured, "Not even the man who fathered your child?"

"Nay, not even that," Meg answered, stepping close enough to touch him, reaching her fingertips to brush along his cheek and the strong sweep of his jaw, and feeling love rush through her anew as he closed his eyes and tilted his head into her hand. "Alexander is part of my past, Richard," she said. "You are my present—and my future."

"Ah, thank God, lady," he said gruffly, pulling her at last into a fierce embrace . . . pressing his lips to her hair, and taking in a breath like a man who had been very near to drowning. "I feared that I had lost you, even before any battle was waged."

"Nay, Richard, that could never happen," she said, smiling through the blurring heat that swelled in her eyes; her love for him drove away all but the sweetness of being here in his arms. Looking up into his eyes, she pressed a kiss of longing, a kiss of promise to his lips, reveling in the beauty of what they shared together before she pulled back to meet his gaze again in utter seriousness.

"And that is why I must beg a promise from you."

"You know that if it is in my power, I will do anything you ask of me."

"It is in your power, I think, but it will demand much of you—more than I would ever ask, were the circumstances we face not so dire."

She met his gaze directly, with all the force of what she felt for him behind it, so that he would know she was in earnest. "Richard, I want you to promise me that if I am not successful in persuading Alexander to withdraw from your Wager of Battle, you will do what you must, no matter the cost, to be victorious against him." She cupped his face in her hands again, blinking back her tears as she repeated softly, "No matter the cost, Richard, so long as you are safe in my arms again when it is over. Promise me."

She knew what she was asking of him.

Alex had been her first love, and the thought of what this might mean for him had filled her with turmoil this past hour. But she also knew that as painful as it was, there was no other real choice. She loved Richard with her whole heart and soul, and she could not bear the thought of losing him now.

Richard had paused, his own struggle clear and heart-breaking to see. But in the end he just jerked his head in a single nod, his eyes shadowed with the terrible weight of his decision.

"Aye, lady, I will undertake what needs to be done, no matter the cost. I give you my promise."

In the end, Meg had been granted little time to attempt any change in the course of the morning's disaster. After she left Richard's chamber, Braedan had informed her that the wager would indeed be played out within the hour, with Alexander and Richard facing each other, regardless of their former camaraderie or the strain that they, who had only ever fought side by side, would surely know in taking up swords against each other.

God's will would prevail in providing a victor, Frère de Villeroi had insisted, over the protests of King Edward and the body of English clerics who had stepped forward to voice their dismay at the turn the proceeding had taken. But the lead Inquisitor had been firm: They had gone through great trouble to bring to England a champion skilled enough to hold his own against a renowned Templar Knight of the highest order, and they would not alter their course now.

Any effort on King Edward's part to forestall the battle further would be construed as an insult to the French throne and would call into jeopardy the alliance being formed between the two countries through King Edward's upcoming marriage to Philip's daughter, Isabel.

And so it had been settled. It remained only for the moment of doom to arrive.

Meg had not been allowed to see Richard again in the interim, though she'd learned to her relief that he was not alone, but rather surrounded in his chamber by several English priests, good and holy men, who, upon the king's decision to go forth with the impending battle, had joined together to offer a Mass for Richard and tender the blessing of confession to him, to protect his soul in the event of defeat.

Alexander had already received that unction from the French prelates, she had been told; he'd been sent shortly after to the much smaller arms chamber adjoining the larger room where the battle would be waged—a mere entryway, really—to await its advent. And so with Braedan's help and a few more coins for bribes, Meg had found herself at the portal of that tiny chamber, steeling herself to face the man she had once loved, with a plea for the man she knew she could not live without.

"I wondered if you would come to me."

Alexander's low-spoken tones echoed in the silence; the much lighter guard placed with him had moved out of earshot with the encouragement of the coin, and now a perfect hush enveloped the area. The room was bare, except for a small table with benches and a large wooden chest. The entire space was less than ten paces across . . . far too small to pretend she had not heard him. And far too small to avoid the strangeness of standing so close to him again, after all the years and heartache that had come between.

"We must talk, Alexander," she answered, her fingers threading tightly together as she willed herself to be strong through this. Not to think of what was at stake, or to allow her intent to be clouded by old and tender memories.

He turned to face her, a physically powerful, striking man, with rich, dark hair and eyes of deep blue . . . a man she had once loved desperately. To her relief, however, none of that volatile, heady emotion remained as she faced him now; she felt a certain sense of compassion, mayhap, or the subtle affection one would feel for a friend who has been absent for a long while.

The kind of sentiment one would feel, perhaps, for a lover

long estranged, after one's heart had been left cut and bleeding with betrayal.

"My sire told me you were dead," she said levelly, though the startling burst of darker emotion that shot through her in the next breath charged the words that followed, bringing them forth in heated demand. "Why did you allow me to believe it was true, Alexander?" She met his gaze, unflinching, her voice almost cracking as she added, "Why did you abandon me and our child?"

He reacted as though she had struck him, his eyes closing for a moment and a small rush of breath escaping him. After a moment he seemed to gather himself together enough to attempt an answer, and when he looked at her again, she saw sadness and regret shadowed in his gaze.

"I let you believe Lord Welton's lies because I was a coward, Margaret," he said, his voice tinged with self-loathing. "Because I was young and foolish, too stupid—or self-preserving, perhaps—to do what was right."

His sensual mouth quirked in the same familiar half smile that had always sent a melting sensation through her, during their brief and passionate time together. "I did it, I suppose, because I was nothing but a common knight without a farthing to my name, who had fallen in love with the daughter of an *earl*, by God, and there was no way to change that or to give you the kind of life you deserved."

"The only life I wanted then was one with you in it; you knew that well," she said, accusing him with both her words and her gaze.

"Perhaps. But you were young then too, lady, and did not realize how difficult life could be outside the shielding walls of wealth and nobility," he countered.

His own gaze pierced her, pointed and honest, and she

glanced away, unable to deny the glimmer of truth in what he had said. She *had* been innocent to the ways of the world, cosseted and protected from the harsh realities of life. But she had learned. Oh, she had learned.

"After you left, life became much more . . . difficult." She looked down at her hands, her throat tightening. "I was not certain I would survive it, even."

He fell very quiet, and Meg braced herself, knowing what would come next, knowing that he had a right to ask, and yet dreading the moment anyway. Once, long ago, she had yearned to share the pain of it with him, to know the comfort of his embrace in the aftermath. He had been the only one who could truly know what she had felt, being the only one who bore an equal share in her loss. But in time that need had faded, pushed to the background when she had thought him dead, and transformed to bitter anger when she'd seen him alive and well after all these years.

"Our babe . . . ?" he murmured hoarsely, and she knew that she would tell him, whether he deserved to hear it from her now or nay. She clenched her jaw, blinking back the stinging heat behind her eyes.

"We had a daughter. Her name was Madeline." Meg breathed in, squeezing the air past the constriction of her throat, to finish on a near whisper. "But though she was precious to me and perfect in every way, she died within an hour of her birth."

Alexander made a low sound of pain; turning away, he sank to one of the benches at the table. "I—I did not know, Margaret. God help me, I did not. You must believe me."

She gave a jerking nod of her head. And strangely enough she did believe him; for all of his faults, there was good in him too. She had fallen in love with that gentler aspect of his nature, it being far more apparent to her then than his more selfish qualities. Aye, she had overlooked the rest so glibly— she, who had been little more than an immature girl, with her rosy, naive outlook of the world.

"I was sent to Bayham Abbey to begin serving my penance," she continued calmly, "followed by a position at Hawksley Manor, caring for a distant relative, Richard's gravely ill wife, Eleanor." Pausing with the memory of it, she added quietly, "She is gone now, as well."

"And you are in love with Richard."

He announced it, not with resentment, but with a matter-of-fact tone that brought her gaze to his once more.

"Aye, we love each other. And that is the true reason I have come here, Alexander. To ask you—to beg you, if need be— to withdraw from this battle you have been charged to under-take with him." She paced closer, agitated with what was at stake.

"In all honesty, I do not know why you have not done so before this, considering the friendship I have been told that you and Richard shared in the Brotherhood; I do not know why you would wish to support the same Inquisition that has commenced the arrest and torture of so many men with whom you served. But I am pleading with you now to refuse this deed. Do not engage in battle with Richard. Withdraw."

"I wish that I could, Margaret," he said lowly, his voice heavy with regret. "But it is the one thing I cannot do."

"Why? It is as simple as standing up and declaring that you will not lift your weapon against your brother in arms!"

"Because if I do not engage in the Wager of Battle, my true brother, the one of my own flesh and blood, will pay the price for it."

Alex lifted his face to her then, looking worn by the weight of some burden he carried, though his eyes were steely with resolve. "Damien is even now in the hands of the Inquisition in France, lady," he explained. "We were both captured on the night of the mass arrests, but my brother, damn him, refused to bend to their demands . . ."

His words caught then, and to her shock she saw his eyes glisten with tightly held emotion before he cleared his throat. "You must understand that, unlike me, Damien became a Templar with honest reason; he believes in the cause of the Brotherhood above all else. When we were brought into custody, I said what was necessary to save myself, but Damien would not recant his vows; he refused to speak at all, even through the beatings and deprivations we endured. And so they began to employ more painful methods in an effort to wring a confession from him."

Meg bit back a gasp, sympathy rising to blend with the fear she already held in her heart for Richard's safety. Alex stared at her, seeming to hold on to his control by the thinnest of threads as he swallowed convulsively. His gaze sought purchase with hers, grasping in blind need.

"He is stubborn and so true of heart that he never would have bent," he continued hoarsely. "He was suffering the agonies of the damned, and still he would not recant. There was naught else I could do but to agree to become the Inquisition's arm in exchange for their promise to stop his torture. Damien knows nothing of it—he would undoubtedly scorn me even more than he already does for my disloyalty to the Brotherhood if he learned of it—but I could not let it go on longer without trying to help him."

"I am sorry, Alexander . . . I did not realize."

"It is a perverse bargain, Margaret"—he shook his head— "one in which I am well and truly caught. I must fight

Richard in a battle of arms and do my best to defeat him. I can only pray that he will do the same, and that neither of us will die in the trying."

Hopelessness pummeled Meg when he'd finished, and she wrapped her arms tightly around her middle. This was the end of it, then. The battle between them would be waged; there would be no stopping it.

"He will fight you, Alexander, it is true," she said, lifting her hand to pinch the space between her eyes, trying her best to stem the liquid heat that threatened to swell again. She took in a shaky breath, her trembling smile sympathetic as she fixed him with her gaze. "And he will do everything in his power to be victorious. Because on his side it is my life and his own weighing in the balance of the combat."

Pain swept across Alex's face, and he looked down at his hands, clasped loosely in front of him, his forearms leaning onto his thighs, as he murmured, "I feared as much." After a moment he glanced up to her again, and she saw a hint of the devastatingly handsome expression he had employed with such success in the past, simmering in his eyes. "Ah, lady, once again we seem to be facing a predicament where every available solution brings with it naught but suffering."

"Aye, Alexander," she admitted softly, "it would seem so."

A scratching sounded at the door then, followed by the call of one of the guards, who announced that the combatants in the Wager of Battle should ready themselves, for the king was nearing the main chamber, along with the members of the Inquisition and the other witnesses who had been called.

"Our time is up," she murmured.

"Then there is nothing left to say, but that I am sorry." Alex's expression now was somber, and his voice sounded harrowed and resigned. "For everything, Margaret, so help me God."

She nodded, her heart made heavy at the thought of the inevitable anguish ahead for them all. "As am I, Alexander . . . as am I."

Chapter 19

Richard took up his position of readiness in the fighting chamber for the second time that day, the awful certainty of what he was going to have to do sitting like a stone on his chest. When he'd entered the room, he had noted the resignation on Braedan's face; his gaze had slid to Meg then, where she stood next to his brother, and he had seen the slight shake of her head, read the answer he had been seeking in her bleak expression.

Alex would not withdraw.

A silent curse unleashed itself in Richard's mind. He was going to have to do battle with his best friend, a man who had saved his neck on more than one occasion, and whom he had saved in return.

Black fury at the unfairness of it all twisted to life inside him, and he latched on to it, using it to drive away all else. Knowing that if he didn't, he wouldn't stand a chance at mustering the kind of focus he would need to accomplish the intolerable task ahead.

The French Inquisitors, King Edward, and the rest of the religious dignitaries required to witness the bloody proceeding were all present and seated on the dais that had been erected at one side of the chamber. Roped off from the fighting area stood the mass of general spectators, increased by almost half from this morning alone, thanks to the swiftness with which gossip traveled through the court. This new audience had come to watch what promised to be the thrilling spectacle of two Templar Knights, both from the most elite, inner circle of the Brotherhood's already notable warriors, commencing in their efforts to kill each other.

Swallowing the bitter taste that thought inspired, Richard gritted his teeth. It was time to focus; Alex would be entering the chamber soon. Widening his stance, Richard closed his eyes and took in a deep breath, willing his arms to relax and hang loosely at his sides in preparation for the exertion to come. When he opened them again, it was to gaze with steady concentration at the portal through which his opponent would enter the chamber.

He didn't have to wait long.

The door swung open, and Alex strode in to an answering chorus of excited exclamations from the spectators; he was a powerful warrior in his own right, as full and broad as Richard, with the almost identical height that had served as the object of many a jest during their time fighting together as Templars. He wore an expression Richard had seen many times as well, though never before directed at himself, and it set him back a bit; it was a look of utter seriousness; the look of a man prepared to kill.

The very same look Richard knew he bore himself, at this moment.

"Let us begin," King Edward called out, though he was clearly not pleased with the prospect. The chamber quieted, and, standing, the king directed his regal stare at Richard, his gaze heavy as he intoned, "We are here to witness a Wager of Battle between Sir Richard de Cantor and the champion of the French Inquisition, Sir Alexander de Ashby. In accordance with holy law, the battle will be fought until one of the combatants is vanquished or calls out 'Craven!' which will signify surrender and the admission of Sir Richard's guilt, should he call out the word, or his innocence, should Sir Alexander employ it."

The sovereign's mouth tightened, his gaze flicking to Alex for an instant before settling on Richard again. "Are there any who wish to question this further, before we proceed?"

Silence greeted King Edward's question, and he nodded, continuing, "It is time, then, to speak the vow of faith, Sir Richard, which will be repeated by Sir Alexander when you are finished."

Nodding in acquiescence, Richard called out the traditional oath required of all who underwent physical ordeal or combat as a trial of innocence. "Hear this, ye justices, that I have this day neither eat, drank, nor have upon me neither bone, stone, nor grass, nor any enchantment, sorcery, or witchcraft, whereby the law of God may be abased or the law of the Devil exalted. So help me God and His saints."

King Edward looked to the lead Inquisitor, who jerked his chin once in acceptance of the speech, before the sovereign directed Alex to repeat the same vow, so that the battle could begin.

When Alex was finished, de Villeroi stood, as practice dictated, and called out, "Sir Richard, you are entitled to one final opportunity . . . have you aught to say before the ordeal commences? There is yet time to confess and avoid the test to come."

Richard stiffened as he faced the French cleric, absorbing the man's smug, hateful look; the Inquisitor seemed confident that he would hold fast and decline any confession. Perhaps he *hoped* for his stubbornness, even, so that he could witness the bloody wounds and possible death that might come of the battle. But while Frère de Villeroi might well get exactly what he craved before this was all over, Richard thought, setting his jaw mutinously, it would not be without a reminder of the truth and the reason he was standing here before them all.

"I do indeed have something to say, Frère de Villeroi," Richard called out in answer, "something that I think you will find of interest."

With his assertion, murmurs arose once more in the chamber, and he felt a burst of satisfaction at the shock on de Villeroi's face.

"It is a phrase that should be familiar to you, Frère . . . words you would do well to heed here today and in all of the unholy interrogations you undertake in the future—for the men who speak them do so with naught but sincerity and service to God."

Swiveling his gaze to Alex for one piercing moment, Richard looked back to the dais before sinking down on one knee in genuflection, making the sign of the cross, and uttering the Templar maxim aloud—repeating the same words he had spoken with his brothers in arms before every battle in which they had fought and died together. He spoke it clearly, his voice hoarse and tight with feeling, offered as a kind of benediction to those men who were even now enduring hell in foul prisons all across France.

"Non nobis, Domine, non nobis, sed Nomini, Tuo da gloriam."

Shocked silence reigned after the last, ringing word of it echoed to nothingness through the chamber. In that awestruck quiet, Richard lifted his face once more, noticing that Alex looked distraught, while the king had sunk back down into his chair. Shifting his gaze, Richard found Meg in the front of the crowd; she stared at him in silent support, her fingers pressed to her lips to hold back her tears, and love for her filled him, helping his rage to ebb.

With deliberation he stood again to face the row of Inquisitors who were responsible for torturing and maiming so many of his innocent brethren, and he finished his statement, saying gruffly, "May God's will truly be done here upon this hour, my lords, for in the way of every Templar, I am willing to battle unto my death to see it so."

Frère de Villeroi continued to appear astounded, his mouth gaping slightly before he snapped it shut to mutter, "So be it."

And with a wave of the king's wrist, the battle began.

Richard turned fluidly, unsheathing his sword and lifting his shield at the same time that he heard Alex's blade rasp free, though he had little time to do aught else before Alex bore down on him, swinging his weapon hard in from over his head. Richard whipped up his sword horizontally to deflect the blow, and their blades clanged together, the impact of it jarring his arm to numbness and making him reel back several paces.

Grunting with the effort, he parried another thrust that Alex angled at him, recognizing in the move a sequence that the two of them had perfected together in Cyprus. The realization filled him with bitter regret, even as he swung his blade in hard from the right, catching Alex's shield in a stroke that would have broken his friend's ribs and cut through flesh had it made its intended contact.

This was wrong . . . so wrong to be taking arms against Alex . . .

The words echoed in his mind, taunting him, but he could not contemplate them further with the pace of the battle between them. Sweat stung Richard's eyes as Alex came in for another blow, using the force of his body to shove Richard back, even as his elbow swept up to crack with brutal force against his jaw.

With a growl of pain, Richard wheeled away, feeling the hot, metallic taste of blood fill his mouth and grimacing as he stiffened his back to absorb the slamming impact of Alex's body against his own. Their blades locked and they stood, chest to chest, so equally matched in strength and skill that Richard knew they would likely hack each other to death before either would be able to claim victory.

"Give over, Alex," he ground out, his teeth clenched as he struggled to disengage his blade without losing his arm, in their precarious dance of death. "Call 'craven' and let us end this now, before one of us dies for the Inquisition's pleasure."

"Nay, Richard—they have Damien, and I cannot surrender myself or him to their torture again," Alex growled, shoving back against him and breaking free, only to swing in full circle as he raised his sword up, to counter Richard's overhead blow. But he stumbled under the power of Richard's strike, and dimly, Richard heard the crowd gasp before Alex righted himself and stepped warily back a few paces, swiping the back of his arm over his eyes in an effort to clear the sweat from them.

"This is madness," Richard muttered lowly, never taking his stare off Alex. "You know as well as I that Damien would rather be dead than to see you serving as an agent of the Inquisition for his sake."

"Perhaps," Alex countered, his breath rasping from exertion, "and perhaps not. I cannot take that chance."

They both were breathing too heavily to speak more at the moment, but they continued to circle each other, guarded and poised for a new attack. From behind him, Richard could hear the rising murmurs of those watching the battle, sensing their impatience to see the fighting resume.

They could be damned.

"I do not wish to kill you, Alex," he grated at last, when he had sucked enough air to form words again.

"Nor do I wish to die," Alex answered, his familiar half grin flashing forth for an instant, before it faded under the weight of a much harsher expression. "And yet you may fall as easily as I, Richard, so be wary."

And then the temporary lull between them vanished as Alex lunged forward once more, their swords clashing in a volley of strikes so furious that sparks danced off the blades. They both grunted with the effort, and the crowd responded with a hum of excitement.

Of a sudden, Richard hissed in his breath as he felt a searing sting just above the elbow of his sword arm. Blood ran, warm and thick, to soak his sleeve, and he tightened his grip on the hilt of his weapon as he fell back a few paces, knowing that the weakness flooding his limb was more dangerous than anything else . . . knowing that if he could not maintain a front of controlled strength before an opponent as experienced and proficient as Alex, he'd be as good as dead in the next few minutes.

Alex was clearly not deceived. Taking advantage of the opening he'd made by wounding Richard, he pressed forward, catching Richard's blade with a powerful strike that swept it out of his weakened grasp and sent it clattering to the wooden floor. The crowd gasped again, and Richard heard Meg's cry of fear above the other voices swelling around them, as he was forced to parry, empty-handed, away from another of Alex's thrusts—a movement that led him farther away from his own blade.

"What will you do, Alex?" he called, every muscle tensed in readiness to evade another strike. "Attempt to run me through unarmed, or have you had enough of serving as the Inquisition's puppet this day?"

"I have had enough of your mockery, of that I am certain!" Alex called, lunging forward with a growl and nearly slicing into Richard's leg, failing at the last instant only because Richard threw himself to the side, hitting the floor and rolling—just managing to reach his blade and lift it in time to meet Alex's downward stroke.

But Alex's momentum was too great, and the force of his blow toppled him over Richard, providing just the opportunity Richard needed to make his move. With a twist of his body, he righted himself, his wounded sword arm shaking but extended, and his gauntleted hand gripping the hilt with all the strength left to him . . .

With the action pinning Alex to the floor, with the edge of his blade poised at Alex's throat.

The gasps of excitement in the chamber fell to deathly silence; the only sound audible, suddenly, was that of Richard and Alex's labored breathing.

"Finish it, Richard," Alex gasped at last, holding himself very still in response to the proximity of the razor-sharp blade. "Do it, man, for they will never be satisfied with less."

Richard held himself stiffly, muttering a curse under his breath before he suddenly pulled his sword away from his friend's throat and growled back, "Then they can go to hell, for I will not be their instrument in your death."

Lowering his weapon deliberately, Richard turned to the dais to call out, "It is finished. I have bested my opponent and declare my innocence in the charges levied against me and the Brotherhood of Templars."

"Nay, Sir Richard." Frère de Villeroi pushed himself to his feet, his entire body seeming to thrum with rage as he spoke in a voice that made clear he would not be thwarted. "Neither you nor Sir Alexander has cried 'craven,' nor is either of you dead. It is therefore *not* finished. Complete the task, or surrender in the admission of your guilt, for a verdict will not be clear until that moment."

Disbelief and disgust rose up in Richard, obliterating his fatigue, and he rounded on the head Inquisitor, growling, "You have had your bloodletting, Frère." He shook his head. "You cannot command me to carry out what would amount to murder, nor will I confess to heresies that neither I nor any Templar brothers I have known have committed."

"As you wish," de Villeroi said smoothly, shifting his

malevolent gaze to Alex. "I order *you*, then, sir, to finish the combat and prove the Inquisition's right in this matter. Strike now and end it, once and for all."

Meg could not breathe as she watched the scene unfolding before her. She had thought she could feel no worse than she had when she'd witnessed Richard and Alexander battling for their lives. She had been sure that her heart could not choke any higher than it had in her throat, or that her stomach could not churn any sicklier from dread. But as had happened so oft these past few weeks, she had been wrong again. It all rushed upon her anew, intense and awful as she watched Alexander take to his feet, watched him lifting his weapon in preparation to make the killing strike commanded of him by the head Inquisitor.

A killing strike against Richard.

She could hold back no longer; crying out a warning, she broke free from Braedan and the crowd of spectators and took several running steps into the fighting arena.

Richard turned at her cry, but then he froze, unable to come closer because of the person blocking his way. He stared unflinchingly at Alexander, who met his gaze as well from where he stood but a few paces off, an agonized expression on his face, his blade upraised and near enough to do as the inquisitor had commanded, likely in one stroke, should Richard not attempt to move away.

"Please, Alexander," Meg said, her voice catching with the force of her anguish. "Do not do this!"

"You *will* do it, sir, or you will suffer the consequences!" Frère de Villeroi shouted in retort, scowling his furious gaze down on them. "Lay down your weapon, and I will have no choice but to consider it a recantation of confession. You will be arrested again under law and made subject to the harshest interrogation, in a final effort to save your eternal soul from the damnation of—"

"Do what you must, Alex," Richard broke in quietly, sounding so calm as de Villeroi continued to carry on from the dais, that Meg couldn't help marveling at his composure in the face of the glinting death hanging quite literally over his head. "Only be sure," Richard continued, never releasing Alex's gaze, "that it is a decision you can live with, come what may."

Alex seemed to wage a battle inside himself; Meg knew too well the choices haunting him, and she waited, unmoving, suspended on emotional tenterhooks as he decided which way the hand of fate would fall.

At last he uttered a quiet curse. That familiar, sardonic smile of his swept over his lips, and Meg felt a twisting of relief, gratitude, and sorrow for him all at once, as he shook his head, half turning to look at her. "Before I do this, Margaret, I need you to know something," he murmured. "I did love you. For the rest of my life, I will regret what my lack of courage wrought between us. My choices have hurt many, and so I must try a new path. One that Richard would take, were he in my place." He paused, adding huskily, "and that I believe Damien would as well."

He shifted his gaze to Richard, then, his eyes glittering with bittersweet feeling as he finished even more lowly, "Live well with the freedom I am about to buy for you, my friend . . ."

Then he turned, and with a gesture that reminded her so of the colorful, reckless man she had known long ago, Alex dropped his sword, lifting his hands in surrender and calling to the judges in a voice roughened by the knowledge of exactly what he was bringing upon himself, "My lords, I hereby publicly recant my earlier confession of heresy . . . the Templars are innocent, as am I, I swear it. By God, we are all innocent—"

His words cracked then, and Meg felt her heart lurch for him, watching as he struggled to keep a brave face, while Frère de Villeroi sank stiffly into his chair, gesturing for the French guards to place him in custody. The chamber hummed with murmurs and the beginnings of new gossip as Alex was clapped in irons and dragged from the chamber, all the while maintaining his stoic expression. And though she saw a glimmer of fear in his eyes, he did not break—nay, not for as long as she could see, until the door closed tightly behind him. The French contingent stood almost en masse, led by Frère de Villeroi, who swept from the chamber in an effort to maintain some modicum of dignity, offering little more than a curt bow to the king before vanishing without further ado behind the same door through which Alexander had been taken.

Then all fell quiet again. She looked at Richard, reading the sad awareness in his eyes and knowing that neither one of them would ever be able to truly repay the sacrifice Alexander had just made for them—just as she knew that they would try to anyway. First, however, she yearned for nothing more than to run into Richard's arms at last, to hold him and cherish him and tend to the wounds that had been delivered to his body and soul this day.

She would needs wait a little longer to do that, it seemed; Richard knew it too, for he moved not at all, though his gaze sought hers, the muscle in his temple jumping and his eyes speaking so eloquently across the distance between them that she felt as if he voiced his feelings aloud.

But that would not be possible until the king delivered his final decision in the Wager of Battle.

"Sire . . . ?" Richard asked gruffly, swiveling his gaze at last to King Edward. "Will you pass judgment?"

King Edward looked as if it had been he who had suffered the battle; his complexion was pale and his expression looked almost gaunt in his distress. Piers Gaveston, who sat beside him, seemed less affected, but he was unmistakably concerned for the king's reaction, and he pressed an encouraging hand atop the sovereign's own.

"Aye, Sir Richard," the king answered, still clearly emotional as he stood before the assembly, "and it is this: We believe it apparent that the Wager of Battle has proven your innocence . . ."

"Pardon, Your Majesty—but that cannot be!"

Meg's stomach plummeted again, nausea roiling anew at the sight of her father, Lord Welton, with Sir Ector at his side, stepping forward in a final, wicked bid to manipulate the outcome of the proceedings against Richard.

"Sir Alexander de Ashby, bastard despoiler that he is, never called 'craven' in surrender," her sire complained, flicking a dark gaze at Meg. "There is therefore no proof of innocence or guilt in regards to Sir Richard in their battle. The opponent recanted a personal confession of heresy, it is true—but that has naught to do with the question over which we were called to witness."

The body of English priests and bishops who had been called forth at the time of the original Wager of Battle reacted with exclamations of both dissension and agreement, huddling together to discuss the validity of Lord Welton's claims.

"Good God, man, have you not seen enough yet this day?" the king asked him, incredulous at his persistence.

The most senior of the English bishops stepped forward. "Pardon, sire, but Lord Welton is correct in his complaint, for though there are those among us who would belie the need to pursue this further, it is difficult to feign ignorance now to the detail that has been raised so publicly."

King Edward seemed staggered by this latest development. "What would you have Us do, then?" he croaked in dismay. "The French champion has withdrawn from the proceedings, and the wager is played out in full. Do you mean to tell me that We are exactly where We were a full sennight ago, as if none of this—this *ordeal* had taken place at all?"

"I am afraid so, sire," the bishop said regretfully. "No resolution of innocence can be made, as there was no clear victor in the match. It stands as it did before the wager was undertaken."

"Demand, sire," Lord Welton called out coolly, "that Sir Richard confess to the crimes of heresy levied against him as a Templar Knight, with suitable penance charged for it—or else hand him over to the custody of the French, so that they might question him and get to the bottom of his transgressions, for the sake of his eternal soul."

Lord Welton's expression flattened with malicious triumph, as he added the final nail to the tomb he had carefully constructed for Richard with his words. "I would wager to say that, though they made haste to leave the scene of this day's debacle, the Inquisitors would welcome the boon of such a gift as Sir Richard to bring home to France with them; the gesture might even mollify Frère de Villeroi enough to prevent him from delivering what is sure to be an unfavorable account of your court to King Philip."

"You bastard," Richard growled, his sentiments echoed by Braedan, who was still standing in the crowd as a witness to the proceedings. Several guards were forced to rush forward to restrain the two brothers, as they separately made violent advances in Lord Welton's direction.

Meg's fists clenched, all the despair and animosity of a lifetime converging to a moment of defiance as she let go a cry of pure frustration, calling out, "By all the saints, my lord, when will you cease your destructive meddling? Your own grasping nature has become so twisted that you have lost the right to be called a man of honor. Can you not leave off your intrigues even now, and after all that has passed already?"

Lord Welton recoiled, paling in anger, and the king buried his head in his hands as the chamber erupted at the audacity of such a publicly delivered insult to one of the most powerful noblemen in the kingdom. Meg faced her sire undaunted, however, trembling with rage and knowing that she was doomed to be ostracized for good now; and yet she couldn't bring herself to care overmuch about it, except perhaps for the way it might impact Richard.

Richard.

Swinging her gaze to him again, she felt the bond they shared, like a living, vital force, throbbing in warm response at the very sight of him. He had shaken off the guards to stand very still and silent, clearly unwilling to bend to the forces aligned against him. He would not confess to a lie, even to save himself. He could not. His honor and integrity would not allow it, and she loved him for that, as well as for so many other things.

His gaze locked with hers, then, and she saw that his eyes simmered with empathy . . . with passion and deep, abiding love for *her*. The fullness of it swept through her in a great, humbling rush, and she knew in that instant that she would suffer everything she had endured in her life all over again— aye, she would do anything, no matter how difficult, if only Richard could be free of this noose that her sire kept trying to tighten around his neck.

And as realization dawned, swift and agonizing, she saw what she could do to make this stop; to free the man she loved at last from the shadows that would not, even after all this, give over their battle for him.

Her back felt rigid enough to snap as she stepped forward to face the king, saying only loudly enough to be heard over the turmoil still at work in the chamber, "Sire, I beg your hearing on the matter in place before us."

King Edward swung his gaze to her slowly, weariness dragging at both his voice and his expression. "Speak, then, Lady Margaret, for by the Holy Host, we have exhausted all ideas else to resolve this madness."

"I propose an exchange, Your Majesty—myself for Sir Richard's freedom. I will go with my sire, Lord Welton, and do his bidding, if all remaining charges against Sir Richard are expunged and he is freed to go, unhampered by any further incrimination."

"Nay, Meg—nay," Richard called out, before the king or her father could answer. "I would needs be dead to see you handed over to his foul keeping again."

Richard's voice sounded hoarse as he spoke, Meg noted, but he did not sound dismayed; even as Lord Welton stiffened further, and the gathered nobles once more buzzed in titillation over this latest development, she studied Richard, feeling her breath trapped like a bubble in her chest when she saw the fullness of his love for her, clear in his exquisite eyes.

"There is no need to sacrifice yourself for my sake, lady," Richard said more quietly, pulling his gaze from her at last to look at the king and the assembly of priests, "for in truth I *do* have a confession to make in regards to my sins as a Templar Knight—an admission of guilt that I pray will satisfy the demands of the Holy Mother Church, for I make it honestly and with a sincere wish to make reparation for my failings."

Meg's arms had crept up to wrap around her stomach, as if to quell the quaking there, but she realized as she gazed at this man she loved more than her life, that nothing could stem the tide of worry over what he was about to say and at what cost.

"I can in full conscience confess to only one act that bears the taint of heresy," he continued in a calm, clear voice. "Several times on remote battlefields, I accepted the Holy Rite of Reconciliation from a fellow Templar—men who were not priests ordained. We undertook that sin in our desire to be blessed before entering armed conflict that could result in our death, and it was in so doing that we broke the laws of the Church. That is the only heretical act that I or any other Templar I have known has willingly committed."

The bishop nodded gravely. "It is a serious transgression, it is true, and is indeed heretical in form, yet your confession goes far to restore you in the bosom of grace, Sir Richard. You will be assessed a fine, along with a penance of prayer and meditation, but in the accomplishment of that, I deem your transgression wiped clean." He paused, face stern, adding at last, "Is that all you wish to confess, then?"

"Nay," Richard murmured. "There is yet something more I must acknowledge before I can go forth from here; it is not a heresy, but rather an action I committed against Templar law itself, for it is a sin of the flesh, but one for which I swear I will never repent."

Even Meg gasped this time, along with many of the others in the chamber, but Richard continued over their exclamations.

"For though I had not yet been officially released from my term of service with the Brotherhood, I willingly broke my vows of chastity by loving a woman—a magnificent lady whom I have known intimately, I do confess it." His gaze shone with tenderness as he turned his face to Meg, adding more quietly, "But I intend to repair this transgression by marrying Lady Margaret, Your Eminence, if she will have me."

The bishop did not seem to know just how to respond. But Meg did.

"I will, Richard," she answered. "I will marry you by holy law, in reflection of the union I have made with you already in the fullness of my heart."

Astounded at so open a declaration of love, the bishop looked in wonder at Richard, then at Meg and back again to Richard. He must have seen the truth of their avowal in their eyes, however, for he directed his kind stare to Meg again after a moment's reflection, nodding and saying, "Go to him, then, lady, if that is what you wish."

"Aye, please do," King Edward echoed. He looked relieved. "We are satisfied in this resolution, earned at high price," he called out in a commanding voice, ignoring Lord Welton's muffled renewal of protests. "We hereby decree that this matter is resolved, ne'er to be revisited, pray God in His great mercy, so long as We shall live!"

Then the king too nodded to Meg, and reeling with joy, she took several running steps toward Richard, meeting him as he strode forward to her. They fell into each other's embrace then, both laughing and crying all at once, and he pulled her close to him, cradling her head to his chest and pressing his lips to her hair.

Braedan rushed to them as well, gripping Richard by his good shoulder and then swinging him into a hug when Richard turned to him. The relief Braedan showed was almost palpable, Meg thought, and now that her own fears were ebbing, she was able to see fully for the first time just how difficult it must have been for him to stand by and watch his little brother in a battle for his life. Now more than ever, she appreciated the strength and support he'd shown her during these past dark hours, as they'd hoped for the safety of the man they both loved.

Meg accepted Braedan's embrace as well, and then stepped back a bit to allow the two men some time together. But after a moment, Richard's brother nodded his respects, still grinning, before taking his leave to gather what would be needed to clean and wrap Richard's wound.

And then Meg and Richard were once more alone in each other's company; a kind of organized chaos swirled around them, the sounds of the king's official departure from the chamber blending with the din of the dispersing members of court. But the noise and confusion mattered little, Meg knew, joy lifting her spirits higher as she leaned once more into the arms of this man who had faced down a king, a deadly champion, a powerful earl, and the prodigious might of the French Inquisition, all in one day. He had done it for her and for the sake of true justice—and he had come out on the other side, alive and well, with naught but a slight wound that would soon heal.

But that wasn't all, she thought blissfully, for he was gaz-

ing down at her right now, his eyes filled with the complete-
ness of some powerful emotion. With love for *her*, she realized.

"I cannot live without you, Meg," he whispered, still holding her close and smiling as he brushed a kiss over the very
tip of her nose. "You know that, don't you? Never leave me,
lady, for it would kill me more swiftly than any blade or torture the world could devise."

"Aye, Richard," she said, holding him tight. "It is the same
for me—though you have naught to fear, for I will stay by
your side and consider myself the most fortunate woman in
the world for it."

Meg gazed up into Richard's face, lifting her lips for another kiss, this one full of passion and devotion, faith and redemption, brimming with the heady promise of all that was
to come. No words were needed for her to know that part of
that future would include doing whatever was in their power
to free Alex and Damien . . . to work tirelessly to keep the
Templar cause before the eyes and hearts of those who had
the power to see justice done.

But first they had this time to savor together, free of all the
darkness, guilt, and sadness that had held sway over them
both for so long.

"Come," she murmured, smiling more shyly now. She
took his hand in her own, the love she felt for him filling her
beyond the limits of temptation. "Let us retreat to your chambers to tend your wounds—for after that I long to begin
showing you just how much I adore you."

"Only *begin* showing me?" he asked, and the devilish glint
in his eyes sent another rush of warmth straight to her
heart . . . and other places as well.

"Aye, only that." She cupped the strong, smooth lines of

his cheek with her palm, laughing gently as she pressed another kiss to his lips. "For I have a feeling it will take me a very long time to get it right."

"Hmmm . . ." Richard glanced at her playfully. "I have heard that frequent practice is the key in such cases. Time is all that is needed. How does eternity sound, then?"

"It sounds wonderful, my love," Meg answered him, smiling through happy tears. "In fact, I think that will be perfect."

Epilogue

February 1308

The winter wind howled around the turrets of Hawksley Manor, belying the cozy warmth inside the fire-lit bed-chamber where Meg and Richard stood silent before the blazing hearth; Meg leaned more fully into Richard's embrace, relishing the sensation of his broad, strong chest against her back and the cradling comfort of his arms. Tiny ice pellets sizzled and hissed as they blew down the chimney into the fire, and Meg smiled, offering up a happy sigh.

"Ah, wife, you sound mightily pleased for such a stormy night," Richard murmured into her ear, before gently brushing his lips over the spot. It sent delicious tingles shuddering up the back of her neck, making her snuggle into him with a throaty murmur.

"Aye, husband," she answered, "that I am, for the storm pleases me well."

"Does it, now?" he asked in mock surprise, pulling back a bit. "You are certain that it is that barren force of nature which affects you and not . . . *this*?"

As he spoke, he dragged his palm from its warm perch on her waist, up over her ribs in a tantalizing path, making her suck in her breath when he cupped her breast tenderly, adding huskily, "Or *this*?"

His voice was a sensual rumble behind her as he tipped his head forward to press warm, delectable nibbles along her neck.

"Mmmmmm . . ." She stretched against him like a cat, exposing her neck even more as her head tilted to the side, the weight of it heavy of a sudden, in harmony with the sweet, aching heat that swelled anew at the juncture of her thighs. She gripped his hand that was splayed across her ribs, stroking a lazy, teasing pattern over his flesh before grasping his fingers and tugging gently; when he groaned lowly in response, she felt the corners of her lips rise unbidden, for she never ceased to be delighted that she could entice such a sound from him with such a simple touch.

"Unfair," he murmured, and she heard the smile in his voice as well, though she could not see his face.

"Nay—it is naught but turnabout . . . and not nearly as effective as the caresses with which you're plying me, I have to say." Twisting in his embrace at last to face him, Meg wound her fingers into the hair at his nape and lifted her lips for a kiss that began sweetly and finished in breathless and passionate abandon. "Truly, husband," she murmured, once they'd managed to steady themselves, "I will be glad to slip beneath the bedcovers again with you this night—"

He grinned.

"—but before you distract me utterly from remembering

what it is I wished to say, I must needs ask you if you have heard aught yet from John."

"Nay, not yet." He kept her close, but his expression seemed more serious than it had been moments ago. He held her gaze, the beauty of his green and gold eyes taking her breath away as always. "But it has been little more than a fortnight since we secured the Templar treasure in Scotland," he continued. "John has assured me that he knows of men—those in secret support of the Brotherhood in France—who can help to lead us to Alex and Damien. In truth I am expecting word from him any day now."

"And when it comes?" Meg asked softly.

"Then we will go to France, to do what we must to free them from the grasp of the Inquisition."

She nodded, accepting in the necessity of it, even as she worried for Richard's safety. He possessed a writ of absolution from the Holy Mother Church now, it was true, but she feared for him nonetheless, for France was the land most notably hostile toward the Templars, the sovereign there seeming determined to see them destroyed through any means possible.

"There will be naught to fear, Meg," he murmured as if he had read her thoughts, nuzzling his lips to her hair and pulling her closer. "I will take good care and return home safely to you. Do not worry so," he added, and she could not keep from smiling again when he blew a tickling, warm breath into her ear. Laughing lowly, she shook her head and tilted away, looking up once more to meet his gaze.

"I cannot help it, you know," she answered, a teasing smile still pulling at her lips. "There will never be a time when I will not worry for you, Richard. There is no escape for you . . . you are well and truly caught."

"Aye—as are you, my love," he countered, rubbing his thumb over the lower curve of her mouth and sending a familiar thrill of longing through her with his touch. "I am afraid that you shall never be free of my complete attention to your every need and desire." As he spoke he brushed little kisses over her temple and along her jaw, before lifting her hand and turning it over gently to press his lips with tantalizing promise to the sensitive skin of her palm.

"It is grateful I am to hear it," she whispered, leaning into him and resting her cheek against his chest to hear the steady, strong beat of his heart.

"I love you, Meg," he murmured, holding her close before the blazing fire with the wind howling outside and unable to reach them with its icy breath. "I want you to know that nothing will ever change that."

"Aye, Richard," she said softly in reply. "I do know, for it is the same feeling I cherish for you."

And as she stood there, wrapped in Richard's arms, Meg knew that what they'd spoken was the very truth. They would face all that life would bring them, no longer alone, but strong in their unity and their love. *Together*.

And that, she decided with a little sigh of pure contentment, made all the difference in the world.

Author's Note

Templar Knights were the elite warriors of their day, akin to our modern-day Navy SEALs, Green Berets, or other special military units. They were first established in Jerusalem in the early twelfth century to provide protection for pilgrims to the Holy Sepulcher, and were highly trained combatants who followed a strict code of moral conduct and honor, answering to the authority of the pope alone, regardless of their country of origin or residence.

This autonomy, combined with the suspicion concerning what happened during their "secret" meetings, and their perceived wealth (for though their vows prevented them from amassing personal fortunes, they were considered so honest that they served as the world's first international bankers and therefore had in their control vast quantities of gold, jewels, and other valuables), helped to lead to their downfall.

The beginning of the end occurred at dawn, on Friday, October 13, 1307, when King Philip the Fair ordered secret missives that he'd sent to every sheriff and seneschal in the kingdom to be opened and acted upon; by nightfall, several thousand Templars were in dungeons and prisons throughout France—however, approximately twenty men managed to escape the country. These men, and what I imagined they might have experienced as hunted warriors in the days, weeks, and months following the violent and sudden mass arrests, served as the inspiration for my series *The Templar Knights*.

As an interesting aside concerning the date of the arrests, because of the Templars, Western civilization has considered Friday the thirteenth to be a day of ill fortune ever since, regardless of the month in which it falls.

Many of my books seem to include true historical figures, and *Beyond Temptation* is no exception; this of course requires a bit of additional research, and though I have done my best to get the facts right, I will admit to taking some creative license in representing these real people as characters. However, as I tried to portray in the story, England's King Edward II seems to have been sympathetic indeed to the cause of the Templars, not believing them to be guilty of heretical practices. In fact, upon hearing of the mass arrests, he responded by sending letters defending the order to the rulers of Portugal, Castile, Aragon, and Naples.

It wasn't until he received a missive from the pope himself, instructing him to undertake the arrest of England's Templars for questioning, that he reluctantly issued that directive to his sheriffs and seneschals throughout the kingdom—and in this I did change one aspect of factual history for the purposes of my fictional creation. I took the liberty of showing Richard standing trial in England as a Templar, with French Inquisitors present, at a point which would have been sometime in November 1307. In truth, the actual order for arrest of the Templars in England was not issued until January 9–10, 1308, and French Inquisitors did not arrive to participate in the trial of the English Templars until September 13, 1309.

As another point of historical fact within the story, the wedding that I described taking place between Piers Gaveston and Margaret de Clare did indeed occur on November 2, 1307, at Tunbridge Castle in Kent. Piers was a favorite of King Edward II, and the English monarch spared no expense in lavishing gifts, titles, and estates on him while he lived. It was the cause of much upheaval in the kingdom and animosity among Edward's barons, a truth about which Edward seems to have been blissfully unconcerned.

There is so much more that I would love to share with you here concerning the intriguing tidbits and facts that I uncovered as I researched the Templar order, the trials, and the events that take place in *Beyond Temptation*; however, I am afraid that if I indulged myself, this "Author's Note" could turn out to be as lengthy as the book itself.

So I will simply end in saying that by all appearances, the Holy Order of the Poor Knights of the Temple of Solomon is an organization—a brotherhood of warrior-monks—that, though officially suppressed by directive of the pope in 1314, has continued to engage the imaginations of people around the world; perhaps because of their mystique, hidden ceremonies, and accusations of dark rituals—or perhaps thanks to many peoples' conviction that Templars were the guardians of holy relics like the Grail, relics that some say remain hidden in the places the Templars managed to secret them centuries ago—their legacy persists, garnering respect, study, and interest throughout time.

I certainly find them fascinating, and I can only hope that I have done justice to their history—as well as to the unfolding of Meg and Richard's sometimes challenging path to achieving passionate, committed love.

As always, thanks for coming along on the journey.

MRM

Summer nights are hotter than ever thanks to these July releases from Avon Romance . . .

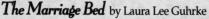

The Marriage Bed by Laura Lee Guhrke

An Avon Romantic Treasure

Everyone in society knows that the marriage of Lord and Lady Hammond is an unhappy one. But all that is about to change, when John, Lord Hammond, begins to see what a beautiful woman he is married to. Now he prays it's not too late to win back the love of his very own wife.

The Hunter by Gennita Low

An Avon Contemporary Romance

In order for Hawk McMillan, SEAL commander, to succeed in his latest lone mission, he needs a tracker, and the best woman for that job is CIA contact agent Amber Hutchens. But when their mission requires Hawk and Amber to risk everything, they've got too much at stake to stay far away from danger . . . or from their passion.

More Than a Scandal by Sari Robins

An Avon Romance

Lovely Catherine Miller has always been timid—until the treachery of unscrupulous cousins threatens her childhood home. To save it, she steals the identity of the notorious "Thief of Robinson Square" who, years ago, preyed on pompous society to help the poor.

The Daring Twin by Donna Fletcher

An Avon Romance

When Fiona of the MacElder clan is told that she must wed Tarr of Hellewyk so the two clans can unite, she is furious. Fortunately, Fiona's identical twin sister Aliss is on her side. The two boldly concoct an outlandish scheme—to make it impossible to tell who is who—and it works. The only trouble is, one of the twins accidentally falls in love with the would-be groom!

AuthorTracker

Don't miss the next book by your favorite author.
Sign up now for AuthorTracker by visiting
www.AuthorTracker.com

REL 0605